Scarlet Wilson wrote her first story aged eight and has never stopped. She's worked in the health service for twenty years, having trained as a nurse and a health visitor. Scarlet now works in public health and lives on the West Coast of Scotland with her fiancé and their two sons. Writing medical romances and contemporary romances is a dream come true for her.

Married to the man she met at eighteen, Susanne Hampton is the mother of two adult daughters, Orianthi and Tina. She has enjoyed a varied career path, but finally found her way to her favourite role of all: Medical Romance author. Susanne has always read romance novels and says, 'I love a happy-ever-after, so writing for Mills & Boon is a dream come true.'

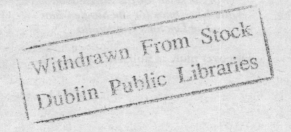

TEMPTED BY THE HOT HIGHLAND DOC

SCARLET WILSON

MENDING THE SINGLE DAD'S HEART

SUSANNE HAMPTON

MILLS & BOON

First Published in Great Britain 2019
by Mills & Boon, an imprint of HarperCollins*Publishers*
1 London Bridge Street, London, SE1 9GF

Tempted by the Hot Highland Doc © 2019 by Scarlet Wilson

Mending the Single Dad's Heart © 2019 by Susanne Panagaris

ISBN: 978-0-263-26971-0

MIX
Paper from
responsible sources
FSC™ C007454

This book is produced from independently certified FSC™ paper
to ensure responsible forest management.
For more information visit www.harpercollins.co.uk/green.

Printed and bound in Spain
by CPI, Barcelona

TEMPTED BY THE HOT HIGHLAND DOC

SCARLET WILSON

MILLS & BOON

To my fab editor Carly Byrne,
for supporting me to write the stories I love—
no matter how crazy!

PROLOGUE

'ABSOLUTELY NO WAY. I'm not doing it.' Kristie Nelson shook her head and folded her arms across her chest.

Louie, her boss, arched one eyebrow at her. 'Do you want to pay your mortgage or not?'

She shifted uncomfortably on her chair. 'I was promised a chance at working with the news team. These puff pieces are driving me nuts, and if you send me in the direction of another quiz show I swear I'll grab that ceremonial sword from behind your head and stick it somewhere nasty.'

Louie let out a hearty laugh. They'd been working together far too long to be anything but straight with each other.

He sighed and leaned his head on one hand. 'Kristie, your last two projects have bombed. You fell out—in a spectacular fashion, I might add—with the producer on the TV series you were scheduled for. I've had to search around for work that might fit with your other obligations.'

She swallowed, her throat instantly dry. Louie knew her well—better than most because she revealed nothing to most people—and, although she didn't tell him so, she did appreciate it.

She stared down at the file he'd handed her. '*A Year in the Life of the Hot Highland Doc*? Really?' Her voice arched upwards, along with her eyebrows. She tried to ignore the involuntary shudder that went down her spine. She straightened her shoulders. 'Sounds like another puff piece to me.'

Louie looked her in the eye. 'A puff piece that involves filming three days a month on the island—paid travel to and from the island, all expenses covered, and a salary better than any news channel would pay you.'

She shifted uncomfortably in her chair. When he put it like that…

Louie continued. 'These streaming TV channels are the ones with the big budgets these days. They're making all the best new TV shows, and they're not afraid to take chances. Don't you think it might be a good idea to get in there, and make a good impression?'

Her brain was whirring. She knew it all made sense. She knew it was an opportunity. How many people really made it onto the terrestrial TV channels? She didn't even want to admit that she'd subscribed to this streaming service too. Some of the shows were addictive.

Louie shrugged. 'Filming is taking place all around the world. There's a volcanologist in Hawaii. A museum curator in Cairo. A quarterback from an American football team. Someone training for the space station.'

'And I get the Scottish doc?' She held up her file, not even trying to hide the disappointment on her face.

Louie didn't speak and the silence told her everything she needed to know. She'd got what was left. Louie had probably had to campaign hard to even get her this gig.

She flicked through the files sitting on Louie's desk. There was also a vet. A firefighter. A teacher. A policewoman.

If she'd had to rank each of the possibilities, she knew the work with the doc would have been last on her list. The thought of being around a medic all day—possibly being in a hospital environment—made her feel sick.

Six years ago as a media graduate she'd thought she was going to take the world by storm. But somehow that storm had changed into a long, hard slog with only a few glimmers scattered throughout. Part of her resented this job already. It wasn't exactly her career goal. But what was?

Things had shifted in the last few years. Real life events had left her jaded and knocked her confidence in the world around her. Sometimes she wasn't even sure what it was she was fighting for any more.

'Isn't describing someone as a Hot Highland Doc considered sexist these days?'

Louie shrugged. 'Who cares? That's the title we liked. It should draw viewers in. Who wouldn't want to see a Hot Highland Doc?'

Her brain was still ticking. She wrinkled her nose. 'Geography isn't my strong point. Hold on.' She pulled out her phone and stuck in the name of the island. 'Arran? That's on the southwest coast of Scotland. That's not even in the Highlands.'

Louie laughed. 'Like I said—who cares? At least it is an island. It's the UK, so trade descriptions can't get us on that one.'

Kristie closed her eyes for a second and thought about the pile of bills currently sitting on her dresser. This was money. Money that would be guaranteed for one year. She would be a fool to turn this down.

'Smile. Arran—who knows? You might even like it. You just need to go there three days a month and film as much as you can. You need enough footage for forty-one minutes of screen time.' Louie waved his hand. 'And if it's boring, do something to mix it up.'

This time it was Kristie that raised her eyebrows. 'Mix it up? What exactly does that mean?'

Louis shrugged. 'I mean, make it interesting viewing. If you work on another show that gets cancelled midway, people will start to think you have the kiss of death.' He met her gaze. 'People won't want to work with you.' He left the words hanging.

She gulped. She knew he was right. TV and media were ruthless. One minute you were the belle of the ball, the next you were lucky to pick up the leftovers—just like she was now.

She gave a slow nod of her head then frowned as she compared her file with some of the others. 'This guy? There's no photo.'

'Isn't there?' Louie had moved over to his appointment diary, obviously ready to move onto his next task.

'And how do you even say his name?'

Louie moved back around the desk and leaned over her shoulder. '"Roo-ah-ree", I think.' He winked. 'At least try and get the guy's name right.'

She stared at the scribbled notes in the folder. Rhua-ridh Gillespie. General Practitioner. Also provides cover to Arran Community Hospital and A and E department.

How did that even work?

She swallowed and took a deep breath. How bad could this be?

'How much preparation time do I have?'

There was a glint in Louie's eyes as he threw something across the desk at her. Flight details.

'A day,' he answered.

'A day?' She stood up as she said the words. 'What do you mean, a day?'

Louie just started talking as if there was nothing unusual at all about what he'd just said. 'You fly into Glasgow, car hire has been arranged—you need to drive to a place called Ardrossan to catch the ferry to Arran. The crossing takes about an hour but...' he paused as he glanced at some notes in front of him '...apparently can be hampered by the weather. So build in some extra time.'

Her brain had gone directly into overdrive. Clothes. Equipment. What was the weather like on Arran this time of year? This was the UK, not the US. She needed to learn a bit more about their healthcare system. And what about this guy? Under normal circumstances she'd take a few days to do some background research on him—to learn what kind of a person he was—what made him tick. Anything that would give her a head start.

She shook her head. Then realised she hadn't asked one of the most important questions. 'Who is my cameraman?'

Louie gave a little cough that he tried to disguise as clearing his throat. 'Gerry.'

'Gerry?' She couldn't hide her dismay. 'Louie, he's about a hundred and five! He doesn't keep up well, his timekeeping is awful, and he always leaves half his equipment behind.'

Louie gave a half-hearted shrug. 'Give the guy a break. He needs the work. And anyway, he knows you better than most.'

She bit her lip as she picked up her bag. Maybe she was being unreasonable. He did know her better than most—he'd been there with her and Louie when she'd got that terrible call. But last time she'd worked with Gerry he'd left her sitting in the middle of a baking desert in Arizona for three hours.

'I swear if he isn't at the airport when I get there, I'm leaving without him.'

Louie waved his hand. 'Whatever.' Louie picked up his phone as she headed to the door. 'And, Kristie?'

She spun back around. 'Yeah?'

He grinned. 'Who knows—you might enjoy this.'

She didn't hesitate. She picked up a cushion from the chair nearest the door and launched it at Louie's head.

CHAPTER ONE

May

THERE WAS NO way that this amount of vomiting could be normal. Maybe it was something she'd eaten on the flight between Los Angeles and London? The chicken had looked okay. But then she'd had that really huge brownie at Heathrow Airport before the departure to Glasgow.

She groaned as her stomach lurched again and the roll of the waves threw her off balance. They weren't even out at sea any more, they were in the middle of docking at the harbour in Brodick, Arran.

'First-timer, eh?' said a woman with a well-worn face as she walked towards the gangway.

Kristie couldn't even answer.

Gerry gave her a nudge. 'Come on, they've already made two announcements telling drivers to get back into their cars. Do you want me to drive instead?'

She shook her head and took another glug of water from the bottle he'd bought her. Poor Gerry. He'd spent half of this ferry journey holding the hair from her face so she could be sick. He was more than double her age, but seemed to have weathered the journey much better than she had—even if he had twice tried to get into the car on the wrong side.

She gave him a half-hearted smile. 'Next time we get on a flight together I'll have what you're having.' He'd popped some kind of tablet as soon as they'd boarded the flight in Los Angeles and had slept until the wheels had set down at Heathrow.

He returned a smile. 'What can I say? Years of experience.'

She watched him shuffling down the stairs in front of her to the car deck. The boat's bow was already opening, preparing for the cars to unload. Kristie ignored a few pointed glares as she made her way to their hire car and tried to squeeze back inside.

The cars in front had already moved by the time she'd started the unfamiliar vehicle and tried to remember what to do with the pedals and the gearstick.

She jumped as there was a loud blast of a horn behind her. She muttered an expletive under her breath as she started the car and promptly stalled it. The car juddered and heat rushed into her cheeks. 'Why is everything on the wrong side?'

Gerry chuckled. 'Just watch out for the roundabouts.'

She bit her bottom lip as she started the car again. The roundabout at Glasgow airport had been like an episode of the *Wacky Races*. The whole wrong-side-of-the-road aspect had totally frazzled her brain and she was sure at one point her life had flashed before her eyes.

'Arran isn't that big,' she muttered. 'Maybe they don't need roundabouts. Crazy things anyway. Who invented them? What's wrong with straight roads?'

Gerry laughed as they finally rolled off the ferry and joined the queue of traffic heading towards a road junction.

'Which way?' she asked.

'Left,' he said quickly. 'The doctor's surgery and hospital are in a place called Lamlash. It's only a few miles up the road.'

Gerry settled back in his seat as they pulled out onto the main road. The sun was low in the sky and all around them they could see green on one side and sea on the other.

'I think I'm going to like this place,' he said with a smile, folding his hands in his lap.

Kristie blinked. Although there were a number of people around the ferry terminal, as soon as they moved further away the crowds and traffic seemed to disperse quickly. There was a cluster of shops, pubs and a few hotels scattered along what appeared to be the main street of the Scottish town, but in a few moments the main street had disappeared, only to be replaced with a winding coastal country road.

'I've never seen so much green,' she said, trying to keep her eyes fixed on the road rather than the extensive scenery.

Gerry laughed. 'You don't get out of Los Angeles often enough. Too much dry air.'

A few splotches of rain landed on the windscreen. Kristie frowned and flicked a few of the levers at the side of the wheel, trying to locate the wipers. The blinkers on the hire car flicked on and off on either side. She let out a huff of exasperation as she tried the other side.

'Road!' Gerry's voice pulled her attention back to the road as an approaching car honked loudly at her. She yanked the wheel back in an instant, her heart in her mouth. The car had drifted a little into the middle of the road as she'd tried to find the wipers. She cursed out loud as she pulled it back to the correct side of the road—which felt like the wrong side. 'Darn it. Stupid road,' she muttered.

Gerry shook his head. 'No multiple lanes here. Get with it, Kristie. Embrace the countryside.'

She pressed her lips together. She hadn't seen a single coffee shop she recognised, or any big department stores. What did people do around here? Her grip tightened on the wheel as the rain changed from a few splats to torrential within a few seconds. Her hand flicked the lever up and then down to quicken the windscreen-wiper speed. It was almost as if a black cloud had just drifted over the top of them. She leaned forward and tried to peer upwards. 'What is this? Five minutes ago the sun was shining.'

She knew she sounded cranky. But she was tired. She was jet-lagged. She wanted some decent coffee and some hotel room service. She didn't even know what time zone she was in any more.

A sign flashed past. 'What did that say?' she snapped.

'Go left,' said Gerry smoothly.

She flicked the indicator and pulled into the busy parking lot in front of her. There was a white building to their right, set next to the sea.

The rain battered off the windscreen and the trees edging the parking lot seemed to be lolling to one side in the strong winds.

Gerry let out a low laugh at her horrified face. 'Welcome to Scotland, Kristie.'

'Tell me you're joking.' He stared across the room at his colleague Magda, who had her feet up on a nearby stool and was rubbing her very pregnant belly. She sighed.

'I signed the contract ten months ago. Before, you know, I knew about this.'

'You signed a contract for filming in our practice without discussing it with me?'

She shot him an apologetic look. 'I did discuss it with you.' She leaned forward to her laptop and scrolled. 'There.' She pointed to her screen. 'Or maybe not quite discussed, but I sent you the email. I forwarded the details and the contracts. So much has happened since then.' She let her voice slow for a second.

He knew what she meant. In the last year he'd gone from helping out at the practice as a locum to taking over from his dad when he'd died. This had been his father's GP practice, and Rhuaridh had been left in the lurch when his father had been diagnosed with pancreatic cancer and died in the space of a few weeks. Due to the difficulties in failing to recruit to such a rural post, he'd spent the last ten months, giving up his own practice in one of the cities in Scotland, packing up his father's house and selling his own, and trying to learn the intricacies of his new role. It was no wonder this piece of crucial information hadn't really stuck.

He ran his hand through his thick hair. 'But what on earth does this mean?'

Magda held up her hands. 'I'm sorry. I meant to talk to you last week when I sent them your details instead of mine—but I had that scare and just didn't get a chance.'

Rhuaridh swallowed and took a look at Magda's slightly swollen ankles. This was a much-wanted baby after seven years of infertility. Last week Magda had had a small fall and started bleeding. It had been panic stations all round, even from the team of completely competent staff in this practice and at the nearby cottage hospital. It seemed that practically the whole island was waiting for the safe delivery of this baby. There was no way he was going to put his colleague under any strain.

He sighed and sat down in the chair in front of her as he ran his fingers through his hair. 'Tell me again about this.'

The edges of her lips quirked upwards. They both knew he was conceding that she hadn't really told him properly at all.

'It's a TV show. *A Year in the Life of...*' She held out her hands. 'This one, obviously, is a doctor. It's an American company and they specifically wanted a doctor from Scotland who worked on one of the islands.'

He narrowed his gaze. 'I didn't know you wanted to be a reality TV star.' He was curious, this didn't seem like Magda at all.

She laughed and shook her head. 'Reality TV? No way. What I wanted, and what we'll get—' she emphasised the words carefully '—is a brand-new X-ray machine for the cottage hospital, with enough funds for a service contract.'

'What?' He straightened in the chair.

She nodded. 'It's part of the deal.'

Rhuaridh frowned. How had he managed to miss this? The X-ray machine in their cottage hospital was old and overused. Even though the staff had applied to the local health board every year for an upgrade and new facilities, NHS funding was limited. While their machine still worked—even though it was temperamental—it was unlikely to be replaced. A new machine could mean better imaging, which would lead to fewer referrals to the mainland for potential surgeries. Fractures could be notoriously hard to see. As could some chest complaints.

A better machine would mean more accurate diagnosis for patients and less work all round.

He looked at Magda again with newfound admiration. 'This is the reason you applied in the first place, isn't it?'

She grinned and patted her belly again. 'Give a little, get a little. You know I hate reporting on dusky X-rays. We'll have a brand-new digital system where we can enlarge things, and ping them on to a specialist colleague if we need to.' She shrugged, 'Just think of all those ferry journeys that won't need to happen.'

He nodded. Being on an island always made things tougher. Their cottage hospital only had a few available beds, which were inevitably full of some of the older local residents with chronic conditions. They had a small A and E department and a fully equipped theatre for emergencies but it was rarely used. Occasionally a visiting surgeon would appear to carry out operations on a couple of patients at a time, but they weren't equipped to carry out any kind of major surgery and any visiting consultant had to bring their whole team.

Whilst their facilities were probably adequate for their population of five thousand, every year the influx of holiday tourists during the summer months took their numbers to over twenty thousand. Slips, trips and falls made the X-ray machine invaluable. Rhuaridh had lost count of the number of times he'd had to send someone with a questionable X-ray over on the ferry to the mainland for further assessment.

'Sometimes I think I love you, Magda,' he said as he shook his head.

She wagged her finger. 'Don't tell David you said that, and just remember that while I tell you the rest.' He smiled. He'd known Magda's husband for the last ten years. He'd watched his friend battle to win the heart of the woman in front of him.

'What's the rest?' he asked as he stood up and stretched his back.

Magda bit her bottom lip. 'The filming happens for three days every month. You don't have to do anything special. They just follow you about on your normal duties. They take care of patient consent for filming. You just have to be you.'

The words were said with throwaway confidence but from the look on Magda's face she knew what was coming.

'Three days every month?'

She nodded. 'That's all.'

He pressed his lips together. It didn't sound like *That's all* to him. It sounded like three days of someone following him around and annoying him constantly with questions. It sounded like three days of having to explain to every single patient that someone was filming around him. He could kiss goodbye to the ten-minute consultation system that kept the GP practice running smoothly. He could wave a fond farewell to his speedy ward rounds in the community hospital where he knew the medical history of most of the patients without even looking at their notes.

'Three days?' He couldn't keep the edge out of his voice. He'd spent his life guarding his privacy carefully. Magda knew this. They'd trained together for six years, then jokingly followed each other across Scotland for a variety of jobs. It had been Rhuaridh who had introduced Magda to the isle of Arran off the west coast of Scotland—a place she'd fallen instantly in love with. It had been Rhuaridh who had introduced Magda to his best friend David, and his father Joe, who'd looked after the cottage hospital and GP practice on the island for thirty years. She knew him better than most. She knew exactly how uncomfortable this would make him.

She put her feet on the floor and leaned forward as best as she could with her swollen stomach. 'I know it's bad timing. I never thought this would happen.' Tears formed in the corners of her eyes. 'I always meant for it to be me that did the filming. I thought it might even be fun. Some of our oldies will love getting a moment on TV.'

He could hear the hopeful edge in her voice. He knew she was trying to make it sound better for him.

He shook his head. 'It...it'll be fine, Magda. Don't worry. You know I'll do it.' He could say the words out loud but he couldn't ignore the hollow feeling in his chest. Three days' filming every month for the next year. It was his equivalent of signing up for the ultimate torture. This was *so* not his comfort zone.

He took a deep breath. 'Okay, it's fine. You concentrate on baby Bruce. Don't worry about anything. We both know you should currently be at home, not here. Leave this with me.'

She gave a half-scowl. 'I am *not* calling my baby Bruce.'

It was a standing joke. David's family had a tradition of calling the firstborn in their family Bruce. David had missed out. He was the secondborn. Once Magda had got past the three-month mark both David and Rhuaridh had started teasing her about the family name.

He laughed. 'You know you are. Don't fight it.' He glanced at the pile of work sitting on his desk. It would take him until late into the night. With Magda going on maternity leave, and no locum doctor recruited to fill the gap, everything was going to fall to him. He was lucky. He worked within a dynamic team of advanced nurse practitioners, practice nurses and allied health professionals. He already knew they would support him as best they could.

Life had changed completely for him once his father had died. He'd felt obligated to come back and provide a health service for the people of the island when the post couldn't get filled. Unfortunately, Zoe, his partner, had been filled with horror at the thought of life on Arran. He hadn't even had the chance to ask whether she thought a long-distance relationship could work. She had been repelled by the very prospect of setting foot on the island he'd previously called home and had run, not walked, in the opposite direction.

All of that had messed with his head in a way he hadn't quite expected. He loved this place. Always had, always would. Of course, as a teenager wanting to study medicine, he'd had to leave. And that had been good for him. He'd loved his training in the Glasgow hospitals, then his time in Edinburgh, followed by a job in London, and a few months working for Doctors Without Borders, before taking up his GP training. But when things had happened and his father died suddenly? That whole journey home on the boat had been tinged with nostalgia. Coming home had felt exactly like coming home should. It had felt as if it was supposed to happen—even though the circumstances were never what he had wanted.

He moved over towards the desk and looked at Magda. 'So, when exactly does this start? In a few months?'

There was a nervous kind of laugh. 'Tomorrow,' Magda said as she stared out the window. 'Or today,' she added with a hint of panic as her eyes fixed on the woman with blonde hair blowing frantically around her face in the stiff Firth of Clyde winds. Rhuaridh's eyes widened and he dropped the file he'd just picked up.

'What?' His head turned and followed Magda's gaze to the car park just outside his surgery window.

The woman was dressed in a thin jacket and capri pants. It was clear she was struggling with the door of her car as it buffeted off her body then slammed in the strong winds. She didn't look particularly happy.

'You've got to be joking—now? No preparation time, nothing?'

Magda gave an uncomfortable swallow, her blue eyes meeting his. 'Sorry,' she whispered. 'I just got caught up in other things.'

He could sense the panic emanating from her. He felt his annoyance bubble under the surface—but he'd never show it.

His brain started to whirl. He'd need to talk to patients. Set up appropriate consultations. Make sure nothing inappropriate was filmed. He wanted to run a few questions past his professional organisation. He knew there had been some other TV series that had featured docs and medical staff, and he just wanted a bit of general advice.

A piece of paper flew out of the hand of the woman outside. 'Darn it!' Even from inside her American accent was as clear as a bell.

Magda made a little choking sound. He turned to face her as she obviously tried to stifle her laugh. Her eyebrows rose. 'Well, she looks like fun.'

Rhuaridh pressed his lips together to stop himself from saying what he really wanted to say. He took another breath and wagged his finger at Magda. 'Dr Price, I think you owe me.'

She held out her hand so he could help pull her up from the chair. 'Absolutely.' She smiled.

Gerry seemed to be taking the wind in his stride. 'Why did we come here first?' she muttered as she opened the boot of the car to grab some of their equipment.

'Best to get things started on the right foot. Let's meet our guy, establish some ground rules, then crash.'

She gave him a sideways glance. Maybe her older colleague was more fatigued than he was admitting. She batted some of her hair out of her face. The sign outside the building read 'Cairn Medical Practice', with the names of the doctors underneath.

'Roo-ah-ree.' She practised the name on her tongue as they made their way to the main entrance. Gerry already had a camera under one arm. One thing for Gerry, he was ever hopeful.

'Roo-ah-ree.' She practised again, trying to pretend she wasn't nervous. So much was riding on this. She had to make it work. She had to make it interesting and watchable. There hadn't been background information on this doc. Apparently he'd been the last-minute replacement for someone else. And if he was anything like the majority of the people on the ferry he would be grey-haired, carry a walking stick, and be wearing a sturdy pair of boots.

The ferry. What if she still smelled of sick? She felt a tiny wave of panic and grabbed some perfume from her bag, squirting it madly around her before they went through the main entrance door.

They stepped into a large waiting area. It was empty but looked…busy. Some of the chairs were higgledy-piggledy, magazines and a few kids' toys were scattered around the tables and floor. She could see some tread marks on the carpet. This place had a well-used feel about it.

She glanced at her watch. There was no one at the reception desk. It was after six p.m. The sign on the door said that was closing time. 'Hello?' she ventured.

There was the slam of a door from somewhere and a tall ruffled, dark-haired man appeared from the back of the building. He had the oddest expression on his face. It looked almost pained.

'Hi, sorry,' he said. 'Just seeing my pregnant colleague out.' His eyes seemed to run up and down the two of them. 'You must be the TV people.'

His accent was thick, almost lilting, and it actually took her a few seconds to tune in and process his words. A frown appeared on his forehead at the delay. 'Rhuaridh Gillespie?' He lifted his hand and pointed to his chest.

Oh, my goodness. She was going to have to concentrate hard—and she didn't just mean because of the accent. He was so *not* what she expected. Instead of an old wrinkly guy, she had a lean, muscled guy with bright blue eyes and slightly too long tousled dark hair. He was wearing a light blue shirt and dress pants. And he didn't look entirely pleased to see them.

Something sparked in her brain and she walked forward, holding her hand out, knowing exactly how dishevelled she looked after their long journey. 'Kristie Nelson. It's a pleasure to meet you, Roo—' She stumbled a little. 'Dr Gillespie,' she said, praying that her signature smile would start working any moment soon.

For a while, that had kind of been her trademark. With her styled blonde locks, usually perfect makeup and 'signature' wide smile, there had been a time on local TV when she'd become almost popular. That had been the time she'd had oodles of confidence and thought her star was going to rise immensely and catapult her to fame and fortune. Instead, she'd fallen to the earth with a resounding bump.

He reached over and took her hand. It was a warm, solid grip. One that made her wonder if this guy worked out.

'Like I said, Rhuaridh Gillespie.' He leaned over and shook Gerry's hand too.

'Gerry Berkovich. Camera, lights, sounds and general dogsbody for the good-looking one.' He nodded towards Kristie.

She slapped his arm. 'As if!'

Dr Gillespie didn't even crack a smile. In fact, he barely held in his sigh. He gestured towards the nearest office. 'Come and have a seat. I've kind of been thrown in at the deep end here, so we're going to have to come to an agreement about some boundaries.'

It was the edge to his tone. She shot a glance at Gerry, who raised one corner of his eyebrow just a little. This didn't sound like the best start.

She swallowed and tried to ignore the fact she was tired, now hungry, and desperately wanted a shower and five minutes lying on a bed and staring up at a ceiling. She'd been travelling for twenty hours. She'd been in the company of other people for more than that. Sometimes she needed a bit of quiet—a bit of down time. And it didn't look like it would happen anytime soon.

Rhuaridh showed them to seats in his office.

Kristie had dealt with lots of difficult situations over the last few years in TV and moved into autopilot mode.

'I'm sure everything will be fine,' she said smoothly. 'Contracts have already been agreed—'

'Not by me,' he cut in sharply, 'And not by my patients. In fact...' he took a deep breath, lifting one hand and running it through his dark scraggy hair '...I'll need to get my professional organisation to take a look at this contract to make sure no patient confidentially will be breached inadvertently.'

He was speaking. But she wasn't really hearing. It was all just noise in her ears.

'This was all looked at—all prepared beforehand.' She could cut in too. As it went, she didn't know a single thing about the show's contracts because she'd had nothing to do with any of this. All she knew was she was on a schedule. She had three days to film enough stuff to get forty-one minutes of usable footage. Much harder than it sounded.

'I've been thrown into this. I won't do anything to compromise my patients, or my position here.' His voice was jagged and impenetrable. She could see him building a solid wall in front of himself before her very eyes. Her very tired eyes.

She'd thought he'd looked kind of sexy earlier. If this guy could do a bit of charm, the ladies would love him. But it seemed that charm and Dr Gillespie didn't go in the same sentence. 'I'm sure that—'

He stood up sharply. 'I won't move on this.'

'But we only have three days...'

Gerry gave a little cough. She turned sideways to look at him and he gave an almost invisible shake of his head.

'I'll get back to you as soon as I can. I suggest you go and check into your accommodation and try and...'

he shot her a glance as if he was struggling to find the right words '...rest.'

He walked over to the door and opened it for them. This time he didn't even meet her gaze. 'I'll be in touch.'

Kristie was feeling kind of dazed. Had she just been dismissed? She wanted to stand and argue with him. Who did this guy think he was? Arrogant so-and-so. She'd travelled twenty hours for this.

But it was almost as if Gerry read her mind. He grabbed hold of her elbow as he led her back to the car.

The sky had got darker again as thick grey clouds swept overhead, followed by the obligatory spots of rain.

She opened the car and slumped into the driver's seat. Gerry started talking. 'I can shoot some of the scenery. Get a shot of the exteriors, the roads, the surgery. Maybe we could get someone to show us around the—what did they call it in the file—cottage hospital? I could even get a few shots of the ferry docking and leaving.'

'That will fill about five minutes of film when it's all edited down,' she groaned. She leaned forward and banged her head on the steering wheel. 'Why didn't I get the museum curator in Cairo? The person who is training to be an astronaut? Why did I have to get the grumpy Scottish doctor?' She thumped her head again, just to make sure Gerry understood just how frustrated she was.

'Kinda good looking, though,' he said unexpectedly.

'What?' She sat back up and shot him a weird look.

'I said, he's kind of good looking. And that cross demeanour? I think some folks might like it.'

Kristie shook her head. 'At this rate the whole first episode will have to be subtitled. Did you hear how fast he talks? And how thick that accent is?'

Gerry gave a slow appreciative nod as he folded his

arms across his chest. 'He's practically got Highland warrior stamped on his forehead.' He twisted towards her and tapped one finger on his chin, looking thoughtful. 'Hey? What do you think your chances are of getting him in a kilt?'

It was no use. Her brain was clearly switching off, and Gerry's was clearly switching on. She just couldn't function.

She let out a kind of whimper. 'Blooming Arran. I need food, a shower and a bed. Tell me you know where our hotel is.'

Gerry smiled. 'It's about a five-minute drive from here. And it's not a hotel. It's a cottage. Apparently accommodation can be tricky here. There're only a few hotels, but some holiday lets. We'll be lucky if we stay in the same place twice.'

Kristie put both hands on the steering wheel and started the engine. 'Just tell me which direction.' Her head was starting to thump. It was probably the jet-lag and a bit of dehydration. If she couldn't get something in the can in the next three days she would be toast. Her career was already dangling by a thread. Another failure against her name and Louie would be right—no one would want to work with her.

She was going to have to try all her Kristie charm on Dr Grump. Because if she didn't, who knew what could happen next?

They were sitting in his waiting room—again. Patients had already started asking questions. Some were even volunteering to be filmed. Three days of this every month for the next year?

He'd checked with his union. Apparently the TV contract was standard, and the appendix regarding patient consent was similar to one used by other TV series. As long as consent was granted and paperwork completed, there was no reason for him not to continue.

Truth was, he'd heard this news one day ago, but still couldn't bring himself to tell the TV crew. The guy—Gerry—permanently looked as if he could go to sleep at the drop of the hat, whereas his counterpart—Kristie—looked more wound up than the tightest spring.

Pam, one of the secretaries, stuck her head around the door. She had a sheaf of messages in her hand. 'Hospital called. X-ray problems again. Mrs McTaggart needs her painkillers upped. John Henderson phoned—sounded terrible—I've put him down for a house call, and...' She paused for a second, giving him a wary look. 'And I've got his permission to take the film crew.'

Rhuaridh's head flicked up from the bunch of prescriptions he'd been signing. Pam sighed. She was another member of staff that he'd inherited from his father, meaning she knew him better than most. 'You did what?'

Pam never pandered to him. 'Magda had already gone through all the patient permissions with me. So I've started getting them. Now hurry up and take that woman out of my waiting room before she spontaneously combusts.' Pam spun around and left, not giving him any chance to respond.

Rhuaridh leaned back in his chair and glanced at his watch. Nearly three p.m. He could do this. A few hours today, then all of tomorrow and he wouldn't have to see them again for another month. He tried to rationalise it in his brain. How bad could this be?

He pasted his best kind of smile on his face and walked outside.

* * *

Finally. He'd finally graced them with his presence.

There were only so many outdoor shots they could film on Arran—and Gerry had shot them all. Filler time, to use around the actual, proper filming. The thing they didn't have a single second of.

For a second yesterday, as they'd sat in the waiting room all day, she'd had half a mind to try and put a secret camera in this guy's room. It wasn't that she didn't know all the unethical issues with this, it was just that she was feeling *that* desperate.

And after two days of waiting, Rhuaridh Gillespie gave them a half-nod of his head. 'I've checked things out. We need to go to the local hospital. You'll need to sort out your permissions with the patients when you get there.'

She refused to let that make her mad. She'd already spent part of the night before meeting the nurse manager in charge at the hospital and sorting out all the paperwork with the long-stay patients.

She hadn't let Gerry see that she'd actually been sick outside before they'd entered. She'd been determined that she had to get the first visit to the place over and done with. Once they'd got inside and made the obligatory introductions she'd stuck her hands in her pockets so no one could see them shaking. If she'd had any other choice, she would have walked away from filming inside a hospital. But the fact was, there wasn't another choice. It was this, or nothing. So she'd pushed all her memories into a box and tried to lock it up tight.

Once the horrible squirming feeling in her stomach had finally disappeared, she'd decided that distraction was the best technique so she'd spent some time talking with some of the older patients, and had already decided to go back and interview a few of them on camera.

So by the time they joined Rhuaridh in his black four-by-four and he drove down the road to the hospital she felt a bit better prepared and that horrible ominous sensation had diminished a little. The journey only took a few minutes.

It became pretty clear in the first moments after they entered the hospital that Rhuaridh wasn't going to give them any chance to prepare, lightwise, soundwise or anything-wise. It was almost as if he was determined to ignore them.

Gerry murmured, 'I can work around him.'

Kristie straightened her spine. If she didn't start to get some decent filming soon she could kiss her career goodbye. But there was a little fire of anger burning down inside her. She didn't let people ignore her. And she'd checked the contract, she knew exactly what Dr Gillespie was getting in return for doing this. He *owed* her three days of filming every month, and if this guy didn't start to deliver, she wouldn't hesitate to remind him.

But Kristie knew, at least for now, she should try and ease him into this filming. Maybe the guy was nervous. Maybe he was shy. Or maybe the guy was just a jerk. Part of her was mad. Did he have any idea how hard she was finding this? Obviously not. But whatever it was that was eating him, she had less than a day and a half to find out.

'So, Dr Gillespie, can you tell me about the first patient we'll be seeing?'

She could see the muscles under his white shirt tense. The ones around the base of his neck were particularly prominent. She nodded to Gerry to keep filming as Rhuaridh muttered a few unintelligible words.

'To the camera, Dr Gillespie,' she said smoothly.

He blinked and turned towards her just as Gerry flicked on their extra light. She almost stepped back. Resentment and annoyance seemed to ooze from every pore. For a second she was sure he was going to say no.

So she moved quickly. 'In fact, let's start with introductions. Face the camera, I'll introduce you, then you can tell the viewers a little about yourself.' She shot him a look, then added in a quiet voice, 'And don't mumble.'

She would never normally do things like this. Usually she would go over all the introductory questions with their subject, check their responses, and make sure everyone was comfortable before they started filming. But the fact was—on this occasion—they just didn't have the time.

Before he had a chance to object she turned to the camera and gave her widest smile. 'Hi, there, folks. It's Kristie Nelson here, and I'm your host for...' She realised her mistake almost instantly, but no one watching would notice it. Did this guy know he was going to be called a Hot Highland Doc for the next year? Maybe better to keep some things quiet, this was already an uphill struggle.

She was smooth. She'd been doing this too long. '*A Year in the Life of...*' She let her voice tail off and held both hands towards Rhuaridh. 'Our doctor. And here he is, this is Rhuaridh Gillespie and he works on the Isle of Arran. Dr Gillespie, can you tell us a little bit about your background and the work that you do?'

Rhuaridh did his best impression of a deer in the headlights. She gave him a little nudge in the ribs and he actually started.

He stared at the camera. Gerry kept it still while

he stuck his head out from behind the viewfinder and mouthed, 'Go,' to him.

Rhuaridh gave the tiniest shudder that Kristie was sure only she could see before he started talking. 'Yes, hi, thanks. I'm Rhuaridh Gillespie. I grew up on this island—Arran—before leaving to train in Glasgow as a doctor, then I've worked in a number of other hospitals, and for Doctors Without Borders. I trained as a GP—a general practitioner—like my father, then came back last year to take over the practice when my father...' he paused for a split second before quickly finding a word '...retired.'

She was surprised. He was doing better than expected, even though he still looked as though he didn't want to be there.

'Can you tell the viewers a little about Arran?' she asked.

'It's an island,' he said, as though she'd just asked a ridiculous question.

She kept the smile firmly in place. 'Can you tell the viewers a little about the people here, and the hospital? What was it like growing up here?' The curses shooting across her brain stayed firmly hidden.

He gave a slow nod as if he finally understood that most people watching wouldn't have a single clue about Arran. 'Growing up here was...' his eyes looked up to the left '...fun. Free. Yeah, as a child I had a lot of free-dom. Everyone knows everyone in Arran...' he gave a half-smile '...so there's not much you can get away with. But a normal day was getting on my bike and disappear-ing into the hillsides with my friends. The lifestyle here is very outdoors.' He gave a small frown. 'Not everyone likes that.'

She wasn't entirely sure what he meant by that but didn't push. 'And the island?' she asked again.

It was almost like his professional face slid back into place. 'The population is around five thousand people, but in the summer months that can quadruple. We have a small cottage hospital with some long-stay beds and a small A and E department. I share the work in the hospital with the other GP on the island.'

'What happens in an emergency?' asked Kristie.

He looked a little uncomfortable. 'If it's a real emergency, then we send the patient off the island by air ambulance. In other circumstances we send people by road ambulance on the ferry and on to the local district general hospital.'

'How long does that take?' She could see a dozen potential stories forming in her head.

Now he was starting to look annoyed. 'The ferry takes around an hour. The transfer from Ardrossan—where the ferry docks—and the local hospital takes around thirty minutes.'

'Wow, that could be dangerous.'

His eyes flashed. 'Not at all. We assess all our patients and make sure they are fit for the transfer before they are sent.'

'What about people needing surgeries or baby emergencies?' She knew there was another word for that but just couldn't think of it.

'Most surgeries are pre-planned and our patients will have made arrangements to go to the mainland. All pregnant women on the island are assessed by both an obstetrician and their midwife. We've had a number of planned home deliveries on the island. Any woman who has a history that would give cause for concern for her, or for her baby, has arrangements made for admission to the mainland hospital to ensure the equipment and staff required are there for her delivery. We haven't had any problems.'

Dull. This place was sounding decidedly dull. All the good stuff—the interesting stuff—got sent to the mainland. But there were a hundred documentary-style shows that covered A and E departments. How on earth was she going to make this show interesting enough for people to keep watching?

She licked her lips and turned to the computer on top of Rhuaridh's case note trolley. 'So, Dr Gillespie, let's go back. Can you tell us about the first patient we'll be seeing?'

She had to keep this moving. Interesting footage seemed to be slipping through her fingers like grains of sand on the cold beach outside. *Please let this get better.*

There was not a single thing about this that he liked. Her American accent was beginning to grate on him. 'Don't mumble' she'd had the cheek to say to him. He'd never mumbled in his life. At least, he didn't think that he had.

That spotlight had been on him as he'd done the ward round in the cottage hospital. Normally it would have taken half an hour, but her incessant questions had slowed him down more than he'd liked.

She'd kept stopping and talking in a quiet voice to her cameraman and that had irritated him probably a whole lot more than it should have.

He was almost chanting the words in his head. *One more day. One more day.*

One of the nurses from the ward came and found him. 'Rhuaridh, there's been a message left to remind you about your home visit.'

'Darn it.' John Henderson. He still hadn't managed to drop in on him. He shook his head and grabbed his jacket and case.

'What? Where are you going?' Kristie wrinkled her nose. 'What's a home visit anyway?'

He stared at the woman standing under his nose who was almost blocking his way to the exit. He felt guilty. He'd meant to visit John before he came here, but this filming thing had distracted him in a way he hadn't been before.

He snapped, 'It's when you visit someone—at home.' He couldn't help the way he said the words. What on earth else could a home visit be?

Kristie only looked insulted for a few seconds. 'You actually do that here?'

Of course. She was from the US. It was a totally different healthcare system. They generally saw a specialist for everything. Doctors like him—general practitioners who occasionally visited sick patients at home—were unheard of.

'Of course.' He elbowed past her and moved out to his car.

'Let's go,' he heard her squeak to her colleague, and within a few seconds he heard their feet thudding behind him.

He spun around and held up his hand. 'You can't come.'

She tilted her chin upwards obstinately. 'We can.' She turned her notes towards him. 'John Henderson, he's on the list of patients that granted permission for us to film.'

Of course. Pam had already put a system in place to keep track of all this.

He couldn't really say no—no matter how much he wanted to. He shook his head, resigned to his fate.

'Okay, get in the car but we need to go now.'

They piled into the back of his car and he set off towards the farm where John Henderson lived.

It was almost like she didn't know when to stop talking. Kristie started immediately. 'So, can you brief us on this patient before we get there?'

Rhuaridh gritted his teeth. It was late, he was tired. He didn't want to 'brief' them on John Henderson, the elderly farmer with the biggest range of health problems in the world. He was trying to work out how he hadn't managed to fit John in before the visit to the hospital. He should have. Normally, he would have. But today he'd been—distracted.

And Rhuaridh Gillespie had never been distracted before. Not even when he'd been a junior doctor juggling a hundred tasks.

He didn't speak. He could hear her breathing just behind his ear, leaning forward expectantly and waiting for some kind of answer. Eventually he heard a little sigh of frustration and she must have sat back as the waft of orange blossom scent he'd picked up from her earlier disappeared.

The road to the farm was like every road to a farm on Arran. Winding, dark, with numerous potholes and part way up a hill. This was why he needed the four-by-four.

He pulled up outside the farmhouse and frowned. There was one light inside, in what he knew was the main room. John usually had the place lit up like the Blackpool Illuminations. They liked to joke about it.

He jumped out, not waiting for his entourage to follow, knocking loudly at the front door and only waiting a few seconds before pushing it open.

'John, it's Rhuaridh. Everything okay?'

There was a whimper at his feet and his heart sank as he turned. Mac, John's old sheepdog, usually rushed to meet anyone who appeared at the farm, barking loudly, but now he was whimpering in the hall.

He bent down, rubbed the black and white dog's head. 'What's up, Mac?'

Even as he said the words he had a horrible feeling that he knew what the answer would be.

He was familiar with the old farmhouse, having visited here numerous times in the last few months. Mac stayed at his heels as he walked through to the main room. It was shambolic. Had been for the last few years, ever since John's wife had died and he'd refused any kind of help.

The sofa was old and worn, the rug a little threadbare. A few pictures hung on the walls. But his eyes fixed on the sight he didn't want to see.

'John!' He rushed across the room, already knowing it would make no difference as he knelt on the floor beside the crumpled body of the old man. Mac lay down right next to John, still whimpering as he put his head on John's back.

John's colour was completely dusky. His lips blue. 'Here, boy,' said Rhuaridh gently as he pushed Mac's head away and turned John over onto his back.

His body was still warm, probably thanks to the flickering fire. But there were absolutely no signs of life. No breathing. No heartbeat. He did all the checks he needed to, but it was clear to him that John had died a few hours before.

It didn't matter that this had been on the cards for a

number of months. With his cardiac and respiratory disease John had been living on borrowed time for a while. But the fact was Rhuaridh had loved this old crotchety guy, with his gnarled hands through years of hard work and the well-weathered, lined face.

He looked peaceful now. His face more unlined than Rhuaridh had ever seen it before. Something inside Rhuaridh ached. John had died alone. Something he'd always been afraid of. If Rhuaridh had got here earlier—if he hadn't taken so long over the hospital ward round—he might have made it in time to hold his hand for his last few breaths.

He lifted John's coldish hand and clasped it between both of his. 'I'm sorry,' he whispered before he moved and closed John's eyelids with one finger. He couldn't help the tear he had to brush away. Mac moved back and put his head on John's chest. He hadn't thought it possible for a dog to look quite as sad as Mac did now.

He pulled his phone from his back pocket and made the obligatory phone call. 'Donald, yes, it's Rhuaridh Gillespie. I've just found John Henderson. Yes, I think he's been dead for a couple of hours. You will? Thank you. I'll wait until you get here.'

He sighed and pushed his phone into his pocket then started at the sound behind him.

Gerry had his camera on his shoulder and Kristie was wide-eyed. She looked almost shocked. A wave of anger swept over him. 'Put that away. It's hardly appropriate.'

Gerry pulled the camera to one side. Kristie seemed frozen to the spot. She lifted one shaking hand towards the body on the floor. 'Is…is that it? There's…nothing you can do?' It was the first time her voice hadn't been assured and full of confidence.

'Of course there's nothing I can do,' he snapped. 'John's been dead for the last few hours.'

He didn't add the thoughts that were currently streaming through his brain. *If she hadn't delayed him at the hospital, maybe he could have been here earlier. If she hadn't distracted him at the doctor's surgery, maybe he would have made John's visit before he went to the hospital.*

He knew this was all irrational. But that didn't make it go away.

Gerry's voice broke through his thoughts. 'Do you have to wait for the police?'

Rhuaridh nodded. 'They'll be here in a few minutes, and the undertaker will probably arrive at the same time.'

He turned his attention back to John and knelt down beside him again, resting his hand on John's chest. He felt odd about all of this. They'd stopped filming but it still felt like they were…intruding. And it was he who had brought them here.

Gerry seemed to have a knack of fading into the shadows, but Kristie? She stood out like a sore thumb. Or something else entirely. He'd been around plenty of beautiful, confident women in his life. What was so different about this one? She felt like a permanent itch that had got under his skin. Probably not the nicest description in the world but certainly the most accurate.

She stood to the side with her eyes fixed on the floor at first as his police colleague arrived then Craig, the undertaker. The unfortunate part of being a GP was that for he, and his two colleagues, this was semi-familiar territory.

When at last things were sorted and John's body was ready to be loaded into the undertaker's car, it was almost like the others knew and stepped back for a few seconds.

'What about Mac?' asked Donald, the police officer.

'Right.' For a few seconds Rhuaridh looked around. There was no one to take care of Mac, and they probably all knew that.

He looked over at the dog lying dolefully on the rug, his head on his paws. It didn't matter how impractical. How ridiculous. 'Give me a second.' He moved back over to John's body and slid his hand in to find the keys for the house in John's trouser pocket. Someone would need to lock up.

He stepped back to allow them to take John's body out to the hearse, then moved through to the kitchen and grabbed a bag, stuffing into it the dog's bowl and a few tins of dog food from the cupboard.

Kristie and Gerry were still hanging around in the hallway, Gerry still with the camera resting carelessly on his shoulder.

'You good?' Donald asked as Rhuaridh appeared back out of the kitchen.

He nodded and walked through to the main room. It was almost as if Mac knew because he jumped up and walked over, tail giving a few wags as he wound his body around Rhuaridh's legs.

'Come on then, old guy,' Rhuaridh said as he patted Mac's head. 'Looks like it's you and me.' He bent down and paused for a few seconds, his head next to Mac's. Mac had lived on a farm his whole life. How would he like living in a cottage by the beach? A wave of sympathy and affection flooded through him as he looked at Mac's big brown eyes. Of course he had to take this guy home.

It only took a few moments to put out the fire, flick the lights switches and lock the main door. Mac jumped into the back seat next to Gerry, who seemed quite happy to pat Mac on the drive back.

He dropped them at their rental and sped off into the dark as quickly as he could. His first day of filming couldn't have been worse. 'Please don't let them all be like this,' he murmured to Mac.

Kristie watched the car speed away. Her feet seemed frozen and she didn't even care about the brisk wind blowing around her. After a few seconds, Gerry slung his arm around her shoulders. She'd just seen her second dead body. And she couldn't work out how she felt about that—except numb. It was evoking memories that she just didn't want to recall. The little old man's house had been so...real. A few hours earlier he'd been there, and then he was just...gone.

This was exactly why she hadn't wanted to do this job. It was touching at places she kept firmly hidden, pulling at strings in her memory that she preferred not to remember. She shivered, and it wasn't from the cold.

Gerry looked at the red lights on the now far-off car. 'Funny kind of guy, isn't he?'

Anger surged inside her. 'He's got a contract. They're getting paid well for this.'

Gerry looked at her in amusement and shook his head, taking his hand off her shoulder and instead tapping the camera in his other hand.

'You haven't realised, have you?'

She shook her head. She had no idea what he was talking about.

Gerry smiled. 'That stiff-faced, crotchety doc guise

that he's pulling. This? This tears it all apart.' He gave another nod of his head. 'Kristie Nelson, in here, we have TV gold.'

CHAPTER TWO

June

THE FERRY WAS much busier this time. It seemed that
hordes of schoolchildren seemed to be going on some
kind of trip.

An older woman sat next to her, sipping a cup of tea.
This time Kristie had been prepared for the ferry crossing, and her anti-sickness tablets seemed to be doing
the trick. The older woman smiled. 'There's an outdoor
centre. They're all going there to stay for a week. I guarantee tonight not one of them will sleep. But after their
first day on Arran tomorrow, they'll all be sleeping by
nine o'clock.'

Kristie nodded half-heartedly. She wasn't really paying attention. Last night she'd watched the edited first
show about the Hot Highland Doc.

For want of a better word—it had been dynamite.

The editing had helped, showing the crabbit doctor—a
definitely unwilling participant in the show—turning to
a melting puddle of emotion at the death of his elderly patient. The final shot that Gerry had sneaked of him connecting with Mac the dog and saying the words, 'Looks

like it's just you and me,' would melt the proverbial hearts of the nation when it was shown in a few weeks.

Louie couldn't contain his excitement. 'Play on the fact he doesn't like you.'

Kristie had been a bit stung. 'What do you mean, he doesn't like me?' She hadn't realised it was quite so obvious to anyone but her.

'The audience will love it. You against him. The sparks are tremendous.'

Kristie bit her bottom lip as the announcement came for them all to head to their cars. Last time she'd been desperate to capture anything on camera.

This time around she felt the pressure. The producers didn't just like it, they *loved* it. Apparently the limited footage they'd captured had been the most entertaining— in a heart-wrenching kind of way—of any of the other *Year in the Life of* shows. They hadn't, of course, shown John Henderson. Gerry had filmed Rhuaridh from the back, leaning over the body, without revealing anything about the identity of the patient.

He'd also filmed 'around' Rhuaridh, capturing the essence of the home and the situation, with a particular focus on Mac, and how the professionals had dealt with everything, without sticking the camera in their faces. Kristie was a tiny bit nervous what people would think about it when it finally aired—but she knew it had squeezed at even her heart.

She climbed into the car with Gerry and gave him a nod, handing him a schedule. 'I've had time to be in touch a bit more. We're spending some time in the A and E department in the cottage hospital and filming one of the regular surgeries this time.'

He gave a nod. 'Here's hoping we get something good.' He raised one eyebrow. 'No pressure, of course.'

She shot him a glare. He was being sarcastic, of course.

'Where are we staying?'

Gerry wrinkled his nose. 'We've got a bed and breakfast this time—just down the road from the surgery.' His eyes twinkled. 'Guess we won't need to live on cereal for three days this time.'

She laughed. Neither she nor Gerry was blessed with cooking skills. 'I've decided. We're eating out every night and putting it on expenses.'

He nodded in agreement, 'Oh, I can live with that.'

They settled into the bed and breakfast quickly and made their way to the surgery for their scheduled filming. It was obvious news had spread since the last time they'd been there as a number of the patients sitting in the waiting room started talking to them as soon as they appeared.

'Are you the TV people?'

'Do you want to film me?'

'When will I be on TV?'

'Oh, you're here.' Her head shot up. It was hardly the most welcoming statement. Rhuaridh was standing in the doorway of his surgery dressed in a white shirt and navy trousers. It looked like he'd caught the sun in the last few days as his skin was more tanned than before.

Her first instinct was to hear a wolf whistle in her head. If her friend Alice had been here she was sure she would have actually done it in real life. One thing was for sure—Rhuaridh Gillespie was like a good old-fashioned prom king standing right in front of her.

But then her mouth dried. For a few seconds all she could remember was how she'd felt last time she'd been around him and he'd been dealing with Mr Henderson's dead body. She tried so hard not to let the others notice her reaction. Of course, Gerry had picked up on it. But he hadn't asked any questions.

The surgery filming went fine. For the first few patients it was obvious Rhuaridh wasn't a natural in front of the camera. Eventually, though, he seemed to forget they were there. But filming blood-pressure checks, medicine reviews, chest infections and leg ulcers didn't exactly make scintillating viewing. Kristie could feel a small wave of panic start to build inside.

By the time the day had come to an end she wasn't sure they had enough for even ten minutes of not very interesting film. She was just about to clarify their arrangements for the next day when Rhuaridh's pager sounded.

He looked just as surprised as she did. He hadn't been wearing one the last time she'd been there. A deep frown creased his forehead. It took him a few seconds to look up and speak once he'd checked the message. He gave his head a little shake. 'I thought it was for the local lifeboat…but it's not…it's Magda.'

He looked around his room blankly for a few seconds. Was this a sign of panic? She would never have suspected it from Rhuaridh Gillespie—and who on earth was Magda? A wife? A girlfriend? He hadn't mentioned either last time and she couldn't help but be a tiny bit disappointed. Within another few seconds the look was gone. He strode quickly across the waiting room, grabbing his bag. Kristie stayed on his heels, waving Gerry to follow. If this was something good, she wanted to make sure they didn't miss it.

He shot her a glance as she opened the back door of his car to climb inside. She saw the words form on his

lips—the words of dismissal—but she completely ignored him, turning to shout to Gerry instead, 'Let's go!'

It seemed for Rhuaridh it wasn't worth the time involved in fighting. Gerry had barely slammed the door
before he took off at speed onto the main road in Lamlash. As they started to drive, his phone started ringing.
He answered with a press on his steering wheel. 'Miriam,
are you with her?'

'Of course. How far away are you?'

'Less than two minutes.'

'Good.' The phone went dead.

Kristie was immediately intrigued. 'Who are you visiting?'

Rhuaridh's jaw was clenched. 'My colleague, Magda.
She's planned for a home delivery but things are looking complicated.'

Gerry shot her a look. There was a gleam in his eye.
This would be more interesting filming than what they'd
already got.

Kristie tried her best to phrase the question carefully.
She obviously wanted the footage—but didn't want to get
in the way if something could go wrong. Even she had a
line that wouldn't be crossed.

'We didn't get to meet your colleague,' she started.

Rhuaridh cut her off. 'You should have—she was the
one who signed up for the show. Her pregnancy was an
unexpected but very happy event.'

Gerry gave her a thumbs-up in the back of the car. If
Magda had initially signed for the show, she might not
object to being filmed. There was something in the way
Rhuaridh said the words. He had an obvious affection
for his colleague.

They pulled up outside a large white house at the end

of a long driveway. The front door was open and Kristie gestured to Gerry to get his camera on his shoulder ready to film.

They jumped out of the car and she hesitated as she heard the voices inside.

'Don't panic, Magda, let's get you out right now and I'll attach a CTG to monitor the baby. Now take a deep breath and try not to worry.'

She glanced at Gerry. Yip. He was already filming, capturing the sound inside.

Rhuaridh strode straight inside. Then stopped dead, meaning Kristie walked into the back of him.

'Oh, sorry.'

The main room of the house appeared to have undergone a complete transformation for the delivery of this baby. Right in the centre of the room was a large birthing pool. Soothing music was playing in the background, the blinds were closed and there were a few lit candles.

A heavily pregnant woman with blonde hair and a black loose wet kaftan was being helped from the pool by a worried-looking man and an older woman.

The woman looked up. 'Give me a hand, Rhuaridh.'

He stepped over quickly, taking the woman's place as she dropped to her knees and pulled a small monitor from a black case.

They eased Magda down onto the nearby sofa. Obviously no one was worried about getting it entirely wet.

'Tell me what's happening,' said Rhuaridh.

Kristie was tempted to clear her throat and remind them all that two perfect strangers were in the room, but the woman she thought was Magda looked up and waved her hand in a throwaway manner. 'Carry on,' she said as she grimaced.

'Another one?' asked the woman quickly.

Magda nodded and gripped tightly onto the man Kristie suspected was her husband.

Rhuaridh finally seemed to remember they were there. He pointed at his friends. 'Magda, David, Miriam, this is Kristie and Gerry from the TV show.'

Since Magda had already waved her hand in permission it seemed like he didn't feel the need to say anything else.

Kristie could see the way that David was looking at Rhuaridh. It was odd. She was brand new to these people but could already see a world of emotion without hearing any words. David was holding back panic, Magda had an edge of fear about her, and Miriam—who must be the midwife—had her professional face in place, while worry seemed etched on the lines on her forehead.

Rhuaridh knelt by the sofa and held Magda's hand. 'I thought you had this planned to precision.'

She patted her stomach, keeping her eyes firmly fixed on Miriam's actions as she attached the monitor. 'It seems Baby Price has his or her own plans.'

Miriam spoke in a low voice as she made the final adjustments. 'Spontaneous rupture of membrane a few hours ago. Labour has been progressing well with no concerns. Magda's around eight centimetres dilated, but she feels baby has stopped moving in the last ten minutes.'

'It's a boy,' said Rhuaridh. 'He's having a little sleep before the big event.' The hoarseness in his voice gripped Kristie around the chest. He was worried. He was worried about his friend's baby.

Magda tutted. 'We don't know it's a boy. We want a surprise.'

She was scared to make eye contact with Gerry. This

was beginning to feel like a bad idea. An old man tragedy she'd almost been able to bear. Anything with a baby? No way.

Miriam flicked the switch and the monitor flickered to life. After a few seconds a noise filled the room. Kristie almost let out a cheer. Even she could recognise the sound of a heartbeat.

But the rest of the room didn't seem quite so joyous. Magda clenched her teeth as she was obviously gripped with a new contraction.

All other eyes in the room seemed fixed on the monitor. Kristie leaned forward, trying to see the number on the screen. Ninety, wasn't that good?

'What's happening?' asked Magda.

There was sense in the room of collective breath-holding. The numbers on the screen and the corresponding beat noises crept upwards.

Rhuaridh and Miriam whispered almost in unison. 'Cord prolapse.'

This was all way above Kristie's head.

Magda let out a small squeak of desperation. 'No.' As a doctor it seemed she knew exactly what that could mean even if Kristie didn't.

Rhuaridh pulled out his phone and dialled. 'Air ambulance. Obstetric emergency.' His voice was low and calm. He moved over to the corner of the room where Kristie couldn't hear him any more. By the time he'd finished, David had walked towards him.

'Tell me what's happening.'

Rhuaridh nodded. 'The cord is coming down the birth canal before, or adjacent to, the baby. It means that every time Magda has a contraction, there's a risk the cord can be compressed and affect the blood flow to your baby.'

'Our baby could die?' David's words were little more than a squeak.

Rhuaridh shook his head, but Kristie could see the tense muscles at the bottom of his neck. The tiny hairs prickled on her skin. She was useless here—no help whatsoever. What did she know about medical emergencies?

She walked over to the window and looked outside, putting her hands on her hips and taking a few breaths.

The midwife's voice cut across momentary panic. 'Magda, we're going to change your position. Kristie!' The voice was sharp—one you wouldn't hesitate to follow. 'Run upstairs to the bedroom and grab me all the pillows on the bed.'

Rhuaridh finished his call and moved over to help move Magda onto her side. Kristie did exactly what she'd been told and dashed up the stairs in the house, turning one way then the other until she found the room with the large double bed and grabbed every pillow on it. She paused for the briefest of seconds as her eyes focused on the little white Moses basket at the side of the bed. The basket that had been placed there with the hope and expectation of a beautiful baby.

She held back the sob in her throat as she ran back down the stairs and thrust the pillows towards Rhuaridh. He and Miriam moved in unison. Rhuaridh spoke in a low voice as he helped adjust Magda's position with some pillows under her left flank and her right knee and thigh pulled up towards her chest. 'The position is supposed to alleviate pressure on the umbilical cord.' His words were quiet and Kristie wasn't sure if he was explaining to her or to David.

Magda's hands were trembling slightly. She was scared

and Kristie's heart went out to her. How must this feel? All of a sudden this felt like a real intrusion instead of a filming opportunity. How dared they be there right now?

Rhuaridh's gaze connected with hers. She wasn't quite sure what she was reading there. His voice seemed a little steely. 'Gerry, the air ambulance will land in the field next to the house—you might want to get that.' Gerry nodded and was gone in the blink of an eye.

She was still looking at those bright blue eyes, trying to control the overwhelming sensation of being utterly useless in a situation completely out of her area of expertise. Right now all she could do was send up a prayer that both Magda and this baby would be fine. It was amazing how quickly a set of circumstances could envelop you. Was this what every day was like for a doctor?

All of a sudden she had a new understanding of her grumpy doctor. This was a situation he could end up in any day, and today it involved a friend. She could almost sense the history in the room between them all. The long-standing friendship, along with the expectations. If something happened to Magda or this baby, things would never be the same again.

The monitor for the baby kept pinging. At least that was reassuring. Miriam and Rhuaridh had a conversation about whether another examination should be carried out. Both agreed not, though Kristie averted her gaze while Miriam did a quick visual check to reassure that no cord was protruding.

Rhuaridh moved over next to her and she caught a whiff of his woody aftershave. 'What's gone wrong?' Kristie whispered. Magda was holding her husband's hand, her eyes fixed on the monitor that showed the baby's heartbeat.

Rhuaridh spoke in a low, quiet voice. 'Magda wasn't at high risk for anything. She'd planned for this home birth within an inch of her life. Cord prolapse is unusual, and Magda has no apparent risk factors. But, right now, every time she has a contraction, the baby's heartbeat goes down, meaning the cord is being compressed.'

'Can't you do anything?'

He shook his head. 'The cord isn't obviously protruding, so we just need to get Magda to hospital as soon as possible. This baby needs to be delivered and Magda will need to have a Caesarean section.' He ran his hand through his hair, the frustration on his face evident. 'We just don't have the facilities here for that—or the expertise.'

'How long does the air ambulance take to get here?'

'Usually not long,' he said, then looked upwards as a thud-thud-thud noise could be heard in the distance.

Kristie's heart started thudding in her chest. Maybe everything was actually going to be okay?

Magda let out a groan, and Kristie held her breath as she watched Rhuaridh and Miriam move to support her as she was hit by another contraction. All eyes were on the monitor, and although the heart rate went down, it didn't go down quite as much as it had before.

Rhuaridh glanced towards the door a few times. Kristie could see him weighing up whether to ask David to go and meet the crew or whether to go himself.

After a few seconds he squeezed Magda's hand. 'Give me a minute.' Then he jogged out the main door and across towards the field. Kristie couldn't help but follow him. Gerry had positioned himself outside to capture the landing and the crew emerging from the helicopter.

They didn't waste any time. Within a few minutes Rhuaridh and Miriam had helped keep Magda into the

correct position as they assisted her onto the trolley. The
CTG monitor was swapped over for another and then
Magda and David disappeared inside the helicopter be-
fore it lifted off into the air.

They all stood watching the helicopter disappear into
the distance, Gerry with his camera firmly on his shoulder.

Once the helicopter finally vanished from view there
were a few moments of awkward silence. They all turned
and looked at the open door of the house. Miriam was
first to move, walking back into the house, putting her
hands on her hips and taking a deep breath.

The space felt huge and empty without Magda. The
birthing pool lay with only its rippling water, monitors,
blood-pressure cuff, the midwife's case and Rhuaridh's,
all alongside the normal family furnishings. Pictures of
David and Magda on their wedding day. The sofa with
the now squelchy cushions. A multitude of towels.

'I guess we'd better clean up,' said Kristie.

She wasn't quite sure where that had come from.
Cleaning up was definitely not her forte.

She bent down and lifted one of the sofa cushions,
wondering if she should take it to the kitchen to try and
clean it off and dry it out.

Miriam had started picking up all the midwifery
equipment.

Rhuaridh appeared in front of her and grabbed the
cushion. 'Leave it. We'll get it. You should just go.'

She blinked. Wondered what on earth she'd just done
wrong. She'd just witnessed a scene that had almost made
her blood run cold. Had she ever been as scared as this?

Yes. Probably. But that part of her brain was compart-
mentalised and knowingly put away. It was better that

way. It felt safer that way. The only time she let little parts of it emerge was when she volunteered three nights a month on the helpline. It was the only time she let down her guard. Virtually no one knew about that part of her life. Louie did. He'd been there for her when she'd got the original phone call telling her to come to the hospital. Gerry had been there too.

Louie had held her hand in the waiting room. He'd put an arm around her when she'd been given the news, and he'd stood at the door as she'd had to go and identify her sister's body.

Her beautiful, gorgeous, fun-loving sister. She almost hadn't recognised her on the table. Her skin had been pale with an ugly purple mark on her neck. When she'd touched her sister's hand it had been cold and stiff. The scars on her sister's wrists and inside her elbows had taken her breath away.

Everything had been new to her. She'd had no idea about the self-harm. She'd had no idea her sister had been depressed. Jess had hidden all of this from her—to all intents from everyone. It had only been a long time afterwards when she'd been left to empty her sister's apartment and go through her things that she'd discovered a frequently phoned number that was unfamiliar. The thing that had pricked her attention most had been the number of times that Jess had phoned—and yet had disconnected the calls in under a minute. That's when she'd discovered the helpline.

It was situated in their city and manned by counsellors and trained mental health professionals, staffed twenty-four hours a day. One visit to the centre had made her realise she had to try and help too. She'd undergone her training, and now manned the phone lines three nights a month. The small hours of the morning were sometimes the busiest in the call centre. She'd learned when to talk, and when not to. She'd learned that sometimes people just wanted to know that someone had heard them cry. Had *heard* them at all.

It always took her back to the fact that she wished Jess had stayed on the line a little longer—just once. It might have made the difference. It might have let her know she was safe to confide how she was feeling and didn't have to hide it.

Occasionally she would get a flashback to part of that first night. Hospitals were a place she'd generally avoided ever since, associating the sights and sounds with the memories of that night. It was part of the reason she'd been reluctant about this gig.

But now she was realising it was something more. Last month, with John Henderson's body, and this time, when she'd glanced at the cot upstairs—patiently waiting for its baby—she'd felt a sweep of something else. Pure and utter dread. The kind that made her heart beat faster and her breathing kind of funny.

Her heart had sunk as the helicopter had disappeared into the distance, not knowing what the outcome would be for Magda and the baby. She didn't care about the show right now. She didn't care about anything.

And all that she could see was this great hulking man standing in front of her with the strangest expression on his face. His hands brushed against hers as he closed them around the cushion, gripping it.

He gave a tug towards himself. 'I think it would be best if you go now.'

She couldn't understand. 'But the room…' She let go of the cushion and held out her hands, looking over at the birthing pool and wondering how on earth it would be emptied and taken down. 'You'll need help to clean up.'

She wanted distraction. She wanted something else to think about. Anything to keep her mind busy until there was news about mother and baby.

'I'm sure Magda and David would prefer that their house be fixed up by friends.' He emphasised the word so strongly that she took a step backwards and stumbled, putting a steadying hand on the window frame behind her.

It was then she saw it. The flash across his face. He needed distraction just as much as she did. Probably more. He must be worried sick. Of course he was.

She'd only just met this pregnant woman. He'd known her for—how long? She wouldn't even like to guess. She knew they'd been workmates in the practice but she hadn't really had a chance to hear much more.

'I want you to go now,' he said as he turned away. 'We'll let you know how things are.'

It was a dismissal. Blunt. She wanted to grab him by the arm and yank him around, ask him who he thought he was talking to. In another life she might have.

But if she fell out with Dr Gillespie the whole show could be up in the air. So instead she pressed her lips together and looked around for her bag, grabbing it and throwing it over her shoulder, walking out the room and leaving the disarray behind her.

Gerry was standing at the door. She didn't care if the camera was on or not. 'I hate him,' she hissed in a low voice as she walked past.

Rhuaridh knew he'd just been unreasonable. He knew that Magda had agreed to the TV crew filming. But none of them had expected the outcome that had just happened.

His heart felt twisted in a hard, angry knot. Every possible scenario was running through his head right now—and not all of them were good.

He wasn't an obstetrician. The limited experience he'd had had been gained when he'd been a junior doctor. He knew the basics. He knew the basics of a lot of things. But island communities were different from most. The water cut them off from the mainland. There was no quick road to a hospital with a whole variety of specialists and equipment at his disposal.

In the last few months there had been a mountain climber with a severe head injury, a few elderly residents with hip fractures, a diver with decompression sickness, and now an obstetric emergency. All situations where he'd felt helpless—useless even. He hated that his patients needed to wait for either a ferry crossing or an air ambulance to take them where they could get the help required. He hated that he had to stand and look into their eyes, knowing that on occasion that help might actually be too late. And today, when it had been his friend and colleague, he had felt as though he was being gripped around the chest by a vice.

He'd snapped needlessly at Kristie. He knew that. But he just couldn't think beyond what would happen next for Magda, David and the baby. And until he knew that, he didn't know what came next.

Guilt swamped him. 'Kristie, wait,' he shouted as he walked out after her.

She spun around towards him. The expression in her eyes told him everything he needed to know. She was every bit as panicked and worried as he was. She was also mad. And no wonder. He knew better than to act like this. He walked over and put a hand on her shoulder. 'I'm sorry,' he said quickly. 'I'm just worried.' He glanced up at the sky. The helicopter was well out of sight. He prayed things would go well. 'I didn't mean to snap. And thank you for your help in there. I just feel so...' He struggled to say the word out loud, not really wanting to admit it.

'Helpless?' Kristie added without hesitation. He could see her eyes searching his face. Wondering if he would agree.

He closed his eyes for a second and nodded as the rush of adrenalin seemed to leave his body all at once. 'Helpless,' he agreed with a sigh. 'I won't be able to think about another thing until I know they're both okay.'

'Neither will I,' she said quickly. Should he really be surprised? It was the first real time since she'd got here that he'd taken the time to really look at her, *really* see something other than the bolshie American TV presenter. There was something there. Something he couldn't quite put his finger on.

Her hand reached across her chest and covered the hand he had on her shoulder. He felt a jolt. It must be the warmth of her palm against his cold skin. She licked her bare lips. All her makeup had disappeared in the last few hours. She didn't need it. Something sparked in his brain. Had he really just thought that?

She squeezed his hand and spoke quietly as she held his gaze. 'Let's just do the only thing we can. Pray.'

His stomach gave a gentle flip as he nodded in agreement and looked back up at the sky. He pushed everything else away. Magda and the baby were all he could concentrate on right now. Anything else could wait.

CHAPTER THREE

July

PEOPLE WERE LOOKING at him a bit strangely, and he couldn't quite work out why. And it wasn't just the people he knew. Summer holidays had well and truly started and, as normal, the island's population had grown, bringing a stream of holidaymakers with minor complaints and medical issues to the island's GP surgery. This meant that he now had a whole host of strangers giving him strange sideways glances that turned into odd smiles.

It took one older lady with a chest infection to reveal the source.

'You're the handsome doc I saw on TV,' she said.

'What?' He was sounding the woman's chest at that point, paying attention to the auscultations of her lungs instead of to her voice.

She gave a loud tut then giggled. 'You really don't like that poor girl, do you?'

He pulled the stethoscope from his ears. 'Excuse me?'

'The pretty one. With the blonde hair. She looked shell-shocked by that death.' The woman leaned over and patted his hand. 'I'm sorry about your friend. How's Mac?'

For a few moments, Rhuaridh was stunned. Then the penny dropped like a cannonball on his head.

'You've seen the TV show?' He hadn't really paid attention to when it would air.

She grinned. 'Yes. It was wonderful. Best episode of that series yet.' She gave him a sideways glance and raised her eyebrows. 'And, yep, it's probably fair that they call you hot. But you really need to behave a bit better.'

He wasn't really paying attention to all her words. 'What do you mean—the death?'

She frowned at him, as though he were a little dense. 'Your friend. The farmer.'

'They showed that?' He felt a surge of anger. How dared they?

The old woman shook her head. 'Well, we didn't really see anything much at all. Just a pair of feet. Nothing else. It was more about...' she held her hands up to her crackly chest '...the feelings, the emotions. The love in the room.' She gave a wicked little shrug. 'And the tension. Like I said, you need to be nicer to that girl. She's very pretty, you know. She looked as though she could have done with a hug.'

Rhuaridh sat back in his chair. He was stunned. He'd kind of thought the TV show would only be shown in other countries—not this one. He hadn't expected people he met to have seen it. And he wasn't happy they'd shown the events at John Henderson's house.

The old woman sat back and folded her hands in her lap. 'Mind you, you brought a tear to my eye when you took Mac home with you. How is he, anyway? You didn't answer.'

It was almost like he was being told off. It seemed that parts of his life were now open to public view and scrutiny. Part of him wanted to see the episode—to check it didn't betray John Henderson's memory. But part of him dreaded to see himself on screen. It seemed like he might not have done himself any favours. His insides cringed. 'Mac's good,' he said on autopilot as his brain continued to whirl. 'He's settled in well.'

The old woman gave another tut and looked at him as though he didn't really know what he was doing. 'Well, are you going to write me a prescription or not? Erythromycin, please. It always works best.'

Rhuaridh picked up his prescription pad and pen. This was going to be a long, long day.

The boat was packed to the brim. There was literally not a single seat to be had, and it was lucky someone at the production company had pre-booked their car space and their rental. 'What is it?' said Gerry. 'Has the whole of mainland Scotland decided to visit the island at once?'

'Feels like it,' muttered Kristie as she was jostled by a crowd of holidaymakers. At least the sun was high in the sky and she'd remembered to take her sea sickness tablets.

She leaned on the rail as the ferry started to dock. 'The reception's been good hasn't it?'

Gerry nodded. 'I've not seen this much excitement in a while. And once they've seen the second episode? I think people will go crazy.'

Kristie blew out a long breath. The next episode was due to air in a few weeks. It was ironic really. The first episode had been all about death, and now the second was all about life. They'd improvised. Once they'd left the island, instead of heading straight back to Glasgow airport, they'd driven to the local maternity unit where they'd got Magda's permission to capture a scene with a beautiful healthy baby girl and two relieved, smiling parents. Even Kristie couldn't hide the tears at that point. But it had captured the story perfectly, and would give the viewers the happy ending they would all crave.

'What about me?' she asked Gerry. 'And what about him, what if he sees me saying I hate him?' Her stomach twisted uncomfortably. The producer had insisted on keeping all those elements in, saying the dynamics between her and Rhuaridh Gillespie were TV gold.

Gerry waved his hand as the gangplank was lowered and people started filing off the boat. 'I doubt he's seen it. And if he has? Too bad.'

They made their way down to the car. The car storage area was hot and claustrophobic. Gerry shrugged off his jacket and tugged at his shirt. 'You okay?' she asked.

He nodded. 'Just get me out into the fresh air.'

The plans were a little different this time. They'd agreed to focus more on Rhuaridh's role at the hospital rather than his role at the GP surgery. It seemed harsh, but if they hadn't had the drama with the delivery for the last episode things might have been a little dry.

But for the first day they were going to do some background filming around the hospital. Kristie wasn't sure how that would work out. Or how interesting it would be. At least this time she felt a little prepared and didn't dread it quite so much.

But she shouldn't have worried. The seventeen patients in the cottage hospital were delighted to see her and participate in the filming. She met an army war veteran who had dozens of naughty stories that had her wiping tears from her eyes. She met a young girl who was in the midst of cancer treatment who'd come down with an infection and was bribing the hospital kitchen staff to make her chocolate pancakes. She interviewed the hospital porter, who was eighty and refused to retire. She met a biker who'd come off his bike and fractured his femur. But he'd timed it just as a visiting orthopaedic consultant was doing his monthly clinic on Arran, so had had his surgery performed in the equipped theatre a few hours later.

All this filming without having to deal with Dr Grumpy—as Kristie had nicknamed him.

They'd arranged filming for a little later the next day as they'd been warned the local A and E could be quieter in the mornings. As they pulled up in the hospital car park they could already spot Rhuaridh's car—along with a whole host of others. 'I take it Friday afternoon is a busy time,' said Gerry as they got out of the car.

Kristie shrugged. 'We're trying to get away from the mundane. He's on call all weekend, so maybe we'll get something unusual.'

As they walked inside Gerry almost tripped. The waiting room was almost as busy as yesterday's ferry. He smiled. 'We might be lucky.'

Kristie looked around. 'Let's interview a few of the people waiting,' she said. The waiting room was full of a range of people. There looked like a whole host of bumps and breaks. A few kids had large eggs on their foreheads, others were holding arms a little awkwardly. Legs were on chairs, and some people were sleeping.

It didn't take long for Rhuaridh to spot them in the waiting room. His perpetual frown creased his forehead, then it was almost like he realised that had happened and he pushed his shoulders back and forced a smile on to his face. 'Kristie, Gerry, come through.'

The normally relatively quiet A and E department was buzzing inside. Names were written on a whiteboard, with times next to them. Three nurses and one advanced nurse practitioner were dealing with patients in the various cubicles.

The charge nurse, June, gave Kristie and Gerry a rundown of what was happening. She motioned to a set of rooms. 'Welcome to the conveyor belt.'

'What do you mean?'

June smiled. 'I mean that slips, fractures and falls are our biggest issue today. Everyone in the waiting room has already been assessed. We generally deal with the kids first, unless something is life threatening, then, if need be, an adult can jump the queue. But most of the people outside are waiting for X-rays, and quite a large proportion of them will go on to need a cast.' She pointed to a room that was deemed the 'plaster room' where one nurse, dressed in an apron, was applying a lightweight coloured fibreglass cast to a kid's wrist. There was another child with a similar injury already waiting outside to go in next.

Another nurse nodded on the way past. 'And I have all the head injuries. So far, nothing serious. But I have four kids and two adults to do neuro obs on for the next few hours.'

Rhuaridh walked up and touched Kristie's arm. 'Do you want to come and film a kid's assessment? He's probably got a broken wrist too, but you could capture the story from start to finish—probably in under an hour.'

Kristie couldn't hide her surprise at his consideration. She exchanged glances with Gerry. 'Well, yeah, that would be great, thanks.'

She was hoping that outwardly her calm, casual demeanour had not shifted. In truth, she could feel the beads of perspiration snaking down her back.

It was stupid. She knew it was stupid. But the A and E department was different from the ward. There was something about the smell of these places. That mix of antiseptic and bleach that sent a tell-tale shiver down her spine. She was counting her breathing in her head, allowing herself to focus on the children around her, rather than let any memories sneak out from inside.

It was working, for the most part, just as long as no one accidentally put their hand on her back and felt the damp spot.

Gerry filmed as they watched the assessment of the little boy, Robbie, who'd fallen off his bike and stuck his hand out to save his fall. Rhuaridh's initial hunch had been correct. It was a fracture that was correctable with a cast and wouldn't require surgery. He even went as far as to relieve Pam in the plaster room and put on the blue fibreglass cast himself.

As he washed his hands and the others left the room, Kristie couldn't help but ask the question that was playing around in her head.

'Why are you being so nice this time?'

He gave a cough, which turned into a bit of a splutter. 'You mean I'm not always nice?'

She choked, and tried to cover that with a cough too. By the time her eyes met his he was actually smiling. He was teasing her.

She put one hand on her hip and tilted her head.

'Okay, so you obviously know that you haven't been. What gives?'

'What gives?'

She nodded and folded her hands over her chest. She couldn't help her distinctly American expressions. It wasn't as if he didn't use enough Scottish ones of his own. Half the time she felt as if he should come with a dictionary. 'What are you up to, and why have you decided to play nice?'

He finished drying his hands and turned to face her head on. Today he was dressed a little more casually. A short-sleeved striped casual shirt and a pair of jeans.

'Someone gave me a telling-off.'

'Who?' Now she was definitely curious.

'An older woman who came to the surgery this morning. She basically told me to behave. I haven't been told that since I was six.'

She shook her head. 'I don't believe that for a second.'

He paused for a second, as if he was trying to find the right words. 'We need to talk about what's been filmed—what it's right for you to show. But there's something else first.'

She'd just started to relax a little, but those words—'what it's right for you to show'—immediately raised her hackles. She didn't like anyone telling her what to do.

She couldn't help her short answer. 'What do you mean—what it's right for us to show?' Part of her brain knew the answer to this already. She'd had a few tiny reservations about the filming at John Henderson's house. But it had just felt too important—too big—to leave out.

She was automatically being defensive, even though she knew she might partly be in the wrong. She'd wanted to pick up the phone—not to ask his permission, just to give him a heads-up. But even though she hadn't done that, something inside her now just wouldn't let her back down. What was it with this guy? It was like he'd drawn her in, almost made her laugh, just so she might let her guard down a little then he could get into a fight with her.

The tone of her voice had obviously annoyed Rhuaridh. The smile dropped from his face and he straightened more. 'I haven't seen it,' he said sharply. 'But I'm not sure I approve of you showing film of John Henderson's death. It seems…' a crease appeared in his brow as he tried to search for the correct word '…intrusive, unnecessary.' He shook his head. 'You didn't have the correct permissions.'

Every word seemed like a prickle on her skin. 'We got permission from Mr Henderson before we visited his home, *before* he died.'

She didn't mean to emphasise the word, but she was all fired up. And as soon as the words left her mouth she realised her mistake.

The look that passed over Rhuaridh's face was unmistakeable. Complete and utter guilt. It was almost like her mouth wouldn't stop working. It was like he'd questioned her integrity and her ethics. She wouldn't let anyone get away with that. Parts of her brain were telling her to stop and think, but her mouth wasn't paying any attention to those parts.

'And we shot everything from the back. You obscured the view of Mr Henderson. The only thing that was seen was his feet. Do you really think we'd show a poor dead man on the TV show?'

'You shouldn't have shown anything at all,' snapped Rhuaridh. 'You might have gained John's permission, but to show him after he died, that's just ghoulish!'

She folded her arms across her chest. 'Don't you dare question the integrity of the show. You admitted yourself you haven't seen it—you don't even know the context in which the scenes were shown.'

'The integrity of the show? You showed a dead man!' His voice was getting louder.

'We didn't!' she shouted back. 'And you have no idea how the public reacted to it. They loved it. They didn't think it was ghoulish. They thought it was wonderful. Emotional. And sad. The whole purpose of this show is to show them something real. You can't get much more real than death.'

Those words seem to bubble up from somewhere unexpected inside her. They came out harshly, because that's what death was to her. She could remember every emotion, every thought, every feeling that had encompassed her when she'd been in that hospital room. All the things she'd been trying to keep locked in a box, deep down inside her.

For the briefest of seconds Rhuaridh looked a bit taken aback. But it seemed he was every bit as defensive as she was. 'Death is private. Death is something that shouldn't be shown in a TV show.' He stepped forward. 'If the same thing had happened to Magda's baby, would you show that too?'

His words almost took her breath away. It was the first time she'd stuttered since she'd been around him. 'W-what? N-no.' She shook her head fiercely. 'No. Of course not. What kind of people do you think we are?'

'The kind of people who intrude in others' lives, constantly looking for a story.'

An uncomfortable shiver shot down her spine. It was almost like Rhuaridh had been in the room with Louie when he'd been telling her to find a story, make a story, stir up a story to keep their part of the show the most popular. Now she was just cross.

'Why did you agree to do this anyway? You obviously don't want to be filmed. You couldn't make it any more apparent that you don't want us here. Haven't you ever watched any of the reality TV shows based in hospitals before? What did you actually expect to happen?'

He put his hand to his chest. '*I* didn't agree to this. Magda did. I had less than ten minutes' notice that you were coming. And I couldn't exactly say no, because my pregnant colleague had already signed the contract and negotiated a new X-ray machine for our department. So don't make the mistake that any of this was my idea. And what makes you think for a second I've watched any reality TV shows?' He almost spat those last words out.

The words burned her—as if what she was doing was ridiculous and worthless. Everything about this guy just seemed to rile her up in a way she'd never felt before. 'Do you think it's fun being around a guy all day who treats you like something on the bottom of their shoe?'

The A and E charge nurse, June, walked into the room. 'What on earth is going on in here? I could hear you guys at the bottom of the corridor. This is a hospital, not some kind of school playground.'

It was clear that June wasn't one to mince her words. Heat rushed into Kristie's cheeks. How humiliating. She opened her mouth to apologise but June had automatically turned on Rhuaridh.

'This isn't like you. Why on earth are you treating Kristie like this? She's only here doing a job and she spent most of yesterday on the ward talking to all the patients. They loved her. They want her to come back.'

Rhuaridh had the good grace to look embarrassed. He hung his head. It was almost odd seeing him like that, his hands on his hips and his gaze downward. He gave a low-voiced response. 'Sorry, June. We're having a bit of a difference of opinion.'

'I'll say you are. This is my A and E department and if you can't play nicely together I'll just separate you. Kristie? I hope you like kids. We've got a few in the room down the corridor who all need some kind of treatment— I've checked with the parents and you can film. Rhuaridh, I've got a potential case of appendicitis I need you to review and a couple of X-rays for you to look at.' She looked at them both. 'Now, hop to it. I've got a department to run.' June turned on her heel and strode back out the door.

For a few seconds there was silence—as if both of them were getting over their outbursts. Rhuaridh spoke first. 'You wouldn't guess she was the mother of twins, would you?'

It was so not what she'd expected to hear, and unexpected laughter bubbled at the back of her throat.

It broke the tension in the room between them.

'I'm sorry,' he continued. 'I haven't been so hospitable and I know that. I guess I felt backed into a corner. This show isn't something I would have agreed to—certainly never have volunteered for. But I can't say no. The hospital needs the new X-ray machine. You can tell that alone just by the waiting room today.' He gave a slow shake of his head as the corners of his lips actually turned upwards. 'And you seem to have really bad timing.'

She let out a laugh. 'What?'

He kept shaking his head. 'I'm beginning to wonder if you're a jinx. First the thing with John Henderson, then the thing with Magda. You always seem to be around when there's a crisis.'

'You mean you never had any crises on Arran until we started filming?' She deliberately phrased the question so he'd realise he was being ridiculous.

He sighed. 'Of course we did. But believe it or not, lots of days are just normal stuff. Nothing that dramatic or exciting, and to be honest…?' He looked away. 'I kind of like those days.'

Now she was curious. She'd done a little more research on Rhuaridh Gillespie since the last time she'd been here. She knew he'd taken over at his father's surgery when they couldn't recruit anyone to the post.

'I'm surprised to hear you say that. I thought you only came here because you had to.'

He looked up sharply, as if he hadn't expected her to know that. 'Recruitment is an issue right across the whole of Scotland. It used to be that for every GP vacancy there would be fifty applicants. Now young doctors just don't want to go into general practice. They don't want to have to own a business—run a business, and take on the huge financial debt of buying into a practice. If they even train to work as a general practitioner, they can make more money working as a locum. Then there's less pressure, less responsibility and…' he shook his head '…absolutely no continuity of care for patients.'

Kristie leaned back against the wall. 'But you trained as a general practitioner. Did you just want to work as a locum?'

He met her gaze with a thoughtful expression, as if he hadn't expected her to ask this many questions. 'I had alternative plans. At my practice in Glasgow I also worked a few days in one of the city hospitals in Dermatology.

I covered outlying clinics across Glasgow, doing lots of minor surgery.'

Her mouth quirked upwards. 'You're a skin guy?'

He held out his hands. 'Biggest organ of the body. Why not?'

'And you can't do that here?'

He shrugged. 'Not as much. Sure, I can do biopsies, freeze moles with liquid nitrogen, or surgically remove anything small and suspicious. But when your population is usually around five thousand, that's not really enough people to only specialise in dermatology.'

She waited a few moments. 'So why didn't you just stay in Glasgow? Couldn't you just have left the practice here with only one doctor?'

Rhuaridh took a step back and leaned on the opposite wall. 'And leave Magda here on her own, covering the hospital and the GP practice? Leaving the community I grew up in and loved with no real service provision? What kind of person would that make me?'

It was like a bright light shining in her eyes. She could feel tiny pieces of the jigsaw puzzle slot into place.

Guilt. He'd felt responsible, and had come back to his home without really wanting to. This had a strange air of déjà vu about it. Wasn't this what had just happened with the TV series? He hadn't chosen to do this either, instead he was taking the place of his colleague unwillingly because he didn't want to let her, or the community, down. Kristie didn't doubt for one second that if he'd reneged on the contract, Arran would never get a new X-ray machine.

No wonder the guy was grumpy. Did he get to make any choices in this life?

She looked across the room into those weary blue eyes and said words she'd never have imagined herself saying. 'I guess it makes you a good person, Rhuaridh Gillespie.'

CHAPTER FOUR

August

MAC WAS LOOKING at him with an expression only a dog could give.

Rhuaridh bent down and rubbed his head. 'I'm sorry.' He meant it. He'd been neglectful. August was part of the summer season on Arran. From the end of June until the middle of August, Arran was full of Scottish, and lots of international, tourists. But come mid-August in Scotland the schools started again. Usually that would mean that things would quieten down.

But, in the UK, the English schools were still out. So, Arran was currently filled with lots of English holiday-makers. The beach had been packed all day. It seemed that croup was doing the rounds and between the surgery and the A and E department, he'd seen five toddlers with the nasty barking cough today alone. Chicken pox also seemed to be rearing its head again. Five members of one poor family were currently covered in the itchy spots.

He glanced at his watch. Kristie was due to arrive at some point and he was feeling quite...awkward.

He wasn't quite sure what had come over him last time around, and he had apologised to her, but they still had nine months of filming left. He counted in days. Twenty-seven more days around Kristie Nelson.

There was something about her. At first he'd thought it was the accent and the confidence. But he'd seen her waver on a few occasions. Her confidence was only skin deep. And that was another thing. To others, she may look like a typical anchor woman for an American TV show. Blonde, perfect teeth, hint of a tan and good figure. And somehow he couldn't help watching the way she flicked her thumb off her forefinger, or made that little clicking noise when she was thinking. It was weird. Even though he told himself she was the most annoying female on the planet, he couldn't help the way his mind would frequently drift back to something she'd said or done.

Mac nuzzled around his ankles. It snapped him back from the Kristie fog and he picked up Mac's lead and grabbed his sweater. 'Let's go, boy.' He opened the main door of his cottage and Mac bounded out towards the beach. He'd adjusted well to the move, and after a few short months it actually felt like Mac had always been there. He'd even employed a dog walker to take Mac out during the day when he was working.

The sun was dipping in the sky, leaving the beach scattered with violet evening hues. There were a few other people walking dogs, someone on a horse and a couple strolling along hand in hand.

The breeze tonight wasn't quite as brisk as it normally was. Laughter carried along the beach in the air. A group of teenagers was trying to set up a campfire.

Rhuaridh moved down closer to the firmer sand at the sea's edge. The beach ran for a few miles and Mac had got used to a long walk in the evening.

They'd only been walking for about ten minutes when

he heard thudding feet behind him. He turned to take a step one way or the other and Kristie ran straight into him.

'Oh! Wow.' She stepped back and rubbed her nose.

He laughed and shook his head. 'Where did you come from?'

She was still rubbing her nose. 'I came by your house. I wanted to chat to you about the schedule tomorrow.'

'You came by my house? I wasn't expecting to see you until tomorrow.' He was surprised. He hadn't known Kristie knew where he lived—and after their last meeting, he was even more surprised she wanted to turn up at his door.

She nodded. 'We ended up swapping flights and coming a day early.'

'Does that mean you're going home a day early?'

She let out a laugh. 'Don't even try to pretend you want me around, then.'

'No.' He cringed. 'I didn't mean it like that. I'm just wondering if you wanted to swap things around.'

She stopped for a second, bending down to pat Mac, who'd bounded back to see why Rhuaridh had stopped walking. 'Hey, guy, nice to see you.'

Mac jumped up, putting two wet sandy pawprints on her jeans. He would have expected her to squirm but Kristie didn't seem bothered at all. She crouched down, letting Mac lick her hands. Kristie looked up at him. 'I thought we should maybe have a chat,' she said, biting her bottom lip.

A heavy feeling settled in his stomach. 'About last time? Yeah, we probably should.'

Her nose wrinkled. 'Not about last time,' she said. 'I thought we sorted that.'

Now he was really confused. 'Well, yeah, we sort of did, but...' He wasn't quite sure what to say next.

She straightened up, wiping her wet hands on her jeans. 'I wanted to talk to you about something else.'

'Okay.' He wasn't quite sure where this was going.

She sucked in a breath, not quite meeting his gaze. 'Let's walk.' She turned and started in the same direction he'd been headed.

'Okay,' he said again, wondering what he was getting himself into.

'You said you hadn't watched the show.'

He shook his head. 'Not my thing—no offence.'

She gave a smile, then stuck her hands in her pockets and turned to face him again. The setting sun outlined her silhouette and streaked her blonde hair with violet and pink light—like some kind of ethereal hue.

'None taken.' She cleared her throat. 'I thought I should probably let you know something.'

'What?'

'I watched the third episode before I came here. It goes out in two weeks' time.'

'And...?' He knew there must be something, why else would they be having this conversation?

She reached up and tugged at her earlobe. A sign she was nervous. He was noticing all these little things about her. Now he knew when she was angry, when she was thinking, and when she was nervous. How many other women did he know those things about?

Had he known them about his ex, Zoe? He couldn't even remember. All his memories of her had just seemed to fade into the past.

Her words came out rushed, as if she was trying to say them all before she could stop herself. 'The show's been really popular. Really popular. Partly because in the first episode it covered John Henderson's death, and in the second it introduced a beautiful baby into the world.'

He wrinkled his nose. He was thinking back to the last time she'd been here. No major events had happened.

'So what's wrong with the third episode? Not enough drama?'

She looked distinctly uncomfortable and fixed her gaze on the teenagers further down the beach. 'Nothing's wrong with it exactly. It's just changed focus a little.'

'Changed focus to what?' He was getting tired with this tiptoeing around. 'Why don't you just say what you need to?'

She pressed her lips together for a second. 'The fight we had? Gerry filmed it. He'd already captured us sparring a little in the episodes before and people had been commenting on social media about it.'

Rhuaridh's brain flashed back to the woman in the surgery, telling him he had to be nicer to Kristie. He groaned. 'Oh, no. I look like a complete and utter—'

She held up her hand and stopped him. 'My producer says it's dynamite. He says everyone is going to love it.'

'They'll love you.' Rhuaridh shook his head. 'I'm the villain. I'm the one who lost his patience.'

He could see her biting the inside of her lip.

'I'm sorry,' he said quickly.

'Don't be,' she said, equally quickly. 'The last few shows I've worked on have all been cancelled. I was beginning to be a bit of bad luck charm. In TV, that kind of reputation doesn't do you any favours.'

He stuck his hands into his pockets. 'So, you want to fight with me? Is that what you're saying?'

She pulled a face and gave a little shrug. 'Well...yes

and no. It seems that a bit of tension is good for viewing—alongside all the medical stuff, of course.'

'I'm not sure fighting on screen does much for me as a doctor. I'm not normally like that.'

She gave a weak smile. 'So it's just me that drives you nuts?'

He looked out over the sea. This was the first time they'd really talked. How did he explain she might be right, without offending her—because if he couldn't understand it, how could she?

'I guess I still need to get used to someone following me around,' he said carefully. 'What are the other shows in the series?' It was a blatant attempt at changing the subject. But he was beginning to think he should have paid more attention to all the TV stuff.

'There's a museum curator in Egypt—apparently she practically doesn't let them into any room that hosts an "artefact", and the guy who is training to be an astronaut is said to be a major jerk. After the first shows they brought in someone new to follow—a guy who's trying to make his name as a country and western singer. I'm reliably informed that his singing is the worst ever heard.'

He couldn't help but laugh again. His foot traced a line in the sand. Mac had long since tired of waiting around for them both and was now chasing the tide, getting his white and black coat well and truly soaked. The smell of wet dog was going to drift all the way through the house.

'I can't imagine what they find so exciting about a doctor on an island in Scotland.'

'Maybe it's the exotic. Half the world just wants to visit Scotland and this makes them feel like they've been there.' She gave him a sideways glance. 'Or maybe they just like the grumpy doc.'

The grumpy doc. Was that what she'd nicknamed him? It wasn't the most flattering description in the world. His stomach twisted a little. He should be worrying about his reputation. He should be worrying about what people might think of him. But, strangely, the only person's opinion he was worried about right now was Kristie's. 'Why are you telling me all this?'

'I know you don't watch the series. But I thought I should forewarn you—in case, once the next episode hits, you start to get some press.'

'Bad press, you mean.'

She gave him a smile. 'Actually, no. I've told you. They love you. I was thinking more along the lines that you might get weird internet proposals, or your dating profile might explode.'

'My dating profile? You honestly think I've got a dating profile?'

She held out her hands and gave him a mischievous smile. 'Who knows?'

He shook his head as they started back down the beach. 'On an island this small I pretty much know everyone. If I had a dating profile, the whole island would know it, and anyway it's a bit hard to meet for dates when you rely on a ferry to the mainland.'

He looked at her curiously. 'Do you have one—a dating profile?'

She threw back her head and laughed. 'Are you joking? I was on TV for about ten seconds before I started getting weird emails. It seems that being on a TV show makes you fair game. Nope. I just try to meet guys the old-fashioned way.'

He looked down at her as they walked side by side.

'And how's that working out for you?' He couldn't pretend he wasn't curious.

She gave him an oblique glance. She knew. She knew the question he was asking. She held out her hand and wiggled it. 'Hmm…'

What did that mean?

She didn't say anything else so he was kind of left hanging.

'So, is everything okay for tomorrow, then?'

He nodded. 'Sure.' At that moment Mac ran up and decided to shake half of the Firth of Clyde all over them.

'Whoa!' Both of them jumped back, laughing, Kristie wiping the huge drops of water from her face and neck.

Rhuaridh took a step closer. 'Sorry.' He looked towards Mac. 'Occupational hazard, I guess.'

He reached forward without thinking. Part of her mascara had smudged just under her lower eyelid. He lifted his thumb to her cheekbone and wiped it away. Her laughter stopped as she looked up, her gaze connecting with his.

His hand froze. It was like all the breath had just been sucked from his lungs. He was so conscious of the feel of her smooth skin beneath his thumb pad. He could almost swear a tiny little zing shot down his arm.

She wasn't moving either. Her pupils dilated as he watched.

It was like every sense inside him switched on. He hadn't been paying attention. He'd been so focused on his work he'd forgotten to see what was right beside him. When was the last time he'd actually dated? Maybe once in the ten months since he'd got here. He couldn't even remember.

He couldn't remember what it was like to let a woman's

scent drift around him like it was now. To look into a pair of eyes that were looking right back at him.

There was a shout behind them and both of them jumped back. It was only one of the teenagers carrying on.

But the moment was gone. Kristie looked a little embarrassed and wiped her hands down on her jeans. 'I'd better get back,' she said quickly. 'Gerry and I need to chat about the filming tomorrow.' She started to walk quickly down the beach, then turned once to look at him. 'I'll see you tomorrow.'

The words seem to hang between them, as if she was willing him to add something else. But he gave a quick nod. 'Sure.'

Kristie broke into a jog back down the beach. He couldn't help but stare at her silhouette. Mac bounded up and sat at his feet, looking up at him quizzically.

If there was mental telepathy between a human and a dog, Mac was currently calling him an idiot.

He kicked the sand at his feet. 'I know, I know,' he said as he shook his head and stuck his hands in his pockets.

He pushed his thoughts from his head. She was from LA. She worked on a TV show. He was crazy to think she might actually be interested in some guy from Arran. His ex had been quick to tell him that Arran was a dull, boring rock in the middle of nowhere. What could it possibly have to interest some woman who was probably two minutes from Hollywood? He stared out as the sun drew even closer to the horizon, sending warming streaks across the sky. He sighed. 'Let's go, Mac,' he said as he turned and headed back to the cottage.

Kristie dressed carefully. For the first time since she'd come to the island she wore a dress. It was still summer here—even though it was much cooler than LA. Her hair didn't usually give her much trouble, so she just ran a brush through it as usual. Her makeup took her no more than five minutes. She'd even applied it once in a dark cupboard with no light.

Gerry gave her a smile as she emerged from her room in their rental. 'Special occasion?'

She shook her head, and pretended she didn't notice the rush of heat to her cheeks. What on earth was she doing? Maybe she'd just imagined that moment on the beach. Maybe it had been nothing at all. She'd only wanted to warn him about the hype. Or had she?

Truth was, she never really watched herself on TV much. It seemed too egotistical. But watching the episode between her and Rhuaridh had brought all those emotions back to the surface. She couldn't ever remember a guy getting under her skin the way Rhuaridh Gillespie had. And on the way over on the ferry this time she'd been nervous. Something else that was unusual for her.

Maybe it was the apparent popularity of the show. She'd already had a few interview requests. Last night when she'd logged onto her social media account she'd seen over four hundred comments about the show. What would happen when the third show went out?

Gerry was leaning against the wall. He looked paler than normal. 'Okay?' she asked.

'Sure,' he said. 'Just a bit of indigestion. It's my age.'

She gave a nod and headed to the stairs. They were filming at the surgery today, covering one of the paediatric clinics and immunisation clinics.

Screaming babies. Just her kind of thing. Not.

Gerry fumbled in his pocket and some lollipops landed

on the floor. Kristie bent and picked them up. 'Since when did you like candy?'

He tapped the side of his nose. 'It's my secret weapon. It's in case we have unco-operative kids at the clinic today.'

She shook her head and held up one of the bright red lollipops. 'It's a pure sugar rush. No way will they let you hand these out. Think of the tooth decay.'

He winked. 'I'm wiser than you think. They're sugar-free.' He started walking down the stairs in front of her. 'Don't let it be said that an old guy doesn't have any new tricks.'

'What about the additives?' She stared at the colour again.

He shrugged in front of her. 'Can't think of everything.'

She shook her head and stuck some in the pocket of her dress. She could always eat them herself.

The clinic was chaos. It was a mixture of development checks, immunisations and childhood reviews.

Most of the mothers were delighted at the prospect of their child being filmed, so permissions were easy.

Rhuaridh was wearing a pale pink shirt today and dark trousers. She hated the fact he always looked so handsome. He moved through the waiting room easily, picking up babies and toddlers and carrying them through to the examination room, all while chatting to their mothers. He seemed at ease here. It was as if he'd finally decided to accept they'd be around and was doing what they'd asked him to do right from the beginning—ignore them.

But it made Kristie's insides twist in a way she didn't like.

Some of babies squealed. She didn't blame them, getting three jabs at once was tough. She didn't have much experience around kids or babies, so watching Ellen, the health visitor, do the development checks was more interesting than she'd thought.

She watched the babies follow things with their eyes, weight bear on their legs, and lift their heads up in line with their bodies. The older ones could grab things, sit up and balance on their own, and babble away quite happily.

Her favourite was a little boy just short of two years old. He came into the room with the biggest frown on his face. When Ellen tried to persuade him to build some bricks, say a few words or draw with a crayon he had the same response to everything. 'No.' His mother looked tired and sat with another baby on her lap, apologising profusely for her son's lack of co-operation.

Ellen took some measurements and laughed and turned to Kristie. 'As you can see, he has a younger sister. I've been in the house a dozen times and know he can do all these things—if he wants to.'

Kristie stopped smiling at the little guy and turned her attention to the mum. She had dark circles under her eyes and looked as if she might burst into tears. Kristie's first reaction was to open her mouth and move into counselling mode but before she could, Ellen gave an almost imperceptible nod of her head towards Kristie and Gerry, and they backed out of the room.

Kristie stood against the wall for a few minutes and just breathed. She had no idea what was going on with that woman, but her own thoughts immediately raced back to her sister. The last few volunteer shifts on the helpline had been quiet. She'd almost willed the phone to ring, then had felt guilty for thinking that. In the end, she'd used the time in an unexpected way.

She'd started writing. She wasn't sure what it was at first, but it had started to take shape into a piece of fiction—a novel, based on her experience with her sister and how suicide affected everyone. Her sister's death had impacted on every part of her life. She'd watched the life drain from her mother and father and their health deteriorate quickly, with them eventually dying within a few months of each other.

Burying three family members in a short period of time had messed with her head so much she found it hard to form new relationships. Hard to find hope to invest in a future that might get snatched away from her. Of course, thoughts like those were irrational. She knew that. But she also knew that the last few men she'd met she'd kept at arm's length. Whether she'd wanted to or not.

She sighed as the door opened again and Ellen crossed the hall to Rhuaridh's room with a slip of paper in her hand.

Kristie's mouth dried as the health visitor took charge of the children, then let the mother go and see Rhuaridh on her own.

She couldn't help herself but follow Ellen to where she was bouncing the baby on her knee and entertaining the toddler, who'd now decided to draw pictures.

'Is she okay?'

Ellen looked up. 'It's likely she has postnatal depression. We screen all new mums twice in the first year. I've visited Jackie at home a lot. She's had two very colicky babies. Lack of sleep is tough.'

Kristie rubbed her hands up and down her arms, instantly cold. That piece of paper. That assessment that they do on all new mums—why hadn't there been something like that for her sister? Would it have worked? Would it have picked anything up?

Maybe she was putting hope in something that didn't exist. But just the thought—that there was a simple screening tool that would have picked up something...

'Do you use it for other people?'

Ellen looked up. She'd started building a pile of bricks on the floor with the toddler. 'The postnatal depression scale? No, it's designed specifically for women who've just had a baby. We've used it for years, though, and I think it's very effective. Even if it just starts a conversation between me and the mum.'

'But you took her through to see Rhuaridh?'

Ellen looked over Kristie's shoulder. 'This is very personal. I have to ask that you don't film anything about this case.'

Kristie nodded. 'Of course not.'

'In that case, the final question in the tool—it's about self-harm. It asks if the mum has ever felt that way. If she answers anything other than no, I always need to have a conversation with the GP.'

Kristie felt her voice shake. 'So, what do you do for mums who feel like that?'

Ellen gave her a thoughtful look. 'It all depends on the mum. Some I visit more, every day if I have to. Some I get some other support—like a few hours at nursery for one, or both of their kids. Some Rhuaridh will see. He might decide to start them on some medication, or to refer them to the community mental health nurse, or even to a consultant. Whatever will help the mum most.'

Kristie leaned back against the wall, taking in everything that was being said. The mum was in with Rhuaridh for a while. By the time she came out, she was wiping her eyes but seemed a bit better. It was as if a little spark had appeared in her eyes again. Maybe she finally felt as if someone was listening.

Kristie waited until the clinic was finished then found Rhuaridh while he was writing up some notes.

'That mum? What did you do for her?'

He looked a little surprised by her question but gestured for her to close the door. 'Sit down,' he said.

She took a deep breath and sat down on the chair next to him. 'I talked to her,' he said quietly.

'That's it?' She couldn't hide how taken aback she felt.

'And I listened,' he added.

'But her questionnaire…' she began.

He held up his hand. 'Her questionnaire is just a little bit of her. It's a snapshot in time. I listened. I listened to how she was feeling and talked to her and let her know that some of this is normal for a new mum. She's beyond tired. She hasn't had a full night's sleep in two years. How do you think that would impact on anyone's mental health?'

'But you let her leave…' Her voice trailed off, as her mind jumped ahead.

'I let her leave with an assurance of some support systems in place. While she was here, she phoned her sister and asked her to take the kids overnight. She's coming back to see me again tomorrow and we'll talk again.'

'Oh.' Kristie sagged into the chair a little. Her stomach still churned.

There was so much here that was tumbling around in her brain. She knew that most of the thoughts she was having weren't rational—they were all tinged by her own experience. That desperate sense of panic.

She took a few breaths and tried to put her counselling head on. The one she used three nights a month. Rhuaridh had taken time to talk to the mother and acknowledge her feelings—usually the single most important act someone could do. Then he'd arranged follow up and support. Just like she would hope and expect from a health professional.

Rhuaridh leaned forward and put his hand over hers. 'Kristie, is everything all right?'

And for the first time in her life she wasn't quite sure how to answer. Should she tell him? Should she let him know she worked as a counsellor and what she'd been through herself?

Her mouth was dry. He was looking at her with those bright blue eyes—staring right at her as though he could see right down to her very soul. To all the things she kept locked away tight. Part of her wanted to tell him. Part of her wanted to share.

But something was stopping her. Something wouldn't let her open her mouth and say those words. So before she could think about it any longer, she got up and rushed out.

CHAPTER FIVE

September

'YOU'VE NEVER WATCHED?'

Rhuaridh shook his head as Magda cradled baby Alice. She gave him a curious smile. 'I can't believe it. You should. I have to admit, I'm almost a little jealous.'

'Of what?'

He was drinking a large cup of coffee while he compared a few notes with her on a few of their chronically ill patients. On Arran, a doctor would never really be off duty, and Magda was far too nosy not to want to discuss some of their long-term cases.

'Of you.' She waved one hand while she fixed her gaze back on her fair-haired daughter while she screwed up her nose and gave a sigh. 'But no. If I'd been in the show that wouldn't have worked anyway.'

Rhuaridh put down his cup and held out his hands. 'Give me my goddaughter and tell me what on earth you're talking about.'

Magda stood up and put Alice into his arms, before settling back and putting her feet up on the sofa. 'It's all about the chemistry.'

'Chemistry? I thought you didn't like chemistry. You always complained about it when we were students.'

She shook her head and looked at him as if he was completely dumb. 'Not school chemistry. *Chemistry.* You know...between a man and a woman. Phew! If I need to teach you about the birds and bees I'm going to question whether you should be working as a doctor.'

He shifted in the chair, realising where this was going to go. He shook his head and Alice wrinkled her face. He stopped moving. He knew who was in charge here.

He spoke quietly. 'I've no interest in watching myself on TV. I know everything that's happened—not all of which I'm entirely proud of.'

She gave a sigh. 'You know. They edit things. And they've edited the show for the drama. To be honest, I'm surprised we've not got women heading to Arran by the boatload.' She raised one eyebrow. 'They always seem to catch your good side.'

'Do I have a bad side?' he teased.

But it was almost as if Magda was still talking to herself. 'Then again, most of the women would know they wouldn't get a look in. The chemistry between you and Kristie...' she kissed her fingertips then flicked out her fingers '...is just off the scale.' She gave him a smile. 'You're doing so much better than the others in the show. I can't even watch the country and western singer. And the astronaut is possibly the most arrogant person on and off the planet.'

His mind was spinning. Was everyone who was watching thinking the same thing about him and Kristie? He felt like some teenage boy under scrutiny. *He* hadn't even really worked out what was going on between them.

He liked her. He knew he liked her. But anything more just seemed...ridiculous.

But was it?

Alice made a little noise in his arms. Magda closed her eyes. 'She didn't sleep a wink last night.'

'Didn't she?'

Rhuaridh looked around and glimpsed the pram near the doorway. 'Do you want me to take her for a walk? Mac is mooching around outside anyway. I was planning on taking him for a walk.'

'Would you?' As she said the words she snuggled down further into the sofa. 'Just an hour would be great.'

Rhuaridh smiled and settled Alice into the pram, closing the door as quietly as he could behind him.

Mac gave him a look. Rhuaridh wagged his finger. 'Don't get jealous, old one. Just get in line. We've got a new boss now.'

'Really?'

Rhuaridh nearly jumped. Kristie was standing behind him with a bag in her hand.

'Where did you come from?'

She grinned. 'LA. You know, America.' She made signals with her hands. 'Then a plane and a boat.'

'Okay, okay, I get it.'

She was wearing a pair of black and white checked trousers and a black shirt tied at her waist. Her hair was loose about her shoulders and she seemed totally at ease as she leaned over him and looked into the pram. 'I came to see my favourite girl, but I see you've already kidnapped her. Whaddya say we share?'

Rhuaridh gripped the pram a little tighter as he smiled back. 'Ah, but this is my goddaughter. And this is the first time I've actually managed to kidnap her.'

Kristie made the little clicking noise she always did when she was thinking. He leaned a little closer and caught a whiff of her light zesty perfume. 'To tell you the truth, I think Mac's a little jealous.'

Kristie dropped to her knees and rubbed Mac's head, bending down to put her head next to his. 'Poor boy. Is he neglecting you again?' She wrapped her hand around Mac's lead. 'How about we take turns? I'll take Mac, then swap you on the way back.'

Rhuaridh gave a nod and they started to walk down towards the town. The weather was bright with just a little edge in the air. Kristie chatted constantly, telling him about plane delays and double-booked accommodation. It didn't take long for her to turn the conversation back to work. 'Have you seen that young mum again?'

Rhuaridh gave her a sideways glance. Last time he'd seen Kristie she'd been more than a little preoccupied about the case. She'd rushed out the room when he'd asked her if something was wrong, and the next day she'd left to go back to LA. He hadn't seen her since.

He'd been curious about why she'd been so concerned. He'd had enough experience in life to know when to tread carefully. People didn't come with a label attached declaring their past life experiences.

'I've seen her quite a lot—so has Ellen, the health visitor. She's talking, and I don't think she's going to feel better overnight, but I think if we have adequate support systems in place, and an open-door policy, I think she'll continue to make improvements. Ellen has visited her at home a lot—talked through how she's feeling about things. They've even been out walking together—like we are today.'

He gave her another glance. He thought he knew what

the next answer would be. 'You haven't included anything in the filming, have you?'

Kristie shook her head. 'Absolutely not. It's mainly just footage from the immunisation clinic and the baby clinic.'

He gave a nod and then changed tack. 'So, what are you and Gerry going to do tonight about food?'

She blinked. 'What do you mean?'

'The place you've booked into after the mix up—they didn't tell you, did they? Their kitchen is out of order. Something to do with an electricity short.'

Kristie let out a big sigh. 'Darn it. I never even asked. We just said we needed beds for the next few days after the mix-up at the other place.'

She nudged him as they kept walking. 'Okay, so give me the lowdown on all the local places.' She wrinkled her nose. 'Though I'm not sure about Gerry. He's been really tired. I think the jet-lag is hitting him hard this time.'

Rhuaridh gave her a cheeky kind of grin. 'Well, if you can promise me that you actually eat, I'll show you my favourite place in town.'

'What do you mean—if I actually eat?'

He laughed. 'You're from LA. Don't you all just eat green leaves and the occasional bit of kale or spinach?'

Now she laughed too. 'You heard about that new diet?' She shuddered. 'Oh, no. Not for me. Anyhow, I'm a steak kind of girl.'

'You are?' He actually stopped walking and looked at her in surprise.

She pointed to her chest. 'What? I don't look like a steak girl?'

He couldn't help but give her an appreciative gaze. 'If steak's what you like, I know just the place.'

She glanced around. They were right in the heart of

Brodick now. There were a number of shops on the high street, a sprinkling of coffee shops and a few pubs.

'Cool. Which one is it?'

He turned the pram around. 'It's back this way.'

Quick as a flash, Kristie came alongside and bumped him out of the way with her hip, taking his place at pushing the pram. 'Don't try and steal my turn. You got the way out. I get the way back.' She bent over the pram and stroked the side of Alice's face. 'She's just a little jewel, isn't she?'

He was surprised at the affection in her voice. 'You like kids?'

'I love kids.' She shrugged. 'Not all of them like me, right enough.'

He stopped walking. 'Where did you pick that up?'

'What?' There was a gleam in her eye.

'"Right enough". It's a distinctly Scottish expression.'

She lifted one hand from the pram and counted off on her fingers. 'I was trying it out for size. Everyone uses it in the surgery. I'm also looking for opportunities to use *drookit*, *minging* and...' She wrinkled her brow. 'What's the one that Mr McLean who comes to the surgery always uses?'

Rhuaridh burst out laughing. 'Wheesht?'

'That's it!' she said, pointing her finger at him. *'Wheesht.'*

It sounded strange in her American accent. But he liked it. He liked it a lot.

She started walking again. 'There's another one I've heard. It might even be used to describe you sometimes.' She gave him a nod of her head.

'I dread to think. Hit me with it.'

This time the glance she gave him was part mysterious, part superior. 'Crabbit,' she said triumphantly.

Part of him was indignant, part of him wanted to laugh. 'Crabbit? Me?' He pointed to his chest. 'No way. No way could I ever be described as crabbit. I'm the nice guy. The fun-loving squishy kind of guy.' He gestured down to Alice. 'The kind of guy who takes his goddaughter for a walk to give his friend a break.' He raised his eyebrows at her. 'Beat that one, LA girl.'

She folded her arms across her chest, letting momentum carry the pram for a few seconds. 'That sounds like a challenge.'

'It is.' He'd never been one to back down from a challenge.

He swooped in and grabbed the pram handle. 'Ms Nelson, I believe you just neglected your duty. I think I should take over again.'

Before she could protest he nodded towards the pub at the other side of the road. 'Billy's Bar. Best steaks in town. They even do a special sauce for me.'

'What kind of sauce?'

'I could tell you. But I'd have to kill you. It's a secret I'll take to my grave. But if you come along with me tonight, I'll let you have some.' The words were out before he really had a chance to think about them.

'Dinner with the doctor,' she mused out loud. 'Just exactly how good are these steaks?'

'Better than you've ever tasted. The cows bred in the Arran hills are special. More tender.'

There was a smile dancing across her lips. 'Okay, then.' She gave him a cheeky wink. 'But only because I might want to put the steak on film.'

Part of him was elated. Part of him was put out. It had

been a casual, not-really-thought-about invitation. But things had seemed to be heading in this direction. But now, had she only said yes because she wanted to film their dinner? Was this something to try and get more viewing figures?

Because that hadn't even crossed his mind.

Kristie kept chatting again. It seemed she had a gift for chat. And she didn't seem to slow down for a second. They were almost back at Magda's house when Rhua-ridh's page sounded.

He took one glance and grabbed his phone. 'Something wrong?' she asked, taking over the pram-pushing again.

He nodded. Listened carefully to the person at the end of the phone before cutting the call. In the blink of an eye he swooped up little Alice, dropping a kiss on her forehead before running inside with her. Kristie was still fumbling with the pram in the doorway as he came back outside.

'Leave it,' he said, running past her. 'And phone Gerry. Tell him to meet us at the wilderness centre.'

Kristie's head flicked one way then the other, as if she should work out what to do next. He was in the car already and, reaching over, flung open the passenger door. 'Now, Kristie!' he yelled.

Her hands were refusing to do what they were told as she tried to phone Gerry. It took three attempts to finally press the correct button. Rhuaridh was driving quicker than she'd ever seen him. He'd already phoned the cottage hospital and given some instructions to the staff.

It seemed that there was only one ambulance on Arran and it was on its way too.

'What's the wilderness centre?'

'It's an experiential learning place. Adults and kids come and learn to mountain climb, hike, swim, canoe, camp, fish and a whole host of other things.'

'So…' She was almost scared to ask. 'What's happened?'

'There's been an accident. There's a waterfall in the hills. One of the instructors and one of the kids have been hurt.'

He turned up a track that led up one of the nearby hills. Now she understood why he had a four-wheel drive. The terrain was rugged. 'Will the ambulance get up here?'

He nodded. 'You haven't seen it yet, have you?'

She shook her head.

'It's not a regular ambulance because of the terrain it has to cover, well, that and the fact a high number of our injuries are around the foot of Goat Fell—'

'Goat Fell?' she interrupted.

He pointed off to the side. 'Arran's highest mountain, more than eight hundred metres tall. Really, really popular with climbers, and it is a real climb. Especially at the end. Some people don't really come equipped for it and end up injuring themselves.'

'Okay,' she murmured. She looked to where he pointed. She couldn't even see the top of the mountain as it was covered with low-hanging clouds.

They were climbing higher, going through trees and bushes. 'Where is this place?'

'Another few minutes.' He gave her an anxious kind of glance, his voice steady. 'Until the ambulance gets here you might need to give me a hand. Are you okay with that?'

Her response was quicker than he expected. 'It's only hospitals that spook me.'

'What?'

He caught one quick glimpse of her face before he had to look back at the path. For a split second he thought she might be cracking a joke, but her expression told him otherwise.

He swore he could see the pathways firing in his own brain. He'd thought she'd been a little unsettled in the hospital. Just something off—something he couldn't quite put his finger on.

'Why are you spooked by hospitals?'

It was totally not the right time to ask a question like that. And speeding up a hill towards an accident scene was not the right place to give an answer. Of course he knew that. But how could she expect him not to ask?

'Past experience,' she replied in a tight voice. 'One I'd rather not talk about.'

He couldn't help his response. 'You must have loved the thought of coming here.'

They reached the crest of the hill and veered down towards the valley where the waterfall lay.

She shot him a wry expression. 'Let's just say I really wanted the museum in Egypt or the astronaut. Lucky old me.'

His gut gave a twist. As they approached the waterfall site he could see an array of people, all dressed in wet-weather gear, crowded around a man on the ground.

He had to let this go right now. He had a job to do.

'Will you be okay to help?' he asked again. For the next few minutes at least he might need to count on Kristie for help. If she couldn't help, she might well be a hindrance and he'd ask her to stay in the car.

Her voice was tight and she glanced at her phone. He reached over and grabbed her hand. 'Be honest.'

She stared for the briefest of seconds at his hand squeezing hers. 'I'll be fine,' she said without meeting his gaze. 'Gerry's messaged. He's just behind us. He was at the hospital and hitched a ride in the ambulance.'

Rhuaridh nodded. He had to take her at her word. He had to trust her. And hopefully it would only be for a few minutes.

'I'll grab the blue bag, you grab the red,' he said as he jumped from the car.

He walked swiftly to the group of people. One of the instructors was on the ground with a large laceration on his head. From one glance Rhuaridh could see that his breathing was a little laboured. But that was the point. At least he was breathing.

'Where's the other casualty?'

A teenage boy pointed to the bottom of the roaring waterfall. 'Under there. He jumped from the top.'

Rhuaridh's heart gave a little leap. 'Under *there*?'

'Not under the water. Under the waterfall. He says he can't feel his legs so no one wanted to move him.'

Rhuaridh was already stripping off his shoes and jacket. He pulled a monitor from one bag, bent over and stuck the three leads on the first guy's chest. It only took a few seconds to check the readings. He knelt down beside the guy, pulled his stethoscope out and made another check. Lungs were filling normally, no sign of damage. 'What happened?' he asked the nearest kid.

'Ross and Des went into the water as soon as Kai jumped and went under. Des got Kai and pulled him into the cave but when Ross tried to climb the rock face he slipped and hit his head on the way down.' The young boy talking gulped, 'A few of us jumped in and pulled him out. He hasn't woken up at all.'

Rhuaridh pulled a penlight from his pocket and checked Ross's pupils, then completed a first set of neuro obs. It was first-line assessment for any head injury. He scribbled them down and handed them to Kristie.

He handed Kristie a radio. 'You keep these.'

'Where are you going?' There was a definite flash of panic in her eyes.

A teenage girl, her face streaked with tears, tugged at his sleeve. 'The other instructor is with Kai. He stayed with him after Ross got hurt, trying to help.'

Rhuaridh started rummaging through the kitbags. He tucked the other radio into his belt. There was no doubt about it—he was going to get very wet.

He bent over next to Kristie, checking the monitor again. He kept his voice low. 'Keep an eye on his breathing. It seems fine and his heart rate is steady. He's given himself quite a bang on the head. If he starts to wake up, just keep him steady on the ground. If he's agitated or confused, radio me straight away.'

Rhuaridh wouldn't normally leave an unconscious patient, but right now he'd no idea of the condition of the child under the waterfall. As the only medic on site he had to assess both patients. He put his hand on Kristie's shoulder. 'The ambulance crew should be here in a few minutes.' He could tell she was nervous, but she lifted her own hand and put it over his.

'Go on, Rhuaridh. Go and check on the kid. We'll be fine.'

Rhuaridh gave a few instructions to some of the other teenagers around. Most were quiet, a few looked a bit shocked but had no injuries. 'Stay with Kristie, she'll let me know if there's any problems.'

He waded into the water. Cold. It was beyond cold. This waterfall was notorious for the temperature as it was based in a valley with little sunlight. By the time he'd waded across to the middle of the pool the water had come up over his waist and to the bottom of his ribs, making him catch his breath.

The instructor had been wearing a wetsuit that would keep his temperature more steady—hopefully the teenager would be too.

The spray from the waterfall started to soak him. He knew this place well enough. There was a ridge on the rocks the falls plummeted over. It was the only way to get access to the cave under the falls and the only way to access that ridge was to wade through the water and try and scale the rock face.

He had nothing. No climbing equipment. No wetsuit. Not even a rope.

He heard a painful groan. Even though the noise from the falls was loud, he could hear it echoing from the cave. He moved sideways, casting his eyes over the rock face, looking for a suitable place to start.

It had been years since he'd been here. As a teenager he'd been able to scale this rock with no problems. It had practically been a rite of passage for any kid that lived on the island. But that had been a long time ago, when he'd probably been a lot more agile than he was now.

The first foothold was easy, his bare foot pushing him upwards. He caught his hands on the rocks above and pulled himself up, finding a position for the second foot.

'Careful, Doc,' shouted one of the kids.

He moved left, nearer the falls. There was a trick to

this, trying to keep hold of the wall, which got more and more slippery by the second as he edged closer. The weight on his back from the backpack and red portable stretcher was affecting his balance, making him grip all the tighter. His knuckles were white as he waited for the right second to duck his head and jump through the falls to the cave behind.

As he jumped he had a millisecond of panic. What if the injured kid was directly in his path? But as he landed with a grunt behind the falls he realised he was clear. He fell roughly to the side, the equipment on his back digging sharply into him.

It took his eyes a few seconds to adjust. It wasn't quite dark in here. Light still streamed through the waterfall.

'About time,' said Des, the instructor, cheekily. He was sitting next to the injured boy, who was lying on the floor of the cave.

The cave was larger than most people would expect, and the grey rock had streaks of brown and red. There was almost room for a person to stand completely upright, and definitely enough room for six or seven people to sit within the cave. This place had been one of the most popular hideouts when Rhuaridh had been a kid and half the island had scraped their initials into the rock. He'd half a mind to flash his torch over the rock to find his own.

Rhuaridh caught the brief nod from Des. They'd been at school together years ago. He moved closer to the boy. 'Kai? How are you? I heard you jumped off the waterfall.'

His eyes were scanning up and down Kai's body. There was an angry-looking projection underneath the wetsuit covering his left foreleg.

He touched Kai's shoulders. 'One of your friends said you couldn't feel your legs, is that still true?'

'I wish!' said Kai loudly as he groaned again.

Des caught Rhuaridh's eye. 'He said at the beginning he couldn't feel his legs but that was literally only for a few moments. He's been feeling pain in his leg ever since, and for obvious reasons I've not moved him.'

Rhuaridh nodded. He knew exactly what he'd find if he cut Kai's wetsuit open. The only question was whether the bone was protruding from the skin. Right now, it was covered by the wetsuit and still protected.

Rhuaridh turned around and tugged the portable stretcher free from its packaging and started opening it out. There was no way Kai would be able to walk or swim anywhere.

Des had worked as an instructor at the wilderness centre for years and was experienced enough to need little direction. He helped unfold the stretcher while Rhuaridh took some time to assess Kai. He held his hands above the injured leg. 'Okay, I promise I'm not going to touch that bit. But I am going to take a look.' He pulled a torch from his backpack and checked the skin colour. 'Can you wiggle your toes?'

Kai grimaced but wiggled his toes while letting out a low yelp.

'Allergic to anything?'

Kai shook his head.

'How old are you?'

'Fourteen.'

'Any medical conditions I should know about? Or any regular medicines you need to take?'

Kai shook his head to both questions.

'Do you know how much you weigh?'

'Why?'

'I'm going to give you something to ease the pain.

We're going to have to help you onto the stretcher, then carry you out through the waterfall. There's no other way out of here.'

Kai shook his head. 'No way. I can't stand the water pounding on my leg.'

Rhuaridh pulled out some kit. 'There's a metal hoop that fits on top of the stretcher. This plastic can go over the top of the hoop. It will keep the water off your leg, and hopefully protect you.' He looked at the water cascading past his shoulder. 'There *is* no other way out of here. We can get you in the stretcher, but we couldn't manoeuvre it upright to slide you through the space at the side.'

He shook his head as he looked at it. 'I had to imitate a spider to get in here, and I still got soaked by the waterfall on the way in.' He turned to Des. 'You've been around here just as long as me. Can you think of any other way to get him out?'

Des shook his head too. 'Not a chance. He's almost the same size as you and me. There's no way we could manoeuvre him. We just need to go straight through the waterfall.'

Rhuaridh calculated how much pain relief to give Kai and administered it quickly. 'We'll give it some time to take effect before we get you onto the stretcher.'

The radio at his waist crackled. 'Rhuaridh? Rhuaridh, are you there?'

Kristie's voice echoed around the cave. 'Who's that?' asked Des.

Rhuaridh pulled the radio from his waistband. 'What's up, Kristie?'

'They're not here yet and he's starting to wake up.'

'The ambulance crew haven't arrived?' He was surprised. He'd expected them to arrive a few minutes after he left.

'No.' Her voice sounded kind of strained. 'Gerry's here. He got dropped back at our car and came himself. Apparently the ambulance had to stop at a road accident. They've taken the people to the hospital.'

Rhuaridh shook his head. Typical. Everything happened at once. The ambulance hadn't been used at all in the last week and now two simultaneous calls.

'Kristie, tell me the numbers on the monitor.'

There was silence for a few seconds, then her voice came through. 'The P is eighty-six. That's his pulse, isn't it?'

'That's fine. What's the other one?'

'It's ninety-seven.'

'That's his oxygen saturation. That's good. It means his breathing and lungs are okay.'

'Uh-oh.'

Rhuaridh sat up on his knees. 'What do you mean, "uh-oh"? Kristie?'

There was a crackle. Then a rumble of voices—all muffled. It was hard to hear anything with the constant background roar of falling water. Rhuaridh exchanged a look with Des. He'd never met the other instructor at the centre. Throughout the year many instructors from different countries came to help at the centre—Des was the only real constant. 'Your guy. Anything I should know about him?'

Des's brow wrinkled. 'Ross?' He shook his head. 'Don't think so. He's been here about three weeks. Worked in a similar place in Wales.'

'Any medical history?'

Des pulled a face. 'To be honest, I can't remember.

But if there had been anything major it would be on his initial application form.'

Rhuaridh knew that all the paperwork for the centre would be up to date. Des's wife dealt with that. But he also knew that Des wouldn't recall a single thing about it. He'd never been a paper person.

'Rhuaridh!' The shout came through the crackling radio and made all three in the cave start.

'Kristie, what's wrong?'

Even though it was difficult, he was on his feet, crouching in the cave. Staring at the rushing water that was currently between Kristie and himself.

'He's thrashing about. I think he's having some kind of seizure, what do I do?'

He could hear the panic in her voice. He signalled with his head to Des, who immediately pulled the prepared stretcher alongside Kai, knowing they would have to get out of there quickly.

'Do you know the recovery position?' he radioed to Kristie.

'W-hat?'

'His side. Turn him on his left-hand side. Get Gerry or some of the older kids to help you if need be. Once he's on his side pull up his right leg slightly and bring his right arm over so his hand is on the ground in front of him.'

And then there was nothing. No reply. No chatter. Just silence as his stomach churned. Either Ross's head injury had caused agitation and Kristie was mistaken, or he was having a full-blown seizure—neither of which were good signs. Kai would already need to be sent to the mainland for surgery. Now it looked like Ross would need to be airlifted. The nearest head injury unit was in

Glasgow—it would take too long to get there by ambulance and ferry.

'Ready, Doc?'

Des had moved to Kai's head and shoulders, ready to slide the lad onto the stretcher. Rhuaridh bent down straight away. 'Sure. Kai, your painkiller should have started working by now. We're going to slide you over onto the stretcher. It should only be a bit uncomfortable, and once you're on the stretcher the metal hoop will mean that nothing will touch your leg.'

He was trying hard to stay very calm, all while his brain wondered how Kristie was doing. He'd left her out there. He knew she wasn't medically qualified at all, but he'd felt duty bound to come and assess his other patient. Would he have left her out there if he'd known the ambulance would be so long?

His mouth was dry. He couldn't help but remember that momentary glance in her eyes when she'd told him hospitals freaked her out. He'd wanted to ask more, but there hadn't been time. He was drawn to this woman. He liked her. He couldn't ignore the flicker of attraction that seemed to permeate the air around them. But the truth was he barely knew her.

He was moving on autopilot. 'Ready?' he asked Kai.

The teenage boy screwed up his face and Des held him by the shoulders and Rhuaridh gently took the weight off his legs. The movement was swift, with only a minor yelp from Kai. Des helped move the plastic casing quickly over the stretcher, zipping it closed, protecting the rest of Kai's body and only leaving his face exposed.

'Who is going first?' Des asked as he eyed the cascading waterfall. Each of them was going to have to step through it carrying the stretcher.

'I'll do it,' said Rhuaridh quickly. He tried the radio again. 'Kristie, how are you? How is Ross? Have you got him in the recovery position?'

There was an agonising pause.

'I think so. But he's still…twitching.'

'I'll be right there.' He could hear the tension in her voice. He wanted to jump straight through the waterfall and be by her side. But he was a doctor. He was so used to taking the emotion out of things and doing the duty he was bound to—like now, when he had to try and take care of two injured patients. Where was that darned ambulance?

Before he had chance to let his brain churn any more he signalled to Kai and Des. 'Are we ready?'

They nodded. Rhuaridh looked at Kai. 'When I give you the signal, take a deep breath. I'll have the front end of the stretcher and we'll literally just need to walk through the waterfall. You know the pond isn't particularly deep. This isn't dangerous. Just a few moments of pounding water around your ears.'

Kai nodded. 'I've been through it once when Des pulled me back in here. I'll be okay. Let's get this over with.'

Rhuaridh put the rest of the equipment back in the rucksack and put it on his back. He jumped down into the pool with the waterfall directly at his back. The noise was deafening, so he used signals to grab the stretcher above his shoulders and gesture to Kai. Des was ready and they moved swiftly through the waterfall and back out into the pool. Water cascaded over them, but it only took a few seconds to be free of the noise and clear their noses and mouths.

From the crest of the hill he could see a flash of bright

green. The paramedics had finally arrived. Most of the kids were still crowded around the sides of the pool. They waded slowly across, setting Kai down gently as his friends surrounded him. One of the paramedics knelt beside him, and the other joined Rhuaridh at Kristie's side.

Her eyes were glinting with fear. 'He's literally just stopped shaking. He seemed to wake up for a few seconds, thrashing his legs and arms out, then he started shaking again.'

There was a red mark on the side of her cheek.

'Did you get caught by his arm?' asked Rhuaridh.

She shook her head. 'I'm fine. It doesn't matter.'

But it did to Rhuaridh.

It only took a few moments to assess Ross and to arrange an air ambulance for him. His pupil reactions were sluggish now and it was obvious the knock to the head had been harsh. He needed proper assessment in a specialist centre.

Rhuaridh then took time to recheck Kai before loading him up in the ambulance with the paramedics, ready for transfer for surgery.

By the time the ambulance had left with both patients, Des had gathered the teenagers together to take them back to the wilderness centre. Gerry was still chatting to a few that he'd caught on film.

Kristie was standing at the side, dirt smudged on her cheek and on the knees of her trousers. Rhuaridh reached out, took her hand and led her off to the side, pulling her down next to him on a large overturned tree trunk that had fallen over years before.

'Are you okay? I'm sorry that I left you.'

She gave a small shake of her head, fixing her gaze on the view ahead.

He hadn't let go of her, enclosing one of her slim hands in both of his. She moved her gaze to meet his.

He held his breath. He couldn't help it. All he could focus on was the blue of her eyes. The hand he held between his was trembling slightly and he gave it a squeeze. 'I didn't mean to leave you alone so long. I thought the ambulance would only be a few minutes.'

Her voice was quiet. 'You had to go and check on the boy. I know that.' She gave a weak smile, 'You're a doctor. It's your job.'

'But it's not yours,' he replied, his voice hoarse.

She'd been shaking. She was pale. Pieces were falling into place. Now he understood why she'd seemed distracted in the hospital. He'd thought she either wasn't that interested or had just had her mind on other things.

She'd been nervous. She'd been scared. And he'd missed it.

'Why don't you tell me why you don't like hospitals, Kristie?'

She licked her lips and shook her head. 'It's not something we need to talk about.'

She looked him straight in the eye and pulled her hand free from his, lifting it to touch his cheek. 'You just scaled part of a rock face and walked through a waterfall, Dr Gillespie. Some people might call that superhero material.'

'What would you call it?' The words were out instantly. Instinct. His gut reaction to that question. Because he really wanted to know the answer. He wanted to know exactly what Kristie Nelson thought about him.

If he'd thought for a few more seconds he'd have realised she'd just avoided his question. The one that might get to the heart of who she was.

'I haven't quite decided yet,' she whispered, the edges of her mouth turning upwards. 'But things are looking up.'

Her hand on his skin was making his pulse race. His eyes went instinctively to her mouth. The mouth he wanted to kiss.

He moved forward, all rational thoughts leaving his brain as his lips firmly connected with hers. She reacted instantly, leaning in towards him and sliding one hand up the side of his neck. He knew she needed comfort. He knew she needed reassurance. This seemed so obvious, so natural and it looked like Kristie thought so too.

Her skin was cold, but her lips were warm. Sweet. Responsive. She didn't seem to mind they were sitting on a log in the middle of the damp countryside. She didn't seem to mind at all, and as her hand raked through his hair he could almost feel the temperature rising around them.

But little alarms were going off in his brain, like red flags frantically waving. How could he kiss her when he knew there was something else affecting her?

He took a deep breath. He reluctantly pulled back. For a moment, neither of them spoke—just stared at each other as if they couldn't quite believe what had just happened.

Rhuaridh pressed his lips together for a second, doing his best to collect his thoughts. The ones he was currently having involved sweeping Kristie up into his arms, into his car and away from this whole place. But she'd said something. She'd revealed a part of herself that she hadn't before and every instinct told him that he had to try and peel back more of Kristie's layers.

'Wow,' she said softly as a hint of a smile touched her lips.

'Wow,' he agreed. His timing was all wrong. He looked at her steadily, keeping his voice even. 'Kristie, I do think we need to talk.'

There was a flash of momentary confusion in her eyes. He could almost see the shutters going down again, as if she knew what was about to come next.

He kept going. 'I think the reason you don't like hospitals is important. I think, when I work with someone, if something significant has happened in the past that affects how they feel or think about something, I should know. I should know not to expose them to a situation that they might find hard.'

She pulled her hand back as if she'd been stung. 'Is that what we're doing, working together?'

It was the way she asked the question—as if those words actually hurt—that made him catch his breath. He could hear it in her voice. The unspoken question. Was that all it was? Particularly after that kiss…

But she didn't wait for an answer. She just brushed off her trousers, stood up and walked away…for the second time.

CHAPTER SIX

October

SHE CLOSED HER social media account. *Will they? Won't they?* seemed to be everywhere she looked. She'd even been invited on a talk show to discuss her blossoming 'relationship' with Rhuaridh Gillespie, the world's hottest Highland doc.

'I'm going to kill you, Gerry,' she muttered.

He was staring out of the ferry window at the thrashing sea, rubbing his chest distractedly. 'No, you're not. You've got the most popular show on the network. You love it.'

'I don't have time to love it. I can't get a minute of peace.' She rubbed her eyes and leaned against the wall.

'What's wrong?' he asked.

She sighed. 'There was a call last night.' She rubbed her hands up both arms. It was cold. Scotland was much colder than LA, but that chill had seemed to come out of nowhere. 'It was hard. I don't know if I helped. I've spent the whole journey wondering if…' Her voice trailed off.

Gerry touched her shoulder. 'Don't. You volunteer. You counsel. You're the person who listens in the middle of the night when someone needs to talk. You do the best that you can. That's all you can do.'

She put her head back on the wall. Fatigue sweeping over her. 'I know that. But I can't help but worry.'

'You don't look that great,' said Gerry.

She closed her eyes for a second. 'I don't feel that great. I forgot to take my seasickness tablets. I'll be fine when we land.'

The truth was she was nervous, and a little bit sad. She wasn't quite sure what to say to Rhuaridh. She'd felt the connection. And she was sure he had too.

Didn't their kiss prove it? But that had been fleeting. Rhuaridh had stopped it almost as soon as it had started. And then he'd pressed about the thing she didn't want to talk about. Wasn't ready to talk about.

And it had haunted her for the last month. Her head even felt fuzzy right now. She loosened the scarf she'd wound around her neck. It was irritating her. They'd started filming earlier, following up on Ross, the instructor with the head injury last month, who'd had emergency surgery. He was staying in Glasgow, recovering well, even though he was pale with a large part of his hair now missing. The young boy, Kai, had his leg in a cast but took great delight in showing them just how fast he could get about on his crutches.

Thank goodness those two parts of filming were wrapped up. It would mean they would need less footage whilst on Arran. She closed her eyes, part of her not wanting to spend too much time in Rhuaridh's company and part of her aching for it.

She was so confused right now. And who was making all that noise? She shivered, pulling her coat closer around her. Rhuaridh. Sometimes thinking about him made her angry, sometimes it made her feel warm all over. Her mind would drift back to that second on the beach…then that second sitting in the woods together. Her life currently felt like a bad young adult romance novel.

'Kristie. Kristie.' Someone was shaking her. 'We need to go. Here, give me the keys. I'll drive.'

'What? No?' She stood up and promptly swayed and sat back down. Had she actually fallen asleep?

Gerry was looking at her oddly. 'You're sick,' he said, holding out his hand for the car key. 'I'll drive. It's the same place as last time.'

She thought about saying no. She knew Gerry didn't like driving 'abroad', as he put it. But she was just so darned tired. She pushed the keys towards him. 'Okay, just once. And don't crash.'

'Kristie? You need to drink something.'

She moved, wondering why the bed felt so lumpy, trying to turn around, but her face met an unexpected barrier. She spluttered and opened her eyes. Dark blue was facing her. What?

She pushed herself back, trying to work out why there was a solid wall of dark blue in the bedroom in the cottage.

The voice started again. 'Kristie? Turn back this way. You need to drink something.'

Her brain wasn't making sense. Was she dreaming?

She moved back around again. Opening her eyes properly. They took a moment to focus. Directly ahead was a flickering orange fire. She pushed herself up, the material underneath her unfamiliar, velvety to touch. She looked down. She wasn't in her bed in the cottage. In fact, she didn't recognise this place at all. 'What? Wh... where am I?'

A face appeared before her. One she couldn't mistake. 'Rhuaridh?'

He nodded and knelt at the side of what she presumed must be his sofa. 'Here.' He held a glass of water with a straw. 'Will you drink something?'

Her throat felt dry and scratchy. She grabbed the straw and took a drink of the cold water. Nothing had ever tasted so good.

She moved, swinging her legs so she was sitting up right. 'Ooh...' Her head felt as if she'd been pushed from side to side.

'Careful. You haven't sat up for over a day.'

She blinked and took a few breaths, looking down at the large, soft white T-shirt she was wearing, along with an unfamiliar pair of grey brushed-cotton pyjama bottoms.

'Whose are these? And...' she looked about again '...how did I end up here?'

Rhuaridh pulled a face. 'The clothes? I guess they're yours. I had to buy emergency supplies for you. And you ended up here because Gerry panicked. He couldn't wake you up or get you out the car after you landed from the ferry. Your temperature was through the roof and you were quite confused.'

'I was?' She hated that she couldn't remember a single thing about this. 'But...you're busy. You don't have time to look after someone.' She was suddenly very self-conscious that she staying in the doctor's house.

He shrugged. 'I'm the doctor. It's what I do.'

Her head was feeling a little straighter. She tugged at the T-shirt self-consciously. 'What's been wrong with me?'

'You've had some kind of virus.'

'You're a doctor, and that's all you can tell me?' she asked, without trying to hide her surprise.

'Yes,' he said as he smiled. 'Your temperature has gone up and down as your body has fought off the virus. It made you a bit confused at times. You needed sleep to give your body a chance to do the work it had to.'

'Why didn't you send me to hospital?'

'Because you didn't need to go to hospital. You needed complete rest, simple paracetamol and some fluids.' He stood up. 'And some chicken soup—which I've just finished making. I'll go and get you some.'

He walked away towards the kitchen then ducked back and gave her a cheeky wink. 'You gave me five minutes of panic, though—you had a bit of a rash.'

She stared down in horror, wondering where on earth the rash had been—and how he had seen it.

All of a sudden she realised that someone had changed her into these clothes and put her others somewhere else. She looked around the room. It was larger than she might have expected. Comfortably decorated with a wooden coffee table between her and the flickering fire, the large navy-blue sofa and armchairs. At the far end of the room next to one of the windows was a dining table and chairs, with some bookshelves built into the walls. Part of her wanted to sneak over and check his reading materials.

Rhuaridh appeared a few moments later carrying a tray. The smell of the soup alone made her stomach growl. He laughed as he sat down next to her, his leg brushing against hers.

He slid the tray over towards her. There was a pot of tea, a bowl of chicken and rice soup that looked so thick she could stand her spoon in it, and some crusty bread and butter.

'Aren't you having some?' she asked, conscious of the fact she'd be eating in front of him. He nodded. 'Give me a sec.' He walked back through to the kitchen then joined her on the sofa as she took her first spoonful of soup.

It was delicious. Not like anything they had in LA. Soup wasn't that popular there. But she'd noticed in Scotland a whole variety of soups seemed a staple part of the diet. 'You actually made this?'

He nodded. 'From an old recipe of my dad's. I can make this one, Scotch broth, lentil and bacon, and tomato.' He frowned as he was thinking. 'I can also make mince and potatoes, stovies, steak pie, and chicken and leek pie. After that? My menu kind of falls off a cliff.'

'Okay, is this where I admit I only know what part of that menu is?'

She was starting to feel a little more alive. Now she'd woken up and orientated herself, she wasn't quite so embarrassed by what had happened. Rhuaridh had looked after a million patients. He was a doctor. It was his job.

She kept on spooning up the soup. 'I think this is the best thing I've ever tasted,' she admitted. 'You'll need to teach me. I can't make anything like this. In fact, avocado and toast is about my limit.'

'What do you eat in LA?'

She grinned. 'Avocado and toast. And anything else that I buy in a store.'

She liked the way he laughed. Deep and hearty.

It didn't take long to finish the soup. She sighed and leaned back on the sofa. 'That was great.'

His hand brushed against hers as he moved the tea

on the table in front of her and lifted her soup bowl. It made her start.

'I wonder… I know it's been an imposition having me here, but could I use your shower before I get ready to go back to my own cottage?'

He pointed to the staircase. 'There's a spare room with an en suite bathroom at the top of the stairs. Some of your things are in there. I only brought you down here when you were so cold—so the fire could heat you.'

He'd carried her. He'd carried her down here. The intimacy of the act made her cheeks blaze unexpectedly.

As Rhuaridh made his way back to the kitchen, she practically ran up the stairs. Sure enough, the white bedclothes were rumpled and there was a bag with her clothes at the side. Her stomach flip-flopped. She grabbed what she could and headed to the shower.

He'd spent the last day worrying about her. When Gerry had turned up at his door, it had taken him all his time to assess her to reassure himself that there was nothing serious going on.

The sigh that Gerry had finally let out when Rhuaridh had told him that it was likely she had some kind of virus her body was fighting off had filled the room. He'd sent Gerry back to the rental, advising him that he'd watch over her.

Against his spare white bedding she'd looked pale, her normal tan bleached from her skin, and her temperature had been raging. He'd had to strip her clothes off, then try and dose her with some paracetamol whilst she'd been barely conscious.

He'd known it would pass. He'd known it was part and parcel of the body fighting off a virus—and sleeping was the best thing she could do. But it didn't stop him settling into a chair in the corner of the room and spending an uncomfortable night there, watching over Kristie.

Next day he'd run out to the nearest shop to buy her something to wear as the virus ran its course and she went from hot to cold. He'd had a heart-stopping minute when he'd pulled back the bedclothes and seen the red rash all over her abdomen. But it had faded just as quickly as it had appeared and he'd pulled the pyjamas onto her.

Now she was awake and showering—and would probably want to leave. And he was struck by how sorry he was about that. He'd never shared this cottage with anyone. Since he'd moved to Arran he hadn't brought anyone back to this space. Mac was watching carefully from the corner. He'd come over and sniffed at Kristie a few times, then nudged her in the hope she'd wake up and bring him food. When that hadn't happened he'd slumped off to the corner again.

It had been over a year since Rhuaridh had lived with someone. The penthouse flat that he'd shared with Zoe in one of the central areas of Glasgow didn't have the charm of this old cottage. Its plain white walls and sterile glass now seemed to Rhuaridh like some kind of indicator of their relationship. Zoe had liked living with a colleague who was doing well. Someone she thought might 'go places'. Of course, that had all come to a resounding crash when he'd told her his intention to return home to Arran as a general practitioner.

He couldn't remember the strength of his feelings back then. If Zoe had been sick, would she even have wanted Rhuaridh to take care of her—the way he had Kristie? It was likely not. There were no similarities between the two women. Zoe didn't have the warmth that Kristie did. Even when Kristie was sick, she'd still occasionally reached out and squeezed his hand.

There was something about that connection. That taking care of someone. Letting them share the space that was essentially yours. Somehow with Kristie it didn't feel intrusive. It just felt...right. He'd never experienced that with Zoe. Instead, he'd just felt like part of her grand plan. One that had come to a resounding halt when he'd said he was moving back to Arran. Rejection always hurt. That, and the feeling of not being 'enough' for someone. He had none of that from Kristie. Instead, it felt like they were pieces of the same puzzle—albeit from thousands of miles apart—that just seemed to fit together. And it didn't matter that long term it all seemed impossible, because right now was all he wanted to think about.

Rhuaridh turned as Kristie came back down the stairs. Her damp hair was tied up, her cheeks looked a bit pinker and she'd changed into the clothes that Gerry had stuck in a bag and brought around yesterday. 'Stole some of your deodorant,' she said apologetically. 'Gerry's idea of toiletries seems to be only a toothbrush.'

'No worries,' he said casually. He pointed to the table. 'I made some more tea. I thought you wouldn't be ready for anything more sociable.'

She eyed the tea and accompanying plate of chocolate biscuits. 'That's about as sociable as I can manage,' she said as she sat back on the sofa and tucked her legs underneath her. 'Hey, Mac,' she said, calling the dog over and rubbing his head, 'I'm sorry, have I been ignoring you?' She bent down and dropped a kiss on his head. 'Promise you it wasn't intentional.'

She let Rhuaridh pour the tea and hand her a cup before he sat down next to her again. The pink T-shirt she was wearing made her look more like herself.

'I'm glad you're feeling better,' he said. And he meant it.

She sipped her tea. 'I'm so sorry. I've really put you out. What about work?'

He looked at her and gave a gentle shake of his head. 'It's Sunday. You arrived late on Friday night and there's been a locum on call at the hospital this weekend.'

Her eyes widened as she realised what those words meant. Her hand flew to her mouth. 'Your first weekend off? Oh, no. I'm so sorry. You must have had plans.'

He shrugged. 'I guess you changed them for me.'

She blinked. Her eyes looked wet. 'I'm sorry,' she whispered, her voice a bit croaky.

'Don't be. You brightened up our weekend. Mac's getting bored with me anyhow. He likes the change of company.'

She gave him a curious glance. 'Do you normally bring patients back to your house?'

He paused, knowing exactly how this would sound. 'There's a first time for everything.'

Her breathing faltered and that made his own hitch. He wondered if she'd say something else but instead she sighed and leaned back against the sofa again. 'We've missed filming. We won't have time to get much more.'

'Gerry didn't seem too worried. To be honest, after his initial moment of panic, he almost seemed relieved. I think the guy might need a bit of a break.'

'You've spoken to Gerry?'

'He's been round a few times.' He didn't add that Gerry might have filmed her while she'd slept. That was for Gerry to sort out. According to Gerry, a host's consent was implicit, it was built into their contract—no matter what the situation.

She shuffled a little on the sofa and rested her head on his shoulder. 'We got some footage before we got here. You know about Kai and Ross?'

He was surprised. He hadn't realised they were being so thorough. 'I knew that you followed up on Magda and the baby, but I didn't know you'd followed up on all the other patients too.'

She lifted her head and looked him in the eye. 'Of course. The viewers love it. They want to know if everyone is okay. Haven't you realised that human beings are essentially nosy creatures and want to know everything?'

He could answer that question in so many ways. He could laugh. He could crack a joke. But he didn't.

He'd looked after Kristie for the last twenty-four hours. And at so many points in that time he'd wished he didn't only get to spend three days at a time with her. He'd wished all their time wasn't spent filming. He'd prefer it if it could just be them, without anyone else, no patients, no cameras.

So he didn't make a joke because this was it. This was the time to ask the question he should have asked before.

'Why don't you tell me?' he said gently.

'Tell me what?'

'Tell me why you don't like hospitals.' He could see it instantly. The shadow passing over her eyes.

She swallowed and stared into the fire for a few moments, then reached up and brushed her hand against her damp hair. She wasn't looking at him. He could see he'd lost her to some past memory. Maybe it was the only way she could do this.

'I don't like hospitals because I had to go there...' her voice trembled '...when my sister died.'

The words cut into him like a knife. Now he understood. Now he knew why he could always tell that something was amiss.

'It's everything,' she continued. 'The lights, the smell, the busyness, and even the quiet. The overall sound and bustle of the place.' Now she turned to meet his gaze and he could see just how exposed she was. 'And it doesn't matter where in the world the hospital is because, essentially, they're all the same. And they all evoke the same memories for me.'

He was nodding now as he reached out and took one of her hands in his, intertwining their fingers. 'This job?' she said, as she dipped her head. 'It was the absolute last one that I wanted. I wanted the Egyptian museum. I wanted the astronaut's life. Not because I thought they were more exciting, just because I knew they wouldn't bring me to a hospital. And you—' she looked straight at him '—were always going to do that to me.'

He kept nodding. He was beginning to understand her a little more. Just like he wanted to. But she hadn't answered the most important question. 'What happened to your sister, Kristie?'

She blinked, her eyes filled with tears. 'I don't talk about it,' she whispered. 'Hardly anyone knows.'

'You don't have to tell me. I want you to trust me, Kristie. I want you to know that I'm your friend.' Friend? Was that what you called someone he'd kissed the way he'd kissed her?

He was treading carefully. He had to. He could tell how delicate this all was for her. Holding hands was as much as she could handle right now and he knew that.

She closed her eyes and kept them that way. 'My sister was unwell. She'd been unwell for a long time, and...' a tear slid down her cheek '...felt that no one was listening. She took her own life.'

The words finished with a sob and he pulled her forward into his arms.

He didn't speak. He knew there was nothing he could say right now that would help. She'd told him hardly anyone knew and she didn't really talk about it, so this had been building up in her for a long time. Pain didn't lessen with time, often it was amplified. Often it became even more raw than it had been before.

He hated Kristie feeling that way, so he stayed there and he held her, stroking her hair and her back softly until she was finally all cried out.

'I'm sorry,' he whispered.

She lifted her head and tilted her face towards his. 'You said we were friends,' she said hoarsely. 'Are we friends? Because what I'm feeling... I don't feel that way about a friend.'

He could feel his heart thudding in his chest. It was almost as if she'd been reading his mind for the past two months—ever since they'd sat on that log together. Since they'd shared that kiss. 'How do you feel?'

She reached up and touched the side of his face. 'How many people have you looked after in your house?' she asked.

'None.'

'How many people have you made chicken soup for?' She tilted her head and smiled at him.

He couldn't help but return that smile. 'None.'

She slid her hand up around his neck. 'Then I'm going

to take it for granted that all of this…' she paused '…means something.'

'I think you could be right,' he whispered as he bent forward and finally put his lips on hers.

And all of sudden everything felt right.

CHAPTER SEVEN

November

'I'M SORRY, MISS. That's the just the way is it. We've cancelled the ferries for the rest of today. We can't take them out in a storm like this. We'd never get docked on the other side, it's not safe for the passengers or the crew.'

She could feel panic start to creep up her chest.

'But you'll sail tomorrow, won't you?'

He shook his head. 'Not likely. The storm's forecast to be even worse tomorrow. And it's to last the next day too. It could be Thursday before the ferries are sailing again.'

She couldn't breathe. She couldn't miss filming—not because of the show but because, if she didn't film, she didn't get to spend time with Rhuaridh. The guy she'd been counting down the last four weeks for. The guy she'd been texting every day. And most nights.

Gerry shook his head. 'Louie won't be happy with this. We'll need to use whatever unused footage we have.' He made a bit of a face and walked away.

The man at the ferry terminal gave her a shrug. 'Sorry, it only usually happens around twice a year. Storms get so bad no one can get off or on the island.'

'But there must be another way? A smaller boat? A helicopter? What if there's a medical emergency?'

The man gave her a look. 'To take a smaller boat out in this weather would be suicide. As for emergencies, everyone on the island knows that this can sometimes happen. If the doc can't fix it, it can't be fixed.'

She stepped back. He'd got her with that word. *Suicide.* She'd been desperate. She'd been ready to run around the harbour to try and charter a smaller boat. But she wouldn't do that now. Not after that word.

She looked out through the glass at the ferry terminal. She couldn't even see Arran on the horizon, just the mass of grey swirling storm, and hear the thud of the pouring rain.

Another month without seeing Rhuaridh again?

It had never seemed so long.

CHAPTER EIGHT

December

HE WAS WAITING at the ferry terminal. It was ridiculous. She would be driving the hire car but he still wanted to see her. Two months. Two months since their second kiss.

Sometimes he felt guilty, thinking he'd taken advantage. But from the stream of messages they'd exchanged since then, there had been no indication that she thought that.

Was it possible to actually get to know someone better by text, email and a few random video chats? Because it felt like it was. He'd learned that Kristie's favourite position was sitting on her chair at home, in her yoga pants, eating raisins.

She'd learned that he was addicted to an orange-coloured now sugar-free fizzy drink that some people called Scotland's national drink. He didn't let many people know that. She'd also laughed as she'd watched him try to follow a new recipe and increase his limited kitchen menu, and fail dismally.

It was only when he was standing on the snow-covered dock that he realised he'd no idea what car she would be driving this time. But she spotted him first, flashing her headlights and pulling to a stop next to him in the car park.

'Hey!' She jumped out of the car with a wide smile on her face. At first she looked as if she was about to throw her arms around him, but something obviously stopped her as she halted midway and looked a bit awkward. Instead, she held out her hands. 'Snow,' she said simply as she looked about.

She lifted her chin up towards the gently falling snow, closing her eyes and smiling as she spun around.

Gerry got out of the car and looked mildly amused.

'You've never seen snow before?' asked Rhuaridh.

'Of course I haven't,' she said, still spinning around. 'I live in LA. It's hardly snow central.'

Rhuaridh looked over at Gerry. 'What about you?'

Gerry shook his head. 'Don't worry about me. I spent three months filming in Alaska. I *know* snow.'

Rhuaridh smiled as he kept watching Kristie. He'd never realised this would be her first experience of snow. 'It's not even lying properly,' he said. 'Give it another day and we might actually be able to build a snowman or have a snowball fight.'

'Really?' She stopped spinning, her eyes sparkling.

He nodded. 'Sure. Now come on, I'm taking you two guys to dinner in the pub just down the road. Let's go.'

'Good for me,' said Gerry quickly, climbing back into the car.

Kristie stepped up in front of him. 'You don't have to do that,' she said, still smiling.

She was so close he caught the scent of her perfume. It was different, something headier. 'But I want to.' He slid his hand behind her, holding her for the briefest of seconds. 'I might have missed having you around.'

'Good.' She blinked as a large snowflake landed on her eyelashes. 'Let's keep that up.'

Part of her was excited and part of her was laced with a tiny bit of trepidation. Louie was massively excited. It seemed he'd taken over production of the episode where she'd been unwell and had included footage of Rhuaridh looking after her, interspersed with a few repetitions of their previous interactions.

It wasn't her favourite episode because it felt so intrusive. The whole episode was literally dedicated to the relationship between them, rather than the life of a Highland doc. But Louie had argued his case well. 'The viewers have been waiting for this. They want it. And what else have we got to show them this month? You didn't exactly do any filming on the island, we were lucky Gerry actually filmed anything at all.'

She knew in a way he was right. But when she'd taken on this role, she hadn't realised the story would become about her too.

Watching the scenes where Rhuaridh had been looking after her had brought a lump to her throat. He was so caring. So quietly concerned. It was a side of him she hadn't seen before. And the way that he'd looked at her at times had made her heart melt. Thank goodness Gerry hadn't been around to film their kiss. She hadn't told him about either of the times they'd kissed. He was already looking at her a bit suspiciously—as if he suspected something—so she didn't plan on revealing anything more.

The pub that Rhuaridh took them to was warm and welcoming, panelled with wood. Every table was taken and the pub was full of Christmas decorations—twinkling lights, a large decorated tree and red and green garlands underneath the bar. Rhuaridh insisted they all eat a traditional Scottish Christmas dinner—turkey, stuffing, roast potatoes, tiny sausages, Brussels sprouts and mashed turnip all covered in gravy. 'This is delicious,' said Gerry. 'A bit more like our Thanksgiving dinner. But I like it. I could eat more of this.'

Kristie leaned back and rubbed her stomach, groaning. 'No way. I couldn't eat another single thing.'

Rhuaridh was watching them both with a smile on his face. 'Well, I'm still trying to make up for the fact you spent a few days here eating hardly anything.'

'Are you trying to take care of me, Dr Gillespie?' she teased.

He shook his head. 'No way. You're far too difficult a patient.' There was a twinkle in his eyes as he said the word. He glanced at Gerry, obviously not wanting this conversation to become too personal. 'What are your plans for filming this time? Do we need to make up for lost time?'

Kristie shifted a little uncomfortably, not quite sure how to tell him about the episode that would go out in a few weeks, but Gerry got in there first. 'Don't worry,' he said with a wave of his hand, 'we've got that covered. We had some old unused footage and just mixed it with the fact that Kristie was pretty much out of action.'

'Oh, okay.' Rhuaridh seemed to accept the explanation easily. 'So what about this time?'

Kristie had given this some thought. 'We've got quite a bit of footage of some of the patients in the cottage hospital. Christmas is a big deal. I know we're not actually here for Christmas Day, but it might be nice if we could get some film of how the staff deal with patients who they know will have to stay in hospital for Christmas.'

Rhuaridh lifted his eyebrows. 'You mean, you actually want some heart-warming stuff for Christmas instead of some kind of crisis?'

Gerry laughed. 'If you can whip us up a crisis we'll always take it, but I think we were going to try and keep with the season of goodwill. On a temporary basis, of course.'

Rhuaridh looked carefully at Kristie. 'Do you feel okay about filming in the hospital?'

Gerry's eyebrows shot upwards. He had no idea that she'd shared her secret with the doc. Kristie cleared her throat awkwardly, trying to buy a bit of time. But she could come up with nothing. It seemed that honesty might be for the best.

'He knows about Jess. I told him.'

She couldn't decipher the look Gerry gave her. 'Okay, then,' he said simply.

She took a few moments. She'd thought about this when Louie had suggested it. Everything previously had seemed like a diktat—it had been required for the show so she'd had to grit her teeth and get on with it. She'd been so fixated on how she felt about hospitals, deep down, that she hadn't taken the time to reconsider how her perspective might have changed a little. 'We're talking about the older patients who are too sick to get home. You know I met some of them before?'

Rhuaridh nodded.

She smiled as things seemed to click in her mind. 'I actually really enjoyed talking with some of them. They're not patients. They're people. People who've lived long, very interesting lives and have a hundred tales to tell.

Maybe we should try and film an update on a few of the people we've spoken to before—and maybe we should ask them about Christmases from years gone by. How did people normally celebrate Christmas on Arran? Are there any special traditions?'

Rhuaridh and Gerry exchanged a glance and looked at her, then at each other again.

Gerry leaned over the table. 'What do you think's happened to her?'

'I think she's turned into some kind of Christmas holiday movie. You know—the kind that play on that TV channel constantly at Christmas.'

Kristie laughed and nudged both of them. 'Stop it, you guys. Maybe I'm just getting into the spirit of things. First time I've seen snow. First time I've been in a place that's cold at Christmas. All my life I've spent my Christmases in sunshine next to a pool. Give a girl a break. I'm just getting in the mood.'

As soon as she said the words she felt her cheeks flush. She hadn't quite meant it to come out like that. Gerry didn't seem to notice, but she knew that Rhuaridh did as he gave her a gentle nudge with his leg under the table.

'It's settled, then,' said Gerry as he raised his pint glass towards them. 'Tomorrow we go be festive!'

Arran in the snow was truly gorgeous. He hadn't paid much attention before because snow in winter was the norm here. But somehow, seeing it through Kristie's eyes gave him a whole new perspective on how much the whole island looked like a Christmas-card scene.

Now, as he looked out of the window as they pulled up at the hospital, he took a deep breath and let himself love everything that he could see. He always had loved this place, but the break-up with Zoe had left him living under an uncomfortable cloud. Her words had continued to echo in his head.

'It's an island in the middle of nowhere. There's not a single thing to do on that place. How anyone can stay there more than one night is beyond me. I'd be bored witless in the first week.'

Those words had continued to wear away at him. The place where he'd grown up and loved hadn't been good enough for the woman he'd loved at that time. *He* hadn't been good enough for her.

His loyalties had felt tested to their limit. The loyalties and love he had for the place he'd called home, and his loyalties to his profession, his future dreams, and the woman he'd lived with.

For the first time he actually realised what a blessing it had been that things had come to a head.

He'd always wondered if the move to Arran again was just a temporary move—to fill the gap until someone else could be recruited for the GP surgery. But in the last two months things had changed and he couldn't help but wonder if the TV show was the cause of that.

For the first time in for ever there had been applicants for the GP locum weekend cover posts that had been advertised for as long as Rhuaridh had been here. That was why he'd had cover the last time Kristie had been here. Other GPs were taking an interest in Arran. He'd had some random emails, one asking about covering Magda's maternity leave, and another from a doctor who wanted to complete his GP training on the island. That had never happened before.

Before, he'd felt he was stuck here.

Now he knew he was choosing to stay here. And that made all the difference.

Kristie had a piece of red tinsel in her hair. 'Are we going in, or are we sitting here?'

He smiled. 'Let's go. I'm going to review a few patients while we're here.'

Gerry tagged behind a little, almost like he was giving them a bit of space. Rhuaridh wondered just how much the cameraman suspected. He'd been so tempted to give Kristie a kiss when she'd first arrived that he wondered if Gerry had noticed that.

Rhuaridh watched as Kristie entered the hospital. Her footsteps faltered a little but she held her head up high and ran her hand along the wall as she entered the building. It was like she was using it to steady herself. He paused for a second, then stopped worrying about who was around and who would see.

She'd shared with him why she was antsy around hospitals. She'd shared a part of herself. He walked alongside her and took her other hand in his, giving it a squeeze. She looked down—surprised—then squeezed back. He didn't say anything. He didn't have to.

They carried on down the corridor.

They were only in the hospital for a few minutes before one of the nursing assistants grabbed Kristie and persuaded her to help put up some more decorations.

'We can't put them in the clinical areas, but we can put them at the entrance and in the patients' day room.'

'No tree on the ward?' he heard Kristie say. She looked quite sad.

Rhuaridh shook his head. 'Infection control issues.

Also allergies—they harbour dust. Health and safety too—they could be a fire risk.'

'Phew.' Kristie let out a huge sigh. 'How do you remember so many interesting rules and regulations?' She rolled her eyes. 'And here was me thinking that Christmas decorations would have a place in hospitals—to improve mental health, lift spirits, and to help orientate some of the older patients to time and place.'

He raised his eyebrows. 'Touché. What have you been reading?'

'Lots.' She smiled. 'I'm not just a pretty face.' Her words hung there as they smiled at each other, then she glanced over her shoulder as the nursing assistant appeared with another box. 'Or just an objectionable reporter,' she added quickly.

He pointed to the half-erected tree. 'This has been here for as long as I have. And, Ms Objectionable Reporter, the stuff you say about lifting spirits and orientating to time and place is right. But...' he paused '...our biggest issue in this season is winter vomiting—also known as norovirus. If we end up with that?' He held up his hands and shook his head. 'There's a huge outbreak cleaning protocol, and something like this would have to be taken down and disposed of if it had been in a clinical area.' He gave a shrug. 'Better safe than sorry.'

She picked up a piece of sparkling green tinsel and draped it around his neck. 'Aw, it's a shame. Maybe you could impersonate the Christmas tree instead?'

'Ha-ha. Now, don't you have patients to film?'

'Don't you have patients to see?'

The nursing assistant's head turned from side to side, smiling at the flirtation and teasing going on before her very eyes. 'Glad to see you two are finally getting on,' she said under her breath.

It gave Rhuaridh a bit of a jolt and he nodded and strode towards the ward. 'Catch up if you can,' he shouted over his shoulder.

He spent the next hour reviewing patients, writing prescriptions and watching Kristie out of the corner of his eye. She seemed easier, relaxed even. By now everyone was used to Gerry hovering around in the background with the camera.

It was nice to see her that way. She had a long conversation with one of the older men who was recuperating after a hip operation. She tried a few Christmas carols with a couple of the female patients. She helped put out cups of tea and coffee, and was particularly interested in the range of cakes that appeared from the hospital kitchen.

'It's like a baker's shop,' she said in wonder.

The nurse near her nodded. 'We find that often appetites are smaller when patients get older. Our kitchen staff are great. The cook was even in earlier, asking people what their favourites were. That's why we have Bakewell tarts, Empire biscuits and fairy cakes.'

Rhuaridh heard Kristie whisper, 'Don't you get into trouble about the sugar?'

The nurse shook her head. 'Not at this point. Calories are important. Look around. Most of our patients are underweight, not overweight. We'd rather feed them what they like than look at artificial supplements.'

Kristie flitted from one patient to the next, squeezing hands and making jokes. Occasionally he glimpsed a far-off look in her eye that didn't last long. The patients loved her.

But the more he watched, the more he had nagging doubts. He couldn't pretend he didn't like her. The whole world could see that he did. But was the whole world also laughing at him? After all, what would a gorgeous girl from LA find interesting about a Scottish island? There were no TV studios, no job opportunities. Most of the time during winter half the island shut down. There was no cinema. No department stores—only a few local shops. There was one slightly posher hotel with a swimming pool, gym and spa but there wasn't a selection to choose from. And there were only two hairdressers on the entire island. Kristie had already told him she loved trying different places.

Zoe's words echoed around his head. Boring. Dull. Nothing to do.

He hadn't been able to maintain a long-term relationship with a woman in Glasgow just over fifty miles away. How on earth could he even contemplate anything with a woman from LA—five thousand miles away? He must be losing his marbles.

Just at that moment, Kristie leaned forward and pressed her head against that of one of the older, more confused patients. He could see she was talking quietly to him. His hands were trembling, and Kristie put her own over his, squeezing them in reassurance. She pointed to the Christmas tree through the doors. She was orientating him to time and place.

And that was it. A little bit of his heart melted. Did it really matter if this would come to nothing? Maybe it was time for him to start living in the here and now.

And the here and now for him was that Kristie would still be visiting for three days a month for the next four months. And if that was all he'd get, he'd be a fool to let it slip through his fingers.

Her anxieties were slowly but surely beginning to melt away. She would always hate hospitals. They would always have that association for her. But somehow, this time, things felt different.

Different because she knew Rhuaridh had her back.

If she needed a minute—if her heart started racing or her breathing stuck somewhere inside her chest—she didn't need to hide it or pretend it was something else entirely. And the weird thing was that none of those things had actually happened.

Maybe it was Bill, the older man, who'd distracted her completely. In a lucid moment he'd just told her about his wife dying fifteen years before and how much it had broken his heart. Then he'd started to gently sing a Christmas carol they'd loved together. Kristie had joined in and when, a few moments later, he'd become confused and panicky, she'd taken his hand and reassured him about where he was, who he was, and what he was doing there.

This could be her. This could be Rhuaridh. This could be anyone that she knew and loved. No one knew what path lay ahead for them, and if she could give Bill a few moments of reassurance and peace then she would.

Rhuaridh came over and placed a warm hand on her shoulder. 'I've just finished. Do you have some more people to film?'

She shook her head. 'Gerry's looking tired. I think we've done enough today. We'll come back tomorrow and finish then.'

Rhuaridh gave a nod. 'Okay. The snow's got a bit

thicker since yesterday. We might be able to scrounge up a few snowballs. Are you game?'

She wrinkled her nose. 'Game? What does that mean?'

He laughed. 'It's like a challenge. It means are you ready to do a particular action—like making snowballs.'

Now she understood. She took a few minutes to say goodbye to Bill, then joined Rhuaridh. 'Okay, then, I'm game.'

Gerry joined them outside, and grabbed the car keys while they plotted. The hospital grounds were large, with a grassy forecourt lined with trees.

'Why go anywhere else?' asked Kristie. She zipped up her new red winter jacket—which would never see the light of day in LA. She kicked at the thick snow on the ground. 'Let's just have our snowball fight here.' She put her hands on her hips and looked around, her breath steaming in the air in front of her. 'Or maybe we should start with a snowman. I've always wanted to build a snowman.'

Rhuaridh pulled some gloves out of his pocket. Kristie winced. Gloves. She'd forgotten about gloves. He walked closer. 'Did you forget the most essential tool for playing with snow?'

She grimaced, hating to start on the back foot. 'Maybe.'

He handed his gloves over. 'Here, use mine.'

She grinned. 'Doesn't you being a gentleman give me an unfair advantage?'

His eyes gleamed. He leaned forward, his lips brushing against the side of her face as he whispered in her ear. 'Yeah, but that would only count if I thought you might actually win.'

'That's fighting talk.' She gave him her sternest glare but she knew he was teasing.

He nodded. 'It is. So let's start. First to make a snow-man wins.'

She looked across at the wide snow-covered lawn and wagged her finger encased in the thick gloves. 'We split this straight down the middle. Don't try and steal my snow.'

'Your snow?'

'Absolutely. This is *my* snow.' She gave him a wary nod. 'I'm the guest.'

'You are, aren't you?' He bent down and scooped some of the snow into his bare hands. 'I haven't told you, have I?'

She frowned. 'Told me what?'

'I might have a bit of a competitive streak. Go!' Something streaked across the dark sky towards her, hitting her squarely on the shoulder and splattering up into her face.

She choked for a second as Rhuaridh's deep laugh rang across the night air. He didn't waste any time. He ran straight into the middle of his patch and started trying to pack snow together.

She shook the snow off her hair and out of her face. 'Cheat! I'll get you for that.'

'Keep up!' he shouted over his shoulder.

She didn't waste any time, running to her own patch of snow and trying to pack it like Rhuaridh was doing. After a few minutes she had pressed enough together to form a giant snowball that she could start rolling across the grass to make it bigger. She couldn't hide her de-light. Within a few minutes she was out of breath. Push-ing snow was harder than she could ever have imagined.

She looked up. Rhuaridh was making it look so easy. Ratfink.

She kept going, loving the whole experience of being

in the snow. Before long she had a medium-sized snow-ball, just about big enough to be a body.

Rhuaridh had already positioned his in the middle of the green and was rolling another. She ran to catch up, ignoring the fact hers already looked a bit smaller than his.

If he thought he had a competitive edge, he had nothing on her.

She stopped for a moment, distracted by seeing him blow on his hands for a few seconds. Just watching him gave her a little thrill. His dark hair, which always looked as if it just about needed cutting, his broad shoulders and long legs. Jeans suited him—though she'd never say it out loud. Even from here she could see the deep concentration on his face as he went back to rolling the second ball for the snowman's head. It gave her the opening she needed. She pulled together her first small snowball and threw it straight at him. It landed right at his feet.

He looked up and smiled. 'Given up already? What's happened to your snowman?'

'I've taken pity on you,' she said quickly, not wanting to admit that she'd no idea how, if she rolled a second ball of snow, she'd actually get it on top of the snowman. She grinned and grabbed some more snow, trying her best to shape a snowball and throw it at him. But it seemed she didn't quite have the technique and it disintegrated in mid-air.

'Seems like you LA girls need some snow training,' he said as he strode towards her. He was laughing at her.

She tried again then started to laugh too when it didn't quite work. 'What is it? Do they teach Scottish kids how to make a snowball at birth?'

He shook his head. 'Much earlier. We learn in the womb. It's a survival skill.'

He was right next to her, his tall frame standing over her. She dusted off the gloves and looked up, taking a step closer. She wanted to hold her breath, to stop steam appearing between them. His hair was in front of his deep blue eyes—and they were fixed on hers. Behind him was the backdrop of the navy sky speckled with stars, followed by the snow-covered outline of the cottage hospital. Right now, it felt like being on a Christmas card.

He lifted one hand and touched the side of her cheek, his cold finger made her jump, and they both laughed. 'Red looks good on you,' he said huskily.

'Does it?' She couldn't help it, she stepped forward. She just couldn't resist. It was as if there was a magnet, pulling them together. They were already close but this removed the gap between them. His other hand went instantly to her waist.

He gave a little tug at the scarf around her neck. 'I guess I should say it now.'

She swore her heart gave a jump. 'Say what?'

His cold finger traced a line up her neck, and across her lips. Teasing her.

His head dipped down towards her. 'It's a little early.'

Yip, her heart had forgotten how to beat steadily.

'Early for what?' she whispered.

He pulled something out of his pocket. She recognised it. It was plastic, green and white, slightly bent, and had come from the decoration box in the hospital.

'What are you doing?' she asked.

'This,' he said, 'is mistletoe. And I thought it was time to say Merry Christmas and introduce you to the Scottish tradition.'

She slid her arms around his waist as her smile grew wider. 'And what tradition might that be?'

His lips lowered towards hers. 'The one of kissing under the mistletoe.'

His lips weren't as cold as his hands and the connection between them sent a little shockwave through her body. Last time they'd kissed had been in his front room. It had been comfortable. Warm. And had felt so right.

This was what she'd been waiting for. This had been the thing that had teased in her dreams for the last two months. Expectation was everything. And Rhuaridh Gillespie was meeting every expectation she'd ever had.

Because kissing the hot Highland doc was like standing in a field full of fireworks. And if things got any hotter, they'd light up the entire island.

CHAPTER NINE

January

'IT'S DYNAMITE! WHY didn't you tell me you two were an item?'

'What?' Kristie rubbed her eyes.

'The film. The backdrop of snow. The two of you silhouetted outside the hospital, kissing. The public will die for this. I tell you, once this goes out, you'll have any job that you want. What *do* you want? A talk show? More reporting? How about something fun, like a game show?'

For the briefest of seconds she felt a surge of excitement. Louie was telling her she could have her pick of jobs. How long had she waited to hear those words?

But her stomach gave a flip and she tried to mentally replay what he'd said.

Her voice cut across his as he kept talking. She could almost feel the blood drain from her body. 'What do you mean—the kiss? The silhouette?'

'You and Gerry must have planned that. Tell me you planned it. It couldn't have been more photogenic. I guarantee you that someone will put that picture on a calendar next year.'

Dread swept over her. 'Is that what you think of me? That I *planned* to kiss Rhuaridh?'

'Best career move ever,' came Louie's prompt reply.

Now she was sitting bolt upright in bed. They'd caught the last ferry to Arran the night before and when she'd gone to Rhuaridh's cottage there had been no one home—not even Mac.

She hadn't managed to see the last lot of the footage. Gerry had some excuse about technical issues. Now she knew why. She'd kill him. She'd kill him with her bare hands.

She stumbled out of bed, her feet getting caught in the blankets. For a few seconds she blinked then glanced at her watch. It was still dark outside. Shouldn't it be daytime? She kept the phone pressed to her ear as she walked over and drew back the curtains, flinching back at the thick dark clouds and mist.

'Don't you dare use that footage. I've not seen it. And I didn't agree to it being used.'

'Of course you did,' said Louie quickly. 'It's in your contract.'

'*Please*, Louie.' She didn't know whether to shout or burst into tears. She'd try either if she thought they might work. 'I let you get away with using my sick footage. But not this stuff. It's not fair on me. And it's not fair on Rhuaridh.'

'Oh, it's not fair on Rhuaridh?' Louie's voice rose and Kristie knew his eyebrows had just shot upwards. 'Well, it's pretty obvious that you like him now. But just remember, you have a job to do. And don't forget exactly what he's getting in return for us filming. And anyway, by the end of all this neither of you two will need to work. You'll spend the next few years touting yourselves around the talk shows. The public will *love* this.'

Her heart plummeted. Everything she'd felt about the kiss, the anticipation, the expectation, the longing, and the electricity—the whole moment had stayed in her mind like some delicious kind of dream. But now it seemed tarnished. It seemed contrived and unreal. She sagged down onto her bed. She'd wanted to keep the kiss to herself. She'd wanted that intensely personal moment to remain between her and Rhuaridh. Because that's the way it should be. Her perfect Christmas kiss.

'Gotta go,' Louie said quickly. 'Got another call. Try and catch another kiss on film—or maybe have a fight. That could really kick the figures up.'

The phone clicked. He was gone.

Her brain was spinning. She'd planned to get up this morning and put the new clothes on she'd bought to meet Rhuaridh. She had the whole thing pictured in her head. The checked pinafore she'd picked up that almost looked tartan, along with the thick black tights and black sweater—again clothing she'd never have a chance to wear in LA. It was amazing how a few days in Scotland a month had started to change her wardrobe. She'd never had much use for chunky tights, warm clothing and thick winter jackets. She even had a few coloured scarves, gloves and hats.

Now the pinafore hanging over the back of the chair in the room seemed to be mocking her. Her jaw tightened. She grabbed yesterday's jeans and shirt, pulling them on in two minutes flat, and marched across the hall towards Gerry's room. She couldn't hide the fact she was anything other than mad.

'You filmed us? You filmed us and you didn't tell

me?' She had burst straight through the door—not even knocking.

Gerry was standing with his back to her, the camera at his shoulder. He spun around and swayed. She stepped forward to continue her tirade but the words stuck somewhere in her throat. Gerry's skin was glassy. She couldn't even describe the colour. White, translucent, with even a touch of grey.

Even before she got a chance to get any more words out, Gerry's eyes rolled and he pitched forward onto the bed.

'Gerry!' she yelled, grabbing at him and fumbling him round onto his back. She knelt on the bed and shook both his shoulders. But his eyes remained closed.

She tried to remember what she'd seen on TV. She felt around for a pulse, not finding anything at the neck but eventually finding a weak, thready pulse at his wrist. She squinted at his chest. Was he breathing? It seemed very slow.

She grabbed her phone and automatically pressed Rhuaridh's number. He answered after the second ring. His voice was bright. 'Kristie, are you—?'

'Help. I need help. It's Gerry. He's collapsed at the bed and breakfast we're staying in.'

She could hear the change in his tone immediately, almost like he'd flicked a switch to go into doctor mode. 'Kristie, where is he?'

'On the bed.' She was leaning over Gerry, watching him intently.

'Was there an accident?'

'What? No. He just collapsed.'

'Is he breathing?'

She paused, eyes fixed on Gerry's chest. 'I… I think so.'

'Has he got a pulse?'

'Yes, but it's not strong…and it's not regular.'

'Kristie, I'm getting in the car. Pam has phoned for the ambulance. Which B and B are you at?'

She glanced over her shoulder to find the name on the folder on the bedside table, reciting the name to Rhuaridh.

'I'll be five minutes. Shout for help. Get someone to stay with you, and tell them to make sure the front door is open.'

It was the longest five minutes of her life. When Rhuaridh appeared at the door, at the same time as the ambulance crew, she wanted to throw her arms around him.

She moved out of the way as they quickly assessed Gerry, then moved him onto a stretcher. Gerry seemed to have regained consciousness, although his colour remained terrible. She darted around to the side of the bed and grabbed his hand. 'Why didn't you tell me you didn't feel well?' she asked.

He shook his head and as he made that movement, parts of her brain sprang to life. The way his colour hadn't been great the last few months, his indigestion, his tiredness.

A tear sprang to her eye. She'd missed it. She should have told him to get checked out. But she'd been too preoccupied with herself, too occupied with the show—and with Rhuaridh—to properly look out for her colleague.

Rhuaridh pulled some bottles from his bag and found two separate tablets. 'Gerry,' he said firmly. 'I need you to swallow these two tablets. It's important. Can you do that for me?'

One of the ambulance crew handed him a glass of

water with a straw. 'C'mon, mate, let's see if you can manage these.'

After a few seconds Gerry grimaced then managed to swallow down the tablets. Rhuaridh opened Gerry's shirt and quickly attached a monitor to his chest.

Kristie reached out and touched his shoulder. 'Gerry, I'm sorry, please be okay.'

Gerry's eyes flickered open. 'Hey,' he said shakily. 'Remember the camera.' He gave a crooked smile. 'Don't want to miss anything.' His eyes closed again and Kristie felt herself moved aside as the ambulance crew member reached for the stretcher.

She gulped then grabbed the car keys as Rhuaridh turned towards her. 'What's wrong?' she whispered.

Rhuaridh's voice was low. 'I think he's had a heart attack. I'll be able to confirm it at the hospital.'

She nodded as a tear rolled down her cheek.

'Hey,' he said softly as he picked up his bag. His other hand reached up and brushed her tear away. 'Don't cry. We'll get things sorted.'

'Doc?' A voice carried from outside the door. One of the ambulance crew stuck his head back inside. 'We might have a problem.'

He was stuck between trying to reassure Kristie and trying to reassure himself.

The weather was abysmal. No helicopter could land on Arran or take off in the next few hours. It seemed he was it.

This happened. This was island life. Thankfully it didn't happen too often, but in the modern age lots of people didn't really understand what living on an island meant.

Kristie was pacing outside as Rhuaridh read Gerry's twelve-lead ECG and rechecked his observations. Normally people with a myocardial infarction would be transported to hospital and treated within two hours. But those two hours were ticking past quickly and Gerry had no hope of reaching a cardiac unit.

Most people with this condition would end up in a cardiac theatre, with an angiogram and stent inserted to open up the blocked vessel. But there was no specialised equipment like that on Arran.

There were monitoring facilities and Gerry was currently attached to a cardiac monitor in one of the side rooms with an extra nurse called in to observe him closely for the next twenty-four hours.

Kristie couldn't stop pacing. He hated to see how worried she was, but the truth was he couldn't give her the guarantee she so desperately needed—that Gerry would be fine.

Rhuaridh put down the phone after talking to one of the consultants in Glasgow. Emergency situations called for emergency treatment.

'What's happening?' Kristie was at his side in an instant.

He ran his fingers through his hair. 'Bloods and ECG confirm it. Gerry's had a massive heart attack. If he was on the mainland he'd go to Theatre to get the vessel cleared and probably have a stent put in to try and stop it happening again.'

It seemed she knew where this conversation would go. 'But here?'

'But here I've given him the first two drugs that should help, and now we'll need to do things the more old-fashioned way and give him an IV of a drug that should break up the clot.'

She frowned. 'Why don't you still just do that? It sounds better than Theatre.'

He gave a slow nod. He had to phrase this carefully. 'Studies show the other way is better. But as that isn't an option, this is the only one we have.'

'That doesn't sound good.' Her voice cracked.

Rhuaridh put his hand on her arm. 'It takes an hour for the treatment to go in, then we have to monitor him carefully. There can be some side-effects, that's why we've called an extra nurse in to monitor Gerry all day and overnight.'

Kristie's head flicked from side to side. 'Right, where can I stay?'

He tried not to smile. He knew she would do this. 'You can stay with me. I'm going to have to stay over-night too. We'll pull a few chairs into one of the other rooms close by. Miriam, the nurse, can give me a shout if she needs me.'

He looked down at her white knuckles gripping the camera in her hand. 'What are you going to do with that?'

She took a few breaths as if she were thinking about it, then she lifted her chin and looked at him. 'I'm going to do Gerry's job. I'll film it.'

There was something in her eyes that struck him as strange. 'Are you okay?'

Her jaw was tight. 'If Gerry was the one out here, he would film. He told me back at the B and B.' She nod-ded as if she was processing a few things. 'And I'll film you. You can explain what a heart attack is and what the medicines are that you've given Gerry.' She paused for the briefest of seconds then added, 'Then you can talk about the weather and why we can't leave. I'll ask you a few questions about that.'

He tilted his head to the side. What was wrong with Kristie? Something just seemed a little…off. He understood she was worried about her colleague. Maybe this was her way of coping—to just throw herself into work.

He gave a cautious nod. 'Of course we can do an interview. But give me a bit of time. I'm going to set up the IV with Miriam and have a chat with Gerry.'

She pressed her lips together and swung the camera up onto her shoulder. 'Carry on. I'll capture what I can.'

Just as he'd finally managed to get used to Gerry constantly hovering in the background with a camera, now everything was flipped on its head and Kristie hovering with a camera was something else entirely. Initially he'd found Gerry's filming intrusive, and probably a bit unnecessary. But Kristie's? That was just unnerving. Gerry had an ability to be unnoticeable and virtually silent. Now he was constantly aware of the scent of Kristie drifting from behind him and the noise of her footsteps on the hospital floor.

Where Gerry had felt like a ghost, Kristie was more like a neon light.

And things were certainly illuminating. It turned out Gerry had been harbouring a history of niggling indigestion and heaviness in his arms and a constant feeling of tiredness. Trouble was, Gerry had worked out himself that all the signs were pointing to cardiac trouble—but instead of seeking treatment he'd kept quiet, out of fear of losing his job.

Rhuaridh wasn't there to judge. Healthcare and insurance in the US was completely different from healthcare in the UK.

He turned to speak to Kristie just in time to notice a big fat tear slide down her cheek. Her eyes were fixed on Gerry's pale face as he lay with his eyes closed on the hospital bed, surrounded by flashing monitors and beeping IVs.

Something inside him clenched. This was her worst nightmare. Of course it was. She hated hospitals and now she was forcing herself to stay to be with Gerry. He knew in his heart that any suggestion he made about her leaving would fall on deaf ears. Rhuaridh slid his arm around her shoulders and pulled her towards him. 'You okay?'

She shook her head then rested it on his shoulder. 'I was mad at him. I went across to his room to shout at him.'

Rhuaridh tilted his head towards her. 'Why on earth did you want to shout at Gerry? You two seem to get on so well. You complement each other.'

She hesitated for a second then pulled a face. 'If I tell you why I was mad, you might get mad too.'

Rhuaridh shook his head. He had no idea what she was talking about. 'Okay, I feel as if I missed part of the conversation here.'

Her eyes lowered, her hands fumbling in her lap. Her voice was sad when she spoke. 'I found out Gerry filmed us kissing outside the hospital in December. I didn't know. He didn't say a word to me. And now my producer, Louie, has seen it, and loves it, so it's going to be in the next episode of the show, no matter how much I begged him not to use it.'

For the first time since she'd got here Rhuaridh felt distinctively uncomfortable. He didn't actually care about being filmed kissing Kristie. What he did care about was the fact she didn't seem to want anyone else to know. All those previous thoughts that he'd pushed away rushed into his head. Why would a girl like Kristie be interested in a guy from a Scottish island?

He took a deep breath and said the words he really didn't want to. 'What's wrong with us kissing?'

Her head turned sharply towards his. 'It's private. It's not something I want to share with the world.'

She was looking at him as if he should understand this. But his stomach was still twisting. His brain was sparking everywhere. He was looking at this woman in a new way. A way that told him she could easily break his heart.

He'd kind of shut himself off from the world since he'd come to Arran—focusing on work had seemed easier than realising he might never get the opportunity to meet someone to share his life with. And even though he knew things were ridiculous and completely improbable, even the fact that he'd thought about Kristie in that context had meant that he'd finally started to open himself up a little again. But it seemed he couldn't have timed things worse.

'We were in a public place,' he said carefully. 'That isn't so private.'

For a millisecond he might have been annoyed with Gerry—just like he had been in the beginning, questioning everything they filmed and the ethics behind it.

But Kristie had already told him. She needed this show to be a hit. If she didn't want the world to know they'd kissed, then at least part of him could be relieved she wasn't playing him.

She looked wounded by his words, her hand flew up to her chest. 'But it's private to me,' she said empathically.

He leaned forward, looking into those blue eyes and then whispering in her ear, 'Kristie, I don't care if the world knows we're kissing.' And he meant it. He glanced at Gerry on the bed. They still didn't know how this would all turn out for Gerry. If he had medical insurance he'd get shipped home once his treatment was complete. But chances were Rhuaridh wouldn't see him again anytime soon. Gerry might not be fit enough to travel like he had been.

He had to admire the canny old rogue. He'd seen the opportunity to film and taken it. Something flashed into Rhuaridh's head. Something he hadn't really processed earlier.

'Gerry asked you to film—and you did. We don't know how this is going to play out yet, Kristie.' He was serious. The IV drug Gerry was currently on could cause heart arrhythmias. It could also lead to small clots being thrown off while the heart was trying to re-perfuse. There were no guarantees right now. 'I'm not sure this is footage you should use.'

He left the words hanging in the air.

She blinked and her body gave a tremble. When she spoke her voice was shaky, 'I'm a terrible person. You know I want Gerry to be okay, don't you?'

He nodded and she continued, 'And I was still angry when he asked me to start filming, so I just automatically did. I've left the camera running at times without actually being behind it. I'm not even sure exactly what's been shot.'

Rhuaridh slid his hand over hers. 'I know what you're thinking. You need to take a breath. Take a moment. If Gerry is fine, then you've covered his work. You can show what happens to people in an island community when there's no possibility of getting off the island. This is a fact of life here. Gerry's had an alternative treatment for his heart attack. We hope it will work. If it does, you have footage.' He squeezed her hand. 'If it doesn't, then you stay some extra days and we'll shoot something else.'

He was trying to give her an alternative. The last thing he wanted was for her to be forced to use footage that would prove to be heartbreaking for her. He whispered again. 'No one needs know it's there.'

She shook her head. 'But it is. Our cameras don't need to go back to the studio to be uploaded. Everything uploads automatically to our server. Even if I don't want to use it, Louie probably will.'

'Surely he's not that heartless? You told me he was the guy that held your hand while you were at the hospital.' He leaned forward. 'Footage of us kissing? That's nothing. But if something happens to Gerry? No way. He couldn't use that. He wouldn't use that.' Rhuaridh wasn't quite sure who he was trying to convince. Her or himself.

She leaned back in against his shoulder and put her hand up on his chest. 'I hope so,' she whispered in reply, as both of their eyes fixed on the pulse, pulse, pulse of Gerry's monitor.

CHAPTER TEN

February

TRAVELLING WITH SOMEONE else felt all wrong. Thea was nice enough, but clearly obsessed. She had around one hundred Scottish travel books and couldn't seem to understand there wasn't time to drive around all the rest of Scotland before they got the ferry to Arran. It seemed she hadn't quite grasped the size of Scotland, or the terrain. By the time they docked in Arran, Kristie had a full-blown migraine.

The last few days at the helpline had been hard. Someone had called and kept hanging up after a few minutes. Every time it had happened, Kristie's thoughts flooded back to her sister. This could be someone like Jess. Someone who needed to be heard but couldn't find the words.

She'd struggled with it so much but she dealt with her feelings by continuing to work on the book she'd started writing a couple of months before. It had been years since she'd tried to write things. Last time she'd done this she'd been in college. But all of that had been pushed aside as her course work had taken priority. Now this story seemed to be shaping itself. All of it was fiction. None of it was based on a real person. Instead, it was an amalgamation of years of experiences. But it all felt real to Kristie. Even though this show was the thing the whole world was excited about, this story was the thing that kept her awake at night—that, and thinking of a hot Highland doc.

She'd also had over a thousand social media messages today alone. Since the kiss had been shown, her social media presence had erupted even more than before. Her conversations with Rhuaridh had continued. He'd been hit with just as many messages as she had—more, probably. And he was feeling a bit shell-shocked by it all. But Rhuaridh seemed able to pull his professional face into place and use his job as a protective shield.

She looked up just in time to meet the glare of an elegant-looking woman with gleaming dark brown hair. She looked out of place on the Arran ferry in her long wine-coloured wool coat, matching lipstick and black high heels. Kristie frowned. Why on earth would that woman be glaring at her?

'Will he be waiting for you at the dock? Should I film that?' Thea asked. Kristie started at Thea's voice and turned just in time to catch Thea shooting her a suspicious look. 'And this thing—it is real? Or is it all just made up for the camera? I have to admit I'm kind of curious.'

Kristie was more than a little stunned. 'You think it's fake?'

Thea was still talking. 'I mean, let's just say I'm asking in principle, because—let's face it—he is *hot*.'

A surge of jealousy swept through Kristie. 'You think Rhuaridh is *hot*?' She said the words almost in disbelief.

Thea threw back her head and laughed. 'Oh, honey, the whole world thinks he's hot.'

Now she wasn't just jealous. Now she was mad. Rhuaridh Gillespie was hers. She could picture herself as a three-year-old stamping her foot. Very mature.

And still Thea kept talking. Did the woman ever shut up? 'And anyway, you're from LA, he's from—what is it called again? Arran? How's that ever gonna work? He might as well be on the moon. I mean, let's face it, in a few months you won't be getting paid to come here any more. I bet these flights cost a small fortune.'

A horrible sensation swept over Kristie. She'd always known this—it's not like she was stupid. But she'd tried not to think about it.

The horn sounded as the boat docked, the sound ricocheting through Kristie's head. She winced and stood up. 'Come on,' she growled at Thea.

Her heart gave a leap as she pulled into the car park of the GP surgery. Rhuaridh was standing outside, waiting for her, his thick blue parka zipped up against the biting wind.

Thea let out a sound kind of like a squeak as Kristie jumped out of the car and ran towards him. She couldn't help it. Four weeks was just too long. Rhuaridh dropped a kiss on her nose and wrapped his arm around her. 'What's the update on Gerry?' he asked straight away.

She gave a sigh. 'Good, but not so good. He's started cardiac rehab classes and is making some progress. He's tired. I think he's frustrated that things are taking longer than he hoped. He's been assured he should make a good recovery, but just has to show some patience.' She pulled a face. 'And the TV channel won't cover his travel insurance until he's been signed off as fit by the doctor. And, to be honest, I think that will take a few months.'

The way Rhuaridh nodded made her realise that he'd known this all along—even if she hadn't. He leaned forward and touched her cheek with his finger. 'You okay? You look tired.'

'I am.' She glanced sideways over her shoulder. 'Thea—I'll introduce you to her in a sec—is exhausting. My head is thumping.'

He paused for a second, giving Thea, who already had the camera on her shoulder, a quick wave. 'And the next show?'

Kristie let out another sigh. Maybe she was more tired than she'd thought. 'The show is going out with Gerry as the star and you and I as background footage. Gerry's fine about it.'

'And are you?'

'I guess I should be happy we're not as front and centre this time. But we're still there. The camera was running at the hospital and it's caught us sitting together, holding hands.'

'I can live with that.' It was as if he chose those words carefully.

She met his gaze, ignoring the way her hair was whipping around her face in the wind. 'So can I.' She couldn't help the small smile that appeared on her face. There was just something about being around Rhuaridh. Not only did he make her heart beat at a million miles a second, he was also her comfort zone. Her place.

She leaned forward and rested her head against his chest for a second. 'Kristie?' he said.

Although she'd told him about her sister, she'd never got round to telling him about the helpline. Things were playing on her mind. She needed a chance to talk to him—but she wanted to do that when they were alone.

She lifted her head. 'Can we go to the pub tonight for dinner?' Tonight was only a couple of hours away. She could wait that long.

'Of course.' He nodded. She watched as he painted a smile on his face and put his hand out towards Thea. 'Gerry, you've changed a little,' he joked. 'Welcome to Arran.'

Three hours later they finally had some peace and quiet. Even though the pub was busy, they were tucked in a little nook at the back where no one could hear them talk.

Rob, the barman, had just brought over their plates of steaming food, steak pie for Rhuaridh and fish for Kristie. Rhuaridh lifted his fork to his mouth and halted.

Kristie followed his gaze. The elegant woman from the boat was crossing the pub, heading directly towards their table. Every head in the room turned as she passed, her wool coat now open, revealing a form-fitting black dress underneath. She was easily the best-dressed woman in the room and she knew it.

Kristie's skin prickled. She could sense trouble. Rhuaridh looked almost frozen as the woman approached.

Kristie tilted her head, pretending she felt totally at ease. 'Can I help you?'

The woman looked down her nose at Kristie. For all her elegance, she wasn't half as pretty when she was sneering at someone. 'Oh, the American.' She said the words as if Kristie were some kind of disease.

Years of experience across cutthroat TV shows meant that Kristie was more than prepared for any diva behaviour. She gave her most dazzling smile. 'I'm afraid you have me at a disadvantage. Who are you?' The words were amiable enough, but Kristie knew exactly how to deliver them. The implication of 'not being important enough to know' emanated from her every pore.

There was a flash of anger in the woman's eyes but Rhuaridh broke in. 'Kristie, this is Zoe.'

'Zoe?'

The woman straightened her shoulders. 'Zoe Brackenridge. Rhuaridh and I are...' a calculating smile appeared on her lips '...very good, old friends.'

The ex. It was practically stamped on her forehead. But Kristie wasn't easily bested.

Zoe seemed to dismiss her, turning her attention to Rhuaridh. 'Rhuaridh, do you think we could go back to the cottage? I think we need to have a private chat.'

'I'm not quite sure there's room enough for three,' said Kristie quickly. Too quickly, in fact, she was in danger of letting this woman make her lose her cool.

But it seemed that Rhuaridh had limited patience too. 'What are you doing on Arran, Zoe? I thought you hated the place.' His gaze was steely.

There was a tiny flicker in the woman's cheek. She wasn't unnerved. She was angry. She looked Rhuaridh straight in the eye, 'Like I said, we need to talk.'

'We talked some time ago. I think you said everything you needed to.'

Zoe leaned forward and touched Rhuaridh's arm, leaving her hand there. Kristie resisted the temptation to stab her with her fork. 'Rhuaridh, I'm sure there are some things we could catch up on.'

'Like what?'

Kristie almost choked. She'd never heard Rhuaridh be that rude before. Funnily enough, she kind of liked it.

Now Zoe was starting to show some signs of frustration. 'I think we have a lot of things to catch up on.

One of the consultants I'm working with was enquiring about you—there could be a job opportunity in Glasgow. It would be perfect for you.' She looked over her shoulder. 'Get you away from this island. Now you've done that show, you should be able to recruit someone else for here. Get your career back on track. Get your life back on track.'

Rhuaridh stood up, his dinner untouched, and reached out for Kristie's hand. 'You've watched the show?'

Kristie felt as if she'd been catapulted back into high school. This seemed like teenage behaviour. Rhuaridh had never really talked about the relationship he'd had with Zoe, but in Kristie's head she could see Zoe watching the show, seeing how captivated the world was with Rhuaridh, and realising exactly what she'd let go. Now she'd shown up like some high school prom queen back to claim her king.

Zoe rolled her eyes, then settled her gaze on Kristie. It was distinctly disapproving. 'It doesn't exactly show you in the best light.' She waved her hand. 'And as for that title…' She gave a shudder and touched his shoulder. 'I think it's time a friend helped you get back to where you should be.'

Kristie ground her teeth. Did this woman even know how condescending she sounded? But she didn't get a chance to say anything. Rhuaridh stepped up right in front of the woman.

He stood there for a few seconds. Zoe cast Kristie a triumphant glance that was short-lived. Rhuaridh spoke in a low voice. 'Let me be clear. We don't have anything to talk about. And you've just rudely interrupted dinner between me…' he paused for the briefest of seconds '…and my girlfriend.'

It was like someone had sucked the air out of her lungs. *Girlfriend*. She liked that word. She liked it a lot.

'Goodbye, Zoe,' he finished as he gave Kristie's hand a tug and pulled her with him as he headed to the door, leaving some money on the bar. 'Sorry about dinner,' he muttered as he kept walking.

She ignored her empty stomach as she cast a look over her shoulder. Zoe looked stunned. It was probably her best look.

'Beans on toast,' said Rhuaridh. 'Fine dining. The staple diet of most Scottish students.'

Kristie raised her eyebrows at him. 'I think we could have got away with taking the plates. No one would have noticed.'

He let out a sigh. She hadn't said a word in the car back to the cottage. It was as if she knew he needed some time to sort out his head. He couldn't believe Zoe had turned up here. There had been a few random emails that he hadn't replied to. But he would never have expected her to show up in the place she'd shown so much contempt for.

There had always been a side to Zoe that hadn't exactly been complimentary—one she tried to keep hidden. Zoe, at heart, was competitive. Whether that was in her career, in her love life, or in her finances. And it was the 'at heart' part that annoyed him most.

He'd been deluged with messages from every direction. Even though he still hadn't watched the show, he couldn't fail to notice its impact. Zoe's competitive edge must be cursing right now. She wasn't here really because she regretted her actions or her words. No, she was here because she wanted a bit of the limelight. This wasn't an act of love. This was an act of ambition.

Kristie pressed her lips together as she picked up her plate and walked over to the sofa. It was clear her mind was somewhere else.

'I'm not sure what you and Thea have planned for footage for this month's filming. I imagine Thea will need to find her way around the surgery and hospital for now so I've not scheduled anything in particular. But I've arranged for filming in the school to happen next month,' he said quickly, trying to pull her away from whatever was giving her that pained expression. 'There's a whole host of immunisations coming up. They're handled by the nurse immunisation team, but I generally try to go along in case there are any issues.'

'What kind of issues?'

'There are usually a few fainters. The odd child who might have a panic attack. Consents are all done before we get there, and all the children's medical histories have been checked.'

'Mmm…okay.'

He put his plate down. 'Kristie, what did you want to talk about earlier?'

She pushed her plate away and pulled her legs up onto the sofa, turning to face him with her head on her hand. She gave her head a shake. 'I'm just tired. It's nothing.'

'It's not nothing. It's something. Tell me.'

She gulped. He could see her doing that so reached out and took her hand. After a few minutes she finally spoke. 'I told you about my sister. But what I didn't tell you was that after she died I contacted the helpline she'd phoned a few times and volunteered. The calls she made were short. She always disconnected. But I felt as if I wanted to do something.' She ran her other hand through her hair. 'I couldn't get it out of my head that when she'd been feeling low, the place she'd called was there, not me.'

Her voice started to tremble. 'And I realised that I could be that person at the end of the phone for someone else. So I volunteered, they trained me, and I've been manning the phone three times a month for the last few years.'

He'd listened carefully. He knew there was more.

'So what's wrong?'

She stared down at her hands. 'The last few nights, someone has been phoning, staying on the line for less than a minute then hanging up. I know that's what Jess did.' Her voice cracked. 'And I can't help but wonder if I'm failing them, just like I failed Jess.'

Rhuaridh didn't hesitate, he pulled her into his arms. 'You didn't fail your sister, Kristie, and you haven't failed this person either. They've called. They've got to take the decision to speak. Sometimes people call six or seven times before they pick up the courage to speak. All you can do is be there. All you can do is answer and let them know that you're prepared to listen whenever they want to speak.'

'But what if offering to listen isn't enough?' Her wide blue eyes were wet with tears.

His heart twisted in his chest. He could see just how desperate she was to save any other family from the pain she'd suffered. He could see just how much she wanted to help.

He put his hands at either side of her head. 'Kristie Nelson, you are a brilliant big-hearted person. But you have to accept that there are some things in this life we can't control—no matter how much we want to. All we can do…is the best that we can. I know that's hard to accept. But we have to. Otherwise the what-ifs will eat us up inside.'

He leaned forward and rested his head against hers. They stayed like that for the longest time. At first he could see the small pulse racing at the bottom of her neck, but the longer they stayed together, the more her body relaxed against his, and the more her breathing steadied and eased. He wanted to give her that space and time to gather her thoughts—just like he was gathering his.

She took another breath. 'There's more,' she said quietly.

'What?'

She licked her lips. 'These last few months I started working on something—a book.'

He was momentarily confused. 'A book?'

She nodded. 'It's fiction. But it's based on Jess, and what happens when a member of your family commits suicide. The impact it has on all those around. It's about a tight-knit family and a group of old high school friends. How they all second-guess themselves wondering if they could have done something—changed things—and how they have to learn to live and move on.'

He pulled back and looked at her, amazed. 'Wow, that sounds…incredible.' He reached forward and brushed back a strand of hair from her face. 'Can I read it?'

She looked surprised. 'Do you want to?'

'Of course. Now. Do you have it?'

A smile danced across her lips as she stood up and crossed the room, picking up her laptop. 'It's still in the early stages. There might be spelling mistakes—grammatical errors.'

He shook his head and held out his hands. 'I don't care. Just give it to me.'

He bent over the bright screen and started reading as she settled beside him.

Three hours later it was the early hours of the morning. Kristie's manuscript. It was beautiful, touching and from the heart. And it smacked of Kristie. Every word, every nuance had her unique stamp on it. He brushed a tear from his eye and nudged her. She'd fallen asleep on his shoulder.

'Kristie, wake up.' He gave her a shake and she rubbed her tired eyes.

'You've finished?'

He nodded and she bit her bottom lip. 'What did you think?'

He held out his hand. 'I think it's brilliant. It's heartbreaking. It's real. You have to finish this. *This* is what you should be doing, Kristie. This is so important. I *felt* for every one of the people in this story. You have to get this out there.'

Her eyes sparkled. 'You think so? Really?'

He nodded. 'Without a doubt. You have a gift as a writer. Do it. I believe in you. Once an agent sees this, they'll snatch it up with both hands.'

A smile danced across her lips. He could see the impact his words were having. The fact he believed in her ability to tell this story. It felt like pieces of their puzzle were just slotting into place.

He couldn't believe that Zoe had shown up today. He'd never seen someone look so much like a fish out of water. But it was almost as if a shadow had been lifted off his shoulders. She'd always intimated that Arran was less, and he was less for being here. He'd compromised his career and his life. And for a time those thoughts had drip-dripped into his self-conscious.

But tonight was like shining a bright light on his life. Everything was clear for him. He was exactly where he wanted to be, and with the person he wanted to be with. Zoe's visit—instead of unsettling him—had actually clarified things for him. He didn't care about the distance between him and Kristie. He had no idea how things would play out. All he knew was that he wanted to think about the here and now. With her.

It was almost as if their brains were in accord. Kristie lifted her head and gave him a twinkling smile. 'I just remembered something you said tonight.'

'What?'

'Girlfriend, hey?' she said as she slid her arms around his neck.

His voice was low as his hands settled on her waist. 'I just remembered something you said too. I heard you tell her the cottage wasn't big enough for three,' he said as his lips danced across the skin on her neck. 'You made it sound like you were staying here.'

'Oh, I am.' She smiled as she pulled him down onto the sofa and made sure he knew exactly how things were.

CHAPTER ELEVEN

March

Don't get too comfortable. Miss LA will get just as sick of the place as any normal human would. How can smoggy hills compare to the glamour of Hollywood? Your success is just your fifteen minutes of fame. You should be asking yourself where your career will be in five years' time. That's what's important.

RHUARIDH SHOOK HIS head and deleted the email. It was sad, really. Zoe was trying to provoke a reaction from him and the truth was he felt nothing. He wasn't interested in her or in anything she had to say.

He looked out the window towards the hills. Were they smoggy? Maybe. Goatfell was covered at the top by some clouds. But Kristie had already said she wanted to climb it with him. Every time she visited she seemed a little more fascinated by Arran and wanted to see more. Her attitude was the complete opposite of Zoe's and that made him feel warm inside. She didn't see Arran as the last place on earth she wanted to visit—she might not want to ever stay here but when she was here, she made it seem like an adventure. And he'd take that.

He picked up the case he had ready to go to the high school. The immunisation team would be setting up right now and he'd arranged to meet Kristie and Thea there as they came straight off the first morning ferry. Chances were they'd be tired—they'd been travelling all night, but a delayed flight had caused them a few problems.

The local school was only a few minutes away. The whole place was buzzing. The immunisation team never failed to amaze him by how scarily organised they were. One of the nurses met him just as Thea burst through the door with her camera at the ready. 'Wait for me,' she shouted.

He shook his head and looked down at the list of children the nurse wanted him to give a quick review. Nothing much to worry about. Kristie stepped in behind Thea. Her cheeks flushed pink and her skin glowing. Every pair of eyes in the room turned towards them.

'Hey,' she said self-consciously, tugging at a strand of her hair.

'Hey,' he replied.

What he wanted to do was kiss her. But he didn't want to do it in front of an audience. As soon as the thought crossed his brain the irony struck him. Thanks to Gerry, the whole world had already seen them kiss.

Kristie slipped into professional mode. Interviewing a few of the nurses, watching the kids come in for their vaccinations and capturing a few of them on camera too.

Everything was going smoothly until one of the teachers came in, white-faced. 'Dr Gillespie. I need some help.' Rhuaridh didn't recognise him. He must be one of the supply teachers.

Rhuaridh looked up from where he was finishing talking to a child with a complicated medical history. 'Can it wait?'

The teacher shook his head. 'No, it definitely can't.' He was wringing his hands together and the worry lines across his forehead were deep.

Rhuaridh was on his feet in a few seconds. Thea was still filming on the other side of the room, so Kristie followed Rhuaridh and the teacher up some stairs to the second floor of the school.

The teacher had started tugging at his shirtsleeve. 'I don't know what to do. She's been up and down. Apparently her father died last year and the school has been worried about her. Sometimes she just walks out of class. But today—she's barricaded herself into one of the rooms. Her friend told us that she said she wanted to kill herself. To join her dad.'

Rhuaridh heard Kristie's footsteps falter behind him. He turned around and raised his hand. 'Maybe you should let me handle this.'

He could see the strain on her face, but didn't get a chance to say anything further as the teacher stopped in front of one of the rooms. 'Here,' he said. 'I've tried everything.'

'Is it Jill Masterton?' Rhuaridh asked. He knew everyone on the island—so unless someone new had just moved over, the only teenager he knew who had lost her father in the last year was Jill.

The teacher nodded. 'I've been talking to her for the last half-hour. I didn't think she was serious. I just thought it was attention-seeking. But...but then she said some other stuff, and I realised...' he shook his head '...whatever it was I was saying just wasn't helping.'

Rhuaridh could see the stress on the teacher's face. 'Have you contacted her mum?'

He nodded. 'She's on the mainland, waiting to catch the first ferry back.'

Rhuaridh took a deep breath. He didn't know this girl well. He hadn't seen much of her in the surgery. He turned to the teacher. 'Do you have any guidance teachers or counsellors attached to the school?'

The teacher shook his head. 'I'm only temporary. I came to cover sick leave. The guidance teacher—you probably know her, Mary McInnes—had surgery on her ankle. She's not expected back for a few months.'

Of course. He should have remembered that. He ran his fingers through his hair. 'Has she told you anything at all?'

The teacher now tugged at his tie. It was clear he was feeling out of his depth. 'She won't speak to me at all. But she doesn't know me. And the teachers that she does know haven't had any reply. Last time someone tried to speak to her she said if anyone else came she would jump out of the window.'

There was a nagging voice of doubt in Rhuaridh's head. He hadn't seen this young girl since he'd got back here. She wouldn't remember him at all. When he'd left the island she'd been barely a baby. He held out his hands. 'I'm a doctor. I can speak to her. But I'm not a psychiatrist, or a psychologist. I don't want to make anything worse. Particularly if she's already made threats.'

'Do you have any other counsellors on the island?' Kristie stepped forward. The teacher shook his head.

She put her hand on her chest. 'Then let me.' She turned to Rhuaridh. 'You know that I've been trained. Let me talk to her. Maybe I can relate. I lost someone I loved too, plus I understand what it's like to be a teenage girl.'

'I don't want you to be out of your depth,' he said quietly. He was thinking about her being upset the other week when the caller to the helpline wouldn't speak.

'I want to try,' she said determinedly.

Rhuaridh turned back to the teacher. 'Maybe we should wait. Maybe we should tell her that her mum is on her way back over on the ferry. Has anything else been happening in the school we should know about—any bullying?'

The teacher shrugged. 'I'm sorry. I just don't know. Nothing obvious.'

Rhuaridh let out a sigh. He was torn. Torn between looking after the girl behind the door and putting the woman he loved in a position of vulnerability.

There was so much at risk here, so much at stake. How would this affect Jill and Kristie if things didn't work out? What if Jill reacted to something that Kristie said—the impact on both could be devastating. He was so torn. He wanted to fix this himself—but he wasn't sure that he could. Maybe Jill would react better to a woman, particularly one who might understand her loss. Ahead of him was the closed door. It was symbolic really—demonstrating exactly how the young girl in there felt. He glanced from the panicked temporary teacher and the determined woman in front of him, his head juggling what was best for everyone. There was a hollow echo in his head.

Kristie straightened up. She'd had enough of this. Enough of waiting. He was trying to protect her—she got that. But she didn't need protection.

On the ferry on the way over here today, all she'd

thought about was how much she wanted to see Rhuaridh.
How much she wanted to be in his arms. For the last four
weeks she'd started to dream in Technicolor—and the
dreams didn't just include Rhuaridh, they also included
this place. Arran, with its lush green countryside, hills
and valleys, and surrounding stormy seas. Even though
she'd had a dozen job offers now and enough money in
the bank to pay the bills for a while, her love of TV was
definitely waning. The book she'd started writing had
taken on a life of its own. Rhuaridh's encouragement
had meant the world to her, and after that the words had
just seemed to flow even easier. She'd shown it to Louie,
who'd shown it to another friend who was a literary agent.
The agent had offered representation already. It was almost like her world had shifted, shaping her future. And
the one thing she'd been sure of was that her heart was
leading the charge. Could she think about a life in Scotland? She hadn't really considered things. Would she
be able to walk away from her TV career, and her work
with the helpline?

She swallowed and turned to both men. 'I'm going
to do this.'

She walked up to the door and stood close, trying to
think of the best way to appeal to Jill. Kids were all over
social media right now. Maybe she should try the *you-
might-know-me* approach?

She gave the door a gentle rap with her knuckles. 'Jill,
it's Kristie Nelson. You know, from the TV show? I've
come to talk to you.'

She could hear sobbing inside the room. The kind that
made the bottom fall out of her stomach. 'I don't want
to talk to anyone.'

Kristie leaned her head back against the door, trying

to think like a teenager these days. Her head was still in the social media zone. Their life revolved around social media. She pulled out her phone and did a search for Jill. Sure enough, it only took seconds to find her. Her online profile had a few selfies, and a few older pictures that showed a little girl laughing, sitting on her father's knee. It made her heart pang.

'How are you feeling?' she started.

'How do you think I'm feeling?' came the angry shout.

Good. She'd had another reply. Her main goal now was to keep Jill talking.

'I know about your dad, Jill. I know how sad you're feeling. Do you want to talk? Because I'm here. I'm here to listen to you.'

The sobs got more exasperated. 'How can you know how I'm feeling? How can you know what's in my head? Have you lost your dad?'

Kristie turned around and slid down the door so she was leaning against it. She may as well get comfortable. She wanted Jill to know that she was there to stay—there to listen. 'I've lost both of my parents,' she answered quietly. 'And I lost my sister three years ago. And I think about her every single day and the fact she's not here. And sometimes it catches me unawares—like when I see something I know she'd like and I can't show it to her, or when I hear something that makes me laugh and I can't pick up the phone and tell her.'

There was silence for a few seconds then she heard a noise. Jill was moving closer to the door. 'Three years?' she breathed.

'Honey, these feelings will get better with time. You won't ever forget, and some days will be sadder than others, but I promise you, you can learn to live with this.

You just need to take it one day at a time. You just need to breathe.'

She could feel empathy pouring out of her as she tried to reach out to the teenager behind the door. The teenager who thought that no one could understand.

The voice was quiet—almost a whisper. 'It would have been my dad's birthday today. He would have been forty-five.' Kristie's heart twisted in her chest. Of course. A birthday for someone who'd been lost. The roughest of days.

She heard the strangled sob again. All she wanted to do was put her arms around this hurting young girl. 'I get it,' she said steadily. 'Birthdays are always hard. I'm not going to lie to you. I've cried every birthday, Thanksgiving and Christmas that my sister hasn't been here.' She took a deep breath. 'Just know that you're not alone, Jill. Other people have gone through this. They understand. You just need to find someone to listen. Someone you feel as if you can talk to. Do you have someone like that?'

The reply was hesitant. 'It should be my mum. But I can't. I can't talk to her because she's so upset herself. She cries when she thinks I can't hear.' There was another quiet noise. Kristie recognised it. Jill had sat down on the opposite side of the door from her. It gave her a sense of hope.

'Okay, I get it. What about if we find someone who is just for you? Someone you can talk to whenever you need to?'

'Th-that might be okay… But…'

'But?' prompted Kristie.

'I don't want to have to go somewhere. To see someone.'

'Would you talk to someone on the phone? Have you tried any of the emotional support helplines around here?'

'M-maybe.'

Kristie sucked in her breath. 'Did you talk?'

There was silence for a few seconds. 'No.'

Tears were brimming in Kristie's eyes.

'I… I just wasn't ready.'

Kristie rested her head on her knees. One of the things that Rhuaridh had said before clicked into place in her mind. About all you can do is the best that you can. She wiped her tears again. 'Are you ready now?' she asked.

'I… I think so…'

'Jill, can I come in?'

There was the longest silence. Then a click at the door. Kristie cast a glance over her shoulder to where the teacher and Rhuaridh were standing. Her heart twisted in her chest. He hadn't believed in her. And for a few seconds it had felt like a betrayal—like the bottom had fallen out of her world. But she would deal with that later. Right now, she was going to do the best that she could.

'Kristie…' The voice came from behind her.

But she just shook her head, opened the door and closed it behind her.

He sat there for hours. First talking to the teacher, then to Jill's frantic mother, who'd practically run all the way from the ferry. He'd managed to get hold of a children's mental health nurse who would come and see Jill tomorrow from the mainland. This wasn't something that could be fixed overnight.

Kristie finally emerged from the classroom with her arm around Jill's shoulder. Jill threw herself into her mother's arms and Kristie waited to talk to both mother and daughter together. Just like he would expect a professional counsellor to do.

She'd been a star today. And he knew she'd been scared. He knew she'd had to expose part of herself to connect with the teenager. And words couldn't describe how proud he was of her right now.

He stood to the side until he was sure she had finished talking, then joined her to let Jill and her mother know the plans for the next day.

The rest of the students had now been sent home so the school was quiet, silence echoing around them. Rhuaridh lifted his hand to touch Kristie's cheek. 'I can't believe you did that,' he said quietly.

She met his gaze. 'I had to. She needed someone to talk to—someone to listen—and I could be that person.'

'I'm so proud of you. I know this must have been difficult.'

Something jolted in his heart. He hadn't wanted to say these words here, but he had to go with the feelings that were overwhelming him. 'I love you, Kristie. I've spent the last few months loving you and was just waiting for the right time to tell you.' He held up one hand, 'And even though it's a completely ridiculous and totally unromantic place, the right time is now.'

He couldn't stop talking. 'And I know it's ridiculous because we live on different continents and both have jobs and careers. I don't expect you to pack up and live here. In fact, the last thing I'd want is for you to come here and resent me for asking you to. But I had to tell you. I had to tell you that I love you and you've stolen a piece of my heart.' He lifted his hand to his chest.

She blinked and he could see the hesitation on her lips and his heart twisted inside his chest. He'd taken her by surprise. She hadn't been expecting this.

For a few seconds she said nothing. He'd said too much.

All his insecurities from Zoe's desertion flooded back into his brain as if he'd just flicked a switch. Her look of disdain and disapproval. Kristie's face didn't look like that—hers was a mixture of panic and…disappointment? She was disappointed he'd told her he loved her?

He was a fool. He should never have said anything. He'd just been overwhelmed with how proud he was of her that he'd obviously stepped across a whole host of boundaries he hadn't realised were there.

There was a laugh beside them and he pulled his hand back sharply.

'Oh, the Hot Highland Doc. I'd heard you were in the school.'

Rhuaridh turned to the teacher who'd just walked up beside them. 'What?'

The teacher just kept smiling. 'The kids talk about you all the time.'

He shook his head, thinking he hadn't heard correctly. 'What did you call me?'

'The Hot Highland Doc. It's a great title, isn't it? Better than the Conscientious Curator or the Star-struck Astronaut. Pity the geography is off.'

She gave a shrug and kept walking on down the corridor.

Rhuaridh tried to process the words. He spun back to face Kristie. 'She's joking, right?'

Kristie looked a little sheepish. 'I… I didn't have any say in it.' They were the first words she'd said since he'd told her he loved her.

He stepped back and looked down at himself. 'Hot Highland Doc? That's how you've described me to the world? Of all the ridiculous descriptions…' He shook his head again. 'And we're nowhere near the Highlands!'

He was overreacting. He knew that. But right now he felt like a fool.

A few things clicked in his brain, comments he'd heard people say but hadn't really picked up on at the time. 'I can't believe you'd let them do that.' Then something else crossed his mind. 'I can't believe you didn't warn me.'

Kristie breathed. The air was stuck somewhere in her throat. He'd just told her he loved her, then almost snatched it back by inferring they could never work. It was like giving her a giant heart-shaped balloon then popping it with a giant pin.

Her stomach was in knots. For a few seconds there she'd thought the world was perfect and their stars had aligned, but then Rhuaridh had kept talking. Was he talking himself out of having a relationship with her? Had she only been pleasant company while the filming was going on?

It was as if every defence automatically sprang into place. 'It's not up to me to tell you. The TV series hasn't exactly been a secret. Most of the island watches it. If you weren't such a social media recluse you would have picked up on it in the first month.'

Her brain was jumbled right now. Everything felt so muddled.

'Was any of this real for you? You tell me you love me one second, then tell me how ridiculous our relationship is in the next? Who does that? What kind of a person does that sort of thing?' The words were just spilling out in anger. No real thought because all she could feel right now was pain. All the things she'd considered for a half a second seemed futile now. Coming to Arran? Accepting the book deal and giving up the TV job? How on earth could she leave LA? She was crazy for even considering anything like that.

There was a flash of hurt in his eyes then his jaw clenched.

The anger kept building in her chest, turning into hot tears spilling down her cheeks.

She stepped back and looked him straight in the eye. Her words were tight. 'And…we're done. Goodbye, Rhuaridh.' She had to get out of there. She had to get out of there now.

Her pink coat spun out as she turned around and strode down the corridor. Her heart squeezed tight in her chest, part hurt, part anger. Why on earth had she thought for even a second that this might work?

He watched her pink coat retreating, trying to work out what the hell had just happened. He'd told her he loved her and she'd walked away.

There was a movement at the end of the corridor. A camera. Thea.

It appeared he'd just been starring in his own worse nightmare.

Fury gripped his chest. He put his hands on his hips for a few seconds, staring down as he took a few deep breaths.

This had all been for nothing. He'd been crazy to think they could ever make this work.

Then he straightened his back and walked in the opposite direction.

CHAPTER TWELVE

April

'I QUIT.'

'You can't quit. The show has just been syndicated.'

'For once, Louie, listen to what I tell you. I quit. I'm not setting foot on that island again.'

'Your contract says you are.'

'So sue me.'

Kristie slammed the phone down just as it buzzed. She turned it over.

Can we talk?

She stared at the name. Rhuaridh. Her hand started to shake.

NO.

She typed it in capital letters.

Last time he'd been this tired he'd been a junior doctor on a twenty-four-hour shift. He'd been delayed at both Glasgow then London airports. The heat hit him as soon as he set foot on the tarmac in Los Angeles. Most people in the UK drove cars with gears. Rhuaridh had never driven an automatic and hadn't quite realised it almost drove himself, meaning when he put the car into reverse in the car park at the airport, he almost took out the row of cars behind him.

He was torn between trusting the air-conditioning and just putting down the window to let some air into the car. It was dry. Scratchy dry.

He hadn't slept a wink on the flights. He'd been too busy thinking about the way they'd left things. Once he'd calmed down he'd tried to find her, but it seemed that she and Thea had caught the first ferry off the island.

He'd spent a few days replaying everything in his head. Trying to work out why things had gone so wrong.

Rhuaridh didn't want to call. He hadn't really wanted to text either, he just wanted to see her. He wanted to be in the same room as her. He wanted to talk to her.

He'd only sent the text once he'd landed, when he'd had a crazy second of doubt that he'd look like some kind of madman turning up at her door uninvited.

His brain wobbled at the number of lanes on the highway. At this rate he'd be lucky to make it there at all. Being called the Hot Highland Doc at least a dozen times between Arran and Los Angeles now seemed like some kind of weird irony. For the first time in his life complete strangers had recognised him. He'd been asked for autographs and selfies. People had asked him to speak so they could hear his accent. And there had been lots of questions about Kristie.

Most people had been completely complimentary— but he was sure that was because there was a lag time of six weeks between filming and the finished episode being shown. Once they saw the next episode that was scheduled—which would surely contain their fight and Kristie walking away—he was pretty sure he'd be toast the world over.

But here was the thing. He wasn't worried about the rest of the world. He was only worried about her.

He pulled up outside an apartment complex in the Woodland Hills area of Los Angeles. It looked smart. Safe.

He lifted his chin and pushed every doubt away. It was time. Time to put his heart on the line and tell this woman—again—just how much he loved her. Just how much he was prepared to do to make things work between them. She might still hate him but he had to try. And he could only try his best.

There was a rumble outside her apartment door, followed by a buzz. Was she expecting a delivery? She didn't think so.

Kristie looked down. She'd been wearing this pink slouchy top and grey yoga pants for the last two days. She hadn't even opened the blinds these last few days. She was officially a slob. She shrugged and headed to the door, pulling it open to let the bright Los Angeles sunshine stream into her apartment.

She squinted. Looked. And looked again. Her breath strangled somewhere inside her. Was she finally so miserable that she was seeing things?

'Hey.' The Scottish lilt was strong. She couldn't be imagining this. 'I thought we should talk.'

Her hand went automatically to her hair, scrunched up in a dubious ponytail. She didn't have a scrap of makeup on her face. Every imaginary meeting between them she'd had in her mind these last few days had been nothing like this.

'Can I come in?' She blinked and looked behind him. Three large cases.

'What are you doing?'

'I'm...visiting,' he said cautiously.

She automatically stepped back. 'I just texted you.'

'I know.' He smiled.

She shook her head. 'I said I didn't want to talk.'

'And if you don't then I'll leave,' he said steadily. 'But I've flown five thousand miles. Can we have five minutes?'

She gestured to her sofa. 'Five minutes.' She moved quickly, picking up the empty wrappers from the cookies and chips that were lying on the coffee table.

Rhuaridh sat down heavily. He'd flown five thousand miles to talk to her.

Her brain was spinning.

She'd replayed their last moments over and over in her head. She'd always known he'd object to the title of the show—*she'd* even objected to it when she'd initially heard it. But because he didn't go on social media, or the streaming network, she'd always secretly hoped he wouldn't find out. She'd been lucky. Up until last week. And the timing had been awful because by that point she'd felt so hurt and angry that she hadn't felt like explaining—hadn't felt like defending the show.

'How's Jill?' she asked.

He nodded. He was wearing jeans and a pale blue shirt that were distinctly rumpled. He gave her a thoughtful smile. 'It's baby steps. And everyone knows that. But she said I could let you know how she's doing. She's seen the CAMHS nurse and a counsellor. Two days ago she told me that she'd phoned the number in the middle of the night when her head was spinning, she couldn't get back to sleep and she'd felt so alone. She told me she'd cried, and that the woman at the end of the phone had spoken softly to her until she'd fallen asleep again.'

Tears pricked at Kristie's eyes. 'It sounds like it's a start.'

'Everything has to start somewhere,' he replied. It was the way he said those words, the tone, that made her turn to face him. 'And so do we.'

He sighed and ran his fingers through his hair. 'Kristie, I'm sorry, I feel as if this all spun out of control and I still can't really work out why. Except...' he paused for a second '...I probably put my foot in my mouth.' He didn't wait for her to reply before he continued. 'The one thing that I know, and I know with all my heart, is that I love you, Kristie. I don't want to be without you. And I don't care where we are together, just as long as we get a chance to see if this will work.'

His words made her catch her breath.

He kept talking. 'I hated how we left things.' He shook his head. 'I hate that we fought over...nothing. I love you. I can't bear it when you're sad. I can't bear it when you're feeling down. I just want to wrap my arms around you and stop it all.' He gave a wry laugh, 'And, yes, I know it's ridiculous. I know it's probably really old-fashioned.' He put his hand on his chest. 'But I can't help how I feel in here.'

He took a breath. 'When I told you that I loved you and you didn't reply, I made a whole host of assumptions. Then my mouth started talking and my brain didn't know how to stop it. I thought it was crazy to dare to hope we could be together. It's what I wanted, but how selfish would I be to ask you to pack up your whole life for me? To move from your home, and your career, to be with a guy you'd spent a few days a month with?

'So…' he gestured towards the cases '…because I'm so hopeless with words I decided to try something different.'

She stared at him, her voice stuck somewhere in her throat.

'So…' he paused and she could tell he was nervous '…I decided that actions speak louder than words. That's why I've packed everything up. Magda is due back at work and we've got a locum for the next few months.' He shook his head. 'The irony of doing the show is that we had about twenty people apply. So…' he met her gaze '…if you're willing to talk, if you're willing to give things a try, just tell me. Tell me where your next job is, and this time I'll come to you. Because I love you, Kristie. I'll love you to the ends of this earth.'

She stared at him. Trying to take in his words. 'You'd move here? To be with me?'

'Of course. I'd do anything for you, Kristie—whatever it takes.'

She sagged back a little further into the sofa, then turned her head to face him. His words were swimming around her brain—the enormity of them. Her heart was swelling inside her chest. Those tiny fragments of doubt that had dashed through her mind when he'd made the suggestions about moving had evaporated. She raised one eyebrow, curiously. 'What makes you think I don't like Arran?'

He shot her a suspicious glance and counted off on his fingers. 'Er…maybe the weather. The ferries. Or lack of them. No supermarkets, no malls.'

She leaned towards him. 'Maybe I like all that. Maybe I like waking up in a place where the view changes daily. Maybe I like a place where most people know each other's names.'

He sat forward. It was obviously not what he was expecting to hear and she could see the hopeful glint in his eyes. 'Can I have more than five minutes?' he whispered.

She licked her lips and took a breath. If this was real, if she wanted this to be real, she had to be truthful—she had to put all her cards on the table.

'I've been angry these last few days. Angry with myself and angry with you. When I came to Arran I wanted to tell you that I loved you too. And when you told me first, then added about how it was all crazy and we could never work…it was like giving me part of my dream then stealing it all away again.'

He grimaced.

'I wanted you to ask, Rhuaridh. I wanted you to do exactly what you're here to do now, for me, without the big gesture. All I wanted you to do was to ask me to stay. To ask me to choose you, and to choose Arran.'

He blinked, a mixture of confusion and relief sweeping over his face. 'I thought that would be selfish. Conceited even, to ask you to give everything up.'

'Just like what you've done for me now?' She held her hands out toward his cases.

He let out a wry laugh and shook his head, reaching over to intertwine his fingers with hers. 'It seems that we both crossed our wires when we were really heading for parallel paths.'

She gave a slow nod of her head. 'I want you to know that I've made a decision.'

He straightened a little. 'What kind of decision?'

'A take-a-chance-on-everything life, love, career decision.'

He opened his mouth to speak but she held up her hand. 'I love you, Rhuaridh. The whole world could see it before I could. I started to dream about getting on that ferry, reaching Arran and never leaving again. I've started to like rain. And I definitely love snow. And my job?' She pulled a face and held up her hands. 'It used to be everything, but it's not been that for a long time. Not since Jess died. My family died. Not since I started volunteering at the helpline.' She looked at him nervously. 'I've had enough of TV. No matter what they offer me right now, the only offer I'm going to take is the book deal.'

'You have a book deal?' His eyes widened. 'That's brilliant!'

She looked up into his eyes. 'You gave me the push I needed, you made me write the book in my heart. And you were right. There's been a bidding war. The publishers love it.'

He stopped for a second and tilted his head. 'Is that the only offer you're going to take?'

She licked her lips. 'That depends.'

'Depends on what?' He'd shifted forward, it was like he was hanging on her every word. Funny, handsome, grumpy, loyal Rhuaridh—her own Scotsman—was hanging on her words.

'I came to Arran to tell you I wanted to stay.' She rested her hand against her heart. 'That I'd lived my last few months in Technicolor. It was the life I'd always wanted. I'd found a man I loved and a place I thought I could call home.' She shook her head. 'I know the title of the show is ridiculous. Of course it's ridiculous. It's a TV show. But honestly? At the time I didn't think it was worth the fight. And…' she pressed her lips together for a second '…I honestly hoped you wouldn't find out.'

He reached over and touched her face. 'Kristie, I don't care about the TV show. I love you. I flew all this way to tell you that. Please forgive me. I'll move anywhere in the world with you. But if Arran's where you want to be, then nothing would make me happier.' The glint appeared in his eyes again. 'Mac will never forgive me if I don't bring you home. He hasn't looked at me since you left.'

She smiled. 'Mac is missing me?'

'He's pining. Like only an old sheepdog can. The only look he gives me these days is one of disgust.'

She edged a little closer. 'Well, when you put it like that, I don't want to see Mac suffer.'

His arms slid around her waist as her hands rested on his shoulders. 'I mean, every dog should have two parents.' Her hands moved up into his hair.

His lips brushed the side of her ear. 'I absolutely agree.' He looked at the three large suitcases at the doorway. 'Now, are you going to help me get those cases home?'

EPILOGUE

One year later

THE BRIDE'S THREE-QUARTER-LENGTH dress rippled in the breeze as she walked towards him clutching orange gerberas in one hand and Mac's lead in the other.

It felt as if the whole island had turned up for this event. The local hotel had hired three separate marquees to keep up with the numbers but whilst the sun was shining they'd decided to get married outside so everyone could see.

Rhuaridh's heart swelled in his chest. Kristie's hair wasn't quite so blonde now, her skin not quite so tanned, but he'd never seen anything more beautiful than his bride. Her grin was plastered from one side of her face to the other.

He leaned over, winking at Gerry, who sat on a chair nearby holding a camera, capturing the ceremony for them, then turned back and held out his hands towards his bride's. 'Now, no fancy moves, no running out on me.'

Her eyes sparkled. 'We're on an island. There's nowhere to go and...' she winked '...I'm not that good a swimmer. I guess you'll have to keep me.'

He slid his arms around her waist. 'Oh, I think I can do that.'

He bent towards her as Gerry shouted, 'Hey! Wait up! It's too early for a kiss.'

The celebrant laughed as Kristie slid her hands around his neck. 'What do you think?' she whispered, her lips brushing against his skin and her blue eyes continuing to sparkle.

Mac let out an approving bark and the whole congregation laughed too.

'Oh, it's never too early for a kiss,' said Rhuaridh, as he tipped his bride back and kissed her while the whole island watched.

* * * * *

MENDING THE SINGLE DAD'S HEART

SUSANNE HAMPTON

MILLS & BOON

To everyone who has ever had their heart broken, only to pick themselves up, dust themselves off and find their *new* happy-ever-after.

And to my amazing new editor, Victoria. It has been a pleasure getting to know you... and I truly love your work!

CHAPTER ONE

DR JESSICA AYERS paused for a moment to secure the weighty oversized handbag slipping from her shoulder. She needed to gain some level of composure before she stepped from the thirty-six-seat twin-propeller plane that had just endured a somewhat bumpy landing at Armidale Airport. The landing, however, was the least of her concerns, since 'bumpy' was on a par with the rest of her life anyway.

Drawing a deep breath to fill her lungs, she attempted to quell the rising anxiety she always felt when she arrived in unfamiliar surroundings. Constantly moving to new places was by her own design, but it still unnerved her a little and gave her an overwhelming sense of déjà-vu. One that she feared would never end. Another town. Another short-lived new beginning. In six weeks she would move on again.

Her willingness to fill in for local paediatricians on leave across the country allowed Jessica to move regularly around Australia. There was never time to plant roots or get comfortable. And that was how she wanted it to be, because neither were in her plans. Not any more. The idea of long-term in any part of her life was gone. Badly hurt, and carrying a level of shame for loving the

wrong man, Jessica had decided there was no such thing
as a happily-ever-after for her. She was now a rolling
stone. Gathering no moss and with no ties to anyone.

And falling in love again was definitely not going to
happen. It only brought heartache. And Jessica didn't
want any part of that. Not ever again.

She doubted she was strong enough to survive another disappointment, unlike her best friend, Cassey,
who seemed to rush back onto the online dating scene
after each failed relationship. And there had been many.
Jessica wasn't sure if that had compounded her opinion
about men and love but it didn't matter. She was over it
all. She knew for certain there was no good man in her
future, only heartache waiting to happen if she travelled
that road again.

Jessica was not an optimist like Cassey.

She glanced up into the overcast sky. It was close to
five o'clock on a June afternoon, it was blowing a gale
and the cloud-covered sun was beginning to bid farewell
to the cold winter day. She held onto the rain-dampened
handrail with her woollen glove and quickly realised that
was not the best idea. Now her glove was wet. With a
sigh, she took the seven steps down to the ground, col-
lecting more droplets of water as she held on tightly. The
wind pushed and pulled at her and she struggled to keep
her steps in line as she slipped off one soggy and one dry
glove and made her way over to the pile of small carry-
ons assembled under the wing of the plane. Space restric-
tions in the tiny overhead lockers meant none of the bags
had been allowed in the cabin. Jessica's was easily rec-
ognisable from the pool of small black bags and quickly
she reached down and wrapped her now bare and cold
fingers around the handle of the compact silver hard case

that matched her other luggage. She had always liked the things she could control in her life as it helped to have a sense of order. It was a trait passed down from her father, a military man. It was a pity that was not how she lived any more. Nothing much in her personal life bore much semblance to order.

She attempted to brush away the thick wisps of her hair blowing haphazardly across her face, almost obstructing her view as she walked across the windy tarmac. Still deep in thought, Jessica put one foot in front of the other as she fought hard not to be blown away by the fierce breeze that had made their landing jerky. Her jacket had blown open and the wind cut through her thin sweater as she avoided the puddles of water. Armidale's chill was nothing like the muggy Sydney weather she had left behind.

Silently she questioned with each of her considered steps what she was doing. Not the last hour, taking the flight, nor last month, accepting another temporary Paediatric Consultant position, ironically covering the resident paediatrician's honeymoon, at Armidale Regional Memorial Hospital. No, instead Jessica wondered what she was doing with her life. Her lips wilted at the corners the way they always did when she allowed disappointment in herself to creep back. But a moment's pity was all she would allow. She couldn't afford to fall in a heap because there was no one to pick her up.

She only had herself. Her parents had both passed. Her father had died when she was sixteen and her mother three years ago. As an only child, Jessica had no siblings to turn to now, only cousins and friends, but they were all either settling down and having families or travelling the world *before* they settled down, married and had a family. And Jessica didn't even have a boyfriend, nor would she ever again. Marriage wasn't in the stars for her. She'd thought it was, she had even wandered into wedding gown boutiques to gaze at the stunning white lace and satin creations hanging in rows and pictured which one she would wear when she walked down the aisle to Tom, the man of her dreams.

She had always imagined a flower girl and a pageboy and a stunning bridal bouquet of white roses and a quaint church with the setting sun shining softly through the stained-glass windows. And her groom waiting at the altar, where they would hold hands and make a commitment to love each other for the rest of their lives. But not any more because trust was the foundation of marriage and Jessica didn't trust men. They lied, they made promises they couldn't keep and they broke hearts, sometimes more than one at a time, with their actions.

Biting the inside of her cheek, Jessica dragged her bag into the small terminal. With no romantic dreams, she had to make the best of what she did have and that was a six-week placement in a hospital in the middle of country New South Wales. She'd not worked in a rural city or large country town, and Armidale had been referred to as both. She tugged hard on her bag to lift it over the slight step. It wasn't a particularly heavy bag, as her shoes, clothes and other belongings were packed into her checked luggage; she was just taking out frustration on an inanimate object and potentially using more force than was logically required. Just as the wind outside had been doing to her. Jessica Ayers was being a little unnecessarily rough. It was that simple. She wasn't as patient as she had once been with people, and definitely not with awkward carry-on-sized suitcases.

The weather outside had made her feel as if she had flown in on a broomstick but she knew she would settle in a day or two. She always did. Adapt to her new environment but not stay long enough to get close to anyone—that had been her modus operandi for close to a year. It was getting more difficult each time and Jessica had begun to admit to herself that she was growing tired of running. Now she was facing yet another new beginning that wouldn't change a thing or bring her close to being the person she had once been: an optimistic young doctor who loved life and thought she had found the man to love her as much as she loved him.

It had been twelve months, and her heart was still numb and her mind racked with shame for almost tearing a family apart. A family she knew nothing about. She couldn't come to terms with what had happened, nor could she settle her feelings and, as a result, herself geographically. Was she the victim? Or the perpetrator? She still wasn't sure. But the one thing she was sure of was the need to keep moving. Although the disappointment she felt still followed her wherever she went. Disappointment in the man who had deceived her and deceived his wife. And disappointment in herself. She no longer trusted her own judgement.

The idea that she had been the *other woman* tore at her core. Upsetting thoughts about herself and how she should have known better had a way of creeping into her mind and pitching a tent. She felt physically sick when images of Tom making love to her crept back into her mind. The man who, unbeknown to her, had a wife and children waiting at home for him. Each time she moved town she hoped the change of scenery and distance from Sydney, where he was still playing happy family, would hasten some level of amnesia around her actions or perhaps just help her to find acceptance that she couldn't change what had happened and allow her to move on. But that was yet to happen.

Dr Jessica Ayers would spend the next six weeks in a country town where she knew no one and no one knew her. Armidale was not her forever. It was just another stopover, a place where she could hide from the rest of the world until she knew what she wanted to do with her life. A life that would never have the happily ever after she had once thought she had all wrapped up with a perfect bow.

Jessica accepted there was no fairy tale ending for her. She would only have herself and her regrets…and the wish that one day she could learn to trust herself again.

But she doubted that would ever happen.

'Oh, God. Oh, no.' Lost in her maudlin thoughts, Jessica didn't notice, until she felt the bump of her carry-on bag landing on the ground, that she had run over the man's foot as she had struggled to get inside the terminal building. Looking down, she noticed the highly polished leather loafer with a damp imprint of her wheels. 'I'm so sorry—I didn't see you.'

'It's fine,' the deep voice comforted her, adding, 'I'm pretty sure nothing's broken.'

She looked up to see the stranger's lips curve to a half smile. She couldn't help but notice his vivid blue eyes harboured a smile too. Jessica doubted that her actions would have brought about his reaction. Running over someone's foot could not ordinarily incite a happy response. No, this man looked like someone who had found a bowl of cream and had been swimming in it.

His happiness was palpable but she wondered how deep it ran. A new love affair, perhaps? His looks would no doubt have most women swooning. A player with his choice of women to keep that smile firmly secured on his chiselled face, she surmised with absolutely no evidence. She didn't need hard cold facts. Dr Jessica Ayers was ready to judge then quickly hang, draw and quarter each and every man who crossed her path. But, despite her misgivings about the male population, including this stranger, she knew he deserved an apology.

'No, really, I'm sorry. I should've been more careful.'

'Accidents happen. Honestly, don't give it another thought,' he told her with that same smile that once again made his blue eyes sparkle like sapphires against his lightly tanned skin. Perhaps the happiness wasn't a mask. It was emanating from somewhere deep inside. Resonating from his core, his very being, and it was the most genuine smile that Jessica thought she had ever seen. No, not thought, knew. Jessica had never before seen a smile quite like his.

Without saying another word, he walked away, leaving her standing alone and a little stunned, breathless and wondering what on earth had just happened. Looking down at her feet, she shuffled nervously as she tried to bring herself back to reality. And gain some perspective on the situation. A man about whom she knew nothing except he was handsome and had stylish shoes, now with an unfortunate wet tyre imprint from her bag, had taken her breath away.

Why would she be reacting to a complete stranger that way? Or any way? She should have dismissed him as she did all men, but she hadn't. It didn't make sense. There was something different about him. Perhaps his reaction, perhaps something else. She wasn't sure. Edging closer to the baggage carousel, Jessica was a little confused about why she was giving the man more than her usual thirty seconds of considered disdain. Her curiosity about the source of his happiness lingered in her thoughts. It didn't seem put on; it seemed so real.

The call for passengers travelling to Sydney to make their way to the departure gate suddenly brought her back to reality with a thud. The reason for the man's happiness wasn't her concern. She had enough on her plate without thinking about anyone else. She needed to collect her luggage and make her way to the real estate office to collect the keys to her rental. It would be a tight timeline as the office closed at five-thirty. But she couldn't help but watch him walk over to the other side of the small terminal along with the other passengers. She told herself it was her need to find the luggage carousel and not curiosity that had made her eyes follow him. Gingerly she made her way there too. Looking around, Jessica saw families hugging, reunited lovers kissing and a few like herself standing alone with no one to greet them.

There was no one waiting to greet him either.

That she kept noticing him was beginning to irritate her. She assumed it was because he was the first person she had spoken to since arriving at her new temporary home and the first man she had run over with a suitcase. She was definitely overthinking everything she decided and purposely looked away.

Within moments an array of suitcases, predominantly black with an occasional colour variation dotted among them, and oversized backpacks began to push their way through the grey rubber flaps and onto the carousel. A pushchair appeared and even a surfboard. The terminal was too small to have a separate oversized items area. Quickly her fellow passengers retrieved their bags while still chatting to their companions. One by one they began to exit the terminal. She spun around and found the handsome stranger had gone too. She wasn't sure why, but she wished he was still there. Strangely, his disappearance made her feel alone again.

Jessica pulled her concentration back to the job at hand. Finding her bag and doing it quickly so she wasn't homeless that night. With concern mounting, she watched as the carousel emptied one case at a time until there were none in sight. And no one still waiting empty-handed like her. Her stomach fell as she moved closer to the rubber slats. She peered through to see no more bags waiting to emerge. Anxiously her eyes darted about as she chewed the inside of her cheek again. It was becoming a habit she knew she had to shake. Looking out to the tarmac through the expanse of floor-to-ceiling windows, Jessica could see the bags for the next flight out of Armidale being loaded into the plane. The same plane in which she had arrived. It was a one plane airport. There was no more luggage being taken off. She had to accept her bags had clearly never made it onto the plane in Sydney. Or they'd made it onto another plane heading for God alone knew where, the idea of which was far too upsetting for Jessica to consider at that time.

The only possessions she had with her were the contents of her handbag, her laptop and some notebooks tucked inside her carry-on.

A rising sense of loss surged through her and almost brought her to tears. She had no belongings...not even a toothbrush...nothing and no one in the world belonging to her.

Jessica was once again reminded that she was alone. In a strange town far from the place she'd once called home.

Dr Harrison Wainwright stepped from the Armidale Airport terminal and into the now darkening car park. It was cold and crisp, the way he liked it. He had sorely missed the clean fresh country air. It was still damp from a light shower before they'd arrived and that made it even better in his mind as it more readily carried his favourite scents of hay and eucalyptus. He paused for a moment to fill his lungs like a man who had been starved of oxygen. Winter in Armidale was his favourite time of year and he didn't try and mask his happiness. Los Angeles was not his type of town at any time of the year and six days breathing air heavy with smog was six days too many.

With the *Sydney Morning Herald* newspaper he had picked up at the airport that morning tucked under one arm, he steered his suitcase to the cab rank. Harrison was conscious of the lightness of his steps, despite having just had his foot run over by the pretty stranger inside the terminal. Perhaps more than merely pretty, he mused. Beautiful was closer to the mark, he decided as he allowed his mind to slip back momentarily to when he'd noticed the emerald hue of her eyes, the softness of alabaster skin and ash blonde hair that skimmed her shoulders. The windswept curls that framed her heart-shaped face.

But there was something behind her eyes that struck him and played on his mind as he waited for the cab. She was stunning in an almost hauntingly sad way. A little lost. She was not from around the town he called home. She must be travelling through or visiting.

He pushed the image of her face and the questions

he had about the purpose of her travelling to Armidale from his mind. He was not going there again. Curiosity about a beautiful stranger in his town had completely changed the course of his life once before. And almost ruined it. Not to mention threatened his sanity over the years. He would never let himself travel that path again. He was finally closing that horrendous chapter and was ready to move on. It had been five years of something close to hell but he had emerged and would never let his heart rule his head again. He was finally happy… Well, his new version of happy.

With his chin jutted in defiance he waved down the cab that was approaching and banished the stunning stranger's face from his mind. Finally, he was back home with the outcome he had so desperately wanted. And nothing and no one was going to steer him off course again.

With the custody papers in hand and the signed divorce papers on their way to him in the coming days, he would soon be officially a free man. It was as if a burden he had carried for so very long had disappeared overnight. Nothing could make him happier than the knowledge that now he could move on without the possibility of one day losing his son in a custody battle. No threat of his son living across two continents. No arranging proposed maternal visits that never eventuated. No more explaining to the five-year-old boy why his mother promised to visit and never did. He could finally look into his son's innocent blue eyes and know Armidale would be their forever home. And Harrison Wainwright was determined to be the best single dad possible.

He pushed away the surge of anger that threatened to ruin his victory. He had what he wanted and he had to let the hurt and broken promises go. He was determined to release the sadness and disappointment that had consumed his waking moments for years. But Harrison was a realist and he knew it would take time.

Being in a relationship would never again be an option for him. From that day forward, it would just be Harrison and Bryce. There was no need and no room to invite anyone else in their lives. His house and his heart were full.

And he would never risk his son being hurt again.

CHAPTER TWO

'Excuse me, miss. Can I help you?'

Jessica was so preoccupied she didn't hear the male voice behind her. The empty luggage carousel mirrored her life more than she cared to acknowledge. The fact there was nothing to see consumed her attention. The sound of the aircraft engine starting finally forced her to glance over to the thirty-six-seat plane taxiing down the runway in preparation for take-off into the stormy early evening sky. Her missing bags meant she would not be sleeping in her favourite pyjamas that night. And that was assuming she was able to collect the keys to her rental property and actually had a bed for the night.

It was all a little overwhelming and she wasn't entirely sure what she was going to do. That had been a regular state of mind for a while and completely out of character from the old Jessica. She had always known what to do, even as a teenager. Forget having a social life, she had her head in her textbooks, even on weekends. She'd excelled at school every year until the final year. Then she'd graduated top of the class with perfect end-of-year examination results that saw her in the top twenty students across the entire state of South Australia, which meant her higher education study preference of a medical degree was guaranteed along with being presented to the Premier at Government House. Straight out of school, Jessica Ayers had been on her trajectory to becoming Dr Jessica Ayers, Paediatric Consultant. She'd considered specialising in paediatric surgery and did head down that path and gained the skills but, after a year of surgical study, she'd decided that it was the interaction with children offered by the Consultant's position that made her the happiest.

Over the years there had been few boyfriends to distract her. No jam-packed social calendar to compete with her study schedule. Nothing to prevent her from achieving her lifetime goal. Including her vision, from her very first day in medical school, of one day being Head of Paediatrics at a large teaching hospital. Jessica Ayers had been an unashamed planner.

But there were some things in life she couldn't plan. Some things had just occurred without any decision-making by Jessica. Some of them were very sad, such as losing her father while she was still in high school so he never saw her graduate from medical school, and then losing her mother when she was thirty. At least she was grateful that neither had witnessed her fall from grace in dating a married man.

Now she was flying by the seat of her pants in regard to everything and anything…and she wasn't very good at it.

'Miss, I asked if I can help you.'

Jessica turned her attention to the uniformed older man standing behind her; his bomber-style jacket was emblazoned with the Armidale Airport logo.

'My name is Garry; I'm with the airport. I'm assuming you're still waiting here because your bag, or bags, didn't arrive?'

She feared her distracted state might have given the appearance of being dismissive. She felt sure she was on a roll in managing to offend her adopted new town's population one person at a time. Damaging one man's foot and being plain rude to another.

'Bags—there's two of them—and I'm sorry, Garry, I didn't mean to be impolite.'

'Think nothing of it. You seem a little frazzled. Have you been on a long haul flight and then a connection to get you here? A handful of our passengers came in today from Los Angeles. The Armidale Romance Writers group attended a conference in the US and four of them just came back. My sister-in-law is one of them, that's why I know, and one of our doctors was over in America as well, not that he attended the romance conference,' he said with a wry smile. He added, 'It's a country airport, what can I say, there's not much gossip that gets past the ground staff here.'

'Well, I haven't flown too far at all. I've just done fifty minutes from Sydney so I definitely can't blame my poor manners or distracted state on jet lag...'

'You might not have done a long-haul trip but missing bags is a stress all of its own, so let's see if I can help.'

Jessica wondered for a moment if she had entered some parallel universe. Was this town in country New South Wales the friendliest place on earth? This man was being so kind and helpful, just as the man, whose face was still etched on her mind, had been so gallant about her clumsiness. Immediately, she pushed away the image she still had of the first man, the one she'd run over, but she knew it was more than his appearance that was lingering. There was something about him that was not easy to forget, for some strange reason. But she had to do just that. She had to find her bags and get to her accommodation or face being homeless.

'It's been a long day and I have to get to the realtor by five-thirty to get the keys to my rental property…and I have nothing except these,' she told him tilting her head in the direction of her carry-on and her handbag that she was holding up.

'I must apologise that the rest of your bags didn't arrive. It doesn't happen too often, I must say, but that doesn't help you. If I can have your name I'll start the process to find them.'

'Dr Jessica Ayers,' she replied.

'Nice to meet you, Dr Ayers,' he said as he reached for the extended handle of her carry-on bag.

'Please call me Jessica.'

'Certainly, Jessica. Let's get you over to check-in,' he said, pointing to the other side of the terminal. He added, 'I can get some more details and chase the bags up for you. If you can give me the baggage receipt that was issued with your boarding pass, I'll call through to Sydney and make sure that your bags are sent here on the next flight, which is at eleven-thirty—'

'That's late but at least there's another flight coming in tonight,' Jessica cut in with a faint strand of renewed hope colouring her voice. Excitedly she handed over the documents he requested and then followed him from the departure and arrival lounges and in the direction of the main entrance.

The man's brow wrinkled as he shook his head from side to side and with it swept away Jessica's hope of a swift solution.

'Unfortunately, your flight was the final one from Sydney today. There next one arrives at eleven-thirty *tomorrow morning* and I can have your bags couriered to your home,' he said as he maintained a fast pace. He was a man on a mission and that gave Jessica some small level of comfort as she kept up with him.

'My home? I have no idea if I'll have one. I think my deadline to pick up the keys from the realtor is just about to pass.'

He raised his wrist and glanced at his watch as they reached the check-in counter. 'It's five-fifteen but a cab can have you into Armidale in ten minutes. Let me make a call to the agent and ask them to stay back in case you're a few minutes late getting there.'

'Do you honestly think they will?' she asked, confident that in her home town of Sydney there would be somewhere between a fat chance and absolutely none that they would actually remain open for her. Their care factor about her having to find accommodation for a night would be around about the same—zero.

'Do you have the business name?'

'There's more than one in town?'

Garry smirked and shook his head. 'Armidale is actually a rural city and we have hot running water, traffic lights...and more than one real estate agent.'

Jessica felt quite silly. 'I'm sorry.'

'No need to apologise. You're obviously a big city girl. Is this your first visit here?'

Jessica nodded sheepishly as she scrolled through her emails on her mobile phone until she found the realtor's name. 'Dunstan Boyd is the property manager—' she paused as she squinted to read the fine print in the signature block on the email '—at...'

'Boyd and Associates Real Estate,' Garry finished her sentence.

Jessica dropped her chin a little and stared up at him curiously. 'You know them?'

'Yes,' he told her. 'My sister-in-law works there. Not that I thought you'd have any trouble anyway, and we do have some nice motels in town if there was a problem, but I can almost guarantee she, or one of her colleagues, will stay back and you won't be homeless.'

Jessica drew breath and then emptied her lungs just as quickly with relief at Garry's announcement. While she had nothing to wear and she would have to wash her underwear in the basin and dry it over the bath, she would at least have somewhere to do that.

'Now, if you can give me your contact details, someone from the airport will call you tomorrow and arrange to have your bags sent to you when they arrive.' He pulled a pen and paper from the pocket of his bomber jacket.

Jessica took the pen and paper and scribbled down her mobile telephone number, which he then tucked back in his jacket pocket as they walked outside to the cab rank.

'It might be best sending them to the Armidale Regional Memorial Hospital,' she told him as she tugged her jacket up around her neck. The air was even colder than when she'd alighted from the plane. 'I'll be there so they'll be no one at home to collect them, that's assuming you're right and I have a home.'

'You'll have a home, Jessica. Don't worry.'

There was an empty cab already there and no one else waiting. Garry opened the rear door of the cab for Jessica and she quickly climbed in the back as he leant in the open front window and spoke to the driver.

'Can you please take this young lady to Boyd and Associates Real Estate, Twenty-nine Marsh Street.'

'Sure.'

Flooded with a relief she'd thought impossible ten minutes previously, Jessica put the window down. 'Thank
you so much,' she said as the cab pulled away from the
kerb.

'You're very welcome.'

Garry was right; his sister-in-law's colleague didn't mind
staying back and the cab driver waited while she rushed
inside. The young man asked her for identification, had
her sign two documents and then gave her the house
keys and the keys to the rental car that had been left that
morning in her driveway. Jessica had arranged for everything to be in the one place, and it was a glimpse of
her previous attention to detail. Although twelve months
ago she would have shipped clothes ahead and arranged
for the local dry-cleaner to press and hang them in her
closet and have the pantry and refrigerator stocked with
low-fat food. The kind that Tom liked. Tom, the woman-
ising, cheating bastard whose cholesterol levels she had
worried about for the better part of a year.

But, thanks to said two-timing low-life, the Jessica of
late was nowhere near that organised when it came to her
personal needs. On the job, though, she hadn't changed.
She was as dedicated and focused with her patients as
she had ever been.

'Call me on my mobile if you have any questions. It's
a nice little house, clean, tidy and fully furnished, as you
saw in the photos. I think you'll like the street.'

Jessica was not about to be fussy. A bed and bath was

all she needed right now, and a car for the morning to get her to the hospital.

'I'm sure it will be great and thank you again for staying back for me,' she said as she held on tight to both sets of keys as if they were her lifeline.

'Not a problem, happy to help.'

Half an hour later, with two bags of groceries on the back seat, the cab pulled up in the front of the darkened house. The amiable cab driver from the airport pick-up had kept the meter running while Jessica had signed the lease and picked up the keys, then stopped for milk, bread, oatmeal, fresh fruit and other staples, including bubble bath, a toothbrush and toothpaste from the small grocery store that stayed open until ten o'clock every night.

Her new role began bright and early the next day so she wanted to have a nice home-cooked dinner and an early night, followed by a reasonable breakfast. She knew that she would hit the ground running and had no idea if she would get a lunch break so needed to be prepared for a long day on her feet on the wards and potentially even in surgery if required. In a smaller hospital the roles and duties were sometimes less defined and far broader in nature than in the city hospitals and she had the surgical experience if called upon.

Jessica took a brief study of the street as the cab turned in. It was tree-lined and had a simple prettiness about it. Very country, she mused silently as she noticed the houses either side of the one she would call hers for the next six weeks were softly lit from the inside. Lights and probably open fires, she thought. Curtains were drawn but the glow could be seen from the street.

Jessica's new temporary home had nothing to signify life at all. She wasn't surprised. She couldn't expect anything more than that. It wasn't as if she knew anyone in town; there would be no one there to welcome her to the new house. It had been the same wherever she had been posted but generally she chose apartments close to the city hospitals to avoid the harsh reminder every night that she was arriving home to an empty place.

She still had her terrace home in Surry Hills, an eastern suburb of Sydney, that she kept as a base but, since Tom had spent two or three nights a week there during their year-long relationship, she chose not to actually live there any more. She would fly in and out and collect her belongings between assignments. One day she would sell it but she hadn't set a time frame for anything much in life.

Jessica was just glad that she had a key to her rental home and would soon be soaking in a hot tub. The thought of steaming bubbles infused with lavender brought a much-needed calm to her.

The cab driver pulled the carry-on from the boot of the car as Jessica made her way up the driveway, pulling her coat up around her ears against the bitterly cold air. The sensor light switched on as she approached the front porch, showing her the facade of her accommodation. It was very homely and looked freshly painted. It was grey with white shutters and a red wooden front door. Either side of the red door was a topiary tree in a square cement pot and in front of the door was a mat emblazoned with *Welcome*. She was relieved to see the small hatchback rental car was parked under the carport, as she had requested. The colour matched the front door. The garden was simple but sparse with mostly lawn and an edge of low native bushes. There was nothing that looked demanding of her time and that also made her smile. Jessica was not a green thumb so took comfort in the fact she could just engage with a mowing service a few times during her stay and leave the rest to Mother Nature.

'I can take it from here. Thank you,' Jessica said as she put the key in the door. Turning back to the cab driver, she gave him cash to cover the fare and a little extra.

'Are you sure you don't need me to help you get everything inside? You have shopping too.'

'No, I'm fine to do it myself but thank you for offering.' Her response was genuine and ingrained. She could manage on her own. She didn't need a man to help her. Jessica Ayers was more than capable of taking care of herself, despite everyone being so kind since she'd arrived. The friendliness of the locals was almost making her feel at home. Under different circumstances, in another lifetime, she might have even thought it would be a lovely place to live. But everywhere was temporary to Jessica now.

The driver nodded, put the fare in his pocket and, blowing warm breath on his cupped hands, walked briskly back to the cab. Along with not needing his help, Jessica hadn't wanted to delay him any longer. They had chatted during the brief trip and she had discovered it was the end of his shift. He was heading home to his wife and newborn baby boy after he dropped her off and she appreciated he had already waited for her to do the shopping.

With the front door open, the light from the porch illuminated the interior of the house enough for Jessica to find the inside light switch. She quickly found out the freshly renovated house was as simple and tidy inside as it was out. And there was a faint hint of fresh paint and furniture polish but neither were overpowering.

'New start for us both, hey,' she muttered as she carried the shopping bags inside and closed the door on the cold night air and went in search of a heater, a bath and her bed.

An hour later Jessica emerged from the bathroom with her freshly washed hair piled inside a makeshift white towel turban. The central heating had warmed up the house while she had been under the shower. She had decided a soak in a bubble bath could wait as she saw there was a hairdryer in the first drawer, along with samples of shampoo and conditioner, and clean hair might distract from the clothes she would be wearing on her first day on the job. And, much to her joy, she had found a thick white bathrobe folded on her bed. Nice touches, she thought, and decided to make good use of all of them.

If at least her hair looked clean and tidy she hoped everyone might overlook the fact she was wearing jeans and a sweatshirt. Thank goodness it wasn't summer as the T-shirt she wore underneath was a gift from the plumbing service that replaced her hot water tank and their marketing slogan—*If you want clean pipes, look no further*—would not have been well received. Ordinarily she would never have travelled in such casual clothes, let alone considered going to work in them, but she had been pushed for time to get to the airport that afternoon and decided to stay in the clothes she had been wearing to run errands in the morning. And with the missing suitcases and no shops open, other than the grocery store, she now had no choice.

Jessica walked around the house and found it was clean, tidy and had a nice ambience to it. The furniture had character, as opposed to some of her previous rentals that had generic flat-pack-style furniture that had an impersonal motel feel. This house was homely and had recently undergone a freshen-up. All the furniture was in good condition but eclectic in style and age and she suspected it had belonged to others before it came to rest there, and that felt nice. A country home filled with furniture that came with history. One that she assumed would be country-style sweet, not sordid, as she considered her history to be.

Brushing aside thoughts of her past, Jessica made herself dinner and washed the dishes by hand. There was a dishwasher but it would have been a waste to turn it on for one dish, one glass, a knife and fork and two small pans. Besides, she had nothing much to do other than dry her hair and head to bed. She didn't have to spend any time at all deciding what to wear on the first day of her new job—missing luggage had seen to that.

'Are you going away again, Daddy?'

Harrison closed the story book and gently put it on the nightstand beside the bed as he looked down lovingly at his son snuggled next to him. 'No, Bryce. Daddy's not going anywhere.'

'So, when I wake up you'll be here? You won't get on a plane and go away again?'

The innocent questions tugged at Harrison's heart and he knew immediately he'd done the right thing in fighting for custody. For the right to keep his son safe in Armidale with those who loved him. Those who had since the day he was born. And always would.

'I'll be right here when you wake up and then I'll take you over to Granny and Grandpa's house.'

'For breakfast?'

'For a second breakfast, as Granny always likes to make something special for you before school,' Harrison said as he edged off the bed and, pulling the covers up to Bryce's ears, he ruffled his thick black hair.

Bryce giggled. 'I hope she cooks pancakes.'

'I do too,' Harrison said as he kissed his son's forehead, turned off the light and walked quietly from the room, safe in the knowledge that Bryce was right where he needed to be…and nothing and no one would ever put that at risk again.

The alarm clock ensured Jessica woke on time and found her underwear had dried on the coat hanger she had hung on the shower rail. The house had remained toasty warm overnight and she felt unusually relaxed as she lay under the warm covers surveying the room in the daylight that was creeping through the gaps in the heavy curtains. The walls were a very pale blush, so pale that she hadn't even noticed the night before and had thought it to be cream, but now she could see the hint of colour. It was also in the bedspread and the throw cushions that Jessica had placed on the armchair the night before. There were two framed prints, both of birds, and the furniture was made of oak, including the bedhead.

For a rental, it was quite lovely, she thought as she climbed from under the covers. She could have slept in a little longer as she had over an hour before she was due at the hospital but, as always, she wanted to arrive early. She also wanted to call the airport and remind them to send her bags to the hospital the moment the plane touched down, so she could change into something more suitable as soon as possible.

A quick shower and an equally quick breakfast of oats with blue gum honey and a cup of tea followed by an equally quick phone call to the airport saw Jessica lock the front door of her home thirty minutes later. She had checked directions on her phone the night before. When she rented the house, she was made aware that it was less than ten minutes from the hospital. But then in a town the size of Armidale most homes were only that distance from where the hospital was located.

As she stepped outside into the cold morning she couldn't help but notice the scent of the country air envelop her. It stopped her in her tracks for the briefest moment. The perfume from the large eucalyptus tree in the neighbouring yard travelled on the chilly breeze. There was no smog, no smell of heavy early morning traffic or industry. The fresh, naturally scented air was one of life's simple pleasures that she hadn't realised she had been missing.

Until that moment.

She wondered if there was anything else that this country town might remind her that she had been missing. A year of relatively short-term placements arranged by a national medical locum agency was beginning to grow old for Jessica, but she was scared to stop. Scared to consider other options. A sense of safety came from having the decision of what to do next made by a third party. And the security that came from not forming relationships, other than with colleagues, sat well with Jessica. While there was a sense of emptiness that couldn't be ignored, she decided that was better than the pain of heartache that came from getting close and having it fall apart.

Moments later as she drove along, with a little nervousness stirring in her stomach as it tended to on the first day in a new role, she tried to avoid looking down at her clothes. She cringed as she caught sight of her jeans, sweater and grey and lime-green runners and prayed her bags would arrive from Sydney that morning as promised.

'I'm Errol Langridge. It's so lovely to meet you, Dr Ayers, and, speaking on behalf of the Board of the Armidale Regional Memorial Hospital, we're thrilled to have you on staff, albeit for a short time.' The older, impeccably dressed man shook Jessica's hand gently but for the longest time. His clothing had a country feel in the blue and white check shirt and chambray trousers but the quality of both was evident. And the sincerity of his words shone through the smile in his pale blue eyes. 'Quite a coup for us, if I do say so myself. Not often that we have a temporary position filled by someone as experienced as yourself. Short contracts are usually taken up by those straight out of medical school.'

'I'm very happy to be here, Professor Langridge,' Jessica replied, well aware of the status of the older doctor. She had noted his title on the letter he had sent to her when she'd accepted the role. 'And please, Jessica is fine by me.'

'And you must use Errol. Equality for both sexes, plus it makes me feel less than my sixty-eight years if you use my first name.'

'Then Errol it is.'

The Professor smiled a half smile before his expression became serious with the sudden sound of an impending ambulance. The main doors of the hospital opened just as the vehicle pulled into the bay and the sound carried into the foyer. He motioned for Jessica to follow him down the corridor. His steps were fast and purposeful as he turned his head slightly to speak over his shoulder to her.

'I think now is as good a time as any to visit the ER. You'll see our staff doing what they do best. And, once the commotion subsides, I'll introduce you to our Head of ER, Harrison Wainwright. You'll be working closely with him, no doubt, as many of our paediatric patients are admitted from there. He's been at the hospital for so long he's almost an institution, although he's still the good side of forty, unlike most of us in senior roles. He's a tough taskmaster but it works for most; besides, we can't seem to get rid of him anyway.'

Jessica's eyes widened and her mouth drew tight as she quickly caught up with the older man. She hoped it would work for her too. Working alongside a man with an attitude was not on her wish list, particularly one they couldn't get rid of, perhaps due to his connections or watertight contract. She suddenly felt her stomach churn again. Paediatrics was a long way from ER and hopefully their paths would not cross too often during the six weeks.

Without taking a breath, the Professor continued as his eyes wrinkled in laughter, 'You must forgive my sense of humour or, as my wife says, my bad taste in jokes. We are eternally grateful that he's never indicated he wants to leave us. He actually grew up around this part of the world and we're glad he returned. The hospital couldn't function without him. He's brilliant and I can't praise him enough and the medical students and patients love him. The nurses do too, but for very different reasons, I'm sure.'

Jessica wasn't quite sure how to take the Professor's conflicting character reference for her colleague as she followed him into the Emergency Department. While he'd quelled her concerns on one hand, she certainly didn't want to go near the reason the nurses loved the man.

A stretcher suddenly rushed past them, making Jessica draw in her breath as if that would give them more room. It was a silly reaction and made no sense to her, particularly as a doctor accustomed to the Emergency Department of a great number of hospitals, but not much had made sense in the last few days. The first patient, a young woman, had been immobilised with a cervical collar, so a neck injury had clearly been suspected by the paramedics, and her right leg was in a splint; by her appearance, Jessica assumed she was a teenager. She stepped back again quickly as a second barouche approached them.

'Motor vehicle accident,' the paramedic began as they wheeled the patients into bays opposite each other as directed by the nursing staff. 'Two passengers. Female suspected spinal cord injury, broken ankle and minor lacerations. Male with lacerations to hand and forehead. No other visible or apparent injury.'

The second accompanying young male patient had a bandage to his head but he was alert and firing questions at everyone. His hand was also bandaged but other than that he appeared unscathed by whatever incident had occurred. A female paramedic attempted to calm and comfort him but it appeared to be to no avail. Quickly the medical team approached and an immediate hand-over ensued. The second patient was assigned two nurses and a young doctor, whom she suspected was an intern, while the first with the serious injuries had the attention of many more of the ER staff. The alert patient was distressed but appeared under control.

Suddenly another stretcher entered the ER with two paramedics in tow. 'Hit and run on Mundy Street. Suspected fractured femur. Female, seventy-three years of age.'

'Dr Steele, once you assess your patient, if there's no immediate risk, please leave him with the nurses and attend to our elderly patient,' a deep voice called out from beside the young female patient in the adjacent bay. Jessica could see the back of a tall man in a white consultant's coat. He stood over six foot, close to six foot two, she guessed. The deepest brown, almost black hair and a commanding presence by the way everyone looked to him for instruction. She suspected he was the Head of ER about whom Errol had been speaking only moments earlier.

Jessica watched the young doctor speak briefly with the two nurses and then, as instructed, head over to the paramedics and the new arrival.

It certainly was a busy Emergency Department, just as Errol had told her only minutes before, but it was running smoothly and that was no easy task as there were already patients in another two bays being attended by staff. Jessica couldn't help but agree the department was a well-oiled machine. No one hesitated or appeared to be second-guessing. The Head of ER was, in Jessica's mind, to be admired. It took a high level of calm, an ability to triage patients and manage staff with a good understanding of their strengths and their skills to maintain a calm environment for the patients.

Jessica watched on in silence as the empty bay was filled with another patient, transferred from the stretcher onto the hospital gurney. That level of synergy and professionalism was exactly what she hoped to maintain in Paediatrics during her time at the hospital.

But within moments that very calm began to dissipate.

The young man left in the nurses' care suddenly tugged his arm away from the petite nurse and attempted to climb down from the bed. His feet were almost on the ground.

'It's all my fault…it's all my fault,' he repeated loudly, the words spurred by unbridled emotion. 'I need to see her. I need to say sorry and see she's okay.'

Jessica was aware the young nurse was struggling to contain the situation and the ER did not need an overly emotional patient breaking free and interfering with another patient's treatment in order to purge his guilt.

Jessica spun around to the dispenser behind her and donned a pair of disposable gloves and a disposable gown from the top of a nearby pile. 'Excuse me, Professor. I'd like to start my shift now, if that's all right with you.'

Errol looked a little confused but nodded as Jessica headed over to the bay where the ruckus was taking place.

'I'm Dr Ayers and I'd like to help you,' she announced as she firmly placed her hand on his legs and then lifted them back onto the gurney.

The nurses both looked at Jessica in surprise and she picked up on their confusion.

'I thought you could use some assistance. I'm locum Paediatric Consultant. I commenced at the hospital this morning and must apologise that I've not been issued with my ID yet,' she told them as she motioned towards Errol, aware her current clothing, still visible under the thin blue gown, made her look anything but a medical professional. 'Professor Langridge can vouch for me.'

The older nurse glanced over at Errol, who was nodding his consent, while the younger one took Jessica at face value and together they attempted to control the situation.

'Can you please give me your name?' Jessica asked the young patient while she assessed the proximity of the medical equipment within the bay. A stethoscope lay on the portable trolley nearby so she scooped it up and popped it around her neck. The young man began to calm slightly as if he knew fighting was futile as the nurse attached the monitors to him to record his heart rate, blood pressure and oxygen saturation.

'I want to help you while the medical team in the bay opposite help the young woman who came in with you. Her injuries clearly appear more serious but we will be undertaking a medical examination of you to ensure that yours are in fact only superficial. In motor vehicle accidents you can sustain internal injuries that are not instantly apparent. Before I begin, can I have please have your full name and age?'

'Cody Smith, and that's my girlfriend over there,' he said as he raised his hand and pointed to the other bay.

'Can you please give me her name and age?' the young nurse asked. 'So I can pass that information onto the ER team looking after her.'

'Let me tell them,' he said, trying to pull away from the nurses again. 'I just want to say I'm sorry to her.'

'That won't be happening. Please remain still; I need to check your eyes.' Jessica's words were firm and to the point as she held his chin and shone the light into the young man's left eye and then the right one.

'My eyes are fine. They're not bleedin' or nothing.'

'Cody, as I said before, some injuries are not obvious so there won't necessarily be bleeding, but a mild head injury can still be sustained from a car accident. You may have suffered whiplash and it can result in impaired vision or other problems and symptoms are varied. Do you have trouble focusing your eyes when switching your gaze between near and far objects?'

'Nah, I'm good,' he replied. 'I can read the exit sign and her name thing.' He pointed to the nurse's identification tag.

'Do you feel nauseous, as if you are going to vomit when you look around?'

'Nah, I'm all good, I told you already. It's me girlfriend I'm worried about.'

'No, Cody. That is not an option,' she continued. 'Even if you are fine, you need to understand that if you were to rush over there to help her, you would in fact be doing just the opposite. You could get in the way of the medical team and put your girlfriend at risk.'

'I don't wanna do nothing but help her.'

'Then, as the nurse said, you can help her by giving us her name and age.'

'Ginny Randolf. She's seventeen.'

'Thank you,' Jessica said as she continued the examination and noted his response to the light stimulation was within normal limits.

'I'll pass on her details and come right back,' the younger nurse said as she headed over to the other patient.

'And how old are you?' Jessica enquired while checking the young man's pupils for dilation.

'I'm sixteen.'

'Okay, Cody, we are going to have to take some blood samples and check your alcohol level. Have you been drinking?'

'No. I'm on my probationary licence. That's not why

we crashed. Is that what you think happened? Do you think I was drink-driving?' His voice was shrill and once again Jessica needed to placate him.

'I'm not assuming anything.' Her voice was low and calm as she met his eyes. 'This is routine and *not* because I suspect anything, Cody. It's just that with any motor vehicle accident a blood test for alcohol and other drugs is mandatory.'

'I can't drink on a probationary licence. I'm an apprentice chippy. I'm not looking to lose my job with a baby on the way. Ginny's nine weeks pregnant.'

Jessica and the nurse immediately looked at each other and, without a word exchanged, the second nurse disappeared to pass on the crucial information. Pregnancy would certainly complicate the situation if there were suspected internal injuries and the chance of miscarriage was a concern.

'We found out a few weeks ago.'

He rested back down on his elbows, not taking his eyes off the opposite bay but seemingly finally accepting the need to comply—and the fact a towering male nurse had just approached to assist would not allow him to do otherwise.

'We were arguing about when she would tell her parents. They don't like me. I wanted her to hold off a bit longer so they didn't try to force her to get rid of the baby. She told me she was gonna tell them tonight and I got scared and distracted and I didn't see the merging lane. We went off the road and hit the fence.'

A nurse suddenly pulled a curtain around the young man's girlfriend.

'What's happening? Why are they doing that? Is she

okay?' Cody's questions came flying at Jessica and the nurse as he sat bolt upright again.

'Your girlfriend is in good hands,' Jessica told him. 'And, thanks to you, the team know there's another tiny life growing inside of her so they will be doing everything possible to treat them both.'

'Please can you go and check? I need to know what's happening. I'm freaking out here. She's gotta be okay.'

Jessica reluctantly agreed. She wasn't even officially on staff yet so not keen to overstep protocols further than she already had but she knew Cody's anxious state was escalating by the minute with the curtain obscuring his view and it wouldn't end well if he raced over there. The young man was physically fine and the other nurses had returned to monitor his observations so she headed over to enquire about the status of his partner—the mother of his unborn child.

With each step she took, she prayed fate would not change the course of their young lives.

She quietly and tentatively parted the curtain and peered inside the bay to see the back of the doctor undertaking an ultrasound examination of the young woman. He had been informed of her pregnancy and was obviously prioritising the baby. It all seemed calm so she didn't feel the need to interrupt.

'The baby is fine; there's a strong heartbeat and no obvious signs of distress, Ginny,' she heard him say. 'I'm sorry you can't see the screen that I am looking at right now. I can share those images later with you. But for the time being we need to keep you flat until we can properly assess the damage to your neck and back. I believe it is muscular as you do not have any of the symptoms I would expect to see with a spinal injury. I need to send you for an MRI—it's not an X-ray so it's perfectly safe for your baby and it will allow us to assess any neck, spinal or ankle injuries. You and your baby are both paramount to anything we do.'

Jessica agreed with his treatment plan and she thought he had a lovely bedside manner and comforting voice. Deep, masculine but still warm. It sounded familiar but she knew that couldn't be the case. She didn't know anyone in town.

She raised her hand to close the curtain and caught sight of his profile and all but gasped. Her heart took a leap as she recognised him. She did know him. But the last time she'd seen him he wasn't wearing a white consultant's coat. Instead he was wearing the wet imprint of her carry-on luggage on his shoe.

CHAPTER THREE

JESSICA WAS MOMENTARILY SPEECHLESS.

Harrison Wainwright had been on the plane with her, so was he the doctor she had been told had just flown in on the long-haul flight from LA with the romance writers? She imagined the odds were weighted in favour of him being the one, particularly in a country city of this size. But, wherever he had flown in from, he was the one she had managed to run over. The one who'd captured her attention and piqued her curiosity. And the one she had not been able to erase from her mind.

As she closed the curtain there was a stirring in the pit of her stomach. But this stirring was not nerves. It was as if she had been reunited with someone she knew. There was a familiarity with the man that was inexplicable. As if they had a connection. Not from the incident at the airport; it was something more. Something they had once shared…or were about to share. Something that had kept her awake the previous night, thinking about him. But they hadn't shared anything more than a fleeting uncomfortable meeting and they wouldn't share anything more than that, she reminded herself. She didn't know the man, let alone have a connection. Nor did she want one with Dr Harrison Wainwright or any man.

Of that fact Jessica was resolute, but she was also scared and confused by her reaction. She hadn't been able to forget him since their chance meeting the day before and that was something she was trying to ignore. She wished his face hadn't been etched on her mind but she suddenly realised it had subconsciously, or not so subconsciously, been there for almost twenty-four hours.

Taking a deep breath, she tried to exhale feelings that were beginning to stir with him so near to her again. She hadn't felt anything close to what she was feeling at that moment in longer than she could remember and that was by design. She had controlled her emotions, kept them in check without too much effort. It had been safe for her to be around men of her age, or even ten years either side, because she felt nothing but indifference. She didn't trust them in the slightest. In her mind, few had anything other than a desire to get what they wanted at any cost.

Tom had destroyed her trust in men, and love, and the whole damned thing and she was angry. Angry because Tom had taken her innocent view of the world and twisted it into a level of bitterness she had never wanted or expected to ever feel. Never imagined she could feel. He had robbed her of her belief in happily ever after. She wished it wasn't the case but nothing and no one had or would be able to give her reason to change her outlook. Jessica was starting to believe the moulds were broken after her father's generation of men. Those men had treated women with respect and love. And commitment had meant something. But the new generation of men were shallow and insincere and she felt sorry for women who fell in love. She would never do so again.

* * *

Jessica was relieved that Harrison hadn't seen her as he was too distracted with his patient but she quickly realised that she could not avoid the inevitable. Professor Langridge was about to introduce them so she had no choice but to meet him. She couldn't avoid it. They would be working together. To what extent she wasn't sure, but there would be mutual patients during the course of her short tenure.

Her forehead wrinkled slightly with concern at the thought and her heart began to race a little faster than usual. And it had nothing to do with embarrassment over the silly incident. She wasn't sure if he would even remember that. It was more how her body was reacting to being near him. And the feelings were bringing a warmth to her body. Almost a dizzy rush. It was not like her. She hadn't experienced so many conflicting emotions in such a short space of time. Ever. Pre, post or even during her time with the man she'd thought she was going to marry.

The new mysterious man had been consuming her thoughts for no good reason. And with that came an overwhelming concern about her appearance. Her clothes were completely unsuitable for ER. Why had she not travelled in something nicer? Ordinarily Jessica would have prioritised her wardrobe and asked the cab driver to wait, but that morning she had been running a little late and was anxious he might drive off, causing her to miss her flight. She hadn't wanted to risk it, so she'd raced out of the door in an outfit more befitting walking a trail.

It was out of character for the old Jessica, who always made sure that she was well groomed and elegantly dressed. Even if her skirt and blouse were hidden by a consulting coat. At least she knew she was wearing something smart, and her shoes and earrings were in plain sight even if they were very conservative. Some days Jessica would look in the mirror and think that perhaps her clothing was more befitting someone twenty or thirty years older, but it suited the new her. The Jessica who avoided anything overtly feminine. Since discovering she had unwittingly become someone's mistress she had spent many sleepless nights wondering if she had attracted her lover by the way she dressed. Her choice in clothing had never been overly revealing but she couldn't help but question whether he would have looked twice if she had chosen a different look. Perhaps that had nothing to do with it, perhaps it did, but her new wardrobe sent a clear message to everyone.

She was not interested in anything other than being the best doctor she could be and even thinking about a man did not factor into her day.

Until that moment when she'd felt very self-conscious and almost like a giddy teenager, unable to control her emotions. She was so confused. It was so out of character with the reinvented Jessica of late. Perhaps, she thought, it was because she was tired and that made her anxious and unsettled. Not that the bed hadn't been comfortable the night before; it was and she had slept well, all things considered.

No, Jessica's version of tired was different. She was tired of running. Tired of new beginnings that never changed how she felt about herself. And so tired of the unrelenting late-night thoughts of how she should have done things differently. How she could have managed everything better. But she hadn't and she was living with the consequences. Trying to find peace and forget her time as *the other woman*. Focus on her career and forget about love. There was no room for it in her life or her heart. She was all about work. Her sole focus was to live her life as a single professional woman, respected for her work ethic.

But the next step in her professional journey had been thwarted by delayed luggage. Professionalism had flown out of the window and soccer mum had flown in and there was not a damned thing she could do about it.

She made her way back to check on Cody and reassure him that the baby and his partner were both fine.

'Ginny is being taken for an MRI—'

'What's that? Will it hurt her or the baby?'

'MRI is an abbreviation of magnetic resonance imaging. It's a safe alternative to an X-ray and presents no danger to the baby during the first trimester, which is the first twelve weeks of the pregnancy.'

'Why's she having it?'

'The doctor wants to check that Ginny hasn't sustained any neck or spinal injuries as a result of the accident. He can also check the damage to her ankle.'

Just then another doctor appeared and introduced himself. 'I'm John Steele, the ER Resident.'

'Hi, I'm Jessica Ayers, the Paediatric locum.'

'I know—the nurses filled me in,' he replied with a smile that showed he had orthodontic braces in place. 'Welcome aboard and thanks for stepping in. I heard it's your first day and you're already part of the team.'

'Happy to help.'

'You're going to fit right in; we can all tell,' he told her and then picked up Cody's notes. 'The nurses think you're awesome already and they're a pretty tough lot to impress. So, you're off to a flying start if you can manage that in the first five minutes. Have you met Dr Wainwright yet? He's our ER Consultant.'

Jessica shook her head and swallowed. She didn't know what to say. While she hadn't been formally introduced, she had met him in an unconventional way.

'Anyway, we've held you up long enough. I can take over here if you want to head up to Paediatrics?'

'Okay. Great…and it's lovely to meet you, John.'

'Likewise.'

Jessica turned back to find the Professor still waiting for her. He had a warm expression on his face. Ordinarily that, combined with John Steele's welcoming demeanour, would have put her at ease but Jessica felt anything but relaxed. She wished she had gone straight to Paediatrics and not stopped in the ER and she could have delayed the awkward meeting that she knew was about to take place unless there was another rush of patients through the Emergency Room doors. And by the lack of sirens it was clear that wasn't about to happen.

As Jessica pulled free her gown and gloves and dropped them in the bin, she watched Harrison Wainwright walking towards them. She knew she had to simply accept the situation and move on, as she had been doing for the best part of a year.

'Errol, what brings you to the ER?' Harrison asked.

'This young lady, actually,' the Professor replied. 'May I introduce you to…'

'Jessica Ayers—Dr Jessica Ayers.' Jessica couldn't believe that her nerves had caused her to interrupt a professional introduction and repeat her name, adding her title. So now she was both rude and badly dressed. She was mortified by her behaviour and dying a little inside by her own actions. What had happened to the cool medical professional who'd just stepped into the ER and helped out without making a fool of herself? Where was she now? What was going on in her head to make her behave so strangely? She knew the answer. He was standing right in front of her.

The Professor shot a quizzical smile in Jessica's direction, coughed to clear his throat and continued. 'Dr Ayers is our new Paediatric Consultant and very *enthusiastic* to meet everyone, it would appear.'

Jessica wanted to jump into a non-existent hole in the linoleum floor of the ER but there was no such hole, no saviour of the awkward beyond belief moment, so she did what she had been doing for the past twelve months—she saved herself. She drew in a deep breath and extended her hand to Harrison. He met her handshake but she couldn't help but notice that his eyes left hers momentarily and travelled to her feet. She was under no illusion as to what he was thinking, more than likely silently questioning why she had fronted up on her first day dressed as if she was going on a hike. She braced herself for the mention of her inappropriate attire. While Errol had not mentioned it, she felt sure that someone, perhaps Harrison, would say something.

'Welcome aboard, Dr Ayers,' he replied. 'However, this isn't the first time we've met.'

Jessica stiffened. Of course he would remember that the *enthusiastic* locum had also run over his foot the day before. Terrible first impression followed by an unprofessional second impression. She could hardly wait to see how she could trump either. Throwing up from nerves and embarrassment was a possible contender.

'So, you know each other?' Errol asked with his eyes widening.

'No,' Jessica quickly announced.

'Yes,' came Harrison's response only seconds later.

'Well, which is it?' the Professor asked with a quizzical frown. 'Yes or no?'

'Well, we technically don't *know* each other,' Jessica responded.

'We bumped into each other at the airport yesterday. Quite literally,' Harrison explained.

Errol's glance darted back to Jessica for confirmation.

Jessica cringed and nodded in his direction. 'I ran over him.' Then, turning her attention back to Harrison, she continued, 'I'm so sorry. I'm not usually that clumsy.'

'It happens,' he told her with an almost impish smile she didn't want to see in his eyes.

'Well, I must say you're a good sport, Harrison,' Errol stated. 'And clearly you weren't travelling too fast, Jessica, because there's no visible injuries. Were you on a scooter?'

'No, I didn't run *him* over... I *ran over* him...with a suitcase.'

'And there's not a scratch to show for it,' Harrison added.

Jessica felt her skin prickle—his voice was as deep, husky and reassuring as it had been the day before.

'I'm confused so I think I'll leave it there,' Errol said with a frown creasing his brow yet again.

'It wasn't hard to do, particularly in a bustling international airport like Armidale,' Harrison continued, adding a cheeky grin that threw her emotions into free fall.

She didn't say anything. She wanted to pull her eyes away but she couldn't. She stood frozen. Her head and heart were in turmoil. She felt certain she had experienced almost all possible emotions in the previous five minutes.

'Again, I'm still terribly confused and I have a Board meeting in fifteen minutes. I'm going to leave you to get acquainted, or *reacquainted*, whichever the case may be.' With that, Errol stepped away but not before adding, 'Welcome again, Jessica, to the Armidale Regional Memorial. I'm very glad to have you on board. I have a very good feeling about this.'

Jessica feigned a smile as all the while she was thinking just the opposite. There was nothing good about any of it. In fact, she had a very bad feeling. And it had nothing to do with the hospital or Errol. It had everything to do with the man standing before her.

'So, you're our newbie to the hospital then, Dr Ayers?' Harrison asked, leaning in a bit closer.

'Yes, and please call me Jessica,' she insisted then couldn't think of anything to add. She could and would normally drive the conversation but suddenly she was searching for something to say. Her mind was befuddled by thoughts that had no place being there. And senses were coming into play that had been dormant for a long time. His cologne was subtle to the level of being almost impossible to detect by anyone else with the overpowering scent of sanitising products used in the ER but, unfortunately for Jessica, it was not lost on her. His body warmth was bringing out the masculine notes of sandalwood and she could feel the beat of her own pulse reacting.

'If it makes you feel better, my shoes dried without a

mark. Nothing to indicate that I'd been steamrolled by your runaway luggage.'

Harrison smiled a wide smile that lit up his chiselled face. It made him look even more handsome, but Jessica couldn't help but notice that while it was a genuine smile it seemed slightly guarded. She'd thought she was the only one who walked around at war with herself and the world. Then again, perhaps she was imagining something defensive that wasn't there. After all, they were in the ER so his mind would be on the job of managing the rapid response unit of the largest hospital in the New England region.

At that moment she didn't trust her instincts. And that made her uneasy. In fact, everything about her current situation and, more to the point, Dr Harrison Wainwright made her uneasy. She cursed under her breath. Why couldn't her colleague be the same age as Errol? It would have been far more convenient for her because a handsome and now slightly intriguing man who appeared pleasantly surprised that they would be working together was the last thing she needed. Now or ever.

Harrison was surprised by the level of happiness he was experiencing on seeing the mysterious blonde traveller again. And to learn that they would be working together. It should have worried him, but it didn't. Strangely, he felt elated by the idea. He had fallen asleep thinking about her. Wondering if and when he might see her again. She was clearly gorgeous, but there were a lot of gorgeous women in New England and he had casually dated a few over the years. But his attraction to the stranger in town was more than skin-deep. He was intrigued by her. He had no clue why, after such a brief encounter, but it was undeniable.

Not for a moment had he imagined they would be working together. He had so many questions. Her reason for coming to Armidale for one. Skilled enough to impress the Board of the hospital—that meant she would certainly be in demand in other hospitals. So why choose here? he wondered.

He glanced at her hand and then lifted his eyes just as quickly, but not before he noticed there was no ring indicating a husband or fiancé, but that didn't mean she was single. Why did he care? He had no clue but he was pleasantly surprised to see the absence of jewellery on her hand. Harrison wanted to kick himself for having any interest in the paediatrician's relationship status. For five years he hadn't cared about anyone's relationship status; he had been too preoccupied trying to sort out his own. Although he'd known his marriage was just a piece of paper—any love or commitment he felt was solely focused on his child—still, he had taken a long time to officially end it. His wife's decision to walk away from both him and their child had painfully but effectively ended any feelings he'd had for her many years before.

Dr Jessica Ayers was stirring more than curiosity and Harrison was at odds with how he felt and how he believed he should be feeling. They were poles apart.

At that moment the doors to the ER burst open again and two paramedics with a single stretcher rushed in.

'Male, unidentified, suspected methamphetamine overdose,' the taller of the paramedics announced as he steered the barouche past the nurses' station while the other held a cold compress on the young man's head and kept in place another pack that was resting across his chest. Intravenous fluids were being administered and Jessica could see he had been restrained.

'Bay three,' the senior nurse, whom Jessica was yet to meet, announced as she crossed to meet them, signalling for the nurse she had already met while treating Cody and a young woman to follow her. By the third woman's very young and very nervous appearance and the fact that the Armidale Regional Memorial Hospital was a teaching facility, Jessica assumed she was a medical student. Quickly her suspicions were confirmed when the nurse continued, 'Melissa, ask any questions you like; don't be shy. Your first student placement can seem daunting but we're here to help.'

'You have to love the rush of a Monday morning,' Harrison muttered to Jessica before stepping away and crossing to the allocated bay. He donned sterile gloves while the paramedics transferred the patient to the hospital bed and replaced the restraints. 'Fill me in.' His voice was serious and his words short.

'The young man was found slumped by a dumpster just off Beardy Street by one of the store owners ten minutes ago. No ID and he's not known to us, so either not a regular user or new to town, as we know our regulars. It's an area frequented by the methamphetamine crowd after hours. He appeared unconscious initially; however, when we attempted to engage it became obvious he was crashing from some illegal substance. He was suffering from hallucinations and kept referring to ants eating him alive and this presumably initiated the repetitive motor activity in his legs. It then escalated to verbal abuse towards us before he collapsed with chest pain and shortness of breath. He calmed down so I'd say we found him at the end of the crash. Within two minutes of getting him on board his irregular heartbeat came close to normal.'

'Do we have any clues on the amount taken; if it was snorted or smoked; and any idea on how long ago the drug was consumed?'

'Negative to all three. If he had any mates, they took off. If anyone witnessed him crashing they didn't stay to help or fill us in on the details.'

'Why doesn't that surprise me?' Harrison said, shaking his head in frustration. 'Vitals?'

'We recorded an initial elevated body temperature of thirty-nine point five but managed to bring it down slightly with cold compresses. His BPM was also raised but that's stabilised now.'

'Great work, guys,' Harrison replied then turned to the senior nurse. 'Alison, start gastric lavage and administer activated charcoal.'

Harrison continued issuing instructions as he began an examination of the clearly agitated but still restrained patient. He lifted the oxygen mask and carefully inspected the patient's mouth before replacing the apparatus. 'His dentation appears reasonable, as does his weight, which would indicate an acute overdose and a fairly recent entree to meth. Let's hope with counselling we can redirect his path before he heads into chronic misuse and the myriad of psychological and medical issues that would arise over time.'

The younger nurse hooked the IV already in place to a stand and cleared the paramedics to leave. 'Thanks, guys, for bringing him in. And Brian, say hi to Mum for me and see you next weekend.'

Jessica was close enough to hear everything and she was quickly reminded by the level of familiarity between the nurse and paramedic that she was in a country hospital where everyone knew each other on some level.

'Sure will, Phoebe, Tommo's birthday bash should be awesome,' the younger paramedic replied as they exited the ER, but not before stopping at the nurses' station to sign off on the paperwork.

'I want full bloods, an ECG and a urine sample. By the look and smell of this poor boy he's lost control of his bladder and he's wearing his last sample,' Harrison continued. 'He'll pull through but his long-term prognosis isn't good if he doesn't clean up his act. Can you call up and see if there are any beds available? I'd like to admit him and give him time to see a counsellor either today or tomorrow before we let him back on the streets.'

Jessica could see the unkempt young man's trousers were stained and the foul stench coming from his direction made it clear he had either no awareness of self-care or no means by which to maintain any level of hygiene.

'I'll check. We're not at capacity at the moment, so we might be able to keep him overnight,' Alison replied. 'We'll get him into a hospital gown and reach out for some new clothes from the Salvation Army; they're always happy to send in something clean for cases like this.' She swabbed his arm before taking a sample for the blood work; all the while the now compliant patient lay still, albeit for his restless legs that randomly moved away from his imaginary foe.

Harrison stepped away, as did the medical student. As they left the bay, Harrison reached up and closed the blue curtains. Then he turned his attention to the young woman still hovering awkwardly nearby, apparently unsure of what to do next. 'Melissa, now we have the young man stable, what can you tell me about your textbook and hands-on experience with methamphetamine abuse?'

Jessica watched as Melissa shifted a little on her feet.

'Um…nothing first-hand as this is my first hospital placement. But I know the psychosis resulting from a chronic methamphetamine overdose can last up to twelve months sometimes, with permanent effects of paranoia and ongoing memory loss. Meth abuse by the patient can also result in delusions, repeated infections, rotted teeth, weight loss, skin sores, and they can even suffer a stroke or heart attack, no matter their age.'

'That's correct. Recovery from a methamphetamine overdose depends on the amount of drug that was taken, how long it was abused, and how quickly treatment for the methamphetamine overdose symptoms was administered. The earlier a patient gets medical assistance for a methamphetamine overdose, the better the outcome. Anything else you can add?'

'Methamphetamine is classified as a Schedule II stimulant drug, and it works by affecting the central nervous symptom. It's similar in structure to amphetamine but far stronger and also more addictive. Legally it's only available through a prescription and generally prescribed to treat narcolepsy.'

'I'm impressed, Melissa. Is this an area of interest for you?' Harrison commented as he took the clipboard from the senior nurse, who had just approached him to authorise both the tests and the patient's admittance into the hospital. The nurse then left with the signed documents.

'My father's a pharmacist in Tamworth so he always lectured us about drugs and the potential for them to be abused. We saw a lot of it on the streets there when I was growing up. It's everywhere, like a pandemic in the cities and the regions now.'

'Unfortunately, you're right and let's hope this young man stops before he heads down the road of chronic abuse.'

'His chances are, unfortunately, going to be slim at best,' Jessica stated. 'Unless he can extract himself from his current situation and, depending on the depth of his addiction, enter a rehabilitation programme. There needs to be a holistic approach to turning the young person's life around. Without changing the situation, one night in hospital is a band-aid that will, unfortunately, fall off very quickly in the real world.'

Jessica's response was born of experience and she considered Harrison's decision to admit him overnight was textbook optimistic but not practical. She was no longer a bright-eyed, bushy-tailed medical student who thought following procedure ensured a good outcome. At times like this she felt battle-worn. She had seen it all, and couldn't erase the vision of the tiny skeletal frame of one of her patients, nor the wounds on another twelve-year-old's once pretty face, self-inflicted during a bout of hallucinations. She had cried herself to sleep over the injustice and wished she could wrap every child in the warmth of her arms and protect them. But she couldn't. Her professional innocence had been stolen bit by bit as she'd witnessed the children ravaged by drugs and the parents who couldn't help because they had been using themselves.

On all fronts Jessica was a long way from the young medical student standing before her. She acknowledged for a fleeting moment that she had been just like that young woman once, and there were days when she wished she could be again. Wide-eyed and hopeful for the future. But not any more.

Harrison paused to study Jessica. His look was pensive. He said nothing for a moment but she could see he was surprised by her matter-of-fact honesty. Jessica worried it might have been too blunt but she had reason to be harsh when it came to seeing children in her paediatric ward suffering from drug abuse. She felt so sad and helpless at times.

'I couldn't agree more,' Harrison told her, interrupting her thoughts and echoing her feelings. 'Bloody frustrating and such a waste. And I'm fully aware that one night won't do anything more than keep him off the street and stop him OD-ing in the next eight hours. It won't turn his life around, Jessica, but what it will do is buy us some time to schedule an appointment with a counsellor and a social worker, who might be able to make a difference. We heal the bodies and hope our colleagues can begin the process of healing their minds and broken spirits and, with a good deal of luck, lead them away from the destructive path they're on right now.'

Jessica was taken aback by his response. It was honest but heartfelt and far from textbook and naïve. Clearly, he was as frustrated as her and trying his best with the resources he had. Harrison was a realist with a heart.

Harrison turned his attention back to Melissa and the task at hand—educating the next generation of doctors.

'Do you know what they call methamphetamine on the street?' Harrison questioned Melissa.

'Ice?' Melissa asked.

'Yes, and there are other terms their friends may use when they drop them off at the Emergency Department,' he continued.

'I've not heard it referred to by any other name.'

'Speed,' Jessica cut in as she stepped closer. 'Or crank, tweak, Christina, Tina, chalk... Oh, and *go fast*. That's the latest. I think I've heard them all.'

'Well, that's quite a comprehensive list. You've got the street lingo down pat,' Harrison replied with a curious expression on his face. 'You're clearly passionate about the topic but I didn't think you'd see much of it in Paediatrics. I was under the impression that yours was a slightly more protected unit from the effects of drug abuse, at least by the age of your patients. I've not seen any under seventeen present here.'

'How I wish I didn't know quite so much but I've seen it with a regularity that I despise and one that scares me, particularly in the major cities. Some as young as eleven years of age present suffering from drug abuse in Paediatrics.'

'Eleven?' Melissa's voice rose in shock at Jessica's statement.

'Yes, only two months ago I was consulting in a public hospital in Melbourne and a little girl presented suffering the effects of methamphetamine. She was two weeks shy of her twelfth birthday.'

'What about her parents? Where were they?'

'Doing the same, unfortunately. Chronic users.'

'So her environment was stacked against her,' Melissa said flatly.

'In this case, yes, but not always.'

'If only there was some sort of prerequisite or testing to being a parent. It's hard to break the cycle if a child grows up with it,' Melissa commented as she rolled her eyes.

'Yes, parenting is a huge responsibility and a tough

role at times, no doubt, but in my book if you sign on to have a child, then you sign on for life,' Jessica said with conviction. 'Once you're a parent, then I think your own needs have to come second to theirs, but maybe that's an old-fashioned view. And who am I to say, since I don't have any children of my own? I'm sure in this day and age it's not easy raising them and with so many parents doing it alone it must be a struggle at times.'

Harrison said nothing for a moment. Jessica felt his gaze upon her. It lingered and it made her feel very self-conscious but it didn't feel as if he was judging her. Quite the opposite; it was a look of something that felt like pride. Which was crazy because he didn't know her and she worried from her harsh comments that she might be perceived by him as borderline jaded.

He suddenly averted his gaze and turned to Melissa. 'I hope you get a good block of rotation time in our Paediatric Unit with Dr Ayers. I think she'll be invaluable in your journey. She's certainly opened my eyes to many things this morning. There were definitely a few things I didn't expect to hear.'

CHAPTER FOUR

'HAVE YOU UNDERTAKEN the hospital induction or did the Professor just bring you straight to the ER?' Harrison asked, interrupting Jessica's thoughts and his own.

And his own thoughts needed interrupting. They had been filling his mind for longer than just the short time since he and Jessica had been formally introduced. Once again, he silently admitted that he had given the gorgeous doctor more space in his head than he'd planned after their airport encounter and he had hoped their paths would cross again. Maybe at the grocery store or a restaurant. He'd pictured potential scenarios and wondered if she would run over his foot with a shopping trolley...or sit at a table adjacent to his and drop a fork on his shoe. His thoughts did not shift from recalling her beautiful, slightly embarrassed smile when they'd first met and he'd caught himself smiling too. For the first time in a very long time.

He also remembered the sense of relief that had washed over him as he'd alighted the plane, realising that the custody battle was over. His son would never be at risk of being taken from him again. Bryce was too young to understand that the two of them ever being parted had been a threat, but it had consumed Harrison for most of his son's life. Not knowing if or when his son could be taken for months, or longer, to the other side of the world, to a woman his son couldn't remember, but one he would need to acknowledge as his mother.

But those worries were gone. Now all Harrison had to do was lodge the divorce papers once they were sent over from the attorney in the US. He had done his part; now his soon-to-be ex-wife just had to do the same. He knew there wouldn't be a problem, as she had a new partner and wanted to move on, which was why she had agreed to give him full custody. It was almost a cliché. The new man in her life was considerably older, very wealthy, well connected in the film industry and he didn't want anything to do with children.

Last night, as he'd thrown another log onto the open fire, having tucked his son into bed, Harrison had leant on the fireplace staring into flames that danced and leapt and finally enveloped the new wood. He had sipped on his gin and tonic as the wood snapped and split along a jagged crevice, releasing steam and filling the softly lit room with a warm glow and a burst of heat. And he'd felt a glimmer of hope. It wasn't relief; it was more than that. He wasn't sure what he was hopeful of but he knew he felt that he had left his worries behind. And, unexpectedly, he also had something to look forward to and that was just the chance that he might see the mystery woman again. It didn't make any sense to him, but he couldn't pretend his mood hadn't changed in the last twenty-four hours. It had. And he believed there were two reasons.

Perhaps the second had been born of the first. Finally, he could let down his guard. The battle was over and he felt as if he had let the weight of the world fall in pieces on the ground. Pieces so small they were like dust.

And now, in the light of day, he felt he was letting go of the anger and disappointment. Maybe, just maybe, it hadn't been just a chance meeting. Perhaps it had been more than a coincidence.

There was something fragile about Jessica, yet something equally strong. She intrigued him. And after hearing her beliefs about parenting, and knowing how they were aligned to his own, she was getting a little further under his skin. Warmth spread through him, along with a stirring in his gut. It felt good but he couldn't ignore that it still caused him a degree of angst.

The woman, pretty as a picture and clearly a competent doctor, while strangely dressed on her first day, was making him second-guess his resolve never to feel anything close to what he felt at that moment. Quickly he realised it wasn't the leftover melancholy of a lonely winter's night, the relief of having the signed custody papers…or the gin from the night before that made him feel that way. It was a Monday morning in a frantic Emergency Department and she was still bringing feelings to the surface that he'd believed he would never, could never, experience again. But was he actually ready for those feelings? Was he prepared to potentially let someone into his life, on whatever level? In the light of day he suddenly wasn't so sure.

'I said, Dr Wainwright, I haven't undertaken the induction yet.'

Harrison pulled his thoughts together and realised by Jessica's response that she was repeating herself. It was ironic that he had been too preoccupied with thoughts of her to hear her words. He was more than a little unnerved. He was never distracted by a woman, let alone while on duty.

'I'm sorry. I was distracted.'

'Yes, I can see that. As I've only seen the ER, I should probably head up and arrange an induction now.'

Harrison paused for the briefest moment, filling his lungs with air. He was worried. He wanted to say that he would be her guide. He wanted very much to take the opportunity to get to know Jessica better, but he hesitated. In almost five years he had not felt attracted to anyone the way he felt himself drawn to the locum Paediatric Consultant. The speed at which he was feeling so comfortable in her presence was disconcerting. He knew he was putting himself at risk but equally he was struggling to deny that he wanted to get to know her a little better. What harm could come of it? he asked himself. They might be great friends, with so much in common.

A simple display of professional politeness, he told himself, but he knew he was lying. There was so much more behind the way he was feeling and it was unsettling but he pushed those fears away as quickly as they surfaced. Once before, he had travelled at a similar speed and he knew the danger signs but this felt very different and he chose to ignore them. It had been a long time ago and, while he still bore the scars, he had an intangible feeling, a feeling deep down inside his gut, that getting to know Dr Jessica Ayers might be worth the risk. He could hear the alarm bells ringing loud and clear and yet he wanted to know more about this woman, take the time to personally show her around the hospital. He was all too aware that he was heading in a direction that was dangerous but something about Jessica was making that very difficult to refuse. He prayed his fears were unfounded.

'I would be happy to show you around, if you like.'

'Really?'

'Yes, really,' he almost laughed.

'That's very kind of you.'

'I like to get to know new staff. Put it down to my curious nature.' Again, he lied but he could hardly admit the truth. 'I'll ask one of the nurses to direct you to HR on the second floor so you can complete any requisite paperwork and then, once you make your way back down here, I'll take you around the rest of the hospital and introduce you to the senior staff.'

'Thank you. That's very nice of you.'

'We're a friendly country bunch here.'

Harrison watched as Jessica considered him for a moment in silence. He suspected that she could see through him but she seemed happy enough.

'I'd appreciate that,' she finally said with a sparkle in the most beautiful green eyes he had ever seen.

Harrison felt himself teetering on the edge of something that he couldn't define but wanted to explore. It was crazy to feel anything for someone so quickly but it felt right. There was a familiarity about Jessica that he couldn't explain or define.

'No doubt you've done most of the paperwork online but occasionally they need a signature in person,' he said, finally breaking the spell under which he felt himself falling. 'The staff will also provide you with a security pass and a designated car park space if you have a car.'

'I do, a rental for six weeks,' Jessica said as she nodded. 'I parked in the general car park this morning.'

'Six weeks?' he asked curiously.

'Yes, I'm covering long service leave for your Paediatric Consultant.'

'Of course.' Harrison physically withdrew as he spoke, taking a step back from Jessica. He was deflated by the news. It had slipped his mind that Jessica's residency was to be so short. Perhaps she might be testing the water, he wondered. Checking if she liked country life, trying it on for size, so to speak. Seeing if she liked the pace of Armidale.

'I have a short lease on the house too. My next position's in Adelaide in seven weeks' time. That role is just four weeks, but fi-fo suits me.'

'Fi-fo?'

'Fly in, fly out.'

'Of course.' Harrison knew he was repeating his words…just as he had almost repeated his mistake of wanting to know a woman passing through town. God, he was doing it again. Hadn't he learnt his lesson? Last time he had stupidly believed the woman who'd married him and had his baby might actually want to stay. And he had been wrong. So very wrong. Nothing could've been further from the truth. He should have known better and this time he had to make sure he did.

'You're filling in for us while Stan Jefferson and his new bride enjoy their honeymoon to Europe. Some time on the Greek islands and then heading to the French Riviera.'

'So I heard,' she said flatly then continued. 'I mean I knew the purpose of my placement, just not their actual destination. Oh, well, I wish them luck.'

Jessica's monotone, lacklustre reply was not lost on Harrison and his eyes narrowed. Everything he had first assumed about the woman was perhaps not as he had thought. He wasn't expecting her to be gushing about the honeymoon of two people she had never met, but nor had he expected her response to be so devoid of emotion.

'You don't sound too excited for them.'

'I don't know them.'

'That's true.'

Jessica paused. 'Maybe I should have said good luck to them.'

'*Maybe?* That doesn't sound too definite.'

'It's not,' she said, shifting a little on her feet. 'Look, I'm sure the Mediterranean will be superb at this time of year. I'm just…well…you know what—it truly doesn't matter what I think.'

Harrison felt a knot tighten in his gut and a wall rising between them very quickly. She had become almost flippant about the subject and that brought with it a level of concern.

'No, I suppose it doesn't matter what anyone thinks as long as they're happy.' His intuition, together with the cold hard facts, made it clear that Jessica was not the settling-down kind. Not that it bothered him, he reminded himself. He wasn't either now, but it did remind him that he had to keep a professional distance. Jessica had stirred emotions he had forgotten he could feel and he had to rein them in; he felt as if he was stepping into deep waters and he couldn't afford to be swept away. It wasn't something that happened often to him. Quite the opposite—only once before—but, even then, it hadn't been as immediate a connection as he was feeling with Jessica.

Harrison rubbed his chin with his lean fingers. This new side of her seemed cold and detached and abruptly brought back memories of the way his ex-wife had been able to turn her back and walk away from the life he'd thought they would share. And it reminded him that he truly did not read women well at all.

'I'm all about my career. It's my sole focus now and I suspect always will be.'

Harrison had temporarily slipped into a strange space where he had been thinking… Actually, he didn't know what he had been thinking, or feeling, for that matter, but suddenly he realised he should have known better. He felt stupid. Jessica was another career woman. Point-blank. No room for any debate. Her announcement was an unexpected but much needed and timely awakening. It was the cold hard slap back into reality that Harrison knew he needed. He was at least grateful that she was upfront about it. Perhaps his ex-wife had been too but maybe he hadn't looked for the signs back then. He wasn't sure. Perhaps everything that had happened between them had been at such a lightning pace that he couldn't have seen them anyway. With the passing of time came the knowledge that he had to look out for any signs to ensure that he and his son would never be hurt again.

Harrison knew now that he didn't need a woman he found even mildly interesting, let alone intriguing. Certainly not one who wasn't the staying kind. He was doing just fine as a single father and Jessica had brought him to his senses. Being a single parent had sufficient challenges and he knew he didn't need to make it more difficult by letting himself become involved with a woman like her. He had been swept up in a crazy moment he'd thought was serendipity when in fact it was just a distracted locum doctor who had run over his foot. Nothing more. It wasn't a sign of anything other than what it was. An accident. End of story.

No matter how aligned their values and interests had momentarily appeared, they were in fact miles apart. Brick by brick, an impenetrable wall was being erected in his mind. And the construction was happening at breakneck speed. She was everything he didn't need in a woman, all tied up in one beautiful package. Dr Jessica Ayers was heartbreak about to happen for any man who thought long-term or happily ever after. And he wasn't sure why for a split second he might just have been one of those men. He thought he had learnt his lesson and for five years he hadn't thought about love. Then, since meeting Jessica, for some inexplicable reason it had entered his mind again. And he needed to send any thoughts like that packing.

Harrison cleared his throat. 'Actually, I don't think I'll have time today to show you around the hospital after all.'

Jessica's delicately creased brow didn't mask her reaction to his sudden change of heart. 'Is something wrong?'

'No, it's just that I've remembered that I promised to visit a patient later so I won't have time to show you around. I'm sure HR will assign you someone anyway.'

'Of course. I understand…'

'And there's one other thing, Dr Ayers.'

'Jessica,' she corrected him.

'Fine, Jessica.' His eyes narrowed as he spoke. 'As a senior member of the hospital, there is something I need to mention.'

'That sounds serious.'

'Not overly serious, just good professional practice and I think it needs mentioning.'

'Go on,' she said, with the frown slowly creeping over her entire brow.

The tone of Harrison's voice had purposely shifted from warm to aloof. He needed to define their relationship to himself, if no one else. Remind himself that he didn't know the woman standing before him. It didn't matter how almost instantly he had felt a connection. It wasn't real. They were just feelings passing through his mind, just as she was passing through town. Both would be gone in the blink of an eye.

Jessica had folded her arms across her delicate frame. She was preparing for a fight. The irony was that the battle was an internal one, actually going on inside Harrison. His actions were all about setting personal boundaries that he suddenly felt he needed.

'Professionally speaking, I have to tell you that you should have cleared it with me before you acted in any capacity in the ER since you hadn't officially started.' He paused to regroup his thoughts and stay on track. 'There's no delicate way to put it, Jessica, except to say it how it is. You overstepped the mark and I hope it doesn't happen again.'

CHAPTER FIVE

JESSICA FELT THE wind being knocked out of her sails. She had stepped up to help out. She'd hardly expected a medal but she also hadn't expected a dressing-down about it. She could understand if he had called her on her unprofessional attire. That was very real in her mind. But he'd made no reference to her clothing at all, focusing on her stepping in to help.

Could the man have a twin brother? she asked herself silently as she dropped her gaze. If not, then she surmised she must be quite delusional to have thought of him as kind or charismatic in any way. He was abrupt at best and plain rude if she was to be honest with herself. She found herself in a situation that felt so unsettling she wanted to exit as soon as possible. She felt like a teenager being reprimanded. Again, she realised she was a terrible judge of character.

Not that it came as a surprise to her but she had hoped she had improved over time. Clearly not.

Nothing had changed, not her nor the men she found herself drawn to on any level, however fleetingly.

Jessica wasn't sure what to say. Her thoughts ran the gamut from a transfer to another hospital to eating an entire tub of chocolate ice cream or perhaps having a stiff drink at the end of her shift. All of them would solve the problem in very different ways and all were overly dramatic but that was how she felt. Her judgement, she accepted, was below poor before she'd arrived in Armidale but Dr Harrison Wainwright had, in a few minutes, convinced her that her personality assessment skills were hitting a new low. How and why she had even for the briefest moment thought that the man was worthy of head space before she'd fallen asleep the night before was nonsensical.

Drawing breath, she gathered her thoughts. They were threadbare at best. He was condescending in his approach. As a fully qualified professional, she had stepped up to help out. How dare he speak to her that way? She should have taken another role. There was no shortage of locum positions and if she had gone elsewhere there would be no Dr Wainwright and she would be wearing a suit and not something she felt more suited to the stables than a hospital. Alternatively, she could have taken the day off to wait for her clothes and blamed the airline. But no, she'd turned up feeling like Little Orphan Annie, helped out and got a telling-off for stepping up.

She was embarrassed for the third time in his presence. Twice that day and once the day before at the airport. *Three strikes and you're out*, she told herself as she nodded and walked away without saying a word. But in this case he was the one out.

Of any, ever so fleeting, romantic musings she might have harboured for him.

'Dr Ayers,' the hospital orderly called down the corridor to Jessica. It was almost two-thirty by then. Jessica had undertaken her induction and then begun rounds on the

Paediatric ward. Getting to know the nursing staff and her little patients had been her priority.

'Yes,' she said and turned to find the young man tugging her suitcases behind him.

'They told me to find you as these were urgent.'

Jessica couldn't remember ever feeling as relieved and happy as she did at that moment and she had no intention of hiding her elation.

'Oh, my God, thank you so much!' she said as she rushed towards him as if he might disappear with the suitcases as magically as he had appeared.

'No problem,' he replied and released his hold on the bags. 'Apparently they missed the first flight and made it onto the second one.'

'You have no idea how happy this makes me.'

'I think I do,' he smirked before turning back the way he had entered the Paediatric ward.

Jessica could see by his expression that her reaction had been a little over the top but she didn't bother to explain. There was no point. She was happy and had told him as much. Now she could get dressed and forget her Farmer Jane entrée into the hospital had ever happened. What she couldn't forget was Dr Harrison Wainwright's curt and unexpected call on her helping out earlier. It had played on her mind. She really hadn't pegged him for being so rigid and black and white about a situation. Processes were important within a hospital but she had only been trying to help.

Stupidly, she'd thought he had appeared very nice at the airport. Almost chivalrous, she mused as she wheeled her suitcases past the nurses' station, telling them she was changing and would be back in fifteen minutes. And watching him triage and manage the young pregnant patient so compassionately, and then listening to him speak so encouragingly to the medical student had led her to believe he was a decent human being. Then abruptly he had changed and called her out. It was ridiculous.

Men had a habit of doing that around her, she realised. One minute they're single, then the next they're married. In this case, one minute Harrison was a charming, lovely man and the next quite abrupt and rude. His behaviour was odd at best and it had made her realise that her first impression couldn't have been more wrong. She was strangely relieved and almost grateful, she decided as she closed her office door, that he was not the man she'd first thought. If he had been, it might have been a problem. But not any more.

She shook her head, appalled by her borderline hormonal reaction to him, as she unlocked her suitcase and pulled out a pale pink turtleneck sweater and navy trousers that she was relieved to see weren't creased. Although, even if they had been, she would have still worn them.

Focus on what's important, she reminded herself as she tried to stop her thoughts returning to the man who had just delivered her a harsh reality check. Her shoes were in the other suitcase so she quickly closed the first and unlocked the second one that was already lying flat on the floor. Her tights were in a separate compartment and easy to find and she quickly changed.

'Finally,' she sighed as she closed the door to her office and returned to the job at hand. Her tiny patients and their families. And not her stupid daydreams of a man she barely knew—someone who behaved so erratically it had dropped her belief in her own judgement lower than it had already been. *I'd like to show you around the hospital... Actually, come to think of it, no, I won't. Instead*

I'll tell you off for unprofessional behaviour. It didn't make sense but it did help her to rein in her emotions. It was all about her professional reputation. She was grateful that the ER Consultant had, so less than eloquently, reminded her she was done and dusted with giving men the time of day. Her walls were back up and no one was getting close. Any interest in Harrison was gone and she silently thanked him and the universe as she collected the file for her next patient.

Jessica had visited all but one of the patients in the twenty-eight-bed Paediatric ward. Six-year-old Chloe Naughton was the last. She had taken considerably longer with each patient than she would ordinarily but Armidale Hospital was nothing like the busy city wards she had experienced. Between the high number of agency nursing staff and patients from all over, there had been few connections outside the immediate patient-medical staff relationship, with little known about the patient's background if it wasn't on the notes. However, this hospital was very family-centric and the nurses knew almost all the family members, and the paramedics, Jessica remembered from the morning. The community spirit was evident in the close relationships between everyone at the hospital, no matter in what capacity.

It felt good, she admitted, but she knew she had to keep to herself. She wasn't staying and she didn't want to settle in and start feeling too comfortable and risk wanting to stay. That was not an option. When the time came she would leave and start again somewhere else.

'Chloe arrived in the ER two days ago,' the nurse, Rosie, began—she had just started her shift. 'She was convulsing at home and lost consciousness in the ambulance.'

'She's been diagnosed with diabetes, I see.'

'Yes, Dr Ayers,' Rosie responded as the two of them stood outside the patient's room in the corridor so they could speak candidly about the little girl. 'Dr Wainwright ran blood tests and found autoantibodies that are common in type one diabetes, as opposed to type two. Chloe also had ketones in her urine sample so type one diabetes was his diagnosis.'

Dr Wainwright? Of course, Jessica thought. He would have been in ER and been the first point of contact for the family.

'Did you follow up with a glycated haemoglobin test?' Jessica asked as she searched the notes for the answer to her question.

'Yes. Dr Wainwright ordered it when he transferred her to Paediatrics in the afternoon. And the blood test provided us with the average blood sugar level for Chloe for the past two to three months. The percentage of blood sugar attached to the oxygen-carrying protein in the red blood cells was extremely high.'

'I can see here it was close to seven per cent on two separate tests,' Jessica commented as her eyes found what she was looking for. Harrison had been thorough and left nothing to chance. This reinforced that, while he might be a pig of a man, he was a good doctor.

'Any family history?' Jessica enquired as she looked over at the little girl sleeping on the bed while her mother held her hand.

'Paternal grandfather.'

'How are the family taking the news?'

'Not good at all, unfortunately. Her mother, Rachel, hasn't left her side since she was admitted. Chloe is an IVF baby, conceived after five failed rounds. A very wanted and loved little girl.'

'And the child's father; how is he reacting? I hope he's not feeling any sense of guilt over the genetics. It may not be inherited from his side alone.'

'Chloe's father, Sam, was killed in a farm accident a little over six months ago.'

'Oh, my God, I'm so sorry to hear that.'

'It's been a traumatic time for the family,' Rosie replied. 'Sam was ten years older than his wife, in his mid forties when he passed. Rachel's only thirty-five and financially she's going to be okay, emotionally not so much. She's been dealing with the grief of losing Sam, so this has been another blow to her fragile state.'

Jessica paused before she answered. 'She certainly has a lot to manage emotionally. No wonder she hasn't left her daughter's side.'

'We put Chloe in a private room so Rachel can sleep on a roll-out bed.'

'Has a counsellor been to see her?'

'Yes, she has and Dr Wainwright has visited two or three times a day as well. He brings a sandwich or a cup of coffee for Rachel when he comes in. Sam Naughton was like Dr Wainwright's big brother as he grew up. He kept a watchful eye over him so he's returning the favour now.'

Jessica drew in a breath. She really didn't want to hear anything about Harrison. *Complex* appeared to be an understatement about the man. And *close-knit* was equally an understatement about the town.

She pushed thoughts of Harrison aside and focused on the situation at hand. The family had dealt with significant tragedy in a very short timeframe. She wanted to provide hope but she wasn't going to be able to paint a perfect picture or sugar-coat anything. Chloe's condition was serious and, if not managed properly, it could be potentially life-threatening. Chloe needed to be everyone's first priority at this moment.

Chloe's mother lifted her head as Jessica and Rosie approached.

'Hello, Mrs Naughton,' Jessica said softly and extended her hand. 'I'm Dr Ayers, the new Paediatric Consultant, and I'll be looking after your daughter until she is stabilised and can go home in your care.'

'Pleased to meet you, Doctor,' the woman replied, the rims of her eyes still red from rubbing away tears. She was about Jessica's age but her vulnerable state made her appear younger than that.

Jessica felt her heart melt a little, the way it always did and had done from day one. She hadn't liked the feeling as an intern but she was told by one of her mentors early in her career that the day she lost that compassion and empathy was the day she should leave the profession. She always repeated his words in her head when she felt herself struggling with the sadness faced by the families of her tiny patients.

'Chloe's sleeping so perhaps we can step away and I can answer any questions you might have about her treatment plan?'

'I don't want to leave in case she wakes.'

'We can check if Rosie or one of the other nurses can stay with her...' Jessica began.

'Don't bother the nursing staff. They're busy so I'll stay,' a deep male voice echoed behind them. 'You know for a fact that Chloe loves her godfather. And I don't get enough time with her. I haven't seen her at all today because ER's been like a train station, as Dr Ayers knows first-hand.'

Jessica knew the voice. It was Harrison. She didn't need to turn and face him. His voice and the last words he'd spoken to her still rang in her mind. She was confused and didn't want to give him another thought but he was making that very difficult. Her focus was on her patient's mother but his presence was difficult to ignore.

'Are you sure? Aren't you busy in the ER, Harrison?' Rachel asked as she gently prised her fingers free of her daughter's hand, placing it under the soft blanket before she stood up to greet him.

'Never too busy for my two favourite girls,' he told her.

Jessica turned to see the two embrace and a tear trickle down Rachel's cheek. The young mother wiped the tear away as she stepped back and sat down next to her daughter, turning away from him. Jessica suspected it was to prevent him from seeing her crying. Harrison reached into his pocket and handed her his handkerchief over her shoulder. He hadn't missed Rachel's tears or perhaps if he had missed seeing them he had guessed they would follow. He was once again morphing into the gallant man she had met the day before at the airport. Confusion was reigning supreme at that moment but she had to push it aside yet again.

'Please, Rachel,' he continued. 'If you won't do it for yourself, then do it for Chloe. You need to step away and recharge. It's overwhelming in here, not to mention the fact you need to eat. Even if it's cafeteria food, you need to grab something before you fade away.'

Jessica suspected the casual tone in his voice was masking his own concern at the situation. He knew the results of the tests and was aware of Chloe's condition but was clearly responding with Rachel's emotional state at the forefront. The young mother had already dealt with so much, after so many failed attempts to have a baby and recently losing her husband, and he was treading carefully. Jessica's respect for the man standing so close caught her by surprise.

She watched as he leant in and spoke softly. 'I'm serious, Rachel. Take half an hour to grab a coffee and a sandwich downstairs. Maybe Dr Ayers can join you and you can go through the treatment plan in the cafeteria.'

'I'm not sure...' Rachel began.

'Don't make me call in the heavy guns...' Harrison cut in.

'My mother?'

'You got it. I have her number on speed-dial.'

His lips curved into a grin and Jessica was annoyed that it was an appealing grin.

'She's driving down from Brisbane today to be with us anyway, so you can't use that threat, but I am starting to feel hungry.'

'Good, and I could do with a coffee and a sandwich so you'd be doing me a favour too,' Jessica cut in, wanting to help Rachel and eager to leave Harrison's presence. 'I've not had anything to eat since breakfast.'

'Okay, but I'll only be a few minutes, tops,' Rachel said, climbing tentatively to her feet and lifting her bag onto her shoulder. 'I promise, ten minutes at most and I'll be back.'

'Take thirty. I'll still be here when you get back,' he said as he looked towards Jessica with a guilty expression. 'I want to apologise before you leave, Dr Ayers. Your willingness to jump in and help out was admirable and I was out of place for calling you on it. I'm sorry if I was rude. No, not *if* I was rude—I *was* rude; that's not up for debate.'

'What are you taking about, Harrison?' Rachel asked, tilting her head.

'I'm apologising to Dr Ayers. I behaved poorly earlier in ER.'

'You, rude? You've never been rude to anyone in the whole time I've known you.'

'I guess there's a first time for everything and, unfortunately for me, it was this morning.'

Jessica felt the weight of two sets of eyes fall upon her. She wanted to say that she would not accept his apology and she wanted nothing much to do with the man. Ever again. But she couldn't. She had to accept Harrison's apology as politely as he had offered it. Perhaps his behaviour had been as out of character as her dress sense that morning, which to her surprise neither Harrison or anyone else at the hospital had mentioned. There had been no judgement on that level from anyone, just herself. She started to wonder if she was her own biggest critic. She wasn't sure but at that moment she knew she had to respond courteously and work out the truth later about herself…and Harrison.

'Accepted,' Jessica finally announced. 'Now, let's get you downstairs for something to eat.' She wanted to dismiss any thoughts she was having about Harrison. She didn't need any complications. Giving her best to the patients for the next six weeks was her priority. Nothing else.

'Okay, but promise me, Harrison, that you'll call me if Chloe stirs.'

'I'll call you *and* page Dr Ayers, I promise.'

Harrison saluted as he sat down and took Chloe's tiny hand in his and brushed a wisp of her golden locks from her pale as porcelain forehead.

And against her will and every wall she had tirelessly erected, he was threatening to once again break them down.

'How would you like your coffee, Mrs Naughton?'

'White, no sugar, and please call me Rachel.'

Jessica left Rachel sitting at the table and approached the counter of the hospital cafeteria. As she stood in the short queue looking back at the table, she watched Rachel looking off to a faraway place. She wondered if the young woman was thinking about her husband, about the plans they'd made to have a family and raise them in Armidale. And about the five babies they had lost on their journey to have the precious little girl who was now lying on the hospital bed. It all seemed so unfair and, compared to her own heartbreak, Rachel's was so much worse. It suddenly put things in perspective, as work always did for Jessica.

She could only imagine the pain and worry that would be consuming Chloe's mother. Jessica knew she had to deliver the good and the bad news but it had to be done in a manner that would not threaten Rachel's already tenuous hold on her emotions.

Finally, she made it to the front of the lunch line and ordered two white coffees and two mixed sandwiches. She reached into her suit pocket to pay at the register.

'It's covered already,' came the rosy-faced woman's thick Scottish reply. 'Dr Wainwright's paid for it.'

'But how?'

'He called down and told me to put it on his tab.'

'Okay, then please put *one* coffee and *one* sandwich on his tab,' Jessica continued, taking money from her wallet and handing it over. 'I'll pay for my own.'

'I think you'd best accept Dr Wainwright's kind offer. It's only a wee sandwich and coffee, which, by the way, is going cold, and there's some other lovely people waiting to be served,' the woman said as she gently pushed the tray in Jessica's direction and smiled. 'I think you'll like your sandwiches. I made them fresh this morning.'

Jessica gave up. Time was precious and she needed to sit down and speak with Rachel. It was just a coffee and *wee* sandwich after all, she reminded herself. In the scheme of things, it wasn't worth fussing over and perhaps it was his way of cementing his apology.

She balanced the tray on the edge of the table while she transferred both coffees and sandwiches to the table top.

'Thank you,' Rachel said, glancing at the food but not rushing to have any of it.

'Lunch is Dr Wainwright's treat; he called down and covered it.'

'He's such a sweetheart.'

Jessica couldn't help but shake her head a little as she looked away and rested the tray on a spare seat. *Was he?* She was quite confused—and she hated being confused. She was starting to think that maybe she had actually overstepped the mark and should have sought approval before stepping up in the ER earlier. Was Harrison just being responsible and following protocol and she was being the defensive one? Perhaps her past was impacting on the way she saw everyone. It could be that she was looking for a reason to dislike the man.

It didn't matter. Whether Harrison was the salt of the earth or arrogant bore no relevance. She was done trying to work out men's intentions or personalities. She was just done with the lot of them.

'He's been my rock since my husband died. I don't know what I would've done without him. He took charge of everything, even organising and paying for the funeral. I didn't want him to do it; we had enough savings and my husband had life insurance, but Harrison said he wanted me to keep that tucked away for Chloe's education. He insisted, not in an overbearing way, more a caring big brother way. He's taken on the role of Chloe's godfather very seriously. But that's Harrison. When he commits, he gives it a hundred per cent.'

Jessica had to admit that his management of the ER did reflect that same philosophy. He was clearly a man who wasn't half-hearted or casual about anything. He was a puzzle she didn't expect or think she was equipped to face.

'My life was a blur,' Rachel continued, bringing Jessica back to reality. 'I truly didn't know which way was up and which down. I was drowning in disbelief, shock, worry, all of it, so Harrison stepped in and let me just look after Chloe and myself without the additional burden of the arrangements.'

Jessica nodded. The fact that Harrison had stepped up for Rachel and Chloe when Sam had died was indisputable, just as Jessica's immediate and unexpected attraction to the man was undeniable. But neither mattered now. The task at hand was preparing Rachel for the journey ahead in managing Chloe's illness. Her personal feelings about anything or anyone would, as they always did, take a back seat at this time.

'I can answer your questions about Chloe's ongoing treatment while we eat if you like,' Jessica told her to change the subject.

Rachel nodded and then picked up her coffee and took a sip. 'Thank you.'

'Ask anything you need to know and don't hold back. If for some reason I don't know the answer, I will find out.'

Rachel sat in silence for a moment, her eyes wandering again to somewhere in the distance. Jessica unwrapped her sandwich and took a small bite of the wholemeal bread and vegetarian filling.

'Will my daughter die?' Rachel suddenly asked. Her voice was shaky.

Jessica's hands dropped quietly with her sandwich onto her plate and once again she drew a breath. The question was honest but confronting. So the answer needed to be the same, but tempered with enough bedside manner to not cause unnecessary grief or worry.

'No, not if we manage her condition correctly,' Jessica returned after a moment. She was aware of everything that had transpired in Rachel's life in the past twelve months and, prior to that, with the loss of the other babies and knew the woman needed hope in her life. 'And we have to do that to the absolute best of our ability until Chloe's old enough to manage it herself—and then to see that she does the same. *Never* forgetting the seriousness of her condition is the key to Chloe having a healthy and fulfilling life.'

'But what if we get it wrong? What if we miss something…? I don't know…mess up somehow? What then?'

'We won't. Medical research is advanced and we know what medications are the most effective and we'll have a treatment plan that ensures Chloe's condition does not deteriorate.'

'But what about the times when she's not with me?'

Rachel asked, firing another question about yet another scenario and not hiding how scared she was feeling. Her fear was escalating and Jessica could see she was becoming more overwhelmed by the minute.

'You will educate family and friends and, most importantly, Chloe herself so, for those times you're not with her, she's still safe,' Jessica continued in a calming manner. 'And you want your daughter to enjoy increasing independence as she grows up and, with that independence, comes responsibility for making the right choices.'

'And if she doesn't. What will happen then?'

'She could become seriously ill.' There was no easy way around that question. Choosing honesty was the only response. If Chloe was not responsible as she grew older then the outlook was not good. 'But you don't need to consider that at the moment. You have a six-year-old daughter who is going to learn to adapt. Just as you will.'

Jessica watched Rachel slump a little further into her chair.

'Chloe will fully understand the disease as she grows up and, with a healthy respect for herself, she will ensure she does not take unnecessary risks. It's about balance and each day she will be faced with choices that ordinary children don't have to consider but Chloe will know that she needs to factor in her diabetes.'

'It's a big ask of a little girl.'

'It's a big ask of her mother too but you'll both step up. I have no doubt that your daughter will be as strong as you've been for a long time now.'

Jessica watched as Rachel took another sip of her coffee.

'Please eat something,' Jessica said kindly but with a level of firmness as a health professional. Her eyes travelled down to the uneaten sandwich still on Rachel's plate. 'You'll be no use to Chloe when she needs you if you're rundown and get sick from both worry and lack of nutrition.'

'I guess,' came Rachel's muttered reply before she took a few tiny bites of the sandwich.

Jessica followed suit but there weren't any bite-size mouthfuls. She was hungry and wolfed down the sandwich and coffee in a few minutes. It had been hours since breakfast.

'Would you like me to explain the disease in more depth—and the treatment plan?' Jessica asked as she swallowed the last rushed mouthful.

'Yes. I need to know everything. And as soon as possible.'

Jessica dabbed her mouth with the paper napkin and began. 'With diabetes, a treatment plan is a *lifelong* treatment plan. It may alter over the course of time but it will be a continuous plan, as we will be treating Chloe's diabetes not curing it. Right now, there's no cure for the disease but that's not to say there won't be a cure one day.'

'But she can live a long healthy life, can't she?'

'Most definitely. With proper care, Chloe will look and feel as healthy as any girl her age. And live a long life.'

Jessica watched as Rachel shifted in her seat, her posture improving with the optimistic prognosis. Jessica had never wanted to add to Rachel's stress; however, she did need to explain the seriousness of Chloe's chronic illness.

'Chloe's treatment plan will be based on her very specific needs and the hospital will also provide a diabetes healthcare team.'

'So not just you then, Dr Ayers?'

'No. I'm just standing in for the resident paediatrician's leave. He'll be back in six weeks and, together with a number of medical professionals across the hospital, he will provide advice and support,' Jessica told her, unsure of the identity of the individuals, though she knew the various medical specialties who would be represented in a hospital of that size. 'But, before we get to the team's role, let me explain a little about the illness and the treatment plan.'

Rachel nodded and took another bite of the egg and rocket sandwich.

'Treatment is never the same for every child or adult. The types of insulin given and the schedules for giving insulin each day vary between patients.'

'So Chloe will need an injection of insulin every day?'

'Yes.'

'For ever?'

'Yes. This illness is not something that Chloe will grow out of. It will be something she manages for life.' Jessica paused for a moment. 'I'm sorry that I'm giving you so much to think about now. I thought that it all would have been explained to you yesterday.'

'It was, and I know diabetes is a lifelong condition,' Rachel replied with a look of sheer exhaustion crossing her drawn face. 'I was just too emotional to take anything much in. It washed over me like a tidal wave and I just tried to keep my head above water and focus on Chloe's immediate needs and not break down in front of her.'

'That's understandable,' Jessica reassured her. 'You're doing an amazing job. I'll let you know what's important for now and the rest can wait. I'm mindful you'll want to head back to Chloe.'

And no doubt Dr Wainwright would need to head back down to the ER, she mused. And she wanted to give him a wide berth. Spending as little time with him as possible was her aim for the time she had in Armidale. She feared that he could complicate her life unnecessarily. She prayed he would leave the minute they arrived back in Chloe's room and she could avoid any further awkwardness.

'Harrison did promise he would send a text if she woke,' Rachel replied before she took a deep and worried breath that filled her lungs then deflated just as quickly. 'I think I'm in a better mind-set today. Do you have the time to explain everything to me? I worry that Harrison might leave something out so I don't worry. But I need to know everything.'

Jessica had the remainder of the afternoon free, so she could afford the time. And she didn't care to spend any more time than necessary with Dr Wainwright so she was happy to tell Rachel everything she needed to know.

'Chloe will need insulin to manage her blood glucose level,' Jessica began. 'The blood glucose level is the amount of glucose in the blood.'

'So, is insulin all she needs or are there other things we need to do and how will we manage this when she starts school?'

'If there is a school nurse or first aid officer, they could help until Chloe can do it herself,' Jessica said as she met Rachel's gaze levelly. 'And the hospital will provide ongoing assistance.'

Rachel nodded but didn't look convinced.

'I do feel better knowing I'm not left alone to deal with everything,' she said as she picked some stray alfalfa shoots from her plate and nibbled on them.

'You must ask for additional support if you need it,' Jessica said firmly. 'You can't go it alone on this, Rachel.'

The young woman nodded. 'I won't, I promise. And with all that assistance, I won't have to rely on Harrison as much in the future.'

The mention of his name brought a little knot rushing back to Jessica's stomach.

'He needs a life too. He has a lot on his plate to manage—he doesn't need me on top of everything else,' Rachel continued with a wistful smile. 'He's such a wonderful man and he needs to find someone to share his life and he can't do that if he concentrates on helping me.'

Jessica swallowed. The last thing she wanted to hear was that Harrison Wainwright was eligible and apparently not as dreadful as she had come to believe. On top of the fact he was also, from first impressions in the ER, a highly skilled doctor with a genuinely kind and understanding bedside manner to children and adults alike. All the ingredients for a disaster when she was, for some unknown reason, feeling vulnerable around him.

Suddenly Jessica had been catapulted out of her comfort zone. And she was nervous.

Of him…and of her own feelings.

CHAPTER SIX

THE NEXT FEW days passed quickly. Jessica did her best to avoid Harrison. Her patient load kept her in Paediatrics and away from ER. She passed him in the corridor once or twice, acknowledging him with a polite nod. It was working for her and she hoped to keep it that way for as long as possible. The nights were a little different because, for reasons not understood by Jessica, his face wandered into her mind just before she fell asleep. Every night.

She had almost succeeded in making it to the end of day four without being too close to the handsome medico until he happened upon her in Chloe's room when the little girl was being released into her mother's care.

'Now, you have the hospital number and the individual numbers for each of the diabetic healthcare team,' Jessica told her as she signed the hospital discharge papers and gave them to Rosie.

'Yes,' Rachel answered, patting her oversized handbag. 'It's all in here.'

Jessica watched as Rachel lifted Chloe onto her hip. The little girl clung to her like a baby koala.

'You're going to be fine, both of you. We have a district nurse calling in tomorrow to check up on how you're progressing so you don't have to unsettle Chloe by bringing her back here.'

'Don't forget about me,' Harrison's voice boomed from across the room.

Jessica turned to see his tall silhouette in the doorway. His white consulting coat couldn't hide his muscular physique. The shapeless coat was hanging open but he had a caramel-coloured fine-knit sweater that skimmed and accentuated his toned body. Navy trousers and brown loafers completed the picture that Jessica wished she was not witnessing.

'It's Uncle Harry, Chloe,' Rachel said happily. 'He's come to say goodbye.'

'Is he going on a trip?'

'No.' Rachel laughed as she looked her daughter in the eyes. 'We are. Well, sort of... We're going home. And he'll visit us there soon, I'm sure.'

'Bye, Uncle Harry,' the little girl muttered, then put her thumb back in her mouth and nestled against the warmth of her mother's chest.

Harrison crossed the room with long purposeful steps that covered the space quickly. And with each step Jessica felt the air escaping and her face becoming flushed. She took a few steps back. She was finding the room a little close, and suddenly it became difficult to breathe.

'I will visit you on the weekend. I promise,' he told her and kissed the top of her head before he took a small step back and gently turned her to fully face him. 'Now, you need to be a good girl, the best, in fact, and get lots of rest and do just what Mummy says.'

'Do I have to have needles every day, Uncle Harry?'

Harrison paused for a moment and his gaze wandered over to Jessica. It took her by surprise that he looked a little lost. She'd never expected to see that expression and it tugged at her heart.

'Yes,' Jessica said, moving closer to the three of them again. It was instinctive for her to save him. He was Chloe's godfather and she felt the need to remove the pressure from him. Pressure that he oddly didn't seem to be coping with at that moment. Jessica needed to be the one to deliver the bad news and he could be the one to console the little girl. It was almost as if they had unintentionally adopted aunt and uncle roles.

'But it hurts.'

'I know it does, Chloe. But it's only for a minute and then the little stinging feeling goes away—and you need the medicine to stay healthy and run around like the other children. And Mummy needs you to be healthy so you can help her around the house too. I bet you're a big help.'

'I make my bed and I feed our cat, Snowflake, and—' Chloe paused and her eyes glanced from side to side '—and I give the hens water. We have seven girl hens but no boy hens because they're noisy and wake us up in the morning,' she continued, shaking her tiny head. 'The boys in my class at school are like that too. They're so noisy.'

Jessica smiled at the little girl's words and continued, 'Boys can be noisy and seven hens must keep you busy. And making your bed and feeding Snowflake are all things that Mummy needs help with. If you aren't well because you've not had your medicine, then she'll have to do all of it and—'

'She'll get tired and cry again, like when Daddy died,' the little girl cut in.

Jessica fell silent. She wasn't sure what to say. She had been blindsided by the honesty of Chloe's words. Rachel's emotional state and the recent loss of her husband had momentarily been forgotten in the fuss over Chloe.

Instantly, as if he knew that Jessica was searching for the right thing to say, Harrison cut in. It was a tag team that Jessica hadn't expected to be a part of at all.

'Yes, Chloe. Mummy might get tired and mummies cry when they are tired and sad, so you must try your best to be strong. But if you have days when you're not strong, then you get Mummy to call me and I can help you to look after the cat and the hens. I'm only ten minutes away from the farm,' he told her.

Jessica looked over at Harrison, just as he turned to her. It was a knowing look. A look of gratitude and something more…something that Jessica couldn't quite define.

'Let's get the pair of you out of here and back home before the rain hits,' Rosie added, breaking the moment as she attempted to bustle Rachel and Chloe out of the room.

Jessica wasn't sure if she was relieved or disappointed. But she was confused that she didn't know how she felt. Of that she was certain.

'I'll take you down to Reception to complete the paperwork,' the nurse continued as the three of them headed out, leaving Jessica and Harrison alone.

'Again, I'm sorry about the other day,' Harrison said, running his hand over his forehead. 'You stepped up and, instead of thanking you, I told you off. It was wrong of me. I guess I'm accustomed to running things and I was taken aback. But that's no excuse.'

'You've apologised already and I've accepted. Let's leave it at that,' Jessica responded, eager to get away from the man who was making her pulse race and her heart flutter when she wanted to harbour some sort of negative feelings towards him. It wasn't a fleeting interest that had passed, as she had hoped. Just being near him was causing a reaction that unsettled her. And she didn't want or need to be having that sort of reaction. She didn't need any complications during her short stay in Armidale. She wanted to keep it purely professional and keep him at arm's length. No unnecessary chit-chat, no reason to learn more about him and, as a result, find him even more attractive than she did already. An apologetic handsome man was the absolute last thing on her wish list.

'All righty,' he said, looking taken aback by her dismissive response to his apology.

Jessica immediately felt terrible, suddenly worried that she was now the one overreacting. It was ridiculous that she cared what he thought but she did again. It was all beyond her comprehension and confusing and yet she felt compelled to step in and save it.

'Now it's my turn to apologise. I'm sorry. I—'

Their pagers both went off at the same time, cutting short her words. They looked down simultaneously and saw they were being called to the ER.

'Dr Wainwright, Dr Ayers—' a young ER nurse rushed into the room '—I know you've been paged but I thought I could brief you on the way down. There's been an accident on the New England Highway. A school bus left the road. Four ambulances are on their way here now. Nine seriously injured, eleven others with minor injuries and an unspecified number with cuts and abrasions that are being treated at the scene but may be transported here later. ETA eight minutes.'

'The driver?' Harrison asked as he and Jessica followed the nurse to the lift.

'Pronounced dead at the scene.'

Jessica sighed and closed her eyes for the briefest moment as they all stepped into the lift. 'From injuries sustained in the accident?'

'No, it appears he suffered a heart attack and died at the wheel; that's why the bus left the road,' the nurse continued as the lift reached the ground floor and they all stepped out in unison and headed to the ER. 'He called out to both the teachers as he clasped his chest and tried to keep control of the bus. In the statement to police, the paramedics overheard one teacher say the driver had done his absolute best to slow the bus, but at such a high speed he couldn't prevent them leaving the road. The teachers were at the rear of the bus and couldn't get to the driver in time to take the wheel.'

'What a tragic set of circumstances,' Jessica said solemnly as they entered the doors of the ER.

'Do you have an idea of the age range of the children?' Harrison asked as he scrubbed and donned surgical gloves and gown.

'It was two year five classes on an excursion, so the students are all around nine to ten years of age.'

Jessica followed suit and scrubbed and gowned. 'And the extent of the injuries?'

'Two suspected spinal cord injuries, multiple fractures, lacerations and all are being monitored for internal bleeding.'

'Any fatalities other than the driver?'

'Not yet.'

'Let's make sure we have all bays emptied if possible,' Harrison called out to the ER staff. 'Any non-life-threatening can be triaged to a waiting room. Stat. We have less than two minutes to ETA.'

Jessica watched as four patients were wheeled on their beds out of ER and other beds were quickly wheeled in by orderlies. She suspected that the experienced ER staff had already made that decision and the triaging was well underway before she and Harrison arrived. It was like clockwork and far too quick to have been arranged on his command. They just knew what they needed to do. It was a well-oiled machine that Harrison ran.

One minute later, and one minute ahead of schedule, two stretchers were rushed into the ER. Jessica could see immediately these were two of the serious injuries. Both were in neck braces and bandages had been applied to their heads and one had both legs in splints. A man in his early forties was walking beside one of them. Jessica assumed he was one of the children's teachers. She walked into bay five with the first and Harrison took the second stretcher into bay four.

'Nine-year-old male. Suspected fractures to both legs, potential neck injury and blunt head trauma from hitting the seat in front and being thrown to the ground on impact. No seat belt. We inserted an IV en route and administered pain relief as he was experiencing pain while conscious. While his injuries are extensive, there's no sign of internal bleeding and the pain would indicate no C1-C2 vertebrae damage. He's on a board and we braced him as a precaution.'

'Great job and it does sound promising,' Jessica replied. 'Let's transfer him onto the bed.'

The paramedics and the nurses worked swiftly and carefully to execute the transfer, keeping the board in place before they handed over their notes and exited the bay with the stretcher.

'His name is Trevor Saunders,' the man added. 'I'm his teacher, Gavin Watson. We were on an excursion to Armidale from the Tamworth Elementary School.'

Moments later, two more stretchers arrived with para-medics and they were taken into the adjacent bays, with a third stretcher and two more paramedics following closely behind and being parked in the final empty bay. All nurses and ER staff were engaged and Jessica was aware there were four more serious cases en route.

'Have you been assessed by the paramedics, Mr Wat-son?' Jessica asked before she donned a surgical mask and approached the child.

'I was assessed at the accident site by paramedics and cleared. My seat belt was in place, just as I thought the students' belts were because we have a school travel pol-icy and strict rules. Unfortunately, the boys thought they knew better and I had no way to see they had undone their seat belts just before the accident.'

'Would you be able to help identify the students we are treating? If you make your way over to the desk and explain what you have been asked to do, one of the nurses at the desk will help you. Please stay close so we can call on you if we need anything further,' Jessica said in short staccato sentences. 'I assume the parents have been contacted?'

The teacher nodded. 'My colleague, Ms Forbes, is still at the accident scene with those students not hurt in the accident and the school has called all of the parents,' he said before following her instructions and making his way to the ER desk.

Quickly Jessica turned her attention back to the young patient, who was unconscious but breathing steadily. 'Trevor,' she began in a soft and soothing voice. 'My name is Jessica and I'm a doctor. While you cannot see me, you may be able to hear me. You were in an accident and you've been brought to the Armidale Hospital, about an hour and a half from your school in Tamworth.'

There was no visible reaction to her words.

'We are going to put some monitors on you. If you can hear me, you need to stay very still. You hurt your back and your legs when the bus left the road so we don't want you trying to move.'

The nurses worked quickly to ensure the boy's heart, temperature and breathing were all monitored.

'BP is rising—it's now ninety over forty-five,' the nurse announced, then continued as she looked over the paramedic's notes. 'En route it was eighty over forty.'

The boy's eyelids began to flicker. Jessica could see he was regaining consciousness.

'Welcome back, Trevor.'

His eyes closed again and the flickering stopped for a moment.

'The patient is drifting in and out of consciousness. I need a portal X-ray machine to assess the damage to the lower limbs,' she told one of the nurses in the same calm but lowered voice. 'According to the notes, we have a suspected fracture of right tibia and left femur but the issue for me is the potential for spinal cord injury.'

'BP's a little higher again and oxygen saturation is improving,' the nurse reported.

'Good, his pain must be under control but there's still a risk of lumbar spinal cord damage if he moves so let's not get ahead of ourselves.'

Jessica confirmed the reading on the monitor out of habit and felt silently pleased and confident that she was not dealing with a quadriplegia diagnosis.

The young boy began to open his eyes and they remained open for a few seconds.

'Trevor, I know you are feeling confused and maybe a little scared but you're safe. You're in a hospital and your parents are on their way now to be with you. I'm not sure if you could hear me when you first arrived but my name is Jessica and I'm a doctor.'

The nurse leant in to Jessica and said in a low whisper, 'They left Tamworth twenty minutes ago so their ETA is around an hour.'

'Your parents should be here by the time we've finished these tests, Trevor. Your neck is in a brace so you have limited movement but I need you to keep your body still too. If you can keep your eyes open please do, but if that is difficult then close and rest them as you need. I'll tell you what's happening but again we need you to remain very still. You are flat on a board on a stretcher, as you hit your head on something hard in the bus. You may have also hurt your neck and your back. We're about to take X-rays of your legs. I'll be stepping away for a moment and then I'll come right back. You're not alone.'

Jessica and the nurses stepped away momentarily while the radiologist took the images and then they all returned to find the boy's eyes wide open but staring straight ahead.

'You're doing so well, Trevor,' Jessica continued. 'I know I'm now upside down to you but I need to stand here at your head, so I can check your response to light. I will shine a small torch into your eyes; it won't hurt but I want you to keep looking at my nose.' The nurse handed Jessica the small torch and she shone it in sideways movements across Trevor's line of vision and then slowly in a circular motion. 'I'm going to cover one of your eyes and shine the light in the uncovered eye, then I will do the same to the other eye.'

Jessica completed the examination before turning to the nurse. 'The pupils are equal in size and responsive to light, which is a good sign, but the right eye is a little sluggish, which may be an issue. I just apologise that I don't know all of the consultants at the hospital; is there a neurologist on staff?'

'No, however, our ICU Consultant is on his way down now. A neurologist in Sydney was contacted by Dr Wainwright as his patient is suspected C1-C2 vertebrae damage. The neurologist is flying over tomorrow to assess the boy as he may need airlifting to the Sydney General Memorial Hospital for treatment.'

Jessica nodded her understanding of the situation in the adjacent bay and her appreciation of the ER team's initiative in sending for the ICU Consultant. She quickly returned her attention to her patient.

'You've been very good, Trevor,' Jessica told him and, casting a glance at the nurses' names, she turned back to him, adding, 'Nurse Jan and Nurse Gayle will stay with you and I will check back in a little while. If you have any questions, please ask them. And if you have any pain let them know. We're waiting for another special doctor to come and look at you and, in the meantime, I'm going to help one of your classmates who's been hurt too.'

Jessica discarded her gloves and rushed into the next bay, where an intern was attending another young victim. She had no idea where Harrison was but she could hear his voice and knew he was moving from one bay to the next, doing his best to keep each and every little patient alive.

It was going to be a long day and night for them all and Jessica hoped that no parent would be without their precious child by the end of it.

* * *

'Thank you,' Harrison said as he observed Jessica sign off on the last patient and release the young girl into the care of her very relieved and grateful parents.

His words were few but heartfelt. Jessica could see in his face that the pressure of the previous hours, constantly triaging patients and managing staff, had taken its toll. He was exhausted, mentally and physically.

'You don't need to thank me,' Jessica replied, pulling off her disposable surgical cap and gown, which was splattered with fine spots of her last patient's blood. The young girl had sustained lacerations to her forearm as fragments of plate glass window had cut through her sweater and lodged in her skin, but fortunately not compromised any blood supply. With one of the senior ER nurses assisting, Jessica had painstakingly removed the fine glass and stitched the wounds. It was one of the least serious injuries and, as such, had been left until last to ensure the patients with life-threatening injuries had been treated first.

It had been a long day and night for the ER team and the other medical staff called in from across the hospital as required. They had pulled together professionally and worked tirelessly to save the lives of all the children. While some of the injured students would spend an extended amount of time in hospital with their injuries, they had at least all pulled through. The less seriously injured patients would be transferred to the Tamworth General Hospital the following day to make it easier on family and friends visiting them, but at least two young boys would have to remain in Armidale for an indefinite period. They had not been wearing their seat belts and had, as a result, sustained neck and back injuries that required ongoing monitoring in the ICU as unnecessary travel would not be permitted.

'It's one a.m.,' Harrison commented in passing to the staff who had worked past the end of their shifts to treat the patients. 'Great job—please go home and if you're rostered on tomorrow, don't show up. We'll move staff around the hospital to cover for you. And if any of you usually catch public transport across the New England area, please get a cab and the hospital will reimburse you.'

All the staff thanked Harrison and left for the day. Weary but satisfied with the outcome of the horrific accident. They were all saddened to know the bus driver had lost his life but relieved that the children had not.

'How about you, Dr Ayers? Do you have transport?' Harrison asked Jessica as she made her way to leave.

'Yes,' she said as she turned to face him. 'But thank you for asking. I have my rental in the doctors' car park.'

'If you'd like to get your things from your office, I'm more than happy to walk you to your car. It's a bit isolated out the back, especially at this hour, and not particularly well lit in some places.'

Jessica nodded. 'Thank you; that's very kind of you.'

'It's settled then. I'll grab my jacket and meet you back here in ten minutes.'

Jessica returned to her office and collected her overcoat and handbag. On the way out she called in and caught up with the night staff in Paediatrics and was brought up to speed on her patients. Thankfully, there was nothing to report; all were progressing well with their treatment and Jessica told them she would be back for morning rounds. She returned to the ER to find Harrison waiting, just as he'd said he would. An unexpected warm feeling washed over her. It felt good to have someone looking out for her. She had been doing it alone for the best part of a year and it hadn't bothered her, but seeing Harrison there made her feel unexpectedly safe for the first time in a long time.

And she didn't want to run from that feeling.

'I can't believe how freezing cold it can get in this town. I don't think I've lived anywhere that drops down this low,' Jessica remarked as she dug her hands into the deep pockets of her heavy woollen coat. Her breath was fogging the still night air as she spoke.

'Heads up, Dr Ayers—one in the morning, slap bang in the middle of winter, isn't the best time to get out and about in many places around here!' Harrison laughed as they picked up speed and headed to the doctors' car park at the rear of the hospital. 'And if you didn't already know, Armidale has the highest altitude of any city in Australia.'

'So now I know why almost every house I drive past has a stockpile of wood. They know what they're in for in winter.'

'Yes, and nothing beats an open fire,' he returned, rubbing his hands together as if over the flames.

Jessica smiled and kept walking. The conversation was flowing and she felt at ease…but that was almost making her uneasy.

'At least it's not raining and you don't have far to drive,' Harrison continued.

'That's the joy of not being in a big city. You can drive for what seems like hours in Sydney or Melbourne to get home after a long shift, which isn't pleasant and the last thing you need when all you want is to put your feet up and collapse on the sofa because you have an early start the next morning.'

'So, you're not a lover of big cities then?'

'I'm not averse to living in large cities. I mean it has its advantages but there's the downside too, and I don't have to deal with that here, which is a bonus. I'll be home in five minutes and that's a big plus—particularly at one in the morning, *slap-bang in the middle of winter*!'

Another bonus was being walked to her car by a handsome medical colleague and that hadn't happened in any city placements, but Jessica wasn't about to mention that to Harrison. She was still coming to terms with how her feelings were developing for the man, no matter how hard she fought to remind herself that men were not permitted within a mile of her or her heart. But the more she spent time with Harrison, the more difficult it became to ignore the respect she had for him as a doctor, a godfather and a colleague.

And a chivalrous man.

'So, is Armidale winning over the city girl?'

'I'm not sure,' she replied as she reached inside her handbag for her keys. 'I haven't been here long enough yet…but, from what I've seen of the town over the last few days, it's a lovely lifestyle and such a supportive community spirit.'

Harrison smiled and Jessica wasn't sure if the smile was pride in his home town or something else but she thought it best to leave it at that as she pressed on the small electronic remote key to unlock the drivers' door.

'Thank you, Harrison, for walking me to my car. I really do appreciate it.' The car park was dimly lit in places, just as Harrison had told her, and she had parked her small red hatchback in one of the darkest places.

'It's the least I can do when you just worked a sixteen-hour shift.'

'As did you, and all of the others. I don't deserve any more praise than everyone else.' With that she opened the door and climbed in the car, but not before saying goodnight.

Harrison bid her goodnight and she watched as he walked away to a better lit part of the car park. Cutting a powerful figure with his broad shoulders and long powerful steps, he crossed to a large black four-wheel drive. She couldn't help but stare as he climbed in. She wanted to pull her gaze away but she felt a strange connection to him. It didn't make sense but it was there. Jessica couldn't deny it, nor could she define it.

Within moments he started the car and headed to the exit. Quickly, Jessica was brought back to the task at hand. Getting home and not thinking about Dr Harrison Wainwright. He had walked her to her car, not rescued her from a burning house. She needed to put everything in perspective.

Romance in a rural city was not on the cards. Romance anywhere was not on the cards. End of story.

Then why was she sitting in a dark car park thinking about it?

Quickly she checked her mobile phone for messages. There was nothing urgent so she slipped it inside her handbag on the seat beside her. It was a short drive so she kept her coat on, as she knew the car would barely warm up before she would be pulling up in her driveway. Ready to go, she turned on the ignition. There was nothing. She tried again, but again the engine didn't turn over at all. Nothing happened. She dropped her head on the steering wheel for a moment, realising in an instant that her rental had a flat battery. She wasn't going anywhere.

Harrison had left and she was in the darkest part of the deserted car park with no one in sight. Suddenly feeling safe flew out through the ice-covered window. She tried to pull her tired mind into action. She could run back inside and call a cab, but if Harrison had insisted on walking her to the car, maybe walking back on her own wasn't the best idea. Perhaps she could call roadside assistance, if there was any. It wasn't Sydney and she had no clue if the local provider would be on duty. And what was the number anyway?

Jessica unexpectedly felt a little close to tears. It had been a long day, an incredibly long day, and all she wanted was a nice warm bed for the next six hours. She'd been so relieved that the patients had all survived but managing that stress had taken its toll on her emotional reserves. And now, when she needed sleep almost as much as air, she wasn't sure when she would get to bed. Not to mention the fact that being in the darkness of the car park was starting to add to her angst. She reached down to the glovebox to see if there was any information about who to call in case of a breakdown.

Suddenly there was a tap on the car window.

Jessica screamed and jumped as she turned to see a tall outline standing beside the car door. A towering figure that made her feel more vulnerable by the second and made her heart pick up speed. Her body was instantly in fight or flight mode. She realised this was probably why Harrison had insisted on walking her to the car.

The tapping continued until a mobile phone illuminated the stranger's face.

Only it wasn't a stranger.

'Oh, my God, Harrison!' she exclaimed as she opened the door a little, her hand still visibly shaking and her heart still racing. 'What are you doing here? I thought you'd left—I saw you drive off.'

'I did, but I didn't see your lights in my rear mirror as I turned onto the road so I came back. I thought there might be something wrong. Am I right or did I just scare the living daylights out of you for no good reason?'

'No, you're right,' she said with a rueful half smile. 'I'm guessing I have a flat battery. There's nothing when I turn on the ignition,' she continued, then took a deep breath, encouraging her heart to slow down.

'I suspected car trouble. I didn't think you'd choose to sit in the middle of a deserted car park in the early hours to check your social media,' he said, smiling.

'Not usually.' Her eyes rolled but the smile remained.

'So your car is effectively dead at the moment and, as I don't have any leads to jumpstart your battery, we have two options. We call for roadside assistance and hope they're not caught up elsewhere, which may well be the case as there's not too many service providers after hours, or I drop you home and collect you again in the morning from your home and we call roadside assistance to replace the battery then.'

Jessica nodded. 'Option two sounds much better, if you're sure you don't mind?'

'I don't mind at all. In fact, if you'd chosen option one I would've tried to talk you into option two, just to save my fingers from frostbite.'

Ten minutes later they arrived at Jessica's home. All the houses were in darkness and Harrison insisted on walking Jessica to the door.

'I'm going to make a hot chocolate before I turn in

for the night,' she said as she felt around in her bag for her keys. 'I can just as easily make two, if you would like one?'

She froze as the words slipped from her lips. It scared her that it seemed so natural to ask him in.

Her mind-set on the day she'd arrived couldn't have been further from where it was at that moment. Harrison was like no one she had met before and, while part of her felt she needed her barriers up perhaps even more than usual, there was another part that felt comfortable and relaxed in his presence and, despite the late hour, something was pushing her to spend some time alone to get to know the man who had been so gallant on more than one occasion. He seemed genuinely nice, he was an amazing doctor under pressure and…she silently admitted that, against her better judgement, she was very curious to learn more. It was that simple and nothing about her life had been simple for a very long time.

Harrison hesitated then turned and remotely locked his car.

'I'd like that, but I'm only staying for ten minutes; you need your sleep.'

'And you need yours too,' Jessica replied as she opened the front door and invited him in.

An hour later Harrison stood to leave, not because he wanted to go but because he knew he should. While Bryce was with his grandparents for the night, as he often was when Harrison was working, he wanted to have breakfast with his son the way he always did. Whether they were in their own home or with Harrison's parents, sharing breakfast was a ritual he didn't break often or without good reason. The trip to LA recently had meant they'd missed six shared breakfasts and Harrison didn't want to miss another one.

It was after two in the morning and ten minutes had turned into sixty. Hot chocolate had been accompanied by crumpets with honey and he couldn't remember feeling so comfortable outside his own home. Jessica was sitting on the sofa with him, her legs curled up underneath her. She had excused herself and quickly changed into sweat pants and an oversized jumper while the crumpets were cooking. And, while there was no roaring fire, the central heating had kept them both warm. And the conversation had found Harrison warming to Jessica by the minute and opening up about certain aspects of his life. Each had spoken about their respective journeys to becoming doctors, their reasons for choosing medicine and their experiences on the job, good and bad, including how they dealt with telling the families they had lost their loved one. Both agreed this was the hardest part of their work.

And both had skilfully and purposely avoided the topic of relationships. Jessica hadn't asked about Harrison's past, nor he about hers. It definitely made the evening even more pleasant for him and he suspected perhaps for her too. Bringing Bryce's mother into the conversation would have spoilt everything and brought him back to earth with a thud. And it was too early to mention his son. While Jessica was lovely, unless a miracle happened, she was only in town for a short time and he felt protective of Bryce. There was no need to bring him up yet. Or perhaps ever.

Despite being exhausted, he really didn't want to leave but knew he should for Jessica's sake. 'I've kept you up far too long, and if I don't go now I risk falling asleep on the sofa, not a good look for the neighbours,' he said as he stacked the cups and plates, ready to take them to the kitchen.

He couldn't help but notice Jessica smile a little sheepishly, he assumed at the thought of him staying over. He was suddenly further drawn towards the gorgeous paediatrician who had waltzed into town and made him question much about his life. The idea of staying over was definitely very appealing. She was a stunning conundrum. She had spent the last sixteen hours showing her extraordinary abilities and dedication as a doctor; she was not timid in voicing her opinions; she had a wonderful way of making him feel at ease without trying; and she was gorgeous. Without knowing it, Dr Jessica Ayers was making Harrison question his resolve to only date women who had no further appeal than a great night of sex with no strings attached. He suspected Jessica would come with strings and, for some reason, he wasn't running away. But *she* would be soon enough. She hadn't hidden that fact, yet, despite it, he still didn't want to go.

In fact, it was just the opposite; he was forcing himself to leave. The thought of strings was not a barrier to spending time with her. It was as if he was open to becoming a little entangled, for however long that might be. He would just make sure that it wouldn't involve Bryce. Harrison's personal life would always be kept very separate to his family life.

Together they walked to the kitchen and put everything in the sink. Jessica told him she would wash them in the morning.

'Thank you again for bringing me home,' Jessica said as she followed Harrison to the front door.

'And don't forget to thank me for almost scaring you to death in the car park.'

Jessica laughed. 'It *was* a little horror movie-esque.'

'I promise not to sneak up like that again…'

'Let's hope my car doesn't break down again.'

Jessica reached up and took Harrison's jacket from the wall-mounted coat rail. His hand brushed against hers as he took it from her but, instead of slipping it on, he paused for a moment so close to her. He didn't want to leave. He knew at that moment he wanted more than anything to taste the sweetness of her lips. To pull her body against his and hold her in his arms. It all seemed so natural. There was no doubt, no questions. He didn't need to second-guess. His lips were hovering only inches from the inviting softness of her mouth. The mouth he wanted more than anything to claim, the mouth that suddenly…

Yawned.

Harrison stepped back. 'Oh…that would be my cue to go…'

'Oh, my God, I'm so sorry,' she said and, covering her mouth with her hand, yawned for a second time. 'It's not you…it's just…'

'It's just that you've worked a day from hell and I've kept you up talking for another hour and I almost…' Harrison stopped mid-sentence, raking his hair. He didn't want to admit he had almost kissed her. She knew— they both knew what had almost happened—but he suspected the moment had passed. 'I've almost outstayed my welcome.'

Harrison watched as Jessica's gaze fell to her slippers and then came back to him again. Her eyes were wide and she was smiling, albeit a little embarrassed, just as she had looked at their airport encounter.

'You haven't at all. I've really enjoyed getting to know you.' Her voice was so low that he almost missed what she had said. 'Truly, I've enjoyed spending time with you.'

'I've enjoyed it too,' Harrison said, unsure of many things but realising, yawn or no yawn, he still wanted to kiss her more than he could remember wanting anything. He wasn't going to second-guess himself.

Gently he pulled her close to him and, as his mouth moved towards hers, she tilted her face to him and closed her eyes in anticipation. Their lips met with a tenderness and an almost wonderful familiarity that lovers shared. Such closeness didn't make sense to him, but nothing since meeting Jessica had. She pressed her body against his and his arms held her even more tightly. He didn't want it to end. Swept away by the feelings surging through his body, Harrison wanted to hold her in his arms and feel the warmth of her mouth on his for the longest time. It was a gentle release of feelings, not wildly passionate. Harrison was holding back because he sensed, for reasons he did not yet know, that Jessica needed him to go slowly with her.

Suddenly he felt her stiffen in his arms.

His arm slowly released his embrace as he stepped back and looked at the most beautiful woman he had ever seen. Looking in her eyes, he could see something that wasn't fear but it was close to it. His instincts had been correct.

'Is everything all right?' he asked as he collected himself.

'Yes, it's just that…we should get some sleep,' she said tentatively. 'You need to drive home and we'll have a big day tomorrow, I'm sure, with all the patients to be discharged or transferred to Tamworth.'

Harrison wasn't sure what had happened and why Jessica was pulling away, but he did as he was asked. He wasn't about to press her to find out. Perhaps she was right in pulling away; while he had enjoyed spending time with Jessica, he had not imagined when he drove her home that he would lose perspective and so quickly overstep the boundaries. She was a work colleague and Harrison had, until now, always kept his private life away from the hospital. The entire evening, even wanting to stay for a warm drink in the first place, went against his better judgement. But he had done it anyway. It was obvious to him that there was chemistry between them, but as her actions made him step back he was reminded that what he'd done went against everything he believed. Jessica was only in town for a limited time.

Again, he needed to remind himself, his ex-wife had been in town for a limited time too. The situation screamed déjà-vu and Harrison could not afford to relive that nightmare. He couldn't allow his emotions to get the better of him. He had made that mistake before. Allowed himself to be swept away, falling heart and soul way too soon and then being helpless to prevent it all falling apart. He couldn't travel that road again, but would it be the same road? he wondered. Or was this very different? Harrison's head was telling him to pull back but his heart was saying something very different.

They were two professional people who had spent time getting to know each other outside of work and he had allowed it to go too far. Now he needed to take her cue and set boundaries. Jessica had been upfront about her intentions. Stay six weeks and leave town. There had been no deceit, no false promises. He had to try and colleague zone Jessica immediately and put some distance between them. He had no choice, for his own sake. But he doubted how successful it would be after the kiss they'd shared.

'I'll send a cab for you in the morning at about ten-thirty, if that suits you?'

'A cab?'

'Yes, you deserve a decent sleep, so you can start late. I'll head in earlier and check on our patients before they're transported to Tamworth.'

'I can assist with that...'

'You've done enough.' Enough to unsettle him. Enough to even at that moment make him want to pull her close again. Enough to make him kiss her again. He was so confused, and she had made him think clearly when he'd felt her pull away. Now he had to do it too. 'I'll email hospital admin when I get home and let them know to roster cover for you until eleven. It's not the entire day off, but it's a few extra hours' sleep. I arranged the same for the other staff before I left. And the neurosurgeon is flying in from Sydney mid-morning, to consult on the two suspected spinal cord injury patients.'

'You certainly have everything under control.'

'It's best for everyone that way.' Though Harrison knew he was losing control with Jessica. And that was not the best option for a man who had finally gained control of his life.

His tone had changed and he could see it hadn't gone unnoticed by Jessica. *Torn* best described how he felt. He didn't understand what he had seen in her eyes only moments before. It confused him. Her gorgeously messy blonde hair fell around her beautiful face and she looked less like an accomplished temporary Paediatric Consultant from a large city hospital and more like a fresh-faced country girl. She was so close he could reach out and cup her beautiful face in his hands and kiss her again.

He had to leave before he went mad with the gamut of emotions he was feeling.

Opening the door, he walked into the icy night air without stopping to put on his jacket.

Or saying goodnight.

CHAPTER SEVEN

JESSICA LAY IN BED, staring in the darkness at the ceiling, wondering what on earth had happened. And as she rolled onto her side again and curled her legs up under the warmth of the heavy woollen blankets, she wondered what could have happened if she hadn't pulled away. Gently her fingers pressed against her mouth and for a moment she relived the tenderness of his kiss. A kiss she hadn't imagined would ever happen until just before it did.

Standing so close, when he'd looked into her eyes, her body had rendered her helpless to think logically. To think that she should say no, move away and not give into her feelings. But instead she had surrendered to them. It concerned her that increasingly she was losing perspective and presence of mind around him.

Sleep evaded her for close to an hour, as nothing about her bed was comfortable that night. She tossed and turned all the while, questioning why she'd pushed away every promise she had made to herself about getting close to a man again. She had invited him in for a hot chocolate. And then gave him crumpets. What had she been thinking? And what had he been thinking to accept? And as he'd leant in towards her, she'd known he was going to kiss her. And she'd welcomed the kiss. What if he had wanted to stay longer? What would have happened? Would they have given in to their mutual desire? Or would they have come to their senses? So many questions and absolutely no certainty in the answers swirling about inside Jessica's head.

But one thing was for sure—nothing about the placement was going as planned. Not from the get-go with the lost luggage and then the dressing-down by Harrison. And why on earth would she be interested in a man who turned hot and cold like that? Jessica knew the answer. Because Harrison was like no one she had met before. He was a great doctor, a wonderful leader, an amazingly supportive friend to those who needed him most and... and now she knew he was capable of giving the most amazing kiss. The thought of it made her heart beat a little faster than it should.

She knew for certain that she must have gone mad as she rolled back onto her side, pulled the covers up around her ears and finally succumbed to a restless slumber. Dreams of Harrison's handsome chiselled face so close to hers...dreams of that fateful phone call from the woman whose cheating husband had been her lover...and finally dreams of drowning in a tidal wave that washed over Armidale but claimed only her.

Harrison woke early, showered and drove over to his parents' home to have breakfast at eight o'clock. He had managed to get five hours' sleep but, whether awake or drifting off to sleep, his mind was filled with thoughts of Jessica and the kiss they'd shared the night before... how good it felt to have her in his arms.

While wondering if perhaps everything was moving

too fast, he strongly doubted he could put the brakes on it now. And he wasn't sure if he would if he could.

'Daddy!'

Harrison scooped up the excited five-year-old in his arms and whizzed him around the huge country-style kitchen.

'Be careful,' Harrison's mother, Anthea, said sternly. 'You might break something.'

Harrison kissed the top of Bryce's head before he put him back down. 'We'd better listen to Granny or we'll both be in trouble.'

'That you will. I learnt that about forty years ago,' came a voice from the adjacent sun room.

'Morning, Dad.'

'Morning, Harrison,' his father said as he made his way into the kitchen, popped his newspaper on the bench, pulled out one of the oak chairs and sat down.

'How was Bryce last night? Did he behave and go to bed on time without any protest?'

'An angel, as always,' Anthea cut in, not waiting for her husband to answer as she put a stack of freshly made waffles on the table. There was already butter, jam and cream to be dolloped on the waffles, along with a plate of fresh fruit. She looked at Harrison and Bryce and continued, 'Please, sit down, Harrison, and eat up while I get showered and dressed.'

Harrison sat down and looked over the breakfast spread. 'It's amazing, Mum, but honestly oatmeal would have been enough. You do too much.'

'Don't be ridiculous, Harrison. Bryce loves Granny's waffles. Don't you?' she asked, looking at the little boy.

'I love them!' Bryce answered as he reached for one of the golden-brown breakfast treats.

'Clearly my time spent cooking was justified.' With that, Anthea untied her apron, draped it over an empty chair at the kitchen table and exited the room.

Harrison and his father, David, both shook their heads. There was no point arguing with a doting grandmother.

'So, everything went okay last night?' Harrison asked as he reached for a waffle too. He passed on the jam and cream, instead layering slices of the fresh fruit. He rarely ate an unhealthy breakfast but he didn't want to hurt his mother's feelings and decline the waffle.

'Why do you ask?'

'I just want to know you're okay with it. I mean, if it gets too much having Bryce overnight, let me know.' Harrison's voice was lowered and Bryce was concentrating on the cartoons he could see on the television in the other room and paying little attention to the adult conversation.

'As if he would ever be too much,' David scoffed.

'He'll be back again tonight because of the hospital fund-raising gala at the Art Museum and I don't want you missing out on sleep.'

'We absolutely love having him over and we're looking forward to having him again tonight, even if I lose every game of Go Fish. But he did complain a little about a pain in his tummy before he went to bed. Although he seems fine this morning so it's probably nothing.'

Harrison turned immediately to face his son and bring him back in the chat. 'How are you feeling now, Bryce? Grandpa said you had a tummy ache last night.'

'I did but my tummy doesn't hurt now,' he replied as he spread strawberry jam on a second waffle and turned his attention back to the cartoons.

Harrison looked over at his father. 'By his appetite, I'd say he's okay but I'll take a look at him tonight. Please call me if the stomach ache comes back. It might be a bit of residual anxiety from me being away,' Harrison said, looking from his son and then to his watch before standing and taking his plate to the sink. 'I'd better head in; we had multiple injuries from a bus accident late yesterday and a few are transferring to Tamworth today.'

'Are you going, Daddy?' Bryce asked.

'Yes, I need to go into the hospital. Granny's taking you to school.'

'Will you pick me up?' the little boy continued with an expectant look on his face, his big blue eyes the exact hue of his father's.

'Yes.'

'Yippee.'

'And we'll have a few hours together then I'll need to head out to a party tonight for the hospital, so you will spend another night with Granny and Grandpa.'

'Are you going to a birthday party? Will there be a clown and cake and stuff? Can I come too?'

Harrison smiled. 'No, there won't be cake or clowns and there definitely won't be a bouncy castle. This is a special party where we will talk a lot and raise money to help the hospital to buy new machines to keep people healthy, so I think it would be more fun for you with Granny and Grandpa.'

Bryce tilted his head on one side. 'Okay.'

'But I need you to tell Granny or Grandpa if your tummy starts to hurt again.'

'Okay.'

Harrison kissed his son, put his dishes in the dishwasher and bid farewell to his father. 'I'm sure he's okay but please just keep an eye on him this evening.'

'Will do.'

* * *

Jessica arrived in time to check in on the last three patients still waiting to be transported to their home town. They had improved overnight and she felt confident that after their transfer all three would be released from Tamworth Hospital within days. The two most seriously injured boys, one of whom had the suspected spinal cord injury, had been admitted to Armidale Regional Memorial, along with four other children whose families preferred that they remained in Armidale until they were well enough to be released. They either worked or had family in the town so preferred the children didn't leave hospital until they were completely healed.

Jessica couldn't see Harrison anywhere, which suited her. It had ended awkwardly the night before and, despite a restless night and mixed feelings, she wondered on the short drive to the hospital whether the yawn had been a sign from the universe that the kiss should never have happened. But it had, and she wondered if it would or could stop there. With that thought firmly in her mind, no clue where Harrison was and a decision to keep her distance until she knew how she felt, she headed up to ICU to check on the two boys' progress.

'I can see their vitals are stable. How did they go with pain during the night?' Jessica asked the ICU nurse attending to the boys. The hospital had eleven specialist departments but these did not include a Spinal Injuries Unit so the young patients had been transferred to the Intensive Care Unit rather than Paediatrics. Their injuries were still critical and the monitoring requirements were more aligned to ICU.

'Stable, nothing to worry us during the night,' the nurse replied as she checked the intravenous fluid flow on the patient with the head injury and fractured legs. 'They're on IV pain relief and Dr Jeffries, the neurosurgeon, should arrive here from Sydney within the hour.'

'So still no feeling or movement in the limbs of the C1-C2 vertebrae injured patient?'

The nurse shook her head.

Jessica nodded knowingly but said nothing. It was not going to be an easy road ahead for the young boy or his family if the damage was permanent. Jessica was relieved that the neurosurgeon was on his way. He would at least provide clarity for the family on the next steps.

She returned to Paediatrics and checked in on her patients, all of whom were progressing well and there were thankfully no changes. Four of the children from the bus accident had been admitted and she intended on keeping them for one more day. Suddenly she realised it was Friday and, while she would stay on until late that night, she wasn't rostered on over the weekend. She was on call for emergencies but not physically in the hospital. What was there for her to do in country New South Wales on a weekend? she wondered.

The movies? Dinner? Or stay in and watch cable television? All sounded fine to her, as did sleeping in again for two days. It had been a very busy week and the night before had been exhausting and then confusing so she was relieved that she would have two days to do whatever she wanted and potentially nothing.

'Dr Ayers,' Rosie called as Jessica walked past the administration desk.

'Yes, Rosie?'

'Are you going to the hospital fund-raiser tonight?'

'No, I haven't heard anything about a fund-raiser.'

'I thought you might not know,' the nurse replied,

walking out from behind the desk. 'It's quite a swanky affair at the NERAM. It's to raise funds for the Renal Dialysis Unit. A very worthwhile cause.'

'The NERAM?'

'The New England Region Art Museum; it's lovely and not far from here. Five minutes and loads of parking.'

Jessica smiled and nodded. Rosie was doing her best sales pitch and that didn't go unnoticed by Jessica. 'It certainly is a very worthwhile cause but I didn't start work until almost eleven this morning so I'm not about to leave early to attend an event, besides which I don't have a ticket.'

'The ticket's not a problem. I'm on the social committee and there's still a few remaining tickets so, if you can get the evening off, then I can arrange a ticket.'

'I don't think so. I should be here at the hospital as I'm sure a lot of the hospital staff will be at the event.'

'As they will, my dear, and you're one of them,' a male voice told her.

Jessica turned to see Professor Langridge standing behind her, waving an envelope in his hand. 'Your ticket for tonight's shindig. I should have given this to you on your first day. My apologies. My wife reprimanded me for not giving it to you before now, so you had advance notice. It's apparently a woman thing, to plan what you're going to wear.'

'Professor, its lovely to see you but I really can't take time off. I've only been here for a couple of hours...'

'And a sixteen-hour day yesterday,' he countered. 'I don't know how hard they work you in the big cities, but in this town you get time off after a day like that. We like to keep our doctors alive and well and it's important that you have a work life balance here. Besides, I'd like you to come along and get to meet the other staff you haven't managed to catch up with yet.'

'Oh, I don't know, and to be honest I'm not sure I've brought anything suitable to wear to a charity fund-raiser.'

'Dr Ayers, it's a country fund-raiser; we've got no Royal family members coming along,' Rosie piped up with a smile. 'So, nothing too formal—just a nice dress or suit would be fine.'

Just not jeans and runners, Jessica thought to herself, while acknowledging that no one had so much as muttered a word about her inappropriate clothes. They all really had accepted her as she arrived with no questions asked. The judgement was all hers. She wondered if that extended to other parts of her life. Was she perhaps her own harshest critic? She wasn't sure but she was beginning to think she should relax a little more and just enjoy the country life while she was there.

'Then it's set,' the Professor remarked as he put the envelope on the desk, tapping her name in bold print on the front with his fingers. 'I'll see you there tonight. You can meet my lovely wife and it'll be a good chance to mingle out of scrubs…and, oh, I can arrange a second ticket if you'd like to bring someone.'

Jessica surrendered on the spot. There was no point fighting both of them. She was attending the fund-raiser; that had been settled.

'Thank you, Errol. One ticket is enough. I don't have anyone to bring.'

Jessica worked until a quarter past six. The fund-raiser wasn't until seven-thirty and she wasn't going to be held up in either traffic leaving work or driving to the event at the Museum, only five minutes from home. The convenience of living in the town was starting to grow on Jessica. There was no horrible commute, an extremely friendly bunch of work colleagues and genuine community spirit and, apart from the fleeting belief she was being car-jacked the night before, she felt very safe.

She was glad she hadn't bumped into Harrison all day. It suited her because what had happened worried her.

The kiss had changed everything. It had changed how she felt about getting that close to someone…or where it might lead. He was a single, eligible doctor but was she ready to take it further? She couldn't have been more confused.

Arriving home, she turned on the central heating and made herself a cup of tea and a piece of toast topped with tomato and cheese. Quite often with cocktail parties, the food, while delicious, was difficult to manage along with multiple conversations so she wanted something in her stomach. Jessica wasn't a big drinker but even one glass of wine on an empty stomach never ended well.

With a plate of comfort food in one hand and her cup of tea in the other, she made her way into her bedroom to select a suitable outfit for the event. She had unpacked her suitcase the morning after her first shift and, with everything now hanging in plain sight, she was grateful to see that she had brought her little black winter dress. It was fine wool, with a high collar, long sleeves and skimmed her knees. And being such a quality fabric, it wasn't creased. She found a pair of high black patent court shoes, a small clutch bag and sheer black hosiery. And the look was definitely not flirtatious. Quite the opposite. If there was a name for the style it would be *chic convent*.

With everything laid out on her bed, Jessica stepped into a steaming shower. It felt good to have the hot water wash over her and she silently admitted that a warm sofa and a good movie would have been her perfect evening and given her time to process what had happened the night before but, thanks to Errol and Rosie, she was not to be a master of her own destiny that night.

'It's great that you could make it,' Errol Langridge commented as he met Jessica entering the room, already buzzing with people and conversations. She had dropped her large caramel-coloured winter overcoat at the coat check at the entrance to the Art Museum.

'It was a bit of a surprise but I'm so glad to be here and it's such a worthwhile cause.' As Jessica looked around the museum, which was brimming with artefacts, she realised that it was far better being there than alone at home with a movie. She had plenty of time to do solo nights when she left Armidale.

'And please let me introduce you to my wife. Jessica, this is Grace…and Grace, darling, this is Dr Jessica Ayers, our locum paediatrician who, by all accounts, and I do mean all accounts, is doing a wonderful job.'

'Pleased to meet you,' Jessica said, extending her hand to Grace Langridge. She guessed the pretty woman to be in her early sixties; she had short blonde hair and was wearing an elegant navy dress that skimmed her knees. A single strand of freshwater pearls adorned her neck and she wore matching earrings.

'Lovely to meet you too, Jessica,' Grace replied.

'And thank you, Errol. I'm thoroughly enjoying my

time here; you have such amazing staff and facilities and the final selling point of this placement is the drive to work every day; it's a dream,' Jessica laughed.

'Talking about placements, I thought I should warn you, young lady, we may try to keep you on staff. And there's more than one of your colleagues who would like to see that happen,' the Professor remarked as he took a glass of champagne from the tray being circulated by smartly dressed hospitality staff and handed it to his wife. 'Would you like some champagne, Jessica?'

Jessica nodded and Errol handed her a long-stemmed glass of bubbles, complete with a strawberry dressing the rim.

'Speaking of your fan club, Dr Ayers, the unabashed leader of it just arrived.'

Jessica turned around to see Harrison in the doorway. He took her breath away in his charcoal-grey suit, crisp white shirt and dark patterned tie. And perfect wide smile as he acknowledged one by one people he knew in the room.

He was the leader of her fan club?

She turned back, hoping she wasn't too obviously flushed. She could feel her cheeks warming and she hoped he continued to greet everyone individually, giving her cheeks time to calm down.

'Champagne does turn my cheeks rosy,' she mumbled to Grace and smiled a strained half smile.

'I can't see it, my dear, but then at your age a rosy glow would only make you look even more beautiful. I remember back to being as young as you when I met Errol.'

'Are you from the Armidale New England region or did you both move here?'

'Errol is actually from Uralla, a little town not far

from here. He studied medicine in Sydney and returned to Armidale Regional Memorial as an intern a long time ago. I was in my third year of practice at a leading physiotherapy clinic in Melbourne. Goodness, I loved it and planned on opening my own clinic by the time I reached thirty. I was a city girl with city dreams and then I met a country boy when I was having an evening out with some girlfriends. Errol was in town for a conference. In one night he turned my life completely upside down. In a matter of weeks, I literally gave up everything and moved here.'

'Wow. That is quite a whirlwind romance. I thought that only happened in movies and books.' Jessica was taken aback by Grace's story.

'Yes, it was a wow moment.' She dropped her voice a little, took a sip of her champagne and added, 'My friends and family thought I was completely mad and I must admit I had a few misgivings myself along the way, particularly in the lead up to the move, but once I settled in I couldn't imagine my life anywhere else. I'm truly blessed, Jessica, to have met Errol. He's my soulmate.'

'Well, you certainly took a huge risk and I'm so happy that it worked out so wonderfully for you. I couldn't leave everything for a man I barely knew.'

Grace patted her hand. 'You would for the right man.'

'Ah, Harrison, so good to see you here,' Errol announced as he took a glass of red wine from the waiter circulating with a tray of red and white wines then whispered to Jessica, 'I was wondering when the good stuff would come out; I'm not a bubbles and strawberries kind of man.'

Jessica smiled at Errol's remark but her mind was elsewhere. She suddenly wished she was at home on the sofa with a movie and didn't have to face her own feelings. Feelings that were confusing and scaring her in equal amounts. And all of them about Harrison.

Harrison approached the trio and greeted Errol with a firm handshake, then Grace with an endearing kiss on the cheek. Jessica's stomach did a somersault, wondering how he would greet her. She shifted anxiously on her stilettos and took a gulp of her champagne. Would it be a colleague's handshake, a nod or…? Suddenly her answer came as he stepped forward and gently kissed her on the cheek. A tender kiss that allowed her to feel the softness of his skin as it brushed against hers and for the freshness of his woody cologne to fill her senses. Making her body feel alive with little effort. Just as he had the night before.

'Hello, Jessica.'

'Hello, Harrison.'

Time disappeared for the briefest moment as he stepped back and their eyes locked. The room was empty except for them. She could feel her heart beating and felt herself struggling to breathe. She had to pull herself back from falling into something that scared her to the core so she hurriedly took another sip of her champagne.

'You look gorgeous, Jessica, as do you, Grace.'

'I know,' Errol cut in before the ladies could respond. 'We've certainly got the finest fillies in the room.'

Grace gave a delicate laugh. 'No amount of time spent visiting my family or his many, many years studying in Sydney will take the country boy out of my husband.'

'And would you really want that, darling?'

'Not in a million years.'

Jessica watched as Errol lifted his wife's hand in his, tenderly kissing it as he looked into her eyes. 'And I would not change anything about you, my city born and bred wife either.'

'Would you like to try some kangaroo and salt bush canapés?' a young waiter interrupted as he held out a platter of the tasty delicacies.

'Sounds delicious,' Grace said as she reached for one, as did her husband. 'I've not tried salt bush.'

Harrison looked over at Jessica and again she felt her pulse quickening. 'I'm game to try something new tonight, if you are, Jessica?'

The blue of his eyes seemed to be sparkling even more brightly and she felt drawn in like a moth to a light.

'I've eaten native bush food quite a bit. There's a stall in the market not far from one of the hospitals where I had a placement four months ago and the Indigenous owners have tastings of different herbs and meat. They also tell you how to prepare them at home.' Jessica reached for one of the tiny wafers, dressed with a thin roll of kangaroo and a sprig of salt bush. She took a bite, knowing she would love the salty tang of the greenery and the depth of flavour of the kangaroo.

She watched as Harrison downed the small cracker in one mouthful and waited for his reaction, wondering if he would enjoy it as much as she had.

'That was amazing. Would it be rude to ask for a second?' Harrison enquired of the waiter still hovering near them.

'Not at all. That's why I always wait,' the man said with a smile. 'Because everyone wants more of these.'

The four all accepted the young man's offer and each reached for a second, before Errol and Grace excused themselves to mingle with the other guests, leaving Harrison and Jessica alone.

'You constantly surprise me,' Harrison remarked as he leant against the wall with his glass of red wine.

Jessica dabbed her mouth with a cocktail napkin before taking the final sip of her drink. While she always had a two-drink limit for an entire night, her Dutch courage suddenly needed refilling and her eyes searched the room for a waitress with white wine or something bubbly. 'How so?'

'A city girl who likes bush tucker and knows how to cook it. That's a skill not many would have, whether living in the city or the country. I wouldn't have a clue how to prepare food of Indigenous origins. Maybe I could throw a crocodile sausage on the grill but that would be my limit.'

Jessica laughed. 'I guess deep down I'm pretty much a homebody who loves cooking and it's not very difficult if you are taught by people who have worked with this food for a long time,' she said, trying to mask her borderline nervousness being around him. She found it hard to forget that in the early hours of that day they had kissed. And, more importantly, why they had kissed.

And why, if left alone, they might again.

Harrison broke into her thoughts. 'There's a lot of layers to you, Jessica.'

'I'm not that complex really,' she replied, grateful that he couldn't read her mind or feel her pulse as it was racing.

'I disagree, but how about I get you another champagne and, before the auction begins, show you around the museum, introduce you to some of the hospital staff you may not have met, and enlighten you to some local New England history in an attempt to impress you?'

Jessica found it so strange that Harrison was apparently oblivious to the fact that he had impressed her many times since their first accidental meeting.

Probably most of all when he'd pulled her close and kissed her.

Willingly she allowed him to escort her around the Art Museum and they stopped to greet some of the staff and their respective partners along the way. Harrison soon proved with little effort that he knew a great deal about the artworks and the history of the region. Jessica was at once enjoying her time with Harrison and quickly found herself less and less self-conscious in his presence. Their banter was light and easy and occasionally she felt his hand in the middle of her back as he guided her through the small groups to another piece of artwork. She leant into it and enjoyed the feeling. It made her feel as if she had someone taking care of her, if only for a short while, and it felt good. His attentiveness wasn't forced. Nor was her appreciation of him.

The auction, and the reason they had all come together, finally began. Harrison bid for the third item, a four-night Sydney getaway at one of the finest hotels with flights included, that had been generously donated by the local travel agent. Jessica watched on keenly as the ten bidders were knocked out one by one. Finally, there were two left and Harrison was the one with the leading bid.

'I'm bid ten thousand dollars,' the auctioneer announced. 'Does anyone care to raise that?'

'Ten thousand five hundred,' the other bidder announced with a confident tone. Jessica could see it was all done in good fun, for a good cause, but there was some old-fashioned male rivalry helping to get the bids up.

'Fifteen thousand,' Harrison announced. 'Just so we can get on with the next item.'

The crowd laughed, including the other bidder. 'Fair call,' he said. 'It has been dragging on a bit. It's all yours, Harrison. I'm out.'

The auctioneer called the bid and announced Harrison the winner. He approached the administrator for the night and gave him his credit card details to pay for the item. Then he returned to Jessica and slipped the envelope inside his suit jacket. 'Since I don't know anyone in Sydney, and you know it very well, I might be calling on you to show me around.'

Jessica was speechless. Had he bid an extraordinary amount just to spend time with her? The way he was looking at her, she very much suspected that was the case. Perhaps the kiss they'd shared did mean something more to him.

Jessica wasn't sure about anything except she was growing closer to the man standing next to her by the minute. He was everything she was not looking for when she'd flown into Armidale...but now she felt he was everything she knew she wanted.

'It's only eight-thirty, so not overly late, and I was wondering if you might like to go back to my house and chat some more without that auctioneer's voice drowning us out?'

Jessica drew breath. Her heart was racing at a ridiculous pace. She couldn't think of anything better... or riskier than being alone with Harrison. And that excited her.

'Let's claim our overcoats and exit. Is your car outside?'

'Yes.'

'If you're happy to follow me in your car, my home is literally walking distance from here.'

* * *

Harrison's home was, as he'd said, only three minutes from the Art Museum. It was a large two-storey redbrick home with a sweeping return driveway and beautifully manicured gardens. Jessica was taken aback by the size and grandeur. As she'd not yet driven past that part of the town, she had not seen it before. Harrison pulled his car into the large double garage and walked over to Jessica as she alighted from her car in front of the porch, where she saw an old-style wicker set including a double swing.

It was picture-postcard-perfect and so was Harrison.

'Let's get you inside where it's warmer than out here,' he said, taking her hand, and she felt certain that he intended to take things further than simply repaying her hospitality. She wasn't sure but, with her heart beating so fast, this time she had no intention of pulling away. This time she wanted to forget the past.

She wanted to live in the moment and throw everything else, including logic, out of her mind.

Harrison knew where he wanted to take the evening. He had grown close to Jessica very quickly but his feelings were real. And by the way she was reacting to him, he suspected she felt the same way. He hoped that the night would grow into something more. Suddenly and without reservation he wanted and felt ready to open his heart and his life to the mysterious woman who had arrived without warning. And very soon he planned that Bryce would meet the most amazing woman Harrison had ever laid eyes upon.

He turned on the dim lights and, without hesitation, lifted Jessica's hand to his lips and kissed the inside of her wrist. She was trembling just a little with anticipation, not fear. Tenderly his fingers traced the soft line of her jaw until he reached her chin. Purposefully, he lifted her face to his and his eyes told her everything she needed to know. He wanted her as much as she wanted him.

'I want more than anything to kiss you again. You must know that.'

Jessica nodded and lifted her face towards him. His mouth met hers this time with an urgency she had never felt in any man's kiss before. She met his passion and made it clear that not only her mouth was wanting to be claimed. She was his for the night.

'Are you sure, absolutely sure?' His voice was low and the look in his eyes was piercing her soul.

Jessica nodded and breathlessly she told him, 'Yes.'

'No second thoughts?'

'None.'

Harrison wasn't going to ask again. He didn't need further confirmation that he was not alone in his desire to spend the night together. He didn't need any more encouragement to take her. To make her his own.

He bent his knees slightly to reach around her body and lift her into his embrace. His lips searched for hers again and he hoped the fire in his kiss told Jessica how he was feeling as he carried her into his bedroom then softly but purposely kicked the door closed behind them. This night was for the two of them and nothing and no one was going to take that away from them. No one was going to make him turn away from the most desirable woman he had ever met in his life.

There were many hours until the sun rose and Harrison intended to make use of each and every one of them.

* * *

Harrison woke with Jessica in his arms, her blonde hair flowing over his bare chest and the feeling of her warm soft breath on his skin as she slept soundly snuggled next to him. He didn't want that feeling to end. It was as if an angel had entered his life. An angel he'd never expected to meet.

Suddenly he noticed his cell phone light up. Concerned that it might be the hospital, he slipped from the warm bed and took his phone to the en suite bathroom. He didn't want to disturb Jessica if he needed to make an urgent call. He closed the door and opened the email icon and was instantly jolted into a reality he didn't expect or want.

Hi Harrison,

As you're a board member, I thought you should know that I just had a courtesy call from a colleague at the Eastern Memorial in Adelaide. Jessica was supposed to take on a locum role in six weeks' time, but it appears they are going to offer her the role of Acting Head of Paediatrics with a view to ongoing, providing she's happy to start in one week's time. Sad to be losing her, but a huge opportunity for her in a hospital of that size. I guess we can't compete with that. We'll need to get a replacement as soon as possible.

All the best, Errol

Harrison froze. Jessica would be leaving much sooner than expected. Perhaps, if they'd been able to spend the full six weeks together, they might have been able to see where this was going, might have been able to lay down the foundations of something that had a future. But one week? Impossible. It was a done deal. She would not and should not decline the offer from a large teaching hospital. While Adelaide wasn't the other side of the world, he was a realist. With Jessica's new role, and with his workload and, more importantly, his son, the opportunity to progress their relationship to something more, something deeper didn't exist. And he didn't want to risk it. He wasn't about to make it more and then have it end. That would be dragging out the inevitable and he feared, with a woman like Jessica, he would only grow closer with every minute he spent with her.

Their connection was destined to be one night only and Harrison had no choice but to accept it.

He stepped into the shower, turned on the tap and let the hot water wash over him as he tried to erase the night before. He wanted more than anything to fall back into bed and make love to Jessica again, but he couldn't. She was perfect in almost every way. But one. She wasn't staying in town. And he didn't want to ask her to do it. He had no right to hold her back. He had to treat what they'd shared the night before as something casual. He couldn't let his heart lead his head again.

Jessica's early morning yawn morphed into a wide smile that she couldn't suppress. She stretched in the warmth of the king-sized bed, lifting her arms above her head, arching her back and pointing her toes. It was the most delicious feeling and she couldn't remember feeling that happy. Her mind drifted back to the tenderness and warmth in Harrison's kiss. Her eyes wrinkled softly as her naked skin brushed against the sheets and she remembered the way he had brought every inch of her body to life.

She slid back under the covers, relishing the passion they had shared. Tingles spread over her body with the thought of his body bringing her such guilty pleasure. With a satisfied Cheshire cat grin, she thought back over the last week. So much had happened and, while not all of it appeared to be positive initially, the pendulum had swung back and with it brought so much more joy into her life than she'd thought possible. Harrison, she decided, was the type of man she could potentially fall hopelessly in love with and, surprisingly for her, she wasn't scared of those feelings. A few months ago she would have been so frightened she would have bolted from his bed, his home and, more than likely, the town if she had thought for a moment that she was developing feelings on any level for a man.

But Harrison had somehow changed that. Jessica wasn't sure how it had happened but he had made her feel safe enough to let down her guard and she wondered if, in the process, she might have found her knight in shining armour. She was definitely looking forward to a lot more nights with the country doctor.

And who knew what the future might bring? She thought back to the night before and what the Professor's wife had said about giving up the city life she knew for one in the country. Was that something Jessica could do? She wasn't sure but, the way she was feeling at that moment, she wasn't ruling it out either.

Jessica reminded herself there were still barriers to overcome. Did the country doctor need his heart mended just as much as she did or was his intact? Perhaps she didn't need to know it all. Not at first, at least, but she felt sure this time she wasn't falling for a man who would break her heart the way it had been broken before.

It had been the most amazing night. Ever. Harrison was the most wonderful lover. Giving and tender, yet demanding and strong. He was as complex in bed as he was out of it and that excited her. The night had been so special, so wonderful and she didn't want to allow anything to spoil it. Not the sadness of her past or question marks hanging over the future. She wanted to enjoy whatever it was they had right now and not block out what also might be.

Harrison had slipped from the bed before Jessica had woken. She could hear the shower running and suddenly felt a little disappointed that he hadn't remained in bed. Waking in his arms and making love again would have made the morning as perfect as the night had been, but she knew he was rostered on at the hospital so it was understandable. She hoped she would wake up the next morning in his bed and that he would stay in it with her for many hours.

Quickly but reluctantly, Jessica climbed from the warm, delightfully crumpled bed and gathered her underwear, hosiery and her dress, strewn over the highly polished floors. One by one she picked up the pieces. She would shower at home as she liked the scent of his skin on hers and wasn't in a hurry to wash him away.

'I'm sorry I had to get up but I need to get to work… and I have a stop to make before that.'

Jessica turned to find Harrison standing in the doorway, a plush grey towel hanging low on his hips. Dangerously low. In the soft hue of the morning light his chiselled chest made him look larger than life. Like a Greek statue. Carved and bronze and perfect. It took all of her self-control not to remove her clothes and suggest he call in sick so they could remain under the covers for another few hours.

'I understand completely,' she told him as she averted her eyes and, showing a great deal of restraint, stepped into her dress, the last piece of her clothing that had been thrown across the room the night before. She wasn't sure what he'd meant by *a stop to make before that*. Perhaps he had a patient home visit.

All things considered, she thought as she looked down at her outfit from the night before, she wasn't as dishevelled as she could and should have been. With any luck, her walk of shame might not be noticed by the neighbours after all.

'I wish I could ask you to stay but I have to...'

'Work, I know,' she said, cutting in nervously. Suddenly what they had shared seemed a lifetime ago. In a perfect world he would scoop her up and lay her on the bed and kiss her and tell her that he was falling madly in love with her. But they didn't live in a perfect world. 'It's all good. I have a million things to do today so I need to leave anyway.'

'Last night was great.'

'Yes, it was,' Jessica agreed, suddenly feeling uneasy about the tone of his voice. In the light of day, she sensed that Harrison wanted to put some distance between them. Both emotionally and physically. Perhaps the early morning shower was his way of breaking their intimacy. Waking in each other's arms would have put a very different slant on the situation. He looked ill-at-ease and she sensed it had nothing to do with his nakedness.

His behaviour confused her. He'd been so very certain about everything the night before. He'd been in command and now he looked unsure. She felt a little sick in the stomach by his sudden need to detach.

'I think you're amazing, Jessica,' he began, breaking the strained moment of silence but not bridging the gap she now felt between them.

Jessica felt her heart sink. Only moments before, she had believed she was teetering on something close to falling in love with him but she feared that was not how he saw the situation. She had wanted him so badly that it frightened her and she had let down her guard, only to have him almost disregard it.

'Would you like breakfast or coffee?' he asked as he crossed to his wardrobe. 'I can make you some scrambled eggs once I'm dressed.'

Jessica drew a breath, trying to calm her emotions. She felt a stab of painful awareness. Was she the only one thinking past one night together?

'I think I might leave now,' she said hastily as she felt a tightness in her chest.

'Okay,' he agreed as he laid his clothes on the bed and began dressing. Within moments he donned dark blue jeans, a warm checked shirt and bulky camel sweater.

Jessica had never seen a man dress so quickly. Not that she had seen a man get dressed after a one-night stand as it wasn't something she had done before, but the process did seem hurried. And extremely awkward, considering only hours before that she'd been naked in his bed.

'I'll see you at the hospital on Monday then?' she asked, hoping that he would ask to see her that night. If he did then she would know that she was reading the situation incorrectly. She wanted with all her heart to be proved wrong. So she gave him the opportunity to invite her over again.

'Yes, of course,' he replied. 'I'll see you Monday.'

She was mortified. Her reading was correct.

She'd hoped he might try to convince her to stay but he didn't. He was letting her walk away. She suddenly felt very empty. Even more empty than before she'd slept with him. Before she'd met him. And, unfortunately, those feelings told her that she had given at least a small piece of her heart to him. She'd hoped he deserved it but she was beginning to think perhaps he didn't. She wished it didn't cause an ache inside her, to be walking away from the night they'd shared with no promise of another.

The pain was growing by the minute and heightened as he walked her to the front door. The very place he had first kissed her the night before. The passion in his first kiss, the way he'd carried her into his bedroom and the love they made… It was all gone. He was letting her walk away as if it meant nothing.

What they'd shared was just a one-night stand after all. She hadn't thought that was all it would be as she had lain in his arms but perhaps that was just what he did—made a woman feel there was more without saying it—and perhaps it was unintentional. She was confused and felt let down. She knew she had no right to expect more, Harrison had not promised more, but it still felt wrong to be almost asked to leave.

Was she missing something? Was there something about Harrison she didn't know? She wasn't sure but she was teetering on something close to heartbreak and she didn't need another heartbreak. It didn't take long for Jessica to realise that spending the night with him was quite possibly the biggest mistake she had made in a very long time.

Harrison turned to her as he unlocked the front door. His eyes were filled with emotion that Jessica couldn't define.

'I'll always think of last night as special.'

Jessica couldn't find any words to say. She was just trying to hold back tears that were welling deep inside and threatening to spill onto her cheeks.

'I know you're not planning on staying in town and, believe me, I wouldn't expect or ask you to change your plans, based on one night together. I just want you to know that I think you're an amazing woman, Jessica. Any man would be fortunate to have you in his life. I'm truly sorry the way our lives are destined to be, and that it can't be me.'

CHAPTER EIGHT

JESSICA DROVE HOME in shock. Afterwards, she couldn't remember leaving Harrison's house or driving the short distance to her own rental home. She shouldn't have been on the road, she realised, when she arrived at her door. Her mind was a fog and she had driven in a complete daze. There had been no one on the road and perhaps that was why the drive was so forgettable or perhaps it was because she was so preoccupied with thoughts of the man who had just ended something between them before it had a chance.

She was angry, and sad, and confused and blindsided and...a dozen different emotions she didn't know she could feel. All of them caused by Harrison Wainwright. Why the hell had he invited her home? Was it just to spend one night together? Had he planned all along to kiss her goodbye in the morning for no good reason? Walk her to the door and not want to see her again?

And then to give her a line if translated into Italian would be worthy of a place in an opera. Or at the very least a soap opera. *Any man would be fortunate to have you in his life... I'm truly sorry...it can't be mè.* Who said that? And why? And what did he mean by *the way our lives are destined to be*?

His parting words were coming back to her in a jumbled mess. Her mind was racing at a million miles an hour as she threw her overcoat on the sofa and unzipped her dress and stepped out of it and tossed it on top of her discarded coat before she made her way to the bathroom.

The house was as cold as ice but her blood was boiling as she thought back over their conversations. She wanted to wash any trace of the man from her skin—the scent of his cologne, the scent of his body, she wanted none of it. She turned on the shower and stepped into the steaming water and scrubbed her body with a loofah. All the while she pushed visions of Harrison from her mind and tried to erase the feeling of his arms around her. She couldn't trust that, but the ache in her heart was more real than she cared to admit.

What had gone wrong? Was he really just another bad man? And was she a magnet for men who thought nothing further than how she could meet their own desires?

Or was it her? Was it the barriers she had up when they'd first met? Surely when she was lying in Harrison's bed he would have known the barriers were down. All of them. She reached for the shampoo and, putting her head under the running water, began to wash her hair. His cologne was in her hair and she wanted nothing to remind her of him, nothing to unexpectedly take her back to the hours they'd spent together. Her life felt as if it was unravelling again. The very reason why she'd promised herself not to get involved. She had sworn off men for a very good reason.

Suddenly she thought back to when she'd mentioned she wasn't the marrying kind to Harrison that first day at the hospital. Perhaps she'd made him think she was the one-night stand type with the whole, *I'm not a picket fence kind of woman* statement? But then, the way Rachel Naughton spoke about him, as the doting godfather of her daughter, he was a man who needed a good woman to share his life with. That was not close to a description of the man who'd as good as told her to leave his house the morning after seducing her.

Jessica was close to going mad. She had woken a happy woman, luxuriating in the feeling of what she and Harrison had shared the night before, and now, in the light of day, she was berating herself for going home with him. Maybe she should have taken it more slowly. Maybe she should have said no. Maybe they'd rushed into something that just as quickly had turned into nothing.

As she turned off the shower she told herself that the *maybes* had to stop—she was grasping at straws.

She had to accept they had shared a night. That was where it had started and that was where it would end.

She just had to find a way to erase it from her mind.

Her weekend was filled with thoughts that bounced from regret to acceptance and then back again. It involved a lot of ice cream and more than one call to Cassey, who consoled her and thankfully did not mention online dating as a solution. They made plans to catch up when Jessica was back in Sydney or Cassey made it over to Adelaide.

It was about ten o'clock on Sunday night when she received an email that she wasn't expecting, but one that inadvertently changed the course of her life, even before she received it. It was regarding the role at the Eastern Memorial Hospital in Adelaide. Not as the locum Paediatric Consultant as she had planned in a few weeks but, due to an unexpected resignation, offering the position of Acting Head of Paediatrics if Jessica was interested. There was an opportunity to trial the role for three months and then, if she was successful, the potential to be transitioned into the ongoing position. But the conditions were non-negotiable. She needed to be in Adelaide by Monday of the following week. There was no shifting the time line if she was to accept the position.

It was a role she had dreamed of for so many years and an offer she hadn't expected in her wildest dreams. While she should have been excited by the prospect of achieving a lifelong goal and the opportunities it brought, instead she read and reread the email and thought of it purely as an escape route. There was no elation. Her emotions were flatlined.

Ordinarily she would ask for more time so she could complete her current contract or at least give two weeks' notice, but now those terms more than suited her. Leaving a position with little warning was not what she liked to do and she hoped that Professor Langridge and the hospital Board would understand. What the Head of ER thought didn't matter in the slightest to her. He had not reached out for two days. There had been nothing from him. It was as if nothing had happened between them.

As much as she wanted to accept the new position immediately, Jessica decided to give Errol the courtesy of advising him of her plans in person the next day.

It was two in the afternoon before she could get in to see the Professor.

'I'm not going to lie; I'm very sad to see you go. We've been trying to secure funding to keep you on here, as everyone working with you is so thrilled to have had you on board and they've told me in person. You've made quite an impression with everyone in the space of a week.

Particularly with Harrison Wainwright. He's got to be your biggest fan and the keenest that you should be kept on board.'

Jessica shot the Professor a rueful look but said nothing. The irony of it all. The man who was her supposed biggest advocate was the one who'd hastened her decision to leave.

'In saying that, Harrison was quite adamant that we didn't force your hand or coerce you in any way. From day one, he wanted it to be your choice or not at all.'

Jessica was not buying into anything said by or about Harrison Wainwright. None of it held water in her mind any more and she put it out to the universe that if it could arrange for her to avoid seeing him or hearing his voice for the rest of the week, she would be very grateful.

'Well, again, I'm also sad in many ways but I have to think about my career at this stage in my life and the opportunity to be Head of Paediatrics in Adelaide is just too good to refuse.' *And a damn good exit strategy from Harrison*, she thought.

'It is an amazing opportunity,' came a voice from the doorway. A voice that Jessica recognised only too well. It was the voice of someone who had only a few nights before shared pillow talk with her. 'Too good to refuse, I agree.'

Jessica felt her heart sink, hearing his voice again.

'With your skills and mindset, Jessica, you were never destined to stay long in this town.' With that Harrison exited as quickly as he had appeared.

'A man of few words, our Harrison.'

Jessica didn't respond. In her opinion, Harrison could certainly say all the right words when it suited him.

'We have you on board until Friday then?' Errol asked with a hopeful lilt to his voice.

'I could make it six and work through until late Saturday if that would help? I can arrange flights and accommodation in Adelaide and fly to Sydney and then directly on to Adelaide on Sunday. I'm not starting there until Monday.'

'That's very good of you but certainly cutting it close.'

'Not at all. I'm truly sorry to be leaving early but, all things considered, it's for the best.'

Jessica left Errol's office feeling torn. Letting down the Board and Errol had never been in her plans but then neither was falling for the Head of ER and having her heart broken. All things taken into account, she was doing as well as she could to remain on for another six days. She hoped that Harrison would give her the space to do her job and leave with her dignity intact. She didn't want to tell him what she thought of him or ask for an explanation beyond the empty excuse he'd provided before she'd left his home because that would be letting him know how much he had come to mean to her in a very short space of time. And how she'd mistakenly thought she had come to mean something to him too.

The week passed by quickly. She sent her signed acceptance letter to Eastern Memorial and then organised her flights for the following Sunday morning. It was a nine o'clock flight from Armidale to Sydney with a two-hour layover and an eleven o'clock flight from Sydney to Adelaide. It wasn't difficult to secure an apartment close to the hospital, which meant she wouldn't need to organise a car as she could use public transport and cabs and look into purchasing a car later if needed.

Being organised felt good. Being in control of her destiny felt even better. While the idea of staying in one place was a little daunting after a year of moving around, there was the three-month trial period in the terms of the contract and that was reassuring to her. She might like being in one place, as long as that place was not near Harrison. And if she didn't like being settled, then she would decline the ongoing role and return to her no-madic existence.

It was her second to last day and she had visited all the staff to thank them, as many would not be on duty over the weekend. They had wanted to host a farewell after-noon tea but Jessica declined. While the sentiment was lovely, having to see Harrison at the event and receive his best wishes, or knowing that he might have chosen not to attend, would be far too awkward. And more than a little sad. She found a lovely scarf and beautiful card signed by many of the staff in her office on the Friday night, which she considered was too much for having only been there such a short time. She intended on sending a thank you note from Adelaide. Harrison's name was on the card but his message was brief and nothing could be read into it by anyone, including Jessica.

Walking to her car that night, Jessica felt so many mixed emotions, but predominantly sadness and a sense of loss. She had one more day before she turned her back on the town she knew she would never visit again.

'Jessica, wait.'

She turned to find Harrison standing only a few feet from her.

'I don't want it to end like this,' he told her.

Jessica stared at the man who had broken her heart—

and before she'd met him she hadn't even known her heart had mended enough to love again.

'How did you want it to end?'

'Not at all, to be honest, but I knew it had to.'

Jessica shook her head. She wasn't buying anything he was saying but she was confused why he had bothered to chase her down.

'You are bigger than this town. You deserve this opportunity in Adelaide.'

'Please don't tell me that you know what I deserve after what happened.'

'I did what I thought was best…'

'For yourself. One night with me and you were done. I stupidly thought that what we shared meant something…' she began and then stopped.

'It did but there was no point trying to make it something more. You were always going to leave.'

'I don't want to talk about it any more,' she said, holding back tears.

'No matter what you think now, I want you to understand before you go that the night we shared did mean something.'

'Sure,' she said as she turned and walked away. *But not enough to ask me to stay.*

It was just after ten the following evening. Jessica's last day in Armidale and she was watching television and thinking about heading to bed. The day had gone well. She had not seen Harrison and that brought both sadness and relief to her.

She had closed the chapter on what they had shared.

She looked over at her suitcase and carry-on bag; both were packed and she felt a sense of organisation coming back to her life. A nice pair of trousers, a shirt and jacket for the plane trip were hanging in her room for the trip. If the cases were lost again, she wouldn't be turning up in jeans and a jumper on her first day in Adelaide. She had learnt that lesson the hard way in Armidale. Along with another one. She would lock her heart away for ever.

Suddenly her phone vibrated on the table. She picked it up and saw it was the hospital. She wondered if she had left something there.

'Dr Ayers, it's Jane from ER.'

'Hello, Jane, is everything all right?'

'No, not really. We have a young boy who has presented at the hospital with suspected appendicitis. I'm sorry to bother you; I know you're no longer on staff and you're leaving Armidale tomorrow morning but this is an emergency.'

'Isn't Dr Wainwright on tonight in ER?'

'Yes.'

'Then I'm a little confused as to why you need me. I'm sure Dr Wainwright can handle the case. Unless he has a particularly heavy patient load this evening.'

'No, we've only got two other patients but he's asked me to call you, especially. He knows it's late but he's hoping you might be able to come in and assess the young boy. He said he can meet you in the car park so you don't walk in the dark alone.'

'Please tell him that I don't need him to meet me anywhere. But what I do need is to understand why I'm required. Are there complications? I need some context to this request.'

'I'll pass you on to Dr Wainwright…'

'No, don't do that,' Jessica cut in but it was too late. The last thing she wanted was to hear his voice before she went to bed. She didn't want to be kept awake by thoughts of him. She was doing her best to forget she'd ever laid eyes on him.

The nurse had handed the phone over. 'Jessica, it's Harrison.'

Jessica took a deep breath to steady her nerves. She hadn't thought she'd ever hear his voice again.

'Jessica, are you there?' he asked.

'Yes, Harrison; what's this about? It's late and I don't understand why I'm needed. You have enough experience with suspected appendicitis.'

'I have, Jessica, but this case is quite different. Believe me, I wouldn't be disturbing you if it wasn't urgent.'

'Why—what's different about this patient? Why can't you manage him with the resources you have?'

'Because…' Harrison began and paused '…because, Jessica, he's my son.'

Jessica was dumbfounded and almost dropped her phone. Harrison had a son? They had spoken at length and he'd never thought to mention he had a son? That was a significant piece of information to have kept to himself. Why had he hidden that from her? She felt sick to the stomach. How could she have got it all so wrong? She'd thought she knew him but she didn't know him at all. Why would he hide something so significant from her? He had chosen what he wanted to tell her and clearly kept a number of things to himself. Suddenly he was a father. Where was the child when she'd stayed over? God, how could she have been so stupid to fall for someone like him? Again, she had chosen a man who had lied to her by avoiding a hugely important detail about his life.

'Jessica?' Harrison's voice on the line brought her back

to his call. He needed something or, more accurately, his son did.

'Where was your son the other night?'

'At my parents'. They look after him when I...'

'Have women sleep over. So, what happened between us was premeditated on your part?' Jessica told him flatly.

'No, I didn't plan any of what happened between us... nor do I regret it.'

'Then that makes one of us, because I do,' she spat back angrily. 'And, while we're being honest, do you have a wife as well?'

Harrison did not reply to her question. There was nothing but a deafening silence on the line.

'Oh, my God, you do. You have a wife and a son!' She'd thought she couldn't feel worse than the morning she had left his home but she realised she could, because she suddenly did.

'Bryce's mother is overseas.'

'So that makes it okay to sleep with me? An ocean apart means what happened between us doesn't count?' Jessica felt her blood run cold. Harrison had a wife and he had the audacity to admit it now. It was Jessica's worst nightmare all over again. She felt herself spinning close to the edge and could barely breathe. 'I slept with a married man.' *Again.*

'Stop, please, Jessica; it's not like that. You didn't sleep with a married man. Bryce's mother lives overseas. We're only days away from the divorce being finalised.'

'I don't believe you.'

'It's true. I wouldn't lie to you.'

'Really? You never told me you had a son before now. You led me to believe you were single.'

'I'm a single father, Jessica. Well... I will be by next

week. You didn't sleep with a married man. You slept with a single father.'

'This is all getting too complicated,' she told him with her mind struggling to process everything she had heard. 'Even if it's true, why didn't you mention your son to me? There were plenty of opportunities.'

'I guess I was just protecting him.'

'You were protecting your son from a paediatrician?'

'I know that sounds ridiculous…'

'Because it is.'

Harrison hesitated again. 'I had my reasons, maybe stupid ones, but…'

'Don't go there,' she said angrily. 'Let it go. I'm past it, Harrison.'

'I will go there later. I'm not letting you think that any of what I did or said or didn't say was about you. It was me and I'm trying to let go of the past, I really am.'

Jessica was still not convinced. 'Please just tell me what you want.'

Harrison drew a breath. 'My son is in the ER now. I need a second opinion from a doctor of your calibre. Believe me, I didn't want to put this pressure on you but you're the best doctor I know. I'm worried.'

'There's really no point us talking about this…'

'Please, Jessica.'

'I mean there's no point us talking because I'm on my way…but, just so you know, I'm doing this for your son, not you.' With that, Jessica hung up and grabbed her car keys and overcoat. Despite how she felt about Harrison, she would be there for his son.

Harrison was waiting in the dark car park for her but she chose to ignore any recognition of chivalry, asking only for the cold hard facts about his son's condition. There was nothing more between them.

'Thank you for coming out.'

'Again, this is because I love children and it's why I chose paediatrics. This has nothing to do with how I feel about you. If it did, I'm not so sure I would be here.' Jessica walked briskly in the direction of the main doors of the hospital.

'I know I deserve your reaction,' he told her. 'And, as soon as I can, I want to explain why I behaved the way I did. I owe you that.'

Jessica drew a strained breath, not from the pace of their walking, instead from having to be around Harrison. She'd thought she would never have to lay eyes upon him again and that had suited her just fine. She struggled to speak now, as being near him had brought back so much of what she wanted to forget, but she knew she needed to channel her lingering anger to get through whatever lay ahead. She didn't want to hear his excuses because there was nothing to be gained from it.

'I'm past that, Harrison. I don't care about your reasons. It means nothing to me now. What I care about, in fact *all* I care about, is your son. Nothing else.'

'I'm truly grateful…'

'Please, I don't want to hear anything close to that from you. Just give me the background now,' she said as she picked up speed to get inside. It was starting to rain and she didn't want another of Harrison's chivalrous yet shallow gestures of perhaps taking off his jacket to shield her. She would rather drown.

'Bryce was complaining of a pain in his stomach last weekend and then he lost his appetite. I incorrectly assumed it was nerves about starting school and me being overseas recently.'

'What else?' she asked, filtering out all the superfluous information. Adrenalin was kicking in. There was a little boy's life potentially at stake.

'The pain subsided during the week, so I thought nothing more of it, but it started again yesterday morning and escalated during the day.'

'Understandable, stomach aches are not unusual at that age, but you wouldn't have called me here at this hour if it wasn't serious, so tell me all of the symptoms and the time frame. Any diarrhoea?'

'My mother picked him up when the school called her around lunchtime. He'd soiled his pants and was very embarrassed. The school nurse cleaned him and provided him with some second-hand clothing but, understandably, he wanted to go home,' he replied as they entered the automatic doors of the hospital and continued at breakneck speed into ER. 'He's been at their house for two nights, as he always is if I'm on a late shift, and they didn't want to bother me. They thought it was something he ate. My father finally called me two hours ago when he saw Bryce struggling to get out of the bath and walk into his bedroom. My father's retired but was a military doctor and knew something wasn't right.'

Jessica looked him up and down and didn't hide her disdain. He had an entire family in the town and he'd never bothered to say a thing. She wasn't his keeper and they hadn't known each other for long but, in Jessica's mind, in an open and honest conversation some, if not all, these things would have come up unless he was purposely hiding them.

'Jessica, I know I've screwed up everything with us

and I will try to explain and, if I can, make it up to you but right now I need your help.'

'And you have it. I'm here to help.' At odds with how she was feeling, her voice was unemotional. 'He's five years of age, is that correct?'

'Yes, five years and three months.' He intuitively followed suit, kept to the facts and dropped any reference to them.

'Any other medical conditions?' she asked as they entered the ER.

'No. He's your average young boy. Good weight for his height. The pain has escalated so he's on IV pain relief.'

Jessica quickly scrubbed in, donned a gown and gloves and entered the bay to find a little version of Harrison lying on the bed in a tiny hospital gown. The similarity was uncanny and a little unnerving.

Calmly she approached the little boy. 'Hello, Bryce. I'm Dr Jessica. I work at the hospital with your daddy and I heard you had a tummy ache.'

'Uh-huh, it was bad but the medicine made it better.'

'Was it very bad?' she asked, noting the IV that was administering pain relief.

'Very, very bad,' Bryce replied with the saddest of faces.

'May I have a look at you and try to find out why your tummy's hurting?'

Bryce nodded his mop of thick black hair, again just like his father's.

Pushing away the clear similarities, Jessica continued, 'Did you feel pain anywhere else?'

'Just my tummy, near my belly button.'

Jessica turned to the nurse. 'Is there any fever?'

'His temperature is slightly elevated. Thirty-nine point five.'

'More than likely from the infection,' Jessica replied as she took a stethoscope, warmed it in the palm of her hand for a moment then listened to his chest. Happy with what she could hear, she turned to the nurse again. 'Have you taken bloods to see if the white cell count is elevated?'

'Yes, just waiting on the lab now.'

'We may not have time to wait for that result; please go and put a rush on them.'

The nurse raced from the bay, leaving Harrison and Jessica alone with Bryce.

'Can he raise his right leg?'

'Not without pain,' Harrison replied. 'That was the catalyst for me calling you.'

Gently she lifted Bryce down and began an external examination. There was extra tenderness on his lower right side and nothing elsewhere in his abdomen. She gently replaced the gown and, once the nurse returned, Jessica signalled to Harrison to step outside the bay with her.

'Bryce is presenting with many of the symptoms of appendicitis—the raised temperature, diarrhoea and tenderness near the site. It's not overly common in someone of Bryce's age, but also not unheard of. I think we need to consider an emergency appendectomy rather than risking it rupturing overnight,' she told him as she pulled her gloves free.

'It can't wait till the morning?' Harrison questioned her.

'From what you're telling me, the symptoms have been present for a few days, if not a week already, so my educated guess is we don't have that much time to decide.

The bacteria are rapidly multiplying and, with that pressure, Bryce's appendix could rupture.'

'There's still the possibility that it's not appendicitis.'

'There's always a possibility with any diagnosis but for me that possibility is too small,' she countered. She could sense the fear in Harrison's voice and understood why he had those doubts but she had to push back. Erring on the side of caution was riskier than operating. 'Fairly soon, if I'm right, the decision will be made for us and if that happens then we'll have a whole different set of issues, including the risk to other organs from the resulting peritonitis. And then the emergency surgery will be far more complicated.'

'What would you do in my place?'

'I just told you…'

'Jessica—' he cut in, then continued in a very controlled manner '—I want to know what you'd do if you were not his doctor, but instead his mother. What decision would you make then? Jessica, I'm scared, more scared than I've ever been. I don't want to get this wrong. I can't lose my boy. I need your help.'

Jessica was knocked sideways by Harrison's honesty and vulnerability. Only a few hours before she hadn't known Harrison had a son, and now he was asking her what decision would she make if she was the boy's mother. She wasn't anyone's mother and might never be, so the question was a difficult one. Even more so coming from Harrison. But, as a paediatrician, it wasn't the first time she had been asked a question like this. And each time she understood it wasn't to absolve the parent of their responsibility; it was just a question about gaining perspective. This time was very different though because it was being asked by a man who a few days ago she'd thought might be her world, her future, her everything. A man who'd made her believe in her own judgement and love again, for the briefest of times. But he was also a man who'd turned his back on her. A man who'd broken her heart. And one she wanted to hate. But now, standing so near and learning more, she found that hard to do.

'Harrison, I know it's overwhelming to make a decision for someone you love, but you're the only one who can make it. And if he was my son—' she paused and drew a breath '—I would make the decision to operate tonight.'

Harrison nodded. She could see there was still a battle raging in his head and his heart as he clenched his fingers and an anxious tic stirred in his jaw.

'Then that's what we'll do,' he told her.

'You've made the right decision,' she said and, instinctively and without thinking, she placed her bare hand on his arm in a comforting and reassuring way.

'I hope so,' he said, suddenly putting his hand over hers.

Jessica froze. She hadn't expected that reaction. From a parent, she would understand and not react, but the feeling of Harrison's warm skin against hers brought memories flooding back—memories that she didn't want to deal with again. She pulled her hand free; she was the one who needed space now.

'Do we have a surgeon on call?' she asked back in the direction of the bay where Bryce was waiting.

'Normally we have two general surgeons on call but unfortunately Dr Franklin is down with influenza and Dr Douglas is in Tamworth overnight. He's due back in the morning. It wouldn't usually be a problem because, normally, I would be able to cover.'

'Okay. That certainly changes things.'

'Would you prefer us to hold off and monitor overnight?' Harrison asked as he began pacing.

'No. I understand you want conservative treatment, that's always my aim with my patients, but in this case moderate might, as I said before, be the far riskier option at this point. In the absence of any other choice, it looks like you and I are operating on your son. It's unorthodox at best but it's Bryce's best chance. Have you undertaken an appendectomy recently?'

'One, a few months ago, in similar circumstances.'

'And the age of the patient?'

'Twenty-nine.'

'Twenty-nine, and Bryce is five, so this procedure will be the same…but also very different. You know what I mean. So I'll take the lead. Are you good with that?' Her look was serious as she was preparing mentally for the task at hand. Saving Harrison's son, with his assistance.

'Of course.'

'Bryce,' Harrison said softly as they both re-entered the ER bay. 'Your stomach ache is not going to get any better unless Dr Jessica operates and takes out your appendix.'

'What's that?'

'A little piece of your tummy that you don't need but it is sick and has germs stuck in it and it's giving you the stomach ache.'

'Will the operation hurt?'

'No, you will be asleep and afterwards the nurses will give you medicine to make it better.'

'Then they should give medicine so I don't need an operation, Daddy.'

Harrison appreciated his son's logic. It wasn't correct but it would seem sensible to a five-year-old.

'I wish we could but your appendix is hurting you because it is sick and it needs to be taken out of your tummy. It won't get well with medicine.'

'Will it be put in a jar like Toby's tonsils? He brought the jar in for show and tell.'

'Maybe. We can talk about it later, but first things first and that is getting the sick appendix out of you. And I'll be right with you the whole time.'

'You promise you won't leave me?'

Harrison dropped down to eye level with his son. 'I promise you I'll be right by you. I'm not going anywhere.'

The theatre was prepared and the anaesthesiologist, Dr Martin Barry, arrived fifteen minutes later and was given an overview by Jessica of how she saw the surgery proceeding. She told him that she hoped it would be straightforward laparoscopic procedure and, if so, should be completed within thirty minutes. If there were complications it could take a little longer and they would be prepared for that too.

While Bryce was prepped for surgery, Harrison and Jessica headed in to scrub for the single most important surgical procedure that Harrison would perform in his life. With the water running, they both lathered up and then with the assistance of theatre staff, slipped on gloves, gown, cap and glasses.

'If it becomes too much being in there with your son,' Jessica began, 'please just leave the theatre. Don't hesitate. I can do it alone but it will be better if you at least begin the procedure with me as I'm not entirely sure what we will find going in. It's exploratory and, with any luck, we will find an ever so slightly infected organ that we can take out quickly without any drama and then Bryce will be running around again by next weekend.'

'Let's hope so.'

'At this stage, hoping is all we can do.'

They entered the theatre, where Bryce was resting under the effects of some pre-operative medication with the rest of the late-night surgical team busily preparing for the impending surgical procedure around him. Dr Barry had adjusted the dose of anaesthesia for his height and weight and age as noted on his patient records.

'Daddy's here, just as I promised, with Dr Jessica,' Harrison told the sleepy boy. 'And I'll still be here when you wake up.'

Slowly the little boy drifted into an unconscious state from the anaesthesia.

'You are good to go,' Dr Barry told her.

'Okay, let's get this appendix out and make this young man feel like himself again,' she said as she took the laparoscopic intra-abdominal trocar from the nurse and began the keyhole surgery by making an incision for the umbilical port. Once the trocar had been inserted into the umbilical port, gas was then gently pumped into Bryce's abdomen to inflate the area to enable Jessica to see more clearly what they were facing. Harrison inserted the laparoscope and Jessica could see immediately that the appendix was red and inflamed.

'You were right about the appendix...' Harrison began and then stopped.

Jessica was correct about the appendicitis but there was more and it wasn't good. The theatre staff could all see on the monitor that Bryce's appendix had perforated and the infected contents had spilled out, covering the other organs in his abdomen.

Jessica was concerned but she wasn't going to let Harrison know and she quickly pulled herself back to the task at hand.

'Will we need to change to open surgery?' the theatre nurse asked, preparing to wheel over the other surgical trolley.

'No, I'll continue as planned. I'll insert the other two trocars, then utilise them as a passage into the cavity for the other instruments. I will dissect out the ruptured appendix and mobilise it.'

Jessica gently moved the appendix to one side using the grasper so that she could investigate further his tiny abdomen.

'I can see where it's ruptured; the tissue is necrotic and turning black from the infection,' she explained.

'That is not an overnight occurrence,' Harrison said flatly. 'This is a slightly longer-term infection.'

'Children are good at covering up sometimes, Harrison,' she told him, sensing he was feeling a level of guilt for his son's condition. 'I'll staple off just below the rupture. It will divide the appendix and leave a row of staples across the stump.' Jessica fired one row of staples to divide the appendix from the colon. 'The second row of staples will divide the blood supply,' she explained as she fired another row. 'The staples don't dissolve but they won't cause Bryce any pain or issues in the future.'

Using the graspers again, Jessica checked the staple lines across the stump seal were secure and that there was no leakage or bleeding from the colon. 'I will leave the appendix in there for a moment while I look into the pelvis.'

'There's a lot of pus and murky fluid,' Harrison said, visibly distraught but remaining calm. 'He must have been in so much pain.'

'A great deal, but he's clearly a strong boy,' Jessica responded. 'But after we clean all this fluid and pus out of his pelvis, he'll be feeling like a new little man.' Jessica inserted a suctioning tool and emptied the cavity of the infected material. 'Just to make sure there's nothing remaining there that we can't see, I'll put a drain down into the pelvis and bring it out through the skin. It will need to stay in for four days.'

Jessica ensured all was as she expected and there were no unexpected surprises. 'I can now take out the appendix through the incision.'

Once she had done so, the nurse took the draining tube and attached it to a bulb pump and then Jessica removed all three trocars and began to suture closed the three small wounds. Harrison watched on in awe of her skills. His gratitude was born of the fact that Jessica had saved his son's life; his respect was born of watching such a skilled surgeon.

'I'll leave the port valve in place too for a few days, along with the drain, so that gas can escape from his stomach. If we don't he'll have similar pain again but this time from the procedure.'

With that she stepped back and he watched as she walked from the theatre, leaving the nurses and anaesthesiologist to do their work and take Bryce to Recovery. Harrison chose to stay.

Her work was done.

And now she should be able to walk away…but suddenly her legs felt heavy and her stomach uneasy. Was she walking away from this town too soon? Was Harrison telling the truth? She wasn't sure about anything and she didn't know if she was making the right choice any more. She wondered if she needed to hear him out.

Seeing the depth of love that he had for his son, the trust and belief Harrison had placed in her, suddenly Jessica had more questions than she had answers.

He had based his decision about his son's surgery on what she had said she would do if she were Bryce's mother. An unexpected question and one that made her look at everything a little differently. Including him.

And how he saw her.

CHAPTER NINE

JESSICA FOUND HARRISON outside Bryce's room at six the next morning, understandably dishevelled from a night she suspected had been spent sitting up in a hospital chair. He was looking down at the ground, his head resting in his hands. Just as he'd promised, he'd not left his son's side. Jessica wasn't surprised. His love for his son was undeniable.

'Harrison,' she said softly, so as to not startle him, as she sat on the empty chair beside him. She had barely slept herself but at least what little sleep she'd managed was in her own bed. She was concerned about Bryce and confused about his father. And both had made her toss and turn and wonder if she should get on the plane and turn her back on the man who had hurt her.

Or whether she should stay and see if there was something there worth fighting for.

He raised his head and faced her. His gutted expression cut her to the core. She wished it didn't but it did. He was exposed and vulnerable and her heart went out to him. She wanted to find reasons to hate him. She wanted to not give a damn. But, sitting so close to him, she was struggling to find a reason to hate him—and she did give a damn.

But there was still so much she didn't understand.

'I had to step out. I needed a few minutes...'

'And some black coffee,' she added, handing him one she had picked up at the cafeteria. 'They told me you'd been here all night.'

'I couldn't go home. Bryce needed me here, and I needed to be here.'

'He'll pull through.' She knew they had made the right decision to operate and her earlier call to ICU had confirmed the prognosis for Bryce was optimistic.

The prognosis for her and Harrison was not so certain but she couldn't leave the way it was, with so many questions and so much left unsaid. There was unfinished business. If nothing else, Jessica knew she needed closure or what they had shared and what might have been would haunt her.

'He's all I have, Jessica. Every choice I've made about my life has been based on what's best for my son. I want to shield him from hurt for as long as I can. He's had enough in his life and he's not even fully aware of it yet. He'll have a lot of questions as he grows up and the answers might be painful for him to hear.'

Jessica listened intently, hoping that some of her questions might be answered. Was walking away from her, deciding one night was all they would be, one of those decisions? But why did he not want to see if there could be more? Why would he worry about his son being around her? She loved children and she had devoted her life to providing the best care for children.

'You put Bryce first; it's what devoted parents do,' she told him, wishing she could put her arms around him and comfort him but knowing she couldn't. She wasn't willing to risk showing that level of familiarity or intimacy. 'Bryce will be fine. He's a little fighter.'

'I've been fighting for custody of my son for the last five years.' He raked his hand through his hair. 'Going crazy thinking that I might lose him.'

Jessica was surprised to learn he had been battling to keep his son for so long. The child was only five years of age. She was beginning to understand his level of protectiveness over his son. Harrison had been a single dad for almost Bryce's entire life.

'And now, when I finally get custody, I almost lose him. He was in so much pain and I hesitated. I wanted to leave it until morning. What sort of father does that?'

'One who cares and thinks about things thoroughly and weighs up the risks,' she countered. 'One who doesn't rush in.'

'Oh, I've rushed into things before.'

'Maybe you've learnt a hard lesson about it and that's why you didn't want to rush this time?'

Harrison looked up at the ceiling and drew a deep and thoughtful breath. 'Maybe. But sometimes you have to make quick decisions and hope on a wing and a prayer you get it right.'

'Sometimes you do.' She agreed. *Like the one she had made that morning in coming to see Harrison.*

'If it wasn't for you encouraging me not to be conservative, peritonitis would have most definitely set in overnight and then...' He paused. 'I don't want to think what might have happened. I just wish that I'd acted sooner...'

'There's no point wishing,' Jessica cut in. 'I learnt that a long time ago. You have to accept the situation you're facing and make the right decision at the time with what you know. And afterwards there's no point in looking back because you can't do anything about it. That's what we did last night when we operated.'

'But if only I'd taken more notice of the symptoms two days ago…'

'Harrison, you have to stop this. Look at me. Remember, you can't look back. Bryce is a tough little boy, he managed to hide a simmering appendix from you, and there's no point with the *if only*. God knows, I've spent the best part of a year questioning myself over the mistakes I've made and it doesn't undo what's done.'

Harrison lifted his head and looked at Jessica. His eyes were heavy and tired and filled with fear and something else she couldn't define. 'Jessica, you should have no regrets about anything. I'm the one that should have regrets…particularly where you and I are concerned. Any man would be so lucky to have you and I messed up. I wasn't thinking straight,' he said, his hand moving closer to hers.

Instinctively, Jessica moved her hand out of his reach. It wasn't something she did out of anger. More the need to keep some boundaries for a little longer.

'But I thought I had to push you away, for your sake and mine,' he said, drawing a deep and thoughtful breath.

'I'm not sure I understand. I mean I know you've been in a battle for Bryce, but that has nothing to do with me.'

'I know, absolutely nothing to do with you. It's just that I worried there wasn't enough in this town to hold your interest and I don't want to start something, only to have it end because it wasn't the right thing for you.'

'I love this town, it's amazing and the hospital is as advanced as any I've worked in. Why would you say that?'

'I'm done with convincing anyone that this is where they want to be. I did it once and it ended badly.' He was wringing his hands and staring into another time and place.

Jessica hesitated, then decided there was nothing to lose in knowing the truth. 'Are you talking about Bryce's mother?'

'Yes. I don't think I can face doing it again. Convince you to stay and see where this might lead when you really want to be somewhere, anywhere other than this town. And if it isn't what you want, when you walk away after a few months you won't just take a piece of my heart, you'd take a big piece of Bryce's heart with you. It's not fair for him to pay the price again for his father falling in love too quickly.'

Falling in love? Jessica fell back against the hard chair of the waiting area. He had just said he was falling in love with her? Were his feelings as strong for her as her feelings had been for him? She looked at him, saying nothing, just wanting to know more about what drove him and what made him the man he was.

'I met Bryce's mother and we rushed into a relationship. She was a make-up artist in town for six weeks for a film shoot and we met, hit it off and thought it was love at first sight. One thing led to another and she found out she was pregnant.' He stopped and took a deep purposeful breath. 'It shouldn't have happened, we took precautions, but nothing is one hundred per cent effective. I have Bryce and I wouldn't change anything but his mother didn't feel the same way. I convinced her to stay in Armidale, marry me and raise our son.'

'That was very chivalrous and a little old-fashioned of you.'

'It was the right thing to do and I thought we could be happy and for a while I thought we were. We had our differences but, for the main part, I thought everything was okay until Bryce was three months old and she announced that she was *bored beyond belief with country life*…and me. Those were her words, and they stayed with me. She hated everything about her life here and said she would go mad if she had to stay even another week. That was it; she was leaving.'

'That's such a cruel thing to say to anyone.'

'It was how she felt; she didn't hold back.'

'Did she try and take Bryce?'

'No. She didn't want him. Strangely, while I'm glad she didn't fight me for him initially, it hurt even more that she didn't want Bryce. I couldn't understand it. But over the years she sporadically threatened to take him. If I asked her to make the effort to visit and keep a level of maternal contact that would be beneficial to Bryce as he grew up, she would tell me she was taking him to live with her. It wasn't ever going to be her raising him; it was going to be her parents, who live in San Diego. So I eased off asking her to factor her son into her life.'

Jessica shook her head. 'I don't know what to say. I don't understand how she could not want her baby and then use him to manipulate the situation.'

'She believed that having a child would hold her back. She kept reminding me that she was a city girl, born and bred in Los Angeles, and this town could never compete with that. She belittled everything about it and made no effort to fit in. None. Life here with me, with our son, it was never going to be enough. She wanted to keep moving and not waste her life as the wife of a country doctor. She didn't want the whole picket fence.'

Jessica's eyes widened. It was all falling into place and making sense to her. 'And I said the same to you.'

'And you have every right to want more than this town. I would never want you to stay where you don't want to be.'

'That's not why I said what I did. It was nothing to do with this town...or you. It was someone else. Someone I trusted and loved, who lied to me in the worst possible way. He made me believe that we had a future when all along he knew we didn't. He destroyed my belief in men, marriage and commitment. I thought I had my happily ever after and it all fell apart.'

Harrison turned to face her. 'Is that why you don't want to settle in one place for too long?'

Jessica nodded. 'I didn't want to be lied to again. He was married and never told me. I was clueless but discovered he had a family already. A wife and children. Everything I thought we would have, he already had. So I guess I gave up on believing in that dream pretty darn quickly.'

'I'm so sorry that happened to you.'

'I am too because it has scarred me.'

'I hope the bastard pays one day for what he did to you.'

'Not just me, his family as well. His wife knows; she's the one who called me and told me to walk away.'

Harrison shook his head. His expression was filled with compassion she wasn't expecting.

'You deserve better than that, Jessica. So does his wife. Two innocent women were hurt at the hands of one calculating man. He should rot in hell for his actions. What he did is unforgivable and I'm not surprised it made you feel the way you did.'

Jessica was thrown by his words. There was no hint of judgement and she suddenly felt as if a weight lifted.

The guilt she had been carrying had flowed into every aspect of her life and this man was somehow taking that away, just by the way he looked at her.

'I felt…responsible. I thought I didn't deserve love after that. I didn't want to get close to someone and have my heart broken because I knew I wouldn't survive it again.'

'And that's what I did. I pulled you close and then I pushed you away,' Harrison said with remorse colouring his voice. 'I'm so sorry. I was a fool.'

'We both had our reasons for what we did and said.'

'I shouldn't have rushed us into what we did that night.' He paused. 'But I couldn't stop myself and, while I'm sorry beyond words for how I hurt you afterwards, I don't regret a minute of it. I was the happiest I have ever been.'

Jessica had to agree with everything he had said. She regretted rushing too, but it was the best night of her life. Suddenly she felt that she finally understood the man sitting beside her. He was the man her heart had led her to believe. Not the man that her past had made her want to think he was.

'After everything I did, everything I put you through, I can't believe you're here—shouldn't you be on a plane, Jessica?'

'I should, but some things are more important than a job.'

'You missed your flight to come back to check up on Bryce?'

'And you.'

'But why? You didn't know any of what I just told you,' he said, not taking his eyes away from her beautiful face. 'You compromised your new role without being sure of anything.'

'I guess I took a leap of faith. I saw the depth of your love for your son; I thought that there had to be a reason for your actions. I thought perhaps you needed your heart to be mended too. And if I was wrong, then I'd have learnt another hard lesson about myself.'

'And here I was thinking that if I kept seeing you I would be the one who would get hurt when you packed up and moved on.'

'I don't want to move on, Harrison. I never thought I would say it, but I feel at home here…'

'With me?' he cut in.

'Yes, with you.'

The ICU nurse appeared though the swing doors, pulling free her mask. 'I have wonderful news. Bryce has stabilised. His temperature's back down to thirty-six point five. He's breathing unassisted. Your little boy is going to be just fine.'

Harrison jumped to his feet like a man who had been given a new lease on life. But before he raced in to see his son he reached for Jessica's hand. 'Please come in with me. I want to introduce my son to the most amazing woman in the world and the doctor who saved his life.'

'We did it together, Harrison.'

'Yes, we did and I hope it's just the beginning. I want to spend the rest of my life here with you. I want to fall asleep every night with you wrapped in my arms and wake up the same way.'

Jessica didn't try to hide the smile that was born of her uncontained happiness.

'But it's a big ask, Jessica. I'm a country boy at heart and I want my son to grow up here with his grandparents. But I could commute to see you in Adelaide and you could do the same some weeks maybe, because I don't want you to give up on your dream of being the Head of Paediatrics in Adelaide. That's not fair on you. And I never want you to have to give up something for me and regret that decision…'

'I wouldn't regret anything. I would willingly walk away from that role to be here with you if you're asking me to stay.'

'I am, but…' he said, holding her hand so tightly as if she were his lifeline and he would be hers.

'But nothing—if you want me here then I want to be here more than anything I've ever wanted. And I'd never regret anything,' she promised with tears of happiness welling in her eyes. 'Besides, who says I have to give up on a dream for ever? As the hospital grows I have a feeling there might just be a need for a Head of Paediatrics right here in Armidale.'

Harrison pulled her into his arms and kissed her as passionately as he had that fateful night when their worlds changed for ever.

'I love you, Jessica.'

'And I love you, Dr Harrison Wainwright.'

EPILOGUE

'What a stunning view.'

'Yes, it is,' Harrison said as he looked across at the silhouette of his beautiful bride.

Her blonde hair was swept to one side with an antique clasp his mother had gifted her new daughter-in-law. It was the *something old.* The neckline of the stunning white satin wedding gown with a lace bodice skimmed her bare shoulders. It was the *something new.* On the table nearby was a small white satin purse that Harrison had recognised the moment he'd seen it. It was the one that Rachel had carried on the day she'd married Harrison's best friend, Sam. He knew it because he had bought it for Rachel as a gift. It was the *something borrowed.* Harrison's gaze dropped to the bracelet that caught the light and sparkled as Jessica moved her wrist. It was a gift from Bryce. With help from his grandfather, he had made a bracelet of azure glass beads for his new mummy. It was the *something blue.*

Harrison did not see the Sydney cityscape; he only had eyes for Jessica. She was everything he could ask for and more and he knew he was the luckiest man in the world. And he was not the only one to consider himself lucky.

His family adored her and they'd quickly and warmly welcomed Jessica with open arms.

She turned to face him. 'I guess for that much money you would hope it would be nice,' she laughed.

'Oh, you're talking about what's outside the window,' he said as he crossed the room and pulled her into his arms. 'It was all for a good cause. That auction raised enough for two new dialysis units and will go a long way towards a new wing for the hospital.'

'Well, now we have a baby on the way, you might want to cut back on extravagances like a fifteen-thousand-dollar stay in the big smoke.'

Harrison dropped to his knees and kissed the barely visible bump that would in six months be a new Wainwright.

'I know medical school fees for four of them will cripple us.'

'Four?' she gasped.

'You're right. Between Bryce and this one on the way, we're good for now,' he said, smiling. He loved how easily Jessica had slipped into their lives, how quickly she had formed a bond with Bryce, earning his love and trust in a way that had melted Harrison's heart further.

'Besides,' he said, resuming the thread of their conversation, 'if we have four, maybe not all of them will want to be doctors.'

Jessica laughed as she leant into the strength of her husband's embrace. 'I love you, Harrison Wainwright.'

'I'm glad to hear it because I'm crazy in love with you, Dr Wainwright, and I will spend the rest of my life showing you just how much.'

* * * * *

MILLS & BOON

Coming next month

FROM MIDWIFE TO MUMMY
Deanne Anders

Lana opened her door and stared at the chaos of her living room. Every toy Maggie owned had to be in that room plus what looked like half the clothes from her dresser. She leaned down to pick up the large stuffed elephant in her way then froze. Stretched out on her couch was a sound asleep Trent. He held her sleeping daughter on top of him with one of his arms laid protectively around her. While a wide awake Trent with his powerful frame and those mesmerizing blue eyes of his was a seductive temptation even to her, this version of the man took her breath away. Thick, dark lashes lay resting on copper toned skin, while lips usually turned in a smile relaxed into a soft invitation. She'd felt those lips against hers. She bent down closer. Had they really been that warm, that firm?

Bright blue eyes stared up at her and she jerked away from him.

Heaven help her, had she really been about to kiss him?

No, of course not. She'd never do anything like that.

Lifting Maggie up into her arms, she held her tight against her racing heart as she carried her into her room and laid her in her crib. She took a minute to catch her breath then walked back into the living room where she found Trent sitting up and rubbing the back of his neck.

"I can't believe you did that," he said.

"What?" she said. Her heart sped back up. He'd caught her.

"You got her to stay in her crib," he said.

She watched him walk toward the door, shoulders slumped and feet all but dragging, and she said a silent thank you to a sleeping Maggie.

"Just one of those tricks you learn when you're a mother," she said.

"You're a good mother, Lana," he said. "I just want you to know that. This isn't about me not thinking you can take care of Maggie."

"Then what, Trent? What is it about if not what's best for Maggie?"

She stilled as Trent's hand came up to her face, running the back of his hand down one cheek, then cupping her chin. He pulled her to him and laid a kiss so soft on her lips that she wondered if she'd imagined it. He pulled away, a half smile on his lips, and walked out the door.

Continue reading
FROM MIDWIFE TO MUMMY
Deanne Anders

Available next month
www.millsandboon.co.uk

COMING SOON!

We really hope you enjoyed reading this book. If you're looking for more romance, be sure to head to the shops when new books are available on

Thursday 30th May